I0645292

FAR
OTHER
WORLDS

Far Other Worlds

A NOVEL

Arlene MacLeod

Weymouth Press

FIRST EDITION

Library of Congress Control Number: 2021904683

ISBN 978-0-9978010-3-3 Paperback
ISBN 978-0-9978010-4-0 Ebook

For Bruce always,
and for Morgan, Hannah, and Simon

FAR
OTHER
WORLDS

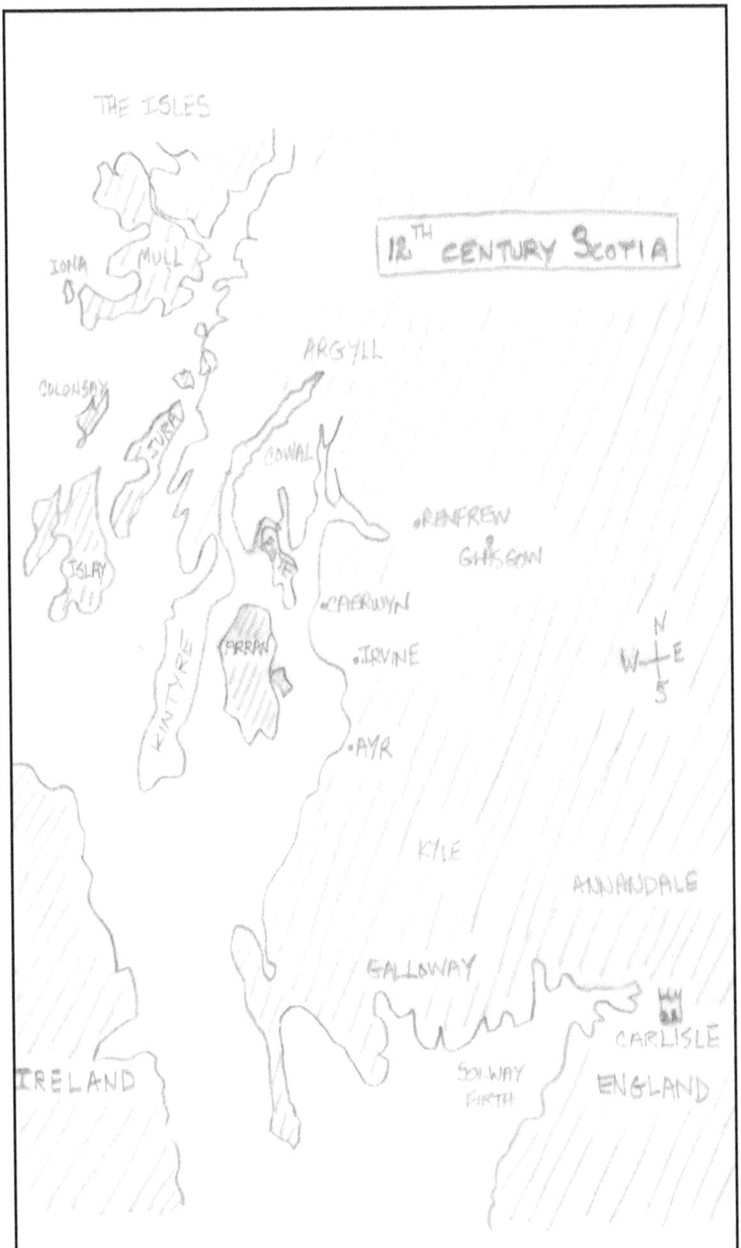

THE ISLES
12TH CENTURY SCOTIA
IONA
MULL
COLONSAY
JURA
ARGYLL
COWAL
ISLAY
RENFREW
GLASGOW
CAERLUYN
IRVINE
KINTYRE
ARRAN
AYR
N
W E
S
KYLE
ANNANDALE
GALLOWAY
CARLISLE
IRELAND
SOLWAY FIRTH
ENGLAND

PART I

CHAPTER ONE

The Western Coast of Scotia, Early Summer, 1135

TWILIGHT, THAT FUGITIVE TIME IN BETWEEN, when strange and stranger events occur. Standing at the wide open window of her bedchamber, wind tangling long hair across her eyes, Ailsa impatiently brushed the strands away and gazed out over the water, toward the rounded hills on the far edge of the bay. She watched, holding her breath, aware she would not see this particular gold light, this familiar slow setting of the sun for some time. Then, just as she was about to turn away, an enormous ship appeared, and silently crossed the still bay, floating on reflections as though on clouds, headed out toward the Far Isles. The hull painted an unusual wine red and the huge sail unfurled, catching all the fitful evening winds. Ailsa smiled as she watched. Tomorrow, at long last, she would herself be set free on just such a ship. Something she had dreamed of, again and again these past five years, since everything had changed.

She waited, unmoving and silent as though caught in a spell, until the strange ship sailed so far west it disappeared into the meeting of sea and far islands and sky. Something fey from a fantastical dream, or an old and wondrous tale. One moment there, and then gone.

Ailsa blinked at this reminder of how quickly one could be here and then gone. Then she shook her head, braided her disheveled hair, and paced her room, refusing any dark thoughts. Tonight was for excitement and hope, only. The hills outside her window darkened and merged with the shadows and the sea. She paced, too excited to sleep, willing the sky to lighten. Her bag was packed long since, she was prepared, and now there was nothing to do but think and remember. Everything she was desperate to forget.

Finally, though not in truth too long after, as it was late into the spring months and the nights very short, a pale light glowed over the eastern hills. She picked up her bag and gave her chamber a cursory glance. She would leave Caerwyn, and her memories, and all her past behind. Only for a while, of course. The past could not be escaped or altered, that she knew well. But she'd be free of it all for the span of one season, a perfect summer of near endless days.

It would be enough. She opened the heavy oak door, creaking on its hinges, and ran down the uneven spiral of stairs.

Out on the shingle, below the cliff edge, the sun peeked over the hills and lit the dew-soaked grasses as though thousands of fireflies wandered lost or searching above the mist. Ailsa paused just once to look back at her home, the manor house built by her grandfather a century back. Gold light gleamed from the two precious glass windows in the chamber above the hall. She stared, caught in a moment of wishing, but the windows were shut tight. No one inhabited that room now. Inside, it would be dark and empty, and the glitter off the glass was only an enchantment.

Scrambling down the cliff path to the beach, she saw at the water's edge, riding up and down on the long swells, her cousin Dugald's galley, already near loaded, men shouting and hefting water barrels. She ran toward them over the sand and stones, skirts and bag flapping, and she felt in that moment she might whoop and soar like the swooping terns overhead.

Dugald hardly glanced her way. Ailsa greeted Meriel, her cousin's brand new wife, who stood well away from the waves with reddened eyes. She bent to give her a quick hug, though in truth she was unlikely to miss her for these few months. Meriel was but fifteen and seemed younger. They had found little to say to each other.

"What are you doing here, cousin," called Dugald, scowling as he approached. His brown hair blew across his face and he thrust it back in the leather cord.

"We've discussed this," Ailsa said, straightening her back.

"We discussed it sure, argued over it night after night, but I don't recall I ever said yes."

"You said yes, you know it," said Ailsa. "If I'd consider marriage again."

"If you'd agree to it, that I recall saying."

"And I have said I'll consider it, after we return in the fall. And so I will." She flicked her braid behind her shoulder. "It is time, I know it too well."

"Past time," said Dugald. He shouted at one of his men, who had dropped a basket of bread loaves into the waves. Impatiently he turned back to her. "But that is neither here nor there. You cannot come."

Wind whipped at Ailsa's skirts, tangling the thick wool around her ankles. "You must take me with you. You cannot mean to leave me behind again." She just managed to keep her voice soft, her tone reasonable.

Dugald shifted his weight. He looked past her, out toward the sea, shining under the pale morning sky. He shrugged and moved toward the boat, fitted with a still-furled sail and six sets of oars. His men were putting the last sacks of fresh foodstuffs on board.

Ailsa yanked off her boots, grasped her skirts, and lifting them over her knees waded out into the freezing water after him. She grabbed the smoothed rails of the oak galley and hoisted herself in. "You know I'll be no trouble to you." She prevented herself from saying she sailed better than he and shoved a lumpy bag of oiled cloth, holding a second wool gown, a quill, and some parchment, under the seat.

Dugald looked over at Meriel, who raised her eyebrows but didn't speak. "I would bring you if I could, cousin." He paused. "Perhaps someday I will take you for a visit to Arran or even one of the Irish ports. But now is not the time. With this crazy bishop Wimond rousing the Isles, pretending he's kin to the old king, threatening the crown. King's men will be here soon, no mistake. Everyone is saying so, they'll be chasing rebels and crying treason." His eyes shifted to the mast, where a strip of bright cloth fluttered in the rising wind. "It's not the time for a woman to be out voyaging."

Ailsa bit her lip. "I'm not afraid of the king's men, nor a bit of trouble. I could be of help to you. You promised me this summer would be different. This time I would come. If I agreed and so I have."

Dugald turned away to his men. "It's final. Climb out."

"Ailsa." Meriel's voice floated to them from the shore. "Do come back, I would so miss you. Surely you won't leave me here on my own."

Ailsa frowned. Meriel's hair was escaping its braids and her blue eyes seemed to plead. She swallowed and turned back to Dugald. "You know I need to go away. For a time only. This one summer, it is all I ask."

"And I have said no. It's dangerous and untimely. With our fathers dead, it is I who must make the decisions and I say you do not go." Dugald moved toward her, wading through the water.

Ailsa rose, rocking the boat in her hurry, suddenly uncertain as rigid lines of anger appeared on her cousin's normally placid face. "You cannot mean it! You cannot mean me to stay here forever, like some sort of prisoner." Surely he would listen to her. This was Dugald, her companion on many childhood adventures. "You know I must," she added in a low voice. "You know why, and also that I will return, and trouble you no more, and do my duty."

Dugald grimaced but said nothing. He reached into the boat, grasped her around the waist, and slung her over his wide shoulder, though she was not small. "Get her bag," he shouted to one of his men.

Hot blood rushed to Ailsa's face. How could he? He'd laughed at first when she'd spoken of summer voyaging with him, in the long winter evenings, but he'd never said no. She thought he, of all people, understood. He would take her this year. Just for a few short months. Just this once.

Dugald dropped her on the sand beside Meriel. "Sorry, cousin, it's for the best." He kissed Meriel, lingering until she stepped back, her eyes bright with pooling tears. Then he called to his men, who scrambled after him, anxious not to displease the chief further. They pushed the blue-painted galley past the swells, then climbed in, grabbing the oars, and soon the rhythmic sound of creaking oak, as they headed toward the wind, filled Ailsa's ears.

She stumbled to her feet and ran after them, into the water. The boat skimmed so gracefully, gliding away from her with the speed of the gulls that rode the winds at the water's edge. "Dugald!" But the boat was already away; the surf drowned her voice as it rushed up the beach. "You must take me!" But Dugald set his face toward the open sea, away from her.

The boat sped on toward the horizon, sail dark against the brilliant water. Smaller and smaller she became and finally she disappeared entirely in the haze of sea and sky. "I must go, I must, I truly must," Ailsa whispered. Suddenly she felt the full bitter cold of the sea washing against her thighs. Her gown, heavy with water, dragged at her waist. She turned, eyes aching. Meriel was still standing on the sand, her cheeks and nose red with the chill air. She started to speak, but Ailsa shook her head. Struggling out of the water, she ran, awkward in her soaked skirts, down the long and desolate curve of stony beach.

Caerwyn was her beloved home, sturdy and safe and sure, until it wasn't. Its timber manor sat comfortably, wedged into a hillside, on the western coast of Scotia, or perhaps on the easternmost lands of the Kingdom of the Isles. A place in between. Near Strathclyde, north of Galloway, East of the Irish, and South of the Norse. A land formed of rough places and ragged edges, where brilliant ever moving seas carved stones into sand, and rocks and pebbles halted the endless wash of the sea. A beautiful and precarious land, of sparkling light and bright danger, where the line dividing solid ground and flowing water was never set nor clear. A place of drifting fogs where sun or land or even a person could dissolve and disappear, unsure which way to go forward.

The beaches rolled and clacked with smoothed stones in the swells as the tide came in and went out; the pastures were dotted with granite boulders and lush grasses. Bog cotton waved in the endless winds. There were long sandy stretches, inlets sheltered from the wind where gold sand melded into glittering sea and dark caves offered mysterious shelter. The people who lived in this land were comfortable in all weather and equally fine on land or on the sea.

The silver tides and banks of fog swept in and swept out and

Caerwyn changed and yet stayed precisely the same. Her own life happened, and for a long time, she was a child and things altered for her and around her, but everything that mattered stayed the same. Even when her father, and Dugald's too, drowned in the sea, even then Caerwyn enclosed her and comforted her. Then, in the space of one season, everything was different. Niall. Niall.

After Niall she grew harder and quieter, she knew it, but she didn't know how to prevent that.

Life is like that, however placid seeming on the still surface. Like a current racing deep beneath the stillness of a windless ocean bay, its waters reflecting only floating clouds and far hills, hiding from sight the forceful moving stream of time and life and death. Endlessly hidden and always flowing.

In this life, one must always be ready for change. If one seeks their own way. If one hopes to be free.

The spring into summer week that followed Dugald's departure passed in a blur of familiar work. Each morning, Ailsa gazed out over a new seeded field. This particular morning, the strip at her feet was planted with barley shoots and the pungent smell of turned earth filled the air. Sun beat unseasonably upon her head. She'd forgotten her hat once again. She lifted her heavy braid off the back of her neck and let the sweat dry.

A shout from one of the men roused her. The workers had gathered at the far edge of the field. Meriel, in a blue gown, straw hat tied firm on her head and ribbons fluttering, had arrived, followed by two maidservants lugging the morning meal in deep baskets covered with linen cloth.

Ailsa set the hoe on her shoulder as she trudged toward them. Her legs ached and her shoulder hurt where the hoe bumped against it with each step. She had not let herself think on Dugald's betrayal. She'd thrown herself into work, rising in the chilly half-light before dawn and riding from field to field, encouraging the workers, making decisions about weather, overseeing quarrels, seeing to the cooking of the huge meals owed when the villagers worked her fields. She flicked at a cloud of midges around her neck and sighed. It was unfair of her, but just seeing Meriel made it all seem harder. She seemed so very content with life. Even with Dugald away, and her marriage only two months old, she went through her day with endless smiles. Ailsa longed for another woman, someone she could truly confide in. What would it be like to have a mother? Her own had died when she was but two, of a winter sickness, a cough that lingered and worsened.

The white glare off the sea made her eyes water. She'd been so sure she could make Dugald take her with him for the summer voyaging this year. When they'd been children together, he'd never cared she was a girl, but let her enter into all his adventures. She hacked at a weed with her hoe. Mirren, her steward, could easily have cared for the crops while she was gone. Such a short time, a few summer months. But so very much she could have seen and heard, as Dugald and his men went from port to port, trading goods and news until the winds shifted in autumn and they headed home. All those new places and even more, the sea itself in all its moods beneath new and different mountains. She'd have seen the far places the bards sang about. Had some small adventures of her own. But now, she was stuck here, where she had been always, mistress of Caerwyn, doing her duty.

She yanked a weed, with its long taproot, and tossed it aside. The annoying truth was she had to make the best of it. She couldn't worry Meriel, who would miss Dugald greatly all the summer months, especially if, as she'd inferred, she might be already with child. Meriel was so calm one couldn't ruffle her surface. It seemed that among the women only she stared out to sea and longed to be away, to go further and further, toward somewhere far and wondrous and new.

Ailsa shook the dust from her woolen skirts. She was her father's heir and Lady of Caerwyn. Nothing could change that. But a few months away from duty, that was all she had asked. One summer, and then she would take up her responsibilities, marry, care for the land and its people, hide her unseemly longing away.

"I'll take that, lass." Mirren appeared at her side and took the hoe. "You look tired."

"I'm sorry," she began and stopped. She had not been sleeping.

Perhaps that's why her thoughts were so dark. "Do you think we did right? Not planting the north field this spring, I mean."

Mirren looked at her, not the north field, and his grey eyebrows drew together. "It's a fine job you're doing here. Isn't many women could run an estate without a man about."

Ailsa smiled, but he had avoided her question. Mirren had been steward on the lands since she could remember. As a child she'd ridden about on his shoulders as he walked the fields for her father. She never could have learned to run Caerwyn without his help. Still, they'd had to abandon three fields in the last two years, for there simply weren't enough men to do the labor. One hundred families had lived here in her father's time. Now, there were barely seventy. It worried her. Mirren was growing old, though he was still healthy, thanks be. But more and more of the younger men had fled, off to the sea trading or to the towns. And what if Dugald were right and troubles did come? It was hard to imagine, here at Caerwyn, where peace had reigned since before she was born.

She sighed loudly and then tried to curve her mouth into a smile. Dugald was always gloomy. She would not become like him. She thanked Mirren as he moved off to organize the men for the afternoon's planting. "I'll take the empty baskets back," she called to Meriel, "you stay out here and enjoy the sun." She lifted the baskets onto her shoulder and headed back toward the manor house. As she walked, she forced herself to stop worrying, to think only of the next task to be done. It was a good day for laundry; with this unusual heat, she'd get the housemaid out in the courtyard and they'd wash the bed linens. There was plenty of the strong soap left. The fresh smell of sunshine on linen was a good solution to any problem.

Ailsa sat on the side of her bed, having slept little once again, her fingers raking through her snarled hair. She felt she couldn't go through another day just like all the last. She yanked a shift from the hook on her door and tossed it on, covering the flimsy linen with a wool gown. Ignoring the laces, she ran down the cold stairs, her feet still bare. At the bottom, she listened. A few rustles and a cough from the hall, where the household slept. With the planting finished, everyone would rise late and take a long day to celebrate. She could hear Mirren snoring in his privileged spot by the banked fire.

She slipped out the side door that led to the kitchens and crossed the yard. The kitchen was dark and empty, and smelled of last night's fire. She cut herself a generous chunk of orange cheese and poured some ale into a skin, then thrust on a pair of heavy boots she found by the door. She wandered outside again with a pleasant sense of escape. No one up yet to prevent her.

She found Nia in her stall, eager to venture out into the morning. She slipped a rope bridle on the mare, whispering into her twitching ears, and led her out the gate, waving to young Kyle, Mirren's grandson, who was yawning and trying to look awake as he let her through.

It was a perfect morning, fields shimmering as the sun's rays penetrated the mist and found the tips of the new grass. They cantered down the beaten path between the twin barley fields toward the sun and the hills, the scent of spring herbs and turned earth filling each breath. They reached the woods, and dense elm and oak trees enclosed them. Pale tree flowers colored the shafts of sunlight greenish as they slanted to the forest floor. The only sounds were the warblers, awakening to the new day, and the soft thud of Nia's hoofs on the wet leaves covering the path.

"Where shall we go this very fine morning," Ailsa murmured, hesitating, then she turned the horse toward her favorite retreat. A stream of crystal water wound down from the hills toward the fields, and in one clearing half up the hills it filled a pool, deep enough for swimming. She rode on, feeling the sun gradually warm her hair and shoulders as it rose. The path was narrow, though not too steep, so they rode slowly. And besides, solitude was a rare treat.

They reached the pool and she slipped down from Nia. Giving her an affectionate pat, and looping her reins over a bush, she left the horse searching for blades of new grass. She strolled toward the pool. Sunlight glimmered down through the green buds and breezes ruffled the water's surface. She dipped her hand in the clear water and laughed. Still ice. Perhaps she'd just wade today. She tugged off the clumsy but warm boots and hiked up her skirts, tying the thick material into an awkward knot, then waded into the clear water, watching her toes sink into the rippled sand. A tiny minnow darted away into a shadow cast by a birch tree leaning over the pool. She stood until her feet turned red and her ankles ached with the cold, then climbed out. She lounged on the damp moss and ate her crumbly cheese as the sun drew overhead.

Deliberately thinking on nothing, eyes closed, she basked in the sun. Her fingers traced the feathery tops of the deep moss, as she tried not to think of what she might be doing this day if she'd actually gotten away. She couldn't stop imagining though. She wouldn't ever be able to convince Dugald. She could see that now. If he wouldn't take her this summer, he wouldn't take her next summer or the one after. He'd be glad to bury her here forever.

Crows cawed, interrupting her thoughts; there was a new sound in the woods. Ailsa tensed and listened, holding her breath. The thud of hoofs, horses coming up the path. She jumped to her feet, grabbed Nia's reins, and urged the mare into a thick stand of hazel. As she peered through the screen of branches, two riders appeared. They were bearded and dressed in the short tunics of Islesmen, with black-haired legs and hardened bare feet and long daggers at their belts. Nia nudged her and she grasped her nose and hoped she would stay quiet.

The men pulled up their horses and stared at the pond and one said something. She didn't understand them, or even recognize their language. The older man said something abrupt and they both kicked their horses and moved on, slowly passing out of sight into the deep forest. They must have watered their shaggy mounts earlier.

Ailsa listened until the clunk of hoofs faded entirely away. It was not the first group of strangers she'd seen this season. Since the snows had melted, men had been traveling, in small groups like this, through the woods. Strangers all. Yet this was the time of summer voyaging and most Islesmen took to their boats for the summer trading, like Dugald, heading west and south to Man, or the Irish ports, where they traded for goods and news and traveled home again in the autumn, loaded with butter and beef and fine ornaments of worked silver and gold. She thought about Dugald's warning, of the bishop Wimond, preaching treason and gathering men, it was said, against the new Scots king. Nia nibbled at her hair and she rubbed the mare's neck and led her out of the bushes. Dugald was always conjuring problems.

All was still once again by the pool, with only the nesting swallows swooping and calling and the distant hum of bees. Ailsa sat down on the moss, uneasy despite herself at the interruption. How aggravating that strangers could dim her pleasure. No, she'd not let this day of precious freedom be spoiled. They'd not be back this way, doubtless they were headed toward Renfrew and the markets. Likely it had nothing to do with Wimond or rebellions or the Isles at all. She was letting Dugald's caution taint her thoughts. Men might be gathering, but it would come to nothing.

Still, she should get back to the manor.

Instead, she pulled off her gown, dropping the faded wool in a careless heap. Tugging the linen shift, softened by many washings, over her head, she shivered at the sudden chill of air on bare skin. She wound her heavy braid on top of her head and tried to knot it into place, but she had no pins. She let it fall down her back, then moved into the water. She stood a moment, enjoying the hot sun on her shoulders and cold water round her ankles, then moved in deeper, gasping as the water reached her thighs. She plunged in, feeling the cold, so icy it felt like fire. She floated on her back for a long moment, ignoring the cold that made her breath come quick, enjoying the blue sweep of sky, tiny puffs of white cloud racing and rolling above the birch boughs. For a moment, it was as though she had no past to weep over, no future to worry about, just herself and the water and wind and so much sky.

Riding back through the warmed meadows, sun high overhead, Ailsa hummed in time with Nia's smooth trot. Her wet braid dribbled water down her back. No matter, it was a glorious day. And nearly the solstice, the start of true summer, when anything wonderful might happen. She sang an old song as she rode. "When crowds of white flowers appear, and green buds light the trees." Suddenly she felt sure something would happen, something unusual and wonderful and strange. Though Dugald would not take her away, still she'd not be buried here on this one plot of land forever, never seeing the incredible wideness of the world.

She touched her heels to Nia. They flew down the curving path and pounded through the manor gate. She waved at Kyle and he gave her a crooked grin as she clattered onto the stone courtyard.

"Lady Ailsa, Lady!" Young Jamie, the stable boy, danced in front of her mare, his long thin arms in the air.

"What is it? Stop, you'll frighten Nia." She slid down. "You look all flustered."

"Aye, my lady, well..." His face wrinkled with distress.

"What is it then?" She handed him the reins. "Is someone injured?"

"Oh no, never say so. It's the Lady Jocelin and her son, they're here, you see."

"Here?" echoed Ailsa. Lady Jocelin was a distant cousin of the great de Morville family and their closest neighbor. Their tower house with its impressive stone walls and cavernous great hall was only a day's ride away, and yet they seldom visited. In fact, since her father's death, she could not recall that Lady Jocelin had appeared at Caerwyn's gates at all.

"Please." Jamie interrupted her thoughts. "She's been waiting here since the midmorning meal and right impatient she is."

Ailsa cast a last glance at the blue sky, then straightened her shoulders. "I'm sure, Jamie. Don't worry yourself, I'll hurry along now."

He smiled, his freckled face lighting up.

Ailsa took a deep breath and pushed open the door to enter the hall. "Lady Jocelin, and Thomas, how very kind of you to pay us a visit."

Meriel, seated on a stool by the hearth, where a small fire burned, smiled. "There you are, Ailsa," she said, relief clear on her transparent face.

Lady Jocelin sat ensconced in the best chair, the one that had been her father's. She was dressed in black wool embellished with black fur, very elegant, but rather warm for such a day. Her long pale face had a faint sheen of sweat. Standing beside her, stiff in his resplendent best, stood Thomas. He was taller than she remembered but his eyes were still kind. They had played together at a few Yule gatherings as children. He bowed to Ailsa in a formal way but said nothing.

"Greetings," began Jocelin in her booming voice. "It is a great pleasure to see you once more."

"And a greater pleasure to entertain you in our home." Ailsa offered the ritual lines of hospitality as her mind raced. She saw Jocelin noting her disheveled clothes and damp hair. She thrust her wet braid over her shoulder but felt her cheeks flush. Thomas suppressed a small grin, then returned to staring at the floor.

"Ailsa, dear. Come sit here beside me. I have something important, and private..." Jocelin stopped and looked pointedly at Meriel, who blushed and rose.

"Of course, pray excuse me, indeed I have just remembered I must see to the dinner preparations in the kitchens." Meriel left the hall, closing the oak door silently behind her.

"Now." Jocelin leaned over and grasped Ailsa's hand. She squeezed it with damp fingers. "Ever since your poor mother died I have taken a great interest in you. And when your brave father perished in that storm, well, you have been often in my thoughts." She paused, her eyes on the ceiling, where a cobweb hung. "I have come to an important decision. You cannot continue here alone, unprotected, unsupervised." She examined Ailsa's wrinkled gown with raised brows. "It's time you had someone to take the heavy load from you, someone to let you be a proper young woman, in truth."

Ailsa wondered why this sympathy had taken so long to be expressed, but she tried to answer politely. "How kind of you to think on me. While it has not always been easy these past years, I am hardly alone or unprotected. I have Mirren, my steward, who is very capable. And Meriel often keeps me good company. And Dugald, of course, is here much in the winter months."

"Yes, yes, dear," interrupted Jocelin, "But let us agree that you have more than reached an age where the proper order of things is to find a husband."

Ailsa felt her face stiffen. Thomas seemed to study the rushes on the floor, trying no doubt to disappear beneath them. She blinked several times. She would not think of Niall now. She would not.

"Indeed what could be more suitable than you and my Thomas here, joining together, what with our adjoining lands. Your own dear father often thought on it, Ailsa, I can assure you of that."

"He did?" Ailsa was taken aback. Surely not. There had been Cathal, her betrothed from the cradle. She had never actually met him, for he'd died in a hunting accident when he was but eleven. After Cathal, even the word marriage had never been uttered by her father.

"Oh yes," continued Jocelin, "he spoke of it often. Indeed, I do believe he was planning on a formal betrothal on his next visit home. Before his unfortunate death, I mean. I would not wish to press you, but young women need guidance and Caerwyn, in these most troubling times, needs a man for its defense. I know you will want to follow your late father's wishes."

Ailsa felt her cheeks burn. Her father had been lax, in truth, loathe to send his darling daughter to a new home, though she had reached and passed the marrying age. And after that awful winter when he died, then she had met Niall, a stranger and so unsuitable to be her husband, but she had decided to marry him nonetheless. She could feel her fingers tremble and she clasped her hands behind her back, so Jocelyn would not see. She felt again the sharp edge of tears and abruptly walked to the window. She stared a moment at the sea, winking blue beyond the greening fields.

"Lady Jocelin," she turned back to the hearth, "and Thomas." She looked at her childhood friend, too content to let his mother talk for him. "I am honored indeed. But I had not thought to marry at this time."

"Whyever not? It is well past time, I would say," said Jocelin, her eyebrows raised.

Ailsa swallowed. Jocelin was right. She was five and twenty in fact, but it was rude.

"Shall we agree, then," Jocelin said, smoothing a thread on her skirts. "You and Thomas will suit well and join the lands to great advantage."

"Indeed, you do me an unlooked-for honor." Ailsa stopped, then said, "You will have to give me time to think on this and consult my relatives. It's an important decision."

Jocelin narrowed her eyes, but she could find no appropriate objection. "Well, it is proper for a girl to seek advice and consider. We will stay with you a few days and help you decide on this matter. In these days," she fingered the silk tassels of her richly embroidered girdle, "it's good to have bonds to English blood. Our good King David ever favors those who do."

"In this house mingle the blood of Gaels and Norse. We have no need of the English here," Ailsa said, then bit her tongue, remembering too late her neighbor's connection with the English de Morvilles, said to be the king's closest of advisors.

Thomas broke in for the first time. "Ailsa, my mother means no offense, I am sure." He glanced at his mother's rigid face, then shrugged and said in a soft voice, "It is true, times are changing, and Norman ways are firm in England, and now come to Scotia too, ever favored by our new king. It's a serious matter to consider. For the sake of your lands, and your peoples."

Ailsa met his gaze, surprised at how earnestly he spoke. He was right in part, though she could not feel so pleased as he that Normans now overran the land. On the coast, the ancient site of Dalriada, the blood of the Gaels and Norse remained strong. And her mother had come from British stock, a people now driven into far Wales by these same Norman interlopers. "I will wait for my cousin to arrive home, for, as you say, it's a weighty matter to consider, one of changing times and loyalties."

His mother flushed and broke in. "Is your cousin Dugald your ward then?"

"I have no ward," said Ailsa curtly. "And we agree that I am no longer a girl." There was an uncomfortable pause. She licked her dry lips and tried to control her voice. "I have no ward, and the decision to wed or not will be mine, as is my right as my father's sole heir to these lands. But I do value my cousin's advice and I will wait to seek it." She glanced at Thomas, who was studying the embroidered hangings on the wall. It was true the political climate had changed, and that she must marry and soon, but she would not be hounded. "I do think we should consider with care, do you not; it takes thinking on most seriously, this matter of marriage."

Thomas regarded her for a long moment, then gave her a slow smile. "An important matter indeed." She smiled back, feeling a moment of communion with him. Yet she noticed, with dismay, that he cast a glance at his formidable mother.

Jocelin stood, her dark skirts dropping in stiff folds. "We will allow Ailsa time to consult her kin." Her face was quite without expression, but red spots flamed on her cheeks. "We shall expect your answer at the end of the Yuletide season then. Dugald will be home and you can discuss matters with him fully, I trust. Now, we must return home."

Ailsa protested, and offered food and drink, but Jocelin gathered her cloak and strode across the clean rushes, newly laid on the earth floor. Thomas followed, but turned at the door, gave her an apologetic smile, then followed his mother into the afternoon sun.

Ailsa trailed after them. "It's becoming late. You must not ride now. Please stay on for the night. You are most welcome here in our home."

Jocelin was helped onto the broad back of her steady mare. "There will be light long yet, and we have plenty of men. Who would dare to stop us?" With this last pointed remark, they passed through the courtyard gates.

Ailsa sighed as she watched them go, then went in, slumping down on the oak bench near the door in the dark hall.

Meriel peered round the corner.

"She wishes him to marry me, Meriel. What think you?"

"Does she know of the curse?" Meriel whispered the words and came to sit beside Ailsa, putting a hand on hers.

Ailsa swallowed. So even Meriel, new to the village, knew the rumors. She shook off Meriel's hand. She had married Niall the summer after her father died and lived with him as a wife for three months. Three sunlit months. Then he had died, in agony, from poison in the blood after a wound from an axe. It was then the villagers began to whisper. First Cathal. Then Niall. Cursed. In the day, she knew it to be chance. But she felt the awful truth of it like a strangling weight on her throat, every night.

"I gather not," Ailsa said. "Nor do they seem to know about my marriage to Niall at all. But it doesn't matter. I suppose I could do worse and apparently, marry I must." She frowned, staring at the oak floor, where the boards were worn with endless footsteps.

"Do you believe it true?" asked Meriel in a small voice. "The curse?"

"Of course I do not. It is but superstitious gossip."

"It has been a long time since your marriage," said Meriel hesitantly.

"Four years is not long," said Ailsa shortly. She stood up and brushed off her skirts. "In any event, I said I must wait on Dugald. For his advice. Till Epiphany."

Meriel nodded. "A good and proper answer. But not one I'd thought to hear you give, in truth. Dugald will be rare pleased you value his wisdom so high."

Ailsa studied Meriel, surprised at this attempt at humor. "Aye, well, I do expect I'll be doing some thinking of my own."

Ailsa left the storeroom where she'd been sorting herbs, deciding what they needed to replenish after the long winter months. The herbs were Meriel's work, and she was more than happy to leave the plants and healing to her. But Meriel had seemed tired at this afternoon's meal, and uncharacteristically downcast. She'd sent her to her bed early.

She stretched her arms over her head; her back ached from bending over the pots for so long. The air was fresh, with a stiff breeze off the sea. She could hear the hum of voices and an occasional excited shout. The turn of the seasons, of course. Midsummer. That visit a week ago had driven all else from her mind. She frowned. What an awful woman Jocelin was. But her son, Thomas, he'd likely be a kind and thoughtful man now. Had her father truly wished it?

She walked round the corner of the storehouse, and stopped in the shadow by the granite wall. Through the courtyard gates she glimpsed a crowd of young women joking and laughing. They had come from all the hamlets about for the celebrations to be held tonight and on until the morn. All wearing their best gowns. Most were shades of blue and they looked beautiful against the green of the lush meadows. The girls were clustered round the circle of old standing stones at the top of the hill, their hair twined with white ribbons fluttering in the breezes off the sea. She caught the smell of green grass and salt.

Ailsa looked down at the gray pot in her hands, filled with dried marjoram; the shriveled leaves fell apart when she touched them with her fingers. The minstrel would sing later tonight, wistful songs of love and great adventure, of ladies and warriors and travels to strange and wondrous lands. She felt the familiar longing to go, to be a part of that wide open world.

She took a deep breath, then walked back to the storeroom. She put the pot on the shelf and closed and locked the heavy door. She mounted the stairs to the walkway along the manor's roof and found her usual protected corner out of the wind, a place she favored, as she could look out over the sea. Soft puffs of white cloud scudded over the flat purple clouds hanging over the water. Her eyes searched the bay and the familiar islands and beyond them, the open sea. If only Dugald had taken her. Surely, she'd be having a fine adventure now, perhaps in an Irish port, filled with ships from every distant land. The colors would be brilliant red and blue and gold against the shifting emerald of the ocean water. And the sounds, people speaking every language and dressed in strange and wonderful cloth, like the silks she'd seen once in Renfrew. She saw herself there too, dressed in a gown of green linen, in a far meadow with unfamiliar bright and beautiful flowers. She fiddled with her long braid.

She was caught, a prisoner to her past and to her duty. She would see nothing, she would grow old and musty, like those miserable herbs in their locked storeroom.

Nothing would ever be the same after Niall. But was her life to be so completely desolate and empty and constrained? She walked back to the wall and stared down at the dancers, their voices blown away from her by the wind, weaving their white ribbons in silent patterns. The bonfire between the stones blazed up toward the clouds. She bit her lip and looked away, toward the empty sea.

21

CHAPTER TWO

King David's Court at Edinburgh, The Yule, 1135

ROBERT NUDGED HIS HORSE over beside his friend Walter and gestured to the timber towers of Edinburgh ahead of them. "What think you? Will we be welcomed?"

"For certain," said Walter. "King David will welcome all who can help hold his lands, what with Henry of England dead. With England weak and fighting amongst all, there's opportunity aplenty." He grinned and adjusted his forest cloak to show the crimson lining to better advantage. "Not so grand as Westminster, for certain." He nodded toward the stockade fence ahead of them.

Robert's brows drew together as he studied the fence and tower. "At least the sun shines, a good omen." They'd been riding for near a week in dampness and fog, ever since they'd crossed the borderlands, but now the sun glinted off the water drops on the branches of the oaks.

"I'll cross over first, I wager." Walter spurred his horse over the bridge and toward the city walls.

Robert laughed and touched Tanet's flanks with his heels and they thundered up the road toward David's seat.

That evening, fresh bathed and dressed in their finest tunics over linen shirts, wet hair combed into place, Robert and Walter sat at the high table watching David, understated in embroidered silk in his huge carved chair. The king was conversing with his son Henry, named after England's recently deceased monarch, and near a man grown. The chair on David's other side was empty; no one sat there since Matilda, his well-loved queen, had died several years back, or so

Walter informed Robert in a low voice. Walter had spent the afternoon joking and talking with men about the castle and he'd learned much in a day. He'd related it all to Robert in a series of entertaining tales, as they soaped the dirt and smell of two weeks riding away in a tub of hot bathwater in a hut behind the kitchens.

Walter gestured with his goblet toward his father, Alain of Dol, who had held vast estates in Shropshire, on the border with Wales. He'd journeyed to Scotia a fortnight ahead of his son to smooth the way, for the crisis over who would be England's next king created uncertainty, and many barons had fled back to Normandy or to the Flemish lands until they saw how matters settled. Walter's father had decided on Scotia and moved quickly, leaving his son to finish some work on his estates and then ride north. "I think we did well to come here. Especially with this latest news." Walter pitched his voice low.

Robert tapped his fingers on the table. Shortly after they'd clattered into the king's courtyard, they'd heard that Stephen of Blois, the late King Henry's nephew, had ridden to Westminster, captured the English treasury, and had himself crowned King of England. Stolen the Empress Matilda's throne, some said, Henry's own daughter, while she tarried overlong in Normandy. It was whispered she'd spent too much time preparing for the grand entrance she hoped to make to her kingdom. It was also whispered she was ragingly angry now, and she had her father's uncontrollable temper, less admired in a woman than in her father. What would come now was anyone's guess.

"We are well out of it," agreed Robert. "Here a man can make a new start. Build with some hope of holding one's gains. But I wonder what the future holds for your father and brother."

"William is right worried," acknowledged Walter. "Does he hold for Matilda or go over to Stephen now. It's a hard choice. But he'll land on his feet, no doubt." Having dismissed his elder brother's dilemma with a shrug, Walter turned to converse with Adam de Brus on his left. He'd already discovered de Brus was the son of an important advisor of the king.

Walter would always land on his feet too. His father was a powerful and wealthy man, already seated near the king at the high table.

Robert sighed. His friend was an opportunist, but he had a good heart and liked a laugh, and besides, he owed him much. They'd fought together in Normandy the past eight years. But he didn't want to think of Normandy now.

Robert turned back toward the king. So much depended on this one man. He liked the intelligent brown eyes and stern face. The king was reputed to be godly to an extreme, and a good lord to serve, fair in his judgments. But he'd been reserving his own judgment; he liked to see a man's face. Now Robert felt his tight shoulder muscles relax, and he stretched his long legs out under the table. He hadn't chosen wrong. And it was past time for his fortune to turn, though he wasn't one to believe in luck. Luck was a matter of assessing a situation and acting.

The crowded hall was noisy, festive with the Yule season. Pages carrying heavy trays and full pitchers darted between trestle tables laid with white cloths, and laden with huge trenchers of venison and pork, pastries filled with mutton and spices, and stone fruits stewed with cinnamon. The scent of roasted chicken mingled with sweet smoke from dozens of beeswax candles and the sharp scent of evergreens decorating the hall. Musicians played harp, bells and drums in one corner, though he could barely hear them over the din of convivial conversations and shouted commands. The king had English tastes indeed. Not strange, for David had been raised in Henry's court, and come home to Scotia only as a man grown, bringing many English and French friends and advisors.

All around, men sprawled, drinking ale and wine, relaxing and making merry. One cheerful serving maid caught his eye, as she carried in a huge bowl piled with sugared oranges. Time to put the past behind and leave the future to itself, Robert chided himself. His life had taken a turn; Normandy lay behind him. Fortune lay ahead for one who could shape it. He meant to finally turn things his way.

Though it was the Yule, the next few days passed in serious discussions with the king's men. As all said, David pondered the affairs of his realm most dutifully. And there was much to consider, with England's throne in contention and Stephen and Matilda both sending urgent messengers to David's court.

Robert sucked in a deep breath of winter air as he walked across the courtyard toward the council chambers. The sky overhead was a clear blue, the wind fresh and he was happy to be out of the stuffy chambers. He stretched his long arms over his head and tarried by the door, just for the pleasure of lingering outside. He watched a groom deal with a spirited black charger, eager to run on such a day. After the groom cantered away, he could find no other excuse, and envying the groom his morning ride, he turned, with a sigh.

As he mounted the steps, a burly man rushed out, already shouting for his horse, and shoved Robert out of his way, cursing. The man glared at the young groom who hurried forward leading a fine horse. Surely there was something familiar about the short figure. As the man pushed the servant away and mounted, the horse swung round and Robert saw him head on. He felt his heart pound. One of fitz John's men. It had been years, near ten years surely, but there was no question. Payn fitz John, who had aided King Henry in his vicious raids into Wales and now ruled there like a king himself. Robert felt again the familiar bleak and futile rage.

"Lord," said a voice behind him, and he swung around, yanked from his dark thoughts, his hand on his sword hilt.

"May I pass, Lord," stammered a nervous housemaid before him.

He dropped his hand from his sword. "I'm sorry." Her eyebrows rose in astonishment. She was slight, pale brown hair trailing in untidy wisps from her cap. She scurried by him.

He turned to the courtyard again. The man, still shouting orders at the grooms, swung his horse round and galloped out the open gate, his men trailing behind. Robert watched him disappear down the road. Fitz John's man, here at David's court. Ignoring the pages who were staring at him curiously, he ran a hand through his hair, thinking. Unlike Walter, he'd never thought Scotia would be a trouble-free haven. But this he had not expected. Face set, Robert strode to the council chamber.

When he entered, he saw that Walter and his father were already deep in discussion with David's lawyers. Land deeds and maps on the table before them, they were tracing the borders for the estate near Renfrew that Walter would soon hold from the king and listing the crops and silver he would owe the bishopric of Glasgow each year in turn. They ignored him, and Robert sat on a bench at the end of the table and braced himself for another tiring day.

The council chamber was shrouded against the sun with deep blue curtains, adding to the gloom. Embroideries depicting classical myths hung on all the walls. An odd choice for a pious king, thought Robert, as he tried to see the embroideries in the dim light. Elsewhere the textiles he'd seen were all of Bible tales and saints. But David was learned in Latin and Greek, tutored in the English king's court. King Henry, dead before his time, of a too ample serving of stewed eels, it was rumored. Spoiled fish, or had he been poisoned? Henry, whose life and even death seemed to reach out and shape his choices. For it was Henry's endless raids into Wales which had taken his father's life and lost him his family lands. And now a man of fitz John's, Henry's powerful arm in Wales, was here, in Edinburgh. Why?

Robert stood up abruptly and walked to the window, flinging open the wooden shutter. The chamber was heavy with the smells of musty wool, spiced wines and perfume. Alain, Walter's father, raised a reproving eyebrow at him, as he continued to discourse with the lawyers. Robert nodded back, but stayed by the window, breathing in the fresh, cold air. Gradually he felt his hands unclench and his heart slow in his chest. The rustle of maps on the table behind him roused him from his dark thoughts. Henry alive had stolen his family lands, and with them his future, but Henry dead was giving him a new chance here in Scotia. He closed the shutter and returned to the table.

David's lawyers droned on, describing the terms under which the lands and castles would come into Walter's estate. As David's man, Walter would be wealthy and powerful indeed. Walter's father's face was stern, not betraying a hint of the satisfaction he must certainly feel to settle a younger son so well. But Alain fitz Flaad of Dol was a powerful man himself, holding lands in Normandy as well as Shropshire, where he held the castle at Oswestry. Robert watched while the men negotiated. He himself had no quarrel with Matilda, nor with Stephen, nor even much interest in the outcome of their contesting for the English crown. He hoped only to find his place far from their struggles. Walter would have grand estates from this Scots king and he, as a much lesser knight with no family lands of his own, would administer them for his friend. He would tie his future to Walter, who tied his own to David. It scarce mattered to him where Walter's lands were, only that he would have a place and a purpose. If Walter was an opportunist, so, in truth, was he. But even Walter knew little of his grave losses to Henry and fitz John. He spoke of his past with no one.

One of the embroidery panels behind the King showed Persephone returning from the underworld, apple blossoms wreathing her waving hair, plums and peaches piled in her arms, and the earth behind her green, lush with new leaves. The stitches and colors were so fine that for a moment Robert imagined he could smell the new earth, the tiny unfurling leaves and the warm peaches in the sun. The women who had stitched this panel were talented indeed. Their work brought back the texture and even the smells of his own lands, now gone forever.

Eight years now he'd fought with Walter, for the causes of the fitz Alain men. Nine years before that he had wandered the tournament circuit and fought for whoever was taking on men in Normandy. He would work for Walter, who worked for the king. But back on the Welsh borders, his own father had walked his orchard in the long twilight evenings of summer and worked for no man but himself.

Some few days later, a hunt was organized in the king's forest. Robert sniffed the early morning air and observed the crowd of fine-dressed courtiers and the huddle of the king's huntsmen, arrayed alike in nut brown wool. He was eager to be out and clear his head of the endless deliberations. The air was bracing; the sun shone bright. Men's voices rose in the still air, along with the smoky scent of the cooking fires, where porridge simmered for their morning meal. He caught the smell of bacon too. Then David himself rode into the clearing on a sturdy silver hunter.

In a short while, well fed, the party of some twenty men set out into the forests, following the beaten pathways where the horses could pass easily. They were headed for a small valley between two forested hills, a good place to drive the deer. It wasn't likely they'd find much today but the hinds. Still, the day promised good sport. Two pairs of the king's greyhounds loped beside the horses, leashed as yet.

Robert pulled up to Walter's side. "Who are those two, up ahead there with the hounds?"

Walter followed his gaze. "That's Hugh de Morville, the king's Constable, and the slim one in black is his eldest son, also Hugh. They arrived late last night from Lauder. He has some interest, so I've heard, in the lands the king grants to me." Walter frowned. "I can't say I like the man. He's stern and without humor. Yet David relies on him."

Robert stared at de Morville. The stiff back and flowing green cloak told him little. "And the son?"

"He said naught of consequence last night. Still, he has a cold look about him." Walter flicked a dead leaf from his leather glove. "They'd not be my choice of neighbors, but it's the nature of things to look to your back. I wager Scotia will be no different in that than Shropshire."

True enough, thought Robert, recalling the surprise of fitz John's man in the king's courtyard. He shook his head. Today was for pleasure and hard riding, not grim thoughts.

They reached the valley and the men dismounted and tied the horses, while a page rushed forward to take the reins from the king. The huntsmen strung their bows, unleashed the hounds and scattered to their line in the woods. The king would have the place of honor, at the head of the valley where the deer would be most likely to appear, running from the hounds and drivers.

Robert handed Tanet's reins to the page with a kind word to the boy, then walked into the thinning woods. The ground was hard with frost underfoot and rolling with with acorns. A few patches of snow lay under the evergreens. He climbed toward the ridge, feeling the pleasure of moving on a perfect winter morning, and gradually the clamor of horses, dogs, and men faded into the silence of the oaks and birches. Finding a small outcrop of granite, he surveyed the forests below, trees stretching into the distance, broken occasionally by the stripe of fields, brown and grey in their midwinter rest. The cooking fire still smoked far below.

Halfway up the slope, the straggling line of men drove through the underbrush, seeking the deer. The faint baying of the dogs filled the air. Robert headed down the far side of the hill, sliding on frost and wet leaves, moving toward the spot where the deer would emerge. He threaded through a stand of birches. Sun patterned the forest floor and gleamed off patches of ice. Shouts came, off to his right.

"Quick now!" It was Walter's voice, guiding the king toward the deer. Robert grabbed his light bow from the strap on his back. He saw the animal, a flash of brown through the trees, and the whirring of arrows from the men below split the air. The deer ran on, unharmed, amid the excited shouts of the men and the thrilled baying of the hounds. Robert plunged back into the trees, outdistancing the others. He hoped to catch the animal against the ridge, holding it there until the king arrived. He heard the animal, crashing in panic, snapping branches ahead. Then came more shouts, from behind. Angry shouts. Robert paused. Perhaps the hounds had flushed another deer, but he could not hear their baying.

Abruptly, he turned and ran back. He burst into a small clearing. Eight or nine men crowded around two hefty fellows, hurling insults at each other. Robert's eyes moved quickly from them, seeking the king. He found him, standing off to one side, frowning. Suddenly an arrow hissed through the air and landed with a thunk into an oak directly behind the king.

"Down!" Robert yelled, running toward David. He leaped onto the king, shoving him to the ground as another arrow hissed by. By now the king's men, though distracted by the fight, were realizing something was wrong. They milled about, yanking their bows out and fired into the bushes. Several rushed into the woods, prodding the brush with their spears, scattered and shouting.

Robert rose to his feet and the king silently got to his feet too, his servants rushing in to brush dead leaves from his clothing. And though they beat the bushes and searched, no one was found, and no clues could be discovered. Robert waited out of the confusion, staring into the forest. Who had dared fire at a king? They had chosen their time well, waiting until the men were distracted. Or had the distraction itself been planned?

The chase was abandoned and a subdued party returned to the castle. David was silent and the men kept their whispers low. As they entered the castle gates, the king shouted for de Brus, called Hugh the Constable to him, and closeted himself in the council chambers. Dinner was a hurried affair, for the king did not emerge.

Robert and Walter went to their pallets early.

"What think you, Robb," asked Walter in a quiet voice.

"It could be anyone." He thought of the hissing arrows and the king's startled face. A king had many enemies, always. And this king had his share. Rebels in the North, only six years before, had risen against David while he tarried at the English court. Angus of Moray had claimed the throne and led the fierce Northmen against the king's old constable, Edward. But Edward had triumphed, for he had Norman and English knights, with chargers and armor. They'd killed Moray himself and beat back his men. But Moray's son, Malcolm MacHeth, had escaped. Robert twisted on his pallet. And caused no end of trouble for four of the last six years. Yet now he too was captured, imprisoned, it was rumored, at the king's castle at Roxburgh, in a dark cell beneath the floors. Imprisoned but not killed. Some whispered it proved he did indeed have royal blood. Some even dared say David's claim to the throne was tainted, for his father stole it through murder of the rightful heir.

He heard Walter sigh and turn over on his pallet, and knew his mind ran through the same dark thoughts. And the North was not the only problem, for in the West too, a young chief was causing concern. Somerled he called himself. The summer voyager, a Viking name, for all he was only part Norse. Named for the powerful ships the Islesmen used to voyage throughout the Isles and on to Ireland on the spring winds and home on the easterlies in the fall. He'd signed a treaty with the Scots king, or so he'd heard it said. But perhaps David's throne was not as secure as it seemed.

Had he gone from the troubles between Matilda and Stephen in England to new and even worse troubles here? Robert sighed. Walter's deep and even breaths signaled that he had fallen asleep. He was not one to worry overmuch about what could not be changed.

After a bad night's sleep, Robert climbed on Tanet and headed into the forest alone. By noon, in a much better mood, he sat by a small fire he'd kindled. Beside him lay three rabbits. Not bad for a morning's hunt, he thought with a pleasant sense of satisfaction. A pheasant roasted on its spit over the coals and he sniffed the combined smells of roasting fowl and wood smoke with appreciation. Now this was better. Endless forests full of game, a winter sky still holding off its snow. The sound of the wind brushing tree branches. He ate the pheasant and a hardened piece of cheese he found in his bag, and then drank at a stream nearby, breaking the crust of clear ice with a rock. He lay down on a pile of oak leaves. Overhead the sky was the color of gray rabbit fur and the tree branches swayed. Soon he was fast asleep.

"Robert, Sir Robert," called a voice.

He was on his feet, pulling his knife. He could see no one, then he heard a crackle in the underbrush and Jos, Walter's man, ran into the clearing. "You're wanted at the castle, long since. You're to wear your best and appear at the high table." Jos paused, and shifted uneasily. "It's fair late, Sir Robert."

Robert frowned, coming fully awake. Kicking some earth over the last coals of the fire, he whistled to Tanet. He took a last look about the peaceful clearing, then jumped on the horse's back. "All right then, let's go," he called to Jos with a grin, and yanked him up behind. They cantered back to the castle, where he handed Jos the sack of game. Jos looked surprised as he peered inside and then he grinned widely and disappeared into the ale-drinking crowd. Robert wished he could go with him.

Music wafted already from the king's hall. Cooking fires roared in the courtyard and boys were turning great haunches of mutton and pork; the scent of the roasting meats and smoke filled the air. Servants bustled back and forth carrying casks of wine, sloshing tubs of ale, and great wheels of orange cheese. Robert hadn't seen such a festive Yule scene in many years. As he crossed the courtyard, he remembered his mother preparing for the holiday. She had always made a special event of all twelve days and nights of the Yule. He hadn't thought of that for a long time.

A pail of water sat by the kitchen door, so he splashed his hands and face.

Walter, arrayed in his best green tunic, stood by the entrance. "Jos found you I see. He's the best tracker around." They moved toward their appointed places at the end of the high table. David hadn't entered yet, so he was sufficiently on time, thanks to Walter and Jos. Robert took a deep drink of the Bordeaux wine and an eager page ran up to refill the goblet. Robert smiled at the boy, remembering his own first days as a page, desperate to please, in the years after he'd run away from his stepfather's reach.

A horn sounded, quieting the noisy throng at the many tables. David entered, dressed in purple wool with a golden circlet, Norman style, on his graying hair. All stood and bowed. David did not sit, as expected, but looked out over the crowded hall. "Tonight we hold our Yuletide Feast." The king's assured voice carried through the high-ceilinged chamber. "I wish to announce a dearly held dream, now coming to fruition. In one week, we march! To Carlisle!" He raised his voice over the exclamations of the men. "There to take the castle that William the Red stole from the Scots. We will return Carlisle and then all Northumbria to Scotia!"

Shouts of approval and much banging on tables and clanking of goblets filled the hall. David smiled calmly through the disturbance. "Ready yourselves, we leave in one week and travel swiftly. Even now, Stephen loiters in Normandy, bargaining with Matilda. While they argue over who would rule England, they leave a gaping hole open for us. We will regain our rightful lands!" Shouts and cheers bounced from the rafters.

Robert wondered at the enthusiasm inspired by David. Though quiet, he pulled men in and made them want to serve him. True, he had picked a popular cause here, one to unite even the prickly Northerners with the Islesmen and the Cumbrians themselves. And one that would give Matilda some apparent aid, seeming to regain the lands from Stephen, but not anger Stephen overmuch, as the lands were but recently claimed. And it was true the lands were stolen from the Scots. He tapped a finger on the table and examined David's face with new respect.

"Enjoy your celebrations, men. Tomorrow we ready ourselves for battle and Carlisle!" The king walked to his carved chair and sat, face serious, amid the clamor of excited voices. Pages appeared, lugging roasted chickens and geese, piles of honey oatcakes, soft wheat bread, stewed apples and plums, and other savory holiday fare. Great pitchers of wine and ale sloshed at every table. Robert grabbed one from a page passing by, and poured wine into his goblet, thinking hard. What would this march to Carlisle mean for him?

He saw David signal a servant, who called Walter to the king. Alain, Walter's father, was tapped too, and they went and stood before him, father and son remarkably alike, sandy hair and blue eyes, round faces with stern chins. Robert glanced at the others at the high table. Hugh de Morville and Robert de Brus. There were others too; he'd learned their names, for he needed to know this new land, if he were to survive and prosper here. There was Paganus de Braose and Prince Henry, of course, laughing at a joke, his face freckled, open and friendly. Young Adam de Brus and Hugh de Morville's son, the younger Hugh, sat together sharing the opposite end of the table. Hugh, with narrowed eyes, was watching Walter with an expression of intense dislike. Robert sucked in a quiet breath. Hugh's black cloak bore a large Celtic brooch of intricate design, highly polished; it flashed in the candlelight. Odd, for the son of a highly placed Norman.

David gestured for quiet at the high table, then announced, "On the eve of my departure to Carlisle, I wish to award to you, my good lords, lands to support your faithful service." He motioned and a page brought a leather parcel and handed it to the king. David nodded to Alain, then gestured to Walter to stand before him as well. He pulled from the leather parcel a small square of parchment and read aloud in Latin:

> *"Walter, son of Alain fitz Flaad of Dol and of Shropshire, I hereby make you my Steward, to serve my household, where-soever I may be. By this charter I grant to you and yours these lands and their wealth -- Renfrew, Mearns, Strathgryfe and North Kyle. I do grant to you and your heirs to hold for me these lands, to make them full productive, and in recognition of these various holdings, I require from you the service of five knights as payment on my call."*

Walter, pale and serious, went down on one knee and thanked the king eloquently, promising loyalty.

"Your duties as steward begin tomorrow," said David, "readying our household for the journey to Carlisle."

"I will be up to the task," said Walter. He returned to his place and grinned over to Robert. Robert waved back, relieved for his friend and for his own future, for though the lands were promised, with kings nothing was sure until it was placed firmly in one's hands.

An elbow dug into his ribs. "They're calling you, man," said the grey bearded lord from the North who sat next to him on the rough bench.

"What?" questioned Robert. But then he heard his name called out. He stood, wondering what this could be about. He made his way up to the high chair and bowed before the king.

"Having spoken with Alain of Dol, I know somewhat of your situation. And having seen your immense ability yesterday," the king continued, "when you saved my life in the clearing..."

"It was little enough and any man would have..."

David silenced him with a stern look. "Any would have, but none did. There are not many retain their wits in crisis to act sensibly and with speed. You showed yourself such a man yesterday and I am full grateful." The king leaned closer and spoke in a low voice. "I need such a man to help hold the West and Isles for me while I am in Carlisle and to help hold your friend the steward's lands as well, whilst he is serving me." David sat back and said, loudly, "I hereby grant you the manor and lands of Caerwyn, on the coast near Dundonald." The king lowered his voice again. "'Twill enable you to oversee Walter the steward's lands, which lie nearby. More, I charge you with building a tower for Caerwyn's defense. You will be able to see over the straits from there to Arran and beyond, and I charge you with acquainting yourself with this bishop some call Wimond. I must know the nature and extent of the threat from the West."

Robert swallowed and nodded. Like all rewards from a king, the prize came with conditions. Expensive and dangerous conditions. But lands, lands of his own, held direct from the king, that had been but a far off hopeless dream.

David waved a hand. A page came forward. "Caerwyn has an heiress. An orphan whose lands escheat to me and of marriageable age. She is my ward, and so I grant her along with her lands to you, for services to me, past and future."

Robert stammered some words of gratitude, bowed, and returned to his bench. Lands of his own. He could hardly think. He grinned at the greybeard, who sloshed wine in his cup and drank cheerfully to his good fortune.

Hearing raised voices at the other end of the table, Robert paused with his goblet in hand. Young Hugh's face was white and angry. His father was gripping his arm and whispering in his ear, but Hugh shook him off, spilling his wine into a pool on the white cloth. David ignored the interruption, and went on smoothly with his conversation with Elizabeth, de Brus's lively wife. The others took their signal from the king and returned to their conversations, forcing jokes to cover the tense scene. Hugh muttered into his son's ear, but the younger Hugh left as soon as the musicians entered the hall and the king rose, permitting people to move about the hall.

"That one may cause you some trouble," commented Walter. He put a hand on Robert's shoulder.

"I will be ready."

Walter grinned, "I know you will." He gave Robert's arm a cuff, his face red. "I'm glad for your good fortune. You deserve it."

Robert shoved him back. "I hardly know what to think of it yet." He grabbed a platter from a page going by. They speared the roasted swan and venison onto their trenchers and ate and drank as the minstrels sang, deep into the night. But when they finally found their pallets for the night, once again Robert lay awake in the dark, listening to the other men snore and rustle as they slept.

The coming days were filled with packing and provisioning. The central courtyard was always crowded with men and women shouting, lugging baskets of food and other supplies, all working on moving the king's household and organizing the military expedition. The knights and foot soldiers were to venture off first, heading south on the old Roman road, and it was planned the household would follow some three days behind, carrying in wooden carts all that was necessary to set up a full court at Carlisle. David intended to establish a firm symbol of his overlordship there.

Walter was so busy with his new duties that Robert barely saw him. But he would be in his element, for he was a born organizer, and good with people, so that men, and the women too, labored overtime for him with no complaint.

Robert ordered provisions for his own journey as well, to his new holding of Caerwyn, but since he would take only a few men, and travel light, all was quickly set in order. He had letters from the king introducing him to the bishop in Glasgow, and to one or two of the lords who hadn't come to David's Yuletide court. And in a packet of oiled cloth, sewn into his tunic, he had the precious parchment, the Latin lettering stating his duties to David for the manor and lands of Caerwyn.

Lady Ailsa of Caerwyn. He had learned her name. Yet it was hard to imagine a wife. His eyes drifted over the courtyard. He would be glad to be on the road again and waited only for the king to leave before heading west himself.

One side of the courtyard was busy with stalls set up by local merchants trying to sell their wares with this opportunity of the king's journey. His eye was caught by one stall with bright ribbons displayed, blowing in the winter breezes under the bright sun. He nodded to the merchant, who turned to help the new customer. "Aye, sir?"

Robert touched some lavender ribbons. "Some of these," he said, wondering at himself, "and these also." He pointed to some emerald strands fluttering in the wind.

"Of course, sir." The merchant packaged the ribbons up and handed him the neat parcel. "Anything else, sir?"

Robert shook his head, puzzled at his own impulse. He handed the man a silver coin from England. Walter appeared at his elbow.

"What do you here?" joked Walter, as Robert thrust the package in his sleeve.

"No business of yours."

Walter laughed. "Have it your way. Soon we'll have Scots coins, the king says, minted at Carlisle. What say you to that? When do you leave for this Caerwyn?"

"Tomorrow morning. When the king marches, I'll go west."

Walter nodded. "You will see my holdings before I do." The two men walked away from the merchant's stall, to a quieter corner by the timber walls. "You must send a report to me."

"Of course," agreed Robert, "I'll visit your lands before I go on."

"That would be helpful, for I'll not get there myself till full summer, I fear." They fell into a discussion of perambulating boundaries, crop selection, and the constant problem of finding men to labor.

Next day, Robert watched the king lead his knights and men onto the Roman road. The weather held bright and clear. The men were cheering and even the horses seemed in high spirits.

"To Carlisle," shouted David, resplendent in a chased hauberk on his gray charger, and the men shouted and shook their spears.

Elizabeth, de Brus' wife, waved and cheered to the men till they were gone from sight. Then she turned to Robert, beside her on the castle walls. "Another long parting," she sighed.

Robert nodded his sympathy. It was said that de Brus and his wife were well suited. "Do you go south as well?" The de Brus holdings were just north of Carlisle.

"Aye, but I am to wait until they send word." She frowned impatiently. Then she turned. "You must bring your new wife to visit, once the king has taken Carlisle. Our seat at Annan is not far at all, just an easy day's ride from the king's castle, and I would like to see her again."

"You know her?" asked Robert.

"I met her some eight or ten years ago. She was but a child yet; she will be quite changed now."

A stable boy led Tanet, coat gleaming in the bright sun, into the courtyard below, the horse excited and nearly toppling the boy. "Your pardon, ladies, I leave now as well." Turning from the women, Robert flew down the stairs.

CHAPTER THREE

Caerwyn, Winter, 1136

AILSA PAUSED, NEEDLE IN HAND, and shifted to a more comfortable position on the hard bench, pulled close to the hearth. She glanced toward the windows and sighed. The narrow slits were covered with stretched sheepskin against the winds, darkening the hall, especially on such a grey day. Impatiently, she pushed the candlestick closer to her work. Her eyes ached with the effort of seeing the fine stitches. Rain drummed down on the stones in the courtyard. It was the day after Epiphany, the Yule over for another year. Last night they had wassailed the oldest apple tree in her small orchard, and lighted twelve candles in the hall, to mirror the twelve fitful fires the men built in the wet fields. She sighed again and stretched her leg, cramped with sitting so long. She had acted her part well enough, but she had not felt festive.

Meriel, huddled under a wool shawl, looked up from her sewing. Her hands were red and rough with chilblains. Still, she insisted on doing her share of the straight sewing and she was mending Dugald's linen tunic. Ailsa looked down at her own hands, at the fine linen she held, dyed a deep blue, the color of the sky in windy September. The colors sprang out deep and satisfying against their background, but she couldn't keep her mind on the patterns. She dropped the cloth and stood, shaking out her skirts.

Meriel paused in her work. "You do sigh so today, why not see to the kitchen? It would give you something to do."

"After the holiday, it always seems so dull and flat."

Meriel smiled. "You mean, this year, it seems especially dreary. Now that Dugald and his friend have gone."

Ailsa glanced at Meriel with suspicion, but Meriel was sewing again, her blue eyes fixed on the material in her hands. It was true she missed the excitement and Dugald's trading partner Torquil was indeed handsome, but even better, a wonderful teller of tales besides. "When do you think Dugald will return?"

Meriel stared at her fingers, counting. "If he has good weather to travel, he might reach Renfrew, do the trading and be back in less than a fortnight. Today's rain will not help though."

"No." If I were a man, Ailsa thought with irritation, I'd go off in midwinter too. January was indeed an endless month, planting over and the new season not yet begun.

Meriel pushed the wisps of fair hair from her forehead. "I noticed you did not yet speak to Dugald about Thomas' offer for you."

"Did you tell him?" Ailsa demanded.

"No," answered Meriel. "It's up to you, after all. But I fear we may see Thomas and his mother at our door any day. You did promise an answer after the Yule. What will you say?"

Ailsa ran impatient fingers through her thick hair. "There's work to be done and I'd best get to it." She grabbed her cloak from the hook by the door, pulled the hood over her hair and pinned it firmly with a silver brooch.

Outside, the cold damp air made her nose tingle. Icy rain slanted down, and puddles of brown water filled the courtyard. She avoided the biggest, and after a moment's pause, headed, not for the kitchen, but toward the outer gate. Nodding to Kyle at the gatehouse, who struggled to jump to his feet as she passed, she strode down the muddy path, shoulders braced against the stiff winds. She didn't know where she was going, but she needed to walk far and fast.

She went in the direction of the woods. Soon, the tall oaks wrapped around her. The creak of bending branches and the sweep of the rain and wind surrounded her. She followed a winding path along the wood's edge, finally reaching a turn where she could glimpse the sea. This was one of her secret places. Close to the manor, yet far away.

Despite the cold she sat on a granite boulder with a conveniently flat top, arranging her wool skirts to keep her warm. Her toes felt chill already in her leather boots, but at least she was out in the fresh air. By midwinter the hall smelled of unwashed bodies and musty air, however clean one tried to be. She tipped her head up, watching grey branches move against grey sky. Not too much rain reached through the thick tangle of boughs.

The fields stretching down to the sea were brown, and the sea was grey as slate and shrouded in mist. No islands could be glimpsed today. The patter of raindrops as they made their way onto the carpet of leaves seemed the only sound. Ailsa stared out at the water, thinking about Dugald's return, and what to do about Thomas, and what to do with her whole miserable life.

Her eye caught the movement of a small boat, riding the swells toward the shore. That was strange; none of Caerwyn's men would be out fishing today. She watched as the boat rowed to the stony beach and two men climbed out. The boat cast off again and headed out, gone soon in the fog. The two men also disappeared, into the trees, with no shouts or even talk she could hear. She listened, but the wind blew in the wrong direction and she couldn't hear even a crack of sticks on the path to tell which way they'd gone.

She thought back to the strangers she'd seen by the pond in the summer. It was disquieting. Torquil and Dugald had talked endlessly of this new leader Somerled in the north and Wimond in the islands to the south. Unrest in far places was one thing, but strangers moving through Caerwyn's lands was another. She bit her lip. It would not have happened in her father's day.

She must tell Dugald. But no. He'd simply forbid her to go out on her own. And she wouldn't give up this small freedom. She had to get away sometimes, even from kind Meriel, be free of all eyes.

She stared at the empty beach, rolling a pebble in her fingers. These troubles would blow over, like a summer storm. Leaving everything the same. Another year past, another begun. I grow old, she thought. But that was not her true problem. Two men, one her betrothed and one her husband, and both now dead. Whispers through the village. That wouldn't have happened in her father's day either. But it wasn't the stares and the furtive crosses that bothered her most. It was Caerwyn. According to Dugald, she needed to marry. These strangers were a sign of worse to come. To him, it was not unfair but more a simple fact. She needed a man who could defend the manor and its people. He could not always be here; his own holdings on Arran were far away. She got to her feet and paced, twigs crunching under her boots. Dugald was right, she knew. But wrong also. And how could she marry again, as though Niall had never been.

Torquil seemed to admire her. Better, he told endless lively stories of all the far-flung places he'd been. Dugald would approve, for Torquil was his long-time trading partner. It would certainly be better than marrying Thomas, with his overbearing mother, or would it? She knew so little of either man really. And no matter who she chose, it would end her dreams of voyaging, of seeing something of the world, of doing something.

A drop of cold water ran down her neck and she sniffed. She needed to get back, see to the food stores; they must make sure there was sufficient to see them through till spring. She turned back toward the manor. At least with the drenching rain, she'd not find Thomas' mother coming up the road toward Caerwyn this day.

When Ailsa reached the manor, a crowd of servants gossiped in the courtyard, oblivious of the cold rain. "What is happening here," she called out.

One of the men turned. "Lady," he said. "News indeed. A messenger from the king!"

"The king!" Ailsa glanced down at her wet attire. "Are you sure?"

"Aye, he waits within."

Ailsa ran for the door to the hall. She yanked off her soaked cloak, handing it to Osla, the housemaid and her friend, who winked at her and returned to staring at the elegant messenger by the hearth.

"Do you come indeed from the king?" asked Ailsa, walking toward the man. "What news might you have for us?" Such a thing had never happened before.

The messenger eyed Ailsa with something like distaste. "I have a private communication for the heir."

"I am the heir," said Ailsa.

The messenger looked confused. "You're a woman," he said, "and my missive is for Dugald of Arran."

Ailsa frowned and stood taller. "I am Ailsa of Caerwyn, and my father's sole heir, as is the custom here in the West." She put a hand out.

The messenger rummaged in his bag. "If you be Lady Ailsa, I have a message for you as well."

"We have heard word of King Henry of England's death," Ailsa said slowly, wondering if this was the news he brought.

"I bring much more recent news than that, Lady," the messenger said, "though it follows on Henry's death. The Scots king marches for Carlisle."

Carlisle, city of King Arthur. She had heard many tales of the legendary castle. "It is kind of you to inform us," she stopped, unsure what to say next. For what exactly had this news to do with them? "Does the king wish Dugald to march with him?" Usually the Islesmen did not fight with the king and his English knights. It was understood they would guard the coast and go about their own business. Perhaps, though, with all this trouble with that rebel bishop Wimond, on the Isle of Man? Was the king testing his Gaelic subjects on the coast?

The messenger interrupted her busy analysis. "My purpose with you is this missive." He handed her a sealed packet, wrapped in oiled leather.

Ailsa hesitated, then took it from his hands. "I'll have the other missive too, as the true heir."

The messenger frowned.

"In any case, my cousin Dugald is away. His wife is here and I can give the package into her safe keeping."

The messenger hesitated but hearing a burst of rain on the slates outside, he handed her the larger packet and bowed himself out.

Ailsa carried both parcels to the bench by the hearth. She took the larger packet, addressed to Dugald, onto her lap.

"Should you?" said Meriel, who crept in from her spot at the doorway. "Isn't it for Dugald? For the men to deal with?"

"I'm the heir," said Ailsa, "and Caerwyn is mine."

"Of course," said Meriel, turning pink, "I only meant."

Ailsa ignored Meriel's confusion and pulled a stiff parchment square from the packet. It was lettered in Latin.

"Can you read it?" asked Meriel, peering over her shoulder.

"I can," said Ailsa, for she had been well taught by Conleth, the tutor her father had brought back with him from Ireland one autumn. For seven years, he'd lived with them, teaching her to read, write a fair hand, calculate, and much music and poetry as well. He'd gone back to Ireland one summer, an old man, wanting to be home before he died. She missed him and the lessons, but most of all the stories he'd told each evening. Stories of all the far-off lands and other seas, of amazing creatures and peoples with strange ways and musical tongues. She missed those tales. She had even tried to conjure some stories herself, but her efforts paled beside his.

She studied the writing, the letters dancing about as she tried to concentrate. She saw the king's own initial at the bottom, a large D in thick scrolled lettering, for David, King of all the Scots.

Know that I, David, King of all Scotia, give and grant by this charter the lands of Caerwyn, between the boundaries of de Morville of Irvine and fitz Alain of Dundonald, to Robert, lately of Shropshire and Normandy, to be held by him and his heirs in return for services to me and the crown. Know also that I give my ward, the Lady Ailsa of Caerwyn, into the hands and the care of the same Sir Robert, as his lady wife. These are the witnesses to my writ.

A long list of unfamiliar English and French names followed, the ink somewhat blurred. Or was it her eyes? Ailsa stood, clutching the parchment in her hands. "Go after that messenger."

"He is gone, Lady," said Kyle from the doorway. "He rode out in haste, saying he had to be away before dark fell."

"What does it say?" asked Meriel.

Ailsa scanned the lines again. "I can read, but I do not believe it," she said in a whisper. "King David is not my ward. I have no ward. These are not English lands here and we do not go by English or Norman law."

She picked up the smaller packet, ripped it open and read. The note was short, on inferior parchment, written by a clerk. It informed her that she was to be made wife to a worthy man, named Robert, a knight of some renown in Normandy. However, should it please her, she might retire to a nunnery instead. She would be, if disinclined to marry, sponsored by the king at the nunnery of Sanquehar."

"A nunnery!" gasped Ailsa.

Meriel pulled on Ailsa's sleeve, her eyes wide and alarmed. "What does this mean? You frighten me!"

Ailsa stared at the two parchment squares in her hands. "It means the king has taken my lands," she said. "He has stolen my lands and he awards me to some English adventurer."

Meriel placed a hand on her shoulder. She gestured to the servants who left the chamber reluctantly.

"To some English or French knight. You know what they are like. Ambitious. Some upstart younger son come to steal my lands. Though I am the heir, the true and only heir. According to all our laws."

"Be calm, dear Ailsa." Meriel patted her shoulder. "Perhaps it would not be so bad. Some of these English must surely be good men, and he may be young too. You might find this offer a good one if you but think on it carefully."

"You can say that Meriel! You, who have a good husband, a proper man from the Isles, one who knows our ways! Do you ask me to accept less?"

Meriel's face flushed. "I do not know. I was never an heiress, as you are. I brought little to our marriage." She looked at the fire, her brows drawn into an unfamiliar frown.

"And Dugald has never cared about that, as you well know, for he has lands aplenty of his own on Arran," answered Ailsa.

Meriel shrugged. "It's true I am fortunate. What can you do

though? It's the word of the king himself." She reached a hand toward Ailsa, but Ailsa was striding away, pacing up and down the hall.

"I'll not allow my lands to be taken and I'll not be sold off like some spineless English woman. We do things differently here, in these Gaelic lands, and the king may as well know it."

"But Ailsa, he is the king, you can't think to go against his word." Meriel clutched her skirts, crumpling the fine wool. "Perhaps it will not be so bad. Wait until you see the man. It's possible all will yet be fine."

"I'll never marry that upstart. Normandy or nowhere, it's all one to me. I'll never give up my home. My life is mine to order." Ailsa threw both parchments onto the floor and stormed out of the hall.

Afternoon sun was sinking over the sea and casting a golden light onto the tops of the waves raised by the light wind. A difficult week had passed. Ailsa rubbed a hand across her aching forehead. She had been up well before dawn, busy preparing their dinner. For surely Dugald would return this day. Dugald, and the handsome Torquil as well. Ailsa fiddled with the wool coverlet over her shoulders and stared at the sea. Meriel had sent her up to lie down. In truth, she had been working too hard, rising early and sleeping late. But how else to deal with the roil inside her?

She reached to the wooden chest beside her bed, resting it on her lap. Inside sat the dread parchments, giving her, her lands, and all her possessions away to this stranger. They were marked with soot, where she'd thrown them down on the hearth. Meriel had rescued them and silently left them on her bed the next morning.

Time was growing short. At first, it had seemed sensible to listen to Meriel's advice. Wait, she said. Dugald will return soon. He will know how to alter this, if you are truly fixed on not marrying this man. But Dugald could easily be late returning from Renfrew, and they had no sure way to get word to him, though she'd sent a boy out with a message. How long could she wait? The Norman stranger might ride through the gate any moment. Each time she heard a shout in the courtyard her heart stood still.

Ailsa swung her legs around and rose from the bed. It was freezing in her chamber, for she'd pulled the shutters back from the narrow window. Yanking the coverlet from the bed, she wrapped it around her and paced up and down.

If only Dugald would return today. Surely, he'd take her away now, out of the king's reach, perhaps to Ireland. The seas were smooth, though it was winter. Then he could get lawyers to fight the king's writ. It was not the custom of the coast or the Isles that she become king's ward and her lands the king's to parcel away. Here, daughters inherited and married as they pleased. Even Dugald had never seen fit to question her about Caerwyn. She must fight this theft, and in this Dugald would help her. He must; he was her closest, her only, kin. She could escape, and in time, recover her manor and her lands.

But if the Englishman got here first. She shivered. The stranger could have their marriage performed and take her. Once consummated, there was no way to go back, that she well knew. Her lands would then be well and truly his. Her only alternative, the veil. And who to stop him? Her men would try, if she asked it. And die in the attempt. The English had horses, metal armor, and sharp weapons. Her men were traders and farmers. She could not ask them; it would be their deaths. She twisted the blanket around her fingers. So he could take her, and none to stop him. She felt like a field mouse, waiting in the tall grass, trying to hide as the hawk flies overhead, its dark wings casting shadows. It was unbearable.

Or perhaps it would all go differently. She swallowed. If the curse were true, if it came upon him. He too would die. Like Cathal, like Niall. She took in a long shuddering breath. She could warn him. But he would ignore her, she knew that much about the English. So proud about their disbelief in the old ways. She shook her head. The curse had no true power; it could not save her.

A loud rap on her door interrupted these unhappy thoughts. She pulled the heavy door open a crack.

"Lady, it's Jamie from the stables. The scouts you sent out have seen Lord Dugald. He'll be here as the sun sets."

Ailsa felt a surge of excitement. Her fingers dropped the heavy coverlet onto the floor.

"Lady, be you there?"

"Aye, thank you," she called out. "Tell Meriel I'll be down directly to help with the meal."

"Aye," said the lad, and she heard his heavy boots knocking away on the stairs below.

She must dress. Torquil would be here too. She stood a moment, biting her lip. Then she threw open her chest, tossing gowns onto the floor. She had many gowns, for she had all her mother's clothes, lovingly saved by her grandmamma, and they were now of a size. And her father had liked to see her in bright colors. Each autumn he had returned from his trading voyages with bright wools and linens. She picked up one of blue-green wool, fine and soft.

She splashed cold water from the basin on her cupboard onto her face and hands. Then she drew the tunic over a linen shift; her fingers fumbled with the blue laces down the sides. But finally, she had them tightened and tied. She grabbed the comb from her table and unbraiding her hair, dragged it through the heavy waves, wincing at the snarls. She pulled a red ribbon from her chest and wound it in as she braided her hair. The thick braid fell down past the small of her back. She pulled her best boots from the chest too, black and of fine soft leather. She tried to peer in the small mirror she kept in her chest, but it was hard to see more than part of her face and impossible to see her gown.

She heard a shout and peered out the window. Could they be here yet? No, she could see no one. Still, she must hurry. She folded the shifts and tunics lying on the floor and secured them in the chest. Noticing the parchments on her bed, she replaced them in the small chest and hurried out.

Meriel was already in the kitchen, a canvas apron tied over her best blue tunic. She smiled at Ailsa. "They must be nearly here," she called. Her face was rosy, from pleasure, Ailsa suspected, as well as the heat of the kitchen fire. She watched Meriel lift a heavy mixing bowl and pour the contents into a pot to be stewed on the fire. The room smelled of smoky bacon, rosemary, and the spicy scent of the apple pudding cooking on the hearth.

Ailsa drew in the good smells; it seemed a long time since they'd had meat, though it was probably only a fortnight. "What can I do?" she asked.

Meriel handed her a tray of apples. "Peel these and we'll make another pudding, one with raisins and some of that cinnamon we have left."

Ailsa tried to watch as Meriel dumped apples and honey and spices into the bowl, for Meriel was a very fine cook, but she couldn't concentrate. Dugald was coming back. Would he agree to take her away? Could Torquil be an answer? Would she have to agree to Torquil for Dugald to take her away? She hardly knew what to think, yet she might have to make up her mind fast.

Shouts rang out from the courtyard, and Meriel handed her bowl to Osla, untied her apron, and ran out to the courtyard. "Dugald!" Meriel called. He ran to her, lifting her to him.

Ailsa, feeling awkward, stepped back.

"And Ailsa, good to see you, cousin," said Dugald, giving her a quick hug. Torquil walked up and bowed to both women.

Flustered suddenly, Ailsa hardly dared look at him. They all passed into the great hall, where a large fire blazed in the center hearth. The scent of greens and savory foods met them.

Dugald sighed with contentment as he peeled off his wet outer clothes. "It's good to be back, in truth." He sank onto a bench near the fire and motioned Torquil to sit beside him. Meriel served each man a goblet of ale.

Ailsa felt she would burst with her news, but how could she raise the matter with Torquil sitting right there? The meal seemed the longest she had ever endured. She must find a way to get Dugald away from Torquil long enough to tell him of the messenger and his news. She fiddled with the heavy white tablecloth, twisting it round her fingers.

"You aren't eating much," whispered Meriel. "Don't worry so, there will be a good moment after the men eat. Dugald will know what to do."

She wished she could be as sure as Meriel that Dugald would have an answer for her.

The men finished off the venison, and the servants took the platters piled with bones off to the kitchen. Osla came in with dried pears and walnuts, heaped in a wooden bowl. A tall boy with a skin of sweet wine followed close behind.

Dugald took the wine and motioned Osla and the boy out. When the room was cleared of the servants, he poured Torquil a goblet and then filled a goblet for Meriel and himself. Sitting back with a contented sigh in his chair, he said, "and have you heard the news yet, of our king?"

"We have heard of his march on Carlisle," answered Meriel.

Dugald looked disappointed.

Torquil jumped in. "We saw the men leaving Renfrew. It was a fine sight, full three score armed men."

"The king intended to move fast," broke in Dugald. "Perhaps he has even now reached Carlisle and she is back in Scots hands."

"That would be a fine thing indeed," said Meriel, "for too long Arthur's castle has been under England's sway." She glanced toward Torquil, who had stood up and was talking with his squire, just come in from the stables.

He looked over. "Forgive me, I must see to my stallion, he has lamed himself with a rock. I will return before long." He was talking to Meriel, but his gaze turned to rest on Ailsa. She felt her face flush. Torquil followed the squire out of the hall.

As the door closed behind him, Ailsa tugged at Dugald's sleeve. "Indeed there is news, cousin. Dreadful news."

"What is this?" he said, concern in his voice. "You look right worried, cousin. Why have you held silent all this while?"

"It is this." Ailsa lowered her voice. She told of the messenger arriving with the parchments. "He means to marry me off to some English or French adventurer. I shall have no say at all, no hold over my own lands." She grabbed his hand. "Please Dugald, you must take me away from here. Take me somewhere over the sea, where I can be safe and fight to regain my lands."

Dugald frowned, his heavy brows meeting. "You opened a message meant for me?" He turned to his wife. "What is all this? How could you allow this, Meriel."

"Don't blame your wife. She had no choice," said Ailsa.

Meriel stared down at the table. "It's true, Dugald. A charter signed by the king himself."

Dugald was quiet, then he shrugged his heavy shoulders. "Not all the new men are so bad, cousin. No doubt David has picked a good man for you."

Ailsa felt her throat seize at his words. "But I cannot marry a knight from England! Someone not of our ways. I cannot marry at all."

Dugald crossed his arms and frowned. "What foolishness is this?"

Meriel placed a calming hand on his shoulder. "She is distraught. It's unexpected."

Dugald put on an expression intended to look patient. "Surely you know it is time to be married. You will like the state well enough once you're in it." He smiled at Meriel, who smiled back.

Ailsa stared at him in disbelief. Had the superstitious whispers in the village never reached Dugald's ears? Niall had been a blacksmith and a poet. Dugald had never met him, for they'd married in the summer, when Dugald was away voyaging, and Niall had died before he returned in autumn. He would never have thought him suitable as a husband, she knew that. Indeed, he preferred to forget she had ever married at all. Ailsa leaned toward her cousin. "These lands are mine. It is my right, as my father's heir. I will not give them up."

"Who is this man the king suggests? What name has he?" asked Dugald.

"I know only this, he is called Robert the knight, and he comes newly from Shropshire with another called fitz Alain, who is to hold the lands south of here."

"Fitz Alain!" said Dugald, tugging at his ear. "Aye, we heard much of him in Renfrew. His holdings will rival de Morville's even, he's been named the king's steward. He travels with David to Carlisle even now." His eyes narrowed. "These are powerful men."

"I care not for their power but for the right. It's my right to hold these lands." She swallowed hard. "It's only their foreign Norman law that says a woman may not inherit. I say the king is not my ward, not by our Gaelic law."

"Have a care Ailsa. You know naught of powerful men and the ways of the world."

"I know you are my kin. You must help me."

Meriel laid a restraining arm on her. "Be calm, Ailsa, harsh words will not solve this or any problem."

The door opened wide, letting a cold gust of wind into the heated room. The candles flickered and Torquil strode in, gold hair awry from the wind. "Just a minor matter, my horse will be fine by tomorrow. I was worried though, I'd not like him come to harm." He paused at the sight of their taut faces.

"Torquil, what heard we of fitz Alain and another called Robert?" said Dugald, his voice loud in the silent chamber.

Torquil came to the fire, pulling off his leather gloves. "Why, all Renfrew was abuzz with the news. Walter fitz Alain's become David's new favorite. The king's given him all the lands hereabout. And this knight Robert secures the lands for the Steward while he marches with the king."

"Our Ailsa here, she has been given, along with her lands, to Sir Robert. By King David himself," said Dugald.

"Dugald!" said Ailsa. "I'll not marry him!"

"Come, Dugald," urged Meriel, a frown on her normally smiling face, and she drew him away, protesting, leaving Torquil and Ailsa alone at the hearth.

Ailsa watched them go and heard the door thud behind them. The fire crackled in the silent chamber.

Torquil sat down on the bench opposite her and looked into the flames a long moment. "Well," he said, strain apparent in his voice. "I'll not deny I returned here with Dugald tonight with some hope to see you again."

"And I am glad you have returned," said Ailsa. She looked at him, eyes downcast, hand clenched around his metal goblet.

"The king himself has ordered this?"

"Aye," said Ailsa, pushing her braid back. "But the king is far away and here we seldom do exactly as the king orders." There was a silence.

"Yet the king grows ever more powerful, even here on the coast and the Isles. And this David is reckoned a good king," said Torquil. He did not look at her.

"Kings can be wrong," said Ailsa, twisting her laces with her fingers, willing him to look up at her. "I would fight this. He is king, but just a man among others, who have their power too."

There was a long pause and Torquil continued to stare into the flames.

"I see," said Ailsa, the color rising to her face. She rose, knocking her wine goblet. Red wine flowed onto the white cloth.

Torquil rose too. "Ailsa ..."

But she escaped his voice, running out the door. Outside the hall, she paused just for a moment, listening. But he did not call again, nor follow her. She felt hot tears well and she wiped them away.

Dugald's voice rumbled in the hall. "Leave the girl be, Meriel. She needs time to think on it. This Robert seems a good husband for her, to tell truth, and for sure, the king's not one to be gainsaid."

Meriel said something in her low calm voice.

"Don't speak of it again," said Dugald. "There's nothing I, or anyone, can do."

Ailsa backed away from their voices. She felt the rough wood of the door behind her, and she pulled the latch and yanked it open. The night was starless and chill. She stumbled out. It seemed no one would stand up to this king.

CHAPTER FOUR

Near Renfrew

"For a woman to rule over men cannot be right, though she
do be Henry's daughter," stated Lord James, his voice loud and
satisfied in the echoing hall of his keep.

Robert clenched his fist under the white cloth of the table. James
was hosting Alain, Walter's father, and Robert had been invited
along. Being too old to fight with the king, Alain intended to go
on to Carlisle once word arrived of the king's victory. But in the
meantime, he visited with friends, especially highly placed friends
who rode freely between Northumberland and the Scots court, men
who could give him useful information.

Alain paused, then his knife continued slicing the venison on his
trencher and he raised a large chunk to his mouth. Robert watched
as he chewed and washed it down with a full goblet of French wine.
Finally, Alain said, "And would you have Stephen made king of
England, then, a man who steals a throne with little claim?"

Grateful that as a mere knight he was seated off to the side, Robert
watched the two lords on their massive chairs. The high-roofed hall
hummed with loud voices and boisterous laughter, as men relaxed
after three days of cold travel.

"Ah no, don't be putting tricky words in my mouth," James said,
sticking a chunk of meat onto his knife with a fat finger. "We're
friends here. Can we not say as we think? There's not a man here
feels different, I'll wager. Henry's daughter or no, that Matilda's not
the sort to get men to love and follow her, as I hear it. Though it's

certain Stephen has his problems too. Too soft for a king, and not one for making up his mind."

"Hard times lie ahead for England, with each man making his own way as best he can." Alain added, "It's why I brought Walter north. Jordan, my oldest will have the lands in Brittany, of course, and William will take over in Shropshire, but Walter, he's not one for the Church, so he must find a place. Here in Scotia, with David, he will have a better chance than with Matilda or Stephen and be well out of the quarreling I fear will come before all this is settled."

James agreed and gulped down more wine and the men turned the talk to the easier subject of hunting. Words and jokes flowed around Robert, and he unclenched his fist under the table. Relax, he chided himself, we came north to rid ourselves of this quagmire of Matilda or Stephen, a plague on them both. He tried to shake off the gloom that sat on his shoulders. Matters were going well enough. Lands and an heiress to boot.

He turned to his neighbor, the lord's nephew, a lad of fourteen. "How goes your training?" The boy's face reddened with pleasure, and soon they were immersed in discussion of swordplay. Several hours passed as he conversed and listened to the minstrels. Then, feeling tired, he rose, meaning to leave the hall. He heard his name called.

"You do not enjoy the subtleties of political talk, I fear," observed James, his dark eyes glittering in the candlelight.

Robert frowned, but said nothing. The man had been drinking steadily, but he would not offend his host.

"Will you truly be able to defend Walter's lands for him, I wonder? He'll be with the king much, and these are unsettled times." James's voice was belligerent and over loud.

Alain broke in. "Robert and Walter go way back."

James turned to Alain. "Those with power and the greed for more will not fade away at a wish. If you want to keep hold of your new lands, you'd best be talking with those who have the king's ear," he continued, in a voice loud enough to reach Robert, "perhaps de Morville, the Constable, for one."

"I've met the man," Alain agreed.

"It's said de Morville has publicly quarreled with that son of his," said James, swirling the wine in his overlarge goblet.

Alain frowned. "He has disowned him?"

"Nay, not quite. Still he is not best pleased with young Hugh." James stabbed another chunk of meat. "Young Hugh leads a cohort at court; they think David goes too slow, especially with changes that would line their pockets. But the king knows he must not anger the Gaelic earls or the Norse traders, though he does mean change, no question of that." James flicked a glance Robert's way and laughed. "Word to the wise, as they say."

Robert left the overheated hall. Outside, the night air was sharp. He sat on a stone bench set near the walls, useful for viewing the kitchen gardens during the day. The stars spread brilliant, scattered wide over a dark sky. He felt the tension between his shoulders easing away. James warned him of something, or tested him, he wasn't sure which. He thought about an odd conversation he'd had before the king and all his court had gone to Carlisle. He'd been out early, hunting again, in the fog and as he returned from the stable the Constable himself had appeared in his path. Dressed all in grey, he'd all but disappeared in the fog and he'd been startled. "You will have to be more careful," the Constable had said, a smile tugging at one side of his mouth. "Scotia appears a placid backwater to you perhaps, coming from Normandy, but much can swirl under the surface of a loch or a sea." A warning certainly, but of what exactly? The Constable had said no more, just thanked him for his efforts with the king, and disappeared back into the fog. When he met him next, in the king's chambers, it was as though they'd never spoken. Robert sighed. What had he hoped to find in the North after all? It would be no different here than anywhere. Greed and grasping and the endless struggle to make a place for oneself.

For a moment, the vision of a sunlit field, green after a late spring rain, blotted out the stars overhead. The smell of scythed grass and new turned earth came unbidden to his nostrils. Home. Lost to him now. He saw his mother standing at the gate, waving farewell, tears shining in her eyes, her new husband by her side. The sturdy manor his father had built, the well-tended fields, all deeded to a new owner. By Henry of England, now dead himself. Though it had been fitz John, Henry's vassal, a vicious, overbearing man with pale narrow eyes, who had arrived with the awful news. And the men to enforce it. He had been a boy, only seven, when fitz John, in a few clipped words, announced his father was dead. The lands reverted to the king. His mother was married off to a new husband within six weeks.

And he had been removed from his Uncle Rhys, where he'd fostered since he was five. Sent off instead to be fostered by some poor relation of his new stepfather, a man who used him as a servant and beat him regularly. He'd run away twice and the third time, when he was eleven, stayed away. Made his way into England, across to the east coast, and taken ship. Eventually he'd found a place of sorts with the fighters in Normandy. Where war was a way of life and the bottomless need for young fighting men let a man rise up the ranks swiftly. He'd never been back. Never saw his mother or uncle again. He twisted the chased gold ring he wore on his third finger. Round and round, frowning into the dark. His mother had died of a winter fever just two years later. The ring she'd always worn had arrived with a curt missive informing him.

A loud clatter and shouts from the kitchens roused him. Best be off to sleep, he thought, running a hand through his hair. What profit in dark memories. Now he was living a new life. Lands were to be his and this time, he was a man. This time, he would hold them. He dreamed still, many nights, most nights in truth, of revenge. Dark dreams, with dark blood flowing. He'd wake, shivering, and stay awake staring until morning. How it would happen, and when, he didn't know, but he would find a way.

Wind swirled under Robert's wool cloak. He cursed under his breath. His head ached, unaccustomed to wines from Bordeaux.

Will, his servant and friend, rode up to his side. "You look like hell," he observed.

Robert cursed again, louder. Then he laughed. Will could always make him laugh.

Will, astride his brown horse, his unruly hair blowing in the wind, laughed too and trotted on ahead.

They cantered along at a fair clip for most of the morning, at least when the path was solid, the horses restive in the snapping air. Robert felt his headache lifting and his mood rising, though the day was gloomy enough, dark clouds racing across the sky. He'd left Alain back at Lord James' manor house, for he'd wanted a few more days of talking politics. "No need to wait for an old man like me," he'd said. Robert ducked under the branches of a big oak above the path. He wondered when he'd see Alain again. The old man and his son had been kind to him these last years. They were the closest thing he had to family.

Thoughts of separation didn't last long, for they reached the borders of Walter's lands and he turned his attention to observing the terrain, fixing landmarks in his mind in this place of rivers, rolling hills and tree covered slopes. They rode slowly through the cluster of buildings called Renfrew. Later in the week, the king's market would be held and the street crowded no doubt. Today, the buildings looked substantial and in decent repair, but all was quiet. Alain would attend to this important burgh for his son, while Robert was charged with seeing to the agricultural lands and small villages beyond, as well as the defenses for the castles on Walter's lands. They stopped once only, to purchase some cheeses and ale from a friendly woman, with a clean apron tied over her gown, who was pleased to chat about the goods to be found on market day. Then they moved on, with an eye to the weather, which looked to blow before afternoon's end. He intended to reach the closest hamlet before halting for the night.

Later, in a curve along the dark flowing river, they pulled to a halt in front of a cluster of sod huts. Robert waited while Will gathered the local men. Women and children crowded behind, curious to see the new lord's representative. They gathered in a circle around him, staring with expressionless faces. Overhead, dark clouds cloaked the sky, and the wind was gusting, but at least it wasn't raining yet. Robert took a deep breath and walked to the front of the small crowd. He looked at their careful faces and at the small children, giggling and darting about in the back, oblivious to their parent's concerns. This was just the first of many such villages he'd have to visit in the next weeks. In all of them, he'd have to gain their trust. Knowing Walter, 'twas unlikely he'd take much interest in the agricultural base of his wealth, for he was ever one to cluster with the great and he'd be much occupied at David's court with his new position. It would fall to him to see to these people, here on Walter's estate, as on his own. He found he did not mind. Already he had ideas that could improve their situation, put food on the table for their children, provide wealth for their master. But change comes hard.

He began telling them about some of the new methods he'd seen in Normandy and in the south of England, new ways to grow crops for higher yields. They listened, faces impassive. Then one man, broad shouldered and tall, with curly black hair, called out a question, his dark brows drawn together. Robert felt his stiffness give way, and he warmed to his topic. Soon they were deep in an animated discussion. A few others ventured questions. He felt the men listening to him, when they saw he respected the information they could give. And they liked the idea that he'd patrol the roads, for most had lost goods and trade had become difficult recently, with strangers from over the water raiding. After the exchange, Robert left, with a promise to return. He wished it could be in a few weeks time, before planting, but that was unlikely. The king's request that he see to the threats from the Isles teased at his mind. It would be longer than he liked before he could return.

Back on Tanet, headed southwest, he realized he felt strangely pleased. With these families and their ordinary concerns of planting and harvesting, surviving, he felt at home. It was a welcome change from the soldiering he'd been doing for so long. Tanet picked up his mood and danced along the frozen path.

A fortnight later, seated by a smoky fire, Robert rubbed the sleep from his eyes. He'd spent long days riding from village to village, checking Walter's lands, meeting the tenants, working on setting up a bond with the men. Though most places scarcely merited the name of village, being merely a few longhouses clustered together, with fields hacked from the woods around. He poked at the fire with a stick. Bacon fat dripped into the fire, sending up a tantalizing aroma. He'd have much to convey to Walter when his friend returned from Carlisle, whenever that might be. How interested his friend would be was another question.

Will came up out of the mist, some wizened apples piled in his arms. "Found these on an abandoned tree." He set about skewering the apples on a pointed stake and held them over the fire to roast.

Robert sniffed with appreciation. The air was so cold it fair crackled, but he was warm here by the fire.

"And when might we be heading to your new lands?" asked Will, his voice carefully casual.

Robert's felt his good humor flow out. "I've a responsibility to see to Walter's lands, as you know. I owe him and Alain a great deal."

Will nodded. "True enough."

"But what," demanded Robert.

Will grinned. "Well, since you ask me and all, you think more of putting another man's lands in shape than of your own." He pulled an apple off the end of the stake and blew on it. "To say nothing of a fine wife to be that waits."

"I have my duty to Walter, which must come before my own lands," Robert responded, in a voice that signaled an end to the conversation.

Will ate his apple and some oatcakes with a chunk of bacon. He washed them down with ale and wiped his mouth with his sleeve. "Women don't always like the waiting, you see."

"And how came you to be such an expert?" Robert sprang to his feet and strode off toward the horses, shouting to his men. "Breakfast is over."

The men got to their feet, still clutching oatcakes.

Later, riding down the twisting path, Robert glared at the blue sky through the bare tree branches. He frowned, hearing Will's banter behind him, laughing with one of the other men. He wasn't angry with Will, who always spoke his mind. They'd been together since he'd arrived in Normandy, half frozen after a winter crossing of the channel and starved. Will was something like an older brother to him, in truth, though he was a servant. But was he avoiding his future somehow? He prided himself on facing his problems head on. Yet lands and a wife were hardly a problem. Curse Will, planting such convoluted ideas in his head. He urged Tanet on. They pounded down the twisting path, and the rhythmic thud of Tanet's hoofs drummed in his ears.

He'd visited all Walter's estate of Strathgryfe now. They had criss-crossed the hills, asking the way to the next hamlet and the next, speaking with as many tenants as possible. Now he intended to work his way down past de Morville's lands and deal with North Kyle, seeing especially to Dundonald. A small castle stood there now, and Walter intended to build it up to be a match for de Morville's castle at Irvine. With Walter's estates dealt with, he planned to then go on to Caerwyn, which lay close by. It was still a good plan, he decided. A responsible plan and logical. He pulled Tanet to a walk and let his men on their slower horses catch up. Will rode up beside him. "Why the long face," Robert asked, "we'll get to Caerwyn soon enough."

"Maybe so," said Will. "Maybe so."

A few days later, Robert sat in the noonday sun, on a huge log hollowed out as a bench, in the enclosed courtyard of a modest house, away from the winter winds. The day promised spring. He found his mind wandering from the matter under discussion, the date for walking the boundary lines, away from the gathering of tenants before him. It was too fine a day to be sitting here talking. "Come," he said, startling the men, "let's walk the boundary now, so I may judge it better."

That evening, his men clustered around a fire, a stew of mutton and onions boiling in the iron pot slung over the flames. Big Fergus was their cook, picked from a village along their wanderings. He favored eating, as his girth showed, and could pull together a good meal from almost nothing. He had the trick of gathering herbs and flavoring the meat and what vegetables could be found this time of year.

Will sat down beside Robert on a log they'd dragged up to the fire. The night air was sharp and overhead the stars already brilliant lights above the tree boughs.

Will cleared his throat.

"What," said Robert, still watching the night skies.

"Robb, I speak to you as your friend."

"Out with it. You've something heavy on your mind."

"I'm wondering why we spend our days wandering about here and there, on Walter's business, when you've business of your own you might be attending to, if you catch my meaning." Will shifted his seat on the log. The fire crackled in the silence. Big Fergus, standing by the fire with a long stick to poke the logs, stopped his singing. Will cleared his throat. "Land such as you've always wanted! You don't talk of it. But I've seen it in your eyes. It lies waiting while we dally about."

Robert frowned. "It's my duty to see to fitz Alain's lands."

"Duty can be an excuse."

Robert jumped to his feet. "You go too far."

Will shook his head and exchanged glances with Big Fergus.

Robert grabbed a blanket from the pack on the ground and strode off into the woods. He found a stand of firs and piled some boughs into a bed. He ticked through the tasks he wanted to accomplish before heading west and gradually felt the calm of the winter evening seep into him again. Avoiding Caerwyn? Hardly likely. Indeed, he was anxious to see the lands he pictured nightly in his mind.

Two days passed and a third. Robert sat in another manor house, this time settled in the hall before a fire. The day was bitter, with dark grey clouds scudding across the sky. Spring now seemed far away. He'd spent the last days indoors, listening to endless variations on the same disputes, for the sleet made other tasks impossible and quarrels more urgent. The room was smoky from the fire, and none too clean. The smell of wet dogs permeated the air. He gave the hounds, huddled by the fire, an irritated glance.

Suddenly he got to his feet, surprising the farmer who was reciting his speech about the tools he'd brought to the smith for repair. He thrust a silver coin into the man's hands, and called to Will. "Find the most responsible man and set him up here as we have done in Walter's other manors. Then take a swift horse and follow me."

"To where?"

"Caerwyn, of course. Haven't you been nagging me this fortnight about it?" He scowled at Will's sudden grin. "You'd best ride quickly." He flung himself out the door. Fresh air chilled his nostrils and he breathed deep. In the stables, he grabbed the bridle from the startled boy tending his horse, gave the boy a grin, then readied Tanet, who picked up his excitement and danced about the barn. He led the horse outside, flung himself on and galloped off, leaving Will and his men to mount and ride behind.

Now that Robert had decided to go straight to Caerwyn, he was in a great hurry. They'd ridden long the day before, stopping only for sleep when the road was so dark the way could not be seen. After a few hours rest, with the slow coming of a wet dawn, he'd nudged the men awake and they'd ridden on.

The grey sky and cold wind meant little to him or his men, dressed in warm fur inside their surcoats. And the sleet had stopped. He urged his stallion on. He was excited, as if all the feelings he'd suppressed in Walter's legal and managerial duties were suddenly released. He grinned into the wind rushing past his head. It was hard to tell the time with the sun so masked, but he thought it close to noon. If he continued at this pace, he'd reach the outskirts of Caerwyn by evening. He wondered what this day would bring.

The path was narrow, but well enough marked, even on such a dark day. He pounded along, enjoying the rhythm of Tanet's hoofs. His men would catch up eventually, but none could match his stallion's speed. They rounded a bend. Tanet pricked his ears. He was on guard, even before he saw the men blocking the path.

Tanet reared. He heard the metallic scrape of swords yanked from leather scabbards. A pack of riders, bearing down on him. He whirled Tanet about; too many to fight alone. They flew back along the path. Robert ducked as branches slashed at his face. Tanet was fast, very fast, but tired from the long morning of swift travel.

Behind, shouts of anger mixed with the frantic neighing of horses as they spurred after him.

Tanet was going like the wind. The stallion's mane slapped against his cheeks. Robert risked a look back. He cursed; they were well mounted and gaining. His eyes raked the path ahead. He needed a good place to make a stand.

They hurled around a boulder and he called halt to Tanet, and wheeled him about, drawing his sword. He had the advantage of surprise now, but little else. The pounding hoofs approached. He rushed at the first pair of surprised riders, separating the pack. He felled the first man with his momentum, and then used his sword on the next. The others pulled up their horses, and approached, more cautiously. He heard a groan and saw the man he had knocked off his horse getting to his feet, blood flowing from his thigh. Robert backed Tanet against a huge oak with a soft command. The swords of the ambushers were dull silver, their faces bound in dark woolen cloths.

With a yell, the men spurred their horses at him. Tanet reared, and struck out with his hoofs, and he thrust at the man charging up on his left. Blood spurted from the man's shoulder and he fell heavily. The others wheeled their horses, yelled, and rushed him again. Robert fought. A sword thrust here, defense there. Having gauged his skill, the men were cautious now, seeking to tire him, for they had the full advantage of numbers. Robert fought, but he was giving ground, the sound of his own breathing harsh in his ears.

Suddenly, the men were backing away, turning their horses. Robert realized, peering through the red haze over his eyes, that his men had arrived. They were fighting already, swords clashing. The smell of blood filled the air. Then a huge man, astride a black stallion, swung around and headed straight towards him. He ducked and parried the other's mighty swing, their swords clanging together. The big man's sword splintered. He threw it down and shouted and the ambushers flung off into the woods, crashing away. All sound of riders or battle faded. Robert stared into the shadows under the trees, but they were gone, vanished like the wind surging through oaks in a gust, passing by and leaving only stillness.

"Robb, are ye harmed." Will rode up and leaned toward him.

Robert looked at his startled face and glanced down at his blood-soaked tunic. He sheathed his sword. "Not mine."

Will nodded, his brown eyes relieved. "Must be that fellow's then." He pointed to one of the men sprawled on the ground. Blood pooled on the frost coated path. Robert whistled, calling his men back. They'd not catch the riders, not in these woods, which the ambushers no doubt knew well.

His men rode in and gathered around him, jostling and joking, relieving their tension after the fight.

"Bold robbers," said Will in a low voice, "to set on you in daytime."

Robert climbed off his horse and bent to examine one of the three bodies sprawled on the ground. It carried no mark of identification, but the clothes were of fine wool and little worn. Will bent down beside him. Robert said softly, "They knew I was alone. They waited for me."

Will was silent. His face screwed into a frown. "They must have been watching. Who could it be?"

"I know not," said Robert. "But I will know, and he will pay."

Will nodded. "What now?"

"We ride on," said Robert. "I would reach Caerwyn."

He turned to his men, and realized one was drooping on his horse, his face white. "Nevin, are ye hurt?"

"Yes, sir," said Nevin, trying to school his face not to show the pain, "though it's nothing much."

"See to him, Will," said Robert. He watched Will, a skilled healer, help Nevin, the youngest of his men, off his horse and gently pull aside his tunic. Bright blood was oozed from a large gash in the man's side. Nevin would not ride tonight. He waited as Will cleaned the wound and bandaged it carefully with a torn chemise.

When Will had gathered up his things, Robert spoke to his men. One he left with Nevin, along with a good horse, with orders to make a lean to of pine boughs for the night. They'd send more men back tomorrow morning, when they reached Caerwyn, to fetch them. The orders given, Robert stood still a long moment, his brows drawn together, and none of the men interrupted his silence. Then, abruptly, he ordered his men to mount.

Robert knelt beside the young man. "You'll be fine, Nevin, for Will's a very skilled healer, as you know," he said, "and we'll see you in a soft bed at Caerwyn tomorrow."

Nevin attempted a smile.

Rising to his feet, Robert caught the worried look in Will's eyes. Fever was likely, with such cases. Warmth and a roof were important now. And answers.

CHAPTER FIVE

Near Caerwyn

RAW WIND WHIPPED HER HAIR and swept under her cloak, billowing the wool and scattering drops of water about. Ailsa tucked the loose cloth under her knees. She pulled her mare Nia to a halt at the top of a rise. "Never mind, we'll reach the manor soon," she murmured to the horse. She unclenched her chilled fingers from the reins as she squinted through the rain down into the valley. She had been riding half the day and now the sky, dim with heavy clouds since morning, was shadowed purple as the sun sank.

"Let us go, Nia," she whispered, "we must reach the gates before full dark." She turned the horse back to the narrow path and urged her to a steady trot. As they went, Ailsa eyed the shadowy woods, thinking of the strangers she'd glimpsed in the hills by the pool, and the others landing secretly on the beach. It had not been unusual for her to ride alone in her father's woods with only Nia for company, though for certain her father had always been telling her it was unsuitable. But he had always smiled his easy smile even as he said it, and Ailsa knew he had been proud. Besides, his men would never have allowed harm to come to his daughter. Sudden tears blurred her eyes. So much had changed. She shook her head. She must concentrate on reaching Thomas' manor. Since Dugald would not help her, she must help herself.

After another spell of cold riding, Ailsa reached the farthest edge of Caerwyn's lands. She paused and looked behind her. Wind blew dark clouds across the wide sky over grey seas, and the fields were dull in their winter brown. Still no sign that anyone followed her.

She felt guilty at the thought of Meriel, waiting for her to come down in the morning, finally coming up to check on her, and finding her gone, only the small note pinned to her blanket. With luck, Meriel would believe she was tired, and let her sleep a long time into the morning, maybe even think she was sulking and give her a chance to improve her mood alone. Perhaps, with real luck she'd not be missed until she was already at the neighboring manor, and she'd had a chance to persuade Thomas.

She was sure she could. If only his mother weren't about. She frowned at the thought of Lady Jocelin, hating the idea of seeming to agree with her schemes.

But ever since her disappointment with Dugald and Torquil she had spent long days and longer nights thinking, thinking, pacing up and down her narrow room, worried always that at any moment the knight would pound at her gate. At the last, she had come to a decision. She would accept Thomas' offer of marriage. For it made sense that if they joined their lands, they'd be able to hold this upstart out of Caerwyn.

He'd be worried about defying the king. Once she told him. But that would be only after they were safely married. She bit her lip. She disliked deceiving him, but Caerwyn's need was pressing. And the king in turn would be placated by Thomas' powerful relatives. His mother was cousin to Beatrice, wife to de Morville, the king's Constable and friend. They'd all be protected from any wrath the king might feel at having his wishes thwarted. It was a good plan, the only plan. She bit her lip again, harder.

It was not the sort of love the bards sang of. But after Niall, such a love would not come again. She didn't want it, in any case. Caerwyn would be secure if she married, even in these uncertain times. The plan was not perfect and Thomas would need to stand up to his mother once the king's writ was known. Nia shook her head at the sudden tightening of the reins. Ailsa gave her a consoling pat on the neck. How sad real life wasn't like fantastical dreams or the romance and adventures and quests of the old stories. She took a deep breath. Caerwyn was her responsibility and she meant to see her people stayed safe.

After another cold bout of riding, Ailsa reached her neighbor's impressive keep. She called out and waved to the guard at the gate. He motioned her through, and she clattered into the courtyard, paved with smoothed stones. She dismounted before the young boy ran up to help her and smiled as she handed him the reins. "For certain I must hurry inside to a warm fire," she said as he looked at her, anxious that he had failed his duty.

He relaxed. "It's a grand gathering tonight too, the cooks have been working all the day."

"For what purpose?"

"To entertain all the guests..."

"Ailsa, what a charming surprise," interrupted a voice. The boy grasped Nia's reins and backed away. "There was no time to send for you. How did you ever hear?" Thomas' mother approached, grand in a furred cloak, wrinkles creasing her brow. "Where are your men? You did not come alone, Ailsa, on this stormy day, in these times?"

Ailsa squared her shoulders. "I have a matter to discuss with Thomas."

"Indeed," said Jocelin, pursing her thin lips. "But how foolish of me, you're freezing and we're standing out here in the wind. Let us go into the warm hall."

Ailsa felt herself pulled along by Jocelin, whose dry hands rasped on the wool of her cloak. Inside, a wall of warm air hit her face, along with the smells of wood smoke, roasting meats, and men's bodies. The large hall was packed with men, and women too, standing near the window seats in small groups, laughing and talking.

"What gathering is this?" asked Ailsa. She thought she recognized some of her father's old friends and surely that was Lord Olaf, from Bute. She turned back to Thomas' mother. "Why..."

"All in good time." Jocelin signaled a servant to take Ailsa's cloak. She stared openly as Ailsa's sturdy linen gown was revealed.

"I was thinking to be warm for the ride," faltered Ailsa. "I did not realize…" She glanced at the colorful crowd in the hall, dressed in their finest outfits of bright wools and furs. Then she frowned. Surely many of these men were dressed in the French style, their hair cropped short and their faces beardless.

"Never mind, we shall fix things. Upstairs with you," ordered Jocelin. She turned to the maidservant hovering by the door. "Take the lady up to my chamber. Find her the blue gown in my chest by the door, and hurry."

The maid took Ailsa's arm and pulled her along. Ailsa cast a desperate look back, searching for Thomas in the huge hall, but she couldn't see him.

"Hurry, Lady," urged the maid, "or she'll have my hide." Ailsa stifled her urge to rush into the hall and search out Thomas immediately. She followed the maid up the timber stairs to the solar. The girl motioned her inside a chamber, heavy with the scent of a flowery perfume, opened a large chest and pulled out a blue gown. The linen was faded and as she held the gown up to Ailsa, it was obvious the gown would be far too big, but it was trimmed with stiff ribbon in deeper blue that perhaps could be tied tight. "I would take it in for you," the maid said, "if there were time."

Ailsa sighed. "I have a perfectly fine gown of my own. Can you send someone to the barns for my pack?"

"Oh no. My mistress said we must hurry," said the maid.

Ailsa shrugged. "I cannot wear what I have on now, so this will do." She pulled off her rough linen gown, worn she saw now along the hem and spattered with mud from her ride. The maid quickly helped her fit the blue gown over her chemise. "What is happening? Why are all these people gathered tonight?"

"It is so exciting." The girl yanked at the laces, knotting one in her hurry. "Men have been riding in all yesterday and today and Cook has…"

"Aye," interrupted Ailsa, "but what is the purpose?"

A banging on the door stopped her. The flustered maid rushed over and opened the heavy door a crack.

"We are here to escort the lady to table," said a loud male voice.

"I come," called Ailsa, anxious to see Thomas, and she gathered her wind tangled hair and pinned it atop her head. "The gown will have to do as is," she said to the maid, whose face expressed her doubts.

Flustered, Ailsa followed the squire down the dark stairs and back into the crowded hall. Flaming torches cast moving shadows on the faces gathered there. She followed close behind as he shouldered his way through the throng, and led her to the hearth at the center, where a group of finely dressed guests gathered.

"Ailsa!" It was Thomas's familiar voice. "How thoughtful of you."

Confused, Ailsa answered, "Of course, Thomas..." She looked into his eyes, and then down at her hands, suddenly shy. "I have come as I promised," she said in a low voice, "after the Yule, to give you my answer." Despite herself, her voice sank lower.

He was staring at her, anxiety plain in his eyes. "Ailsa," he said, "you did get my letter?"

"Letter," she echoed, an uneasy feeling in her stomach beginning. She hadn't expected throngs of people, just Thomas and his mother.

Jocelin, massive in a wool gown, stiff with blue embroidery, swept up, a young woman in her firm grasp. "Let me introduce you," she said loudly, "to Thomas' old childhood friend. They used to play in the tide pools together, a long time ago." She looked meaningfully at her son, who said awkwardly, "Yes, let me present Lady Elinor to you, Ailsa." He stopped a moment, then rushed on. "We are wed this day. How good of you to come to help us celebrate."

Ailsa felt the ground sway under her. She concentrated on the oval face before her, staring into the pale blue-grey eyes. Elinor had hair so light it was nearly white, caught up in a fashionable net on her long swan neck. She extended a slender hand, adorned with three gold rings.

"I am pleased to meet a friend of my husband and hope we shall get to know each other well." The voice was sweet.

Ailsa felt her cheeks flushing hot. She stammered, "I am pleased to meet you as well."

Jocelin grasped her elbow and spun her around. "Come dear, we must find our seats, or the cook will be so aggravated." Thomas started forward, but his mother stopped him with a raised hand. "Please attend to your guests, Thomas."

But Thomas ignored his mother and turned to Ailsa, a puzzled look on his face. "You did receive my letter?" he asked, his voice low and urgent.

"Aye, aye, I did, of course." She forced a smile. "I wish you every happiness, Thomas."

He smiled then, relieved, and turned back to his new wife. "You and Ailsa must indeed become great friends," he said, "living as we do only a day's ride apart." Elinor smiled and agreed they must.

Jocelin tugged her away, and Ailsa was glad to let herself be led to a seat at the far end of the table. She certainly had no desire to talk more to Thomas. She sat down on the bench where she was told, next to Lord Gillechrist, another neighbor.

He patted her arm as she sat beside him, staring at the table. "Here we are, my dear, look at the wonderful feast, and don't they make a fine couple." He was a jovial man, past fifty, with fierce red hair threaded now with grey. He also seemed none too observant, which Ailsa was glad for, and she quickly wiped her eyes with the edge of the tablecloth. Thomas wed!

"If you like an English woman," cut in Lord Malcolm, seated on her other side. He helped himself to a chunk of goose from the platter in front of her. The smell of grease assailed her nostrils.

"Malcolm, so bitter! Such a beauty can be no harm. A man would be lucky to have her, for certain. Young Thomas looks right pleased, does he not?" Gillechrist nodded toward Thomas and his blond lady, her hair gleaming in the candlelight, whispering together. "And she brings much land near Annan into the bargain, so I hear."

Malcolm, a dour man, frowned. "They take our land by gentle faces or mailed knights, it matters not. We lose our lands; they take our workers. They force their customs and their religion on us."

"Leave it for tonight," sighed Gille. "We cannot fight the king himself. David brings his English friends to Scotia. We must bend with the new winds."

"I shall not bend," stated Malcolm curtly. "You may sway as the willow in these breezes, but some of us..."

"No more such talk tonight, you are rash to speak so here. Look about you! And I speak of strong winds and no mere breezes." Gille looked uneasily over his shoulder, then deliberately smiled at Ailsa, took a giant swig of the wine in the goblet between them and switched the talk to hunting. Fierce discussion of hounds flowed over her head.

Ailsa picked at the food on her trencher. Thomas, wed to an English lady. But she could see the way of it. He was so easily led by his mother. Clearly, she'd found a better bargain, with the English becoming ever more powerful at court and even here on the coast. The situation was changing even faster than she'd thought.

She stood up. "I must have some air," she gasped at Macolm's surprised face. She dashed out, leaving the clamor of voices and the stifling smells of meat and candles and perfumes behind.

She found Nia munching oats in the dark, content and welcoming in the warm quiet of the hay scented stall. Ailsa rested her head on the mare's neck. Nia's whiskers brushed her cheek. "You, at least, are a faithful friend," she said. Though that was unfair to Thomas. And he'd tried to tell her. She knew he spoke the truth. It was common enough for a message to go astray or be delayed, and she wouldn't put it past his mother to have kept the note herself. Still, it did not help to acknowledge this. Caerwyn was still in danger. She was still in danger.

Time enough to feel hurt later. Think. She must think. She took the pins out of her hair and shook it down, relieved as the heavy weight stopped dragging on her aching forehead. What were her choices? There are always choices, think beyond the box; she repeated her old tutor's advice.

Her mind ticked off possibilities. I can return home in the morning, there to wait and wed my knight as well. Perhaps the curse would even kill him off. She grimaced. That was a horrible thought, and the king would just send another in his place. I could go back in there, make an enormous fuss. He asked for my hand first; I shall say so in public. It would be humiliating, she thought, the blood rising to her cheeks at the thought of the surprised faces in the great hall, and she would not achieve her end, though Thomas would want to do the honorable thing. She sank back down on the straw, sighing. Thomas's face, aglow with a light she'd never seen there. No, she wouldn't hold him to anything. She hadn't really wanted him, if she were honest. She was the one who'd told him to wait for an answer past the Yule. There had been no legal betrothal. She shredded a piece of straw with cold fingers. She only wanted a way out of this terrible trap.

What else, what other choice was there? There must be something. She heard Conleth's calm voice saying, stop, think, there is always a choice, some strategy you have overlooked, often the most obvious. Or a third path, neither one nor the other. She forced herself to breathe, to be calm. She listened to the darkness around her, the mare chewing her hay, the shouts and cheers from the hall in the distance. The twang of harp strings and the roars of laughter. She emptied her mind, trying to will something new. Her mind refused to settle and flew from one thing to another like a flock of crazed wrens. No answer came. Nothing. She was so tired. She put her head down on the pile of hay, pulled Nia's blanket over her shoulders and then up over her face. She would lie here calmly, and she would come up with a plan. In a moment, she was asleep.

She woke suddenly in the dark. It was very cold and silent. It must be quite late. A shaft of moonlight came through the barn door and lit up Nia's coat. She stared at the light as it glowed and shifted and as she stared, it came to her. A wonderful brilliant image in her mind. Why hadn't she thought of this before? She saw herself, dressed in peacock silks, seated in a great hall lit by enormous torches, the king's own hall at King Arthur's castle in Carlisle. Her breath caught at the daring of the image. But why not? She clenched her hands with excitement. I'll go to King David himself, she whispered. I'll tell him I cannot marry this English knight. She repeated herself out loud and Nia bobbed her head and turned to stare. Ailsa laughed and stroked the mare's nose. They say the king is fair and wise, she thought. He will listen and agree once he hears what I have to say. That it is not our way, here on the coast, to disregard a daughter.

That I inherit my family's lands. That I and I alone have the right. He will look kindly on my request, I know it.

"Ah Nia, why did I take so long," Ailsa said, jumping to her feet. How fortunate after all that Thomas had married and now she was glad for him, so glad he'd found a wife he admired. Nia stopped munching hay and turned to nudge her. Tonight it must be, before morning, which couldn't be far away, before anyone could try to stop her. She would ride to David himself. She would forget Dugald and Torquil and Thomas. Cozying up to these English. Giving in to their power. Well, she would not. She would speak with the king and he would correct this injustice.

The decision made, she sat back down and listed what she would need for the journey. Food certainly, warm clothes, and a weapon. She had her knife, but something larger might be good.

"Lady."

Ailsa started; she hadn't heard anyone approach.

Young Jamie stood at the stall door, the stable hand from Caerwyn. He peered down at her.

"What are you doing here?" she said.

"I saw you leave this morning, and I thought you should have a man with you on such a dark day," he responded. "So I saddled a horse and followed ye." He stopped, worry in his eyes. "Did I do right?"

Ailsa stared at him a long moment. It took courage to tell her he'd followed her. She got to her feet. "Would you help me, Jamie, if I needed something, I mean?" She brushed the straw off her skirt. "Would you go on an adventure with me?"

Jamie's eyes widened. "I would be honored to serve you, Lady," he stammered.

"Good." She detailed her needs. His eyes widened, but he bowed and rushed out of the barn. He was excited to be trusted as a man. She had no fear he'd tell the others.

She left the barn and slipped into the hall, where the male guests snored on rows of pallets. She woke the maid at the door and gave her a message for Jocelin, saying she was heading home very early and wishing Thomas and his new wife well. The maid nodded and fell back asleep, her apron up over her head. Jocelin would think she was slipping away in humiliation. This rankled somewhat. But let her think as she would.

Creeping quietly upstairs to the solar, Ailsa found her old gown. Dragging the huge blue gown off, Ailsa folded it and shrugged into her own comfortable homespun. She listened at the door a moment, but everyone seemed to be sleeping deeply after the late night celebrations. She slipped back out, grabbing her cloak as she went out, and found Jamie already back at the barn. He had a big sack lumpy with provisions.

"How did you get these?"

"There was much food set out, brought back from the feast and meant for the morning meal on the morrow. I thought it proper to take some for us," he said. His eyes waited for her judgement.

"Very proper," she agreed. She was amused to see relief flare in his eyes. "You've done well."

Ailsa, mounted on Nia, rode out through the main gate past the snoring guard. Jamie followed, on a big-boned black horse, the provisions strapped on behind. They headed east, into the hills. Before dawn, the dark silence of the forests enclosed them.

PART II

CHAPTER SIX

The Eastern Hills

Ailsa crouched on a flat slab of granite and tightened her damp cloak around her neck. Wet branches swayed above and dribbled cold water onto her head. Her toes were freezing, and she was feeling very sorry for herself. How unfair that she was forced to this. And, it was so very quiet in the oak forest. She had sent Jamie to find some news at the hamlet they'd passed, and to purchase whatever fresh food he could find. She tired of cheese crusts and damp bannocks.

Jamie had been gone a long while. But she needed to know exactly where the king was now. Had he indeed marched to Carlisle and taken the castle? Or was he ensconced somewhere else along the way? Three days ago, petitioning the king had seemed a logical plan. A fabulous plan. But now she was beginning to wonder.

It was so very still without Jamie's cheerful presence. These unfamiliar forests were nothing like the beech woods she knew so well near her home. Her legs ached and her throat was sore, and she wished for a hot tub of water to bathe. And the king, what exactly would she do and say when she found him? She stared into the tangle of dark twisting boughs and then at the green moss curling around her boots. The pale sky promised more rain. She shivered, stood up, and stamped her feet to warm them.

She must remember why she was here. It was completely wrong for the king to claim her as his ward, steal her estate, and force her to marry a stranger and a foreigner. Gaelic inheritance custom said unequivocally she was her father's heir. There was no question over her land's proper future and her marriage was certainly hers and hers alone to decide.

Ailsa paced up and down the clearing. How would she find the right words to convince the Scots king? Some said he was English to the bone, but her father had called him good and fair. Yet the truth was her father would not have approved this venture, not at all. He'd have been horrified at the thought of his daughter sitting in a winter forest alone, cold, hungry, and far from home. And if her plea to the king failed, what then? She stopped and stared, not seeing, into the dark trees, their trunks stained black with water. If she failed, what life had she left? She would be mistress of Caerwyn in name only, under the power of this stranger. Whatever he was, kind or monstrous, meant nothing. Her land, her home, her body would all be his to control.

She swallowed and made herself resume pacing. What was Meriel doing right now, she wondered. She had intended to come back to Caerwyn triumphant, married or at least betrothed to Thomas, the very next day. Meriel would have found her note, but it simply said she'd gone to visit Thomas. She would think Ailsa was staying on at their neighbor's keep. She'd not be uneasy about her for some days. Yet, here she stood, completely alone in the winter woods. Only silent trees and dripping granite rocks for company.

Of course, King David had actually offered her a choice. A nunnery! He would send her to Sanquehar, which must be fairly near this dismal spot, or to one of the nunneries down in England, dread places where unmarried women or inconvenient wives were imprisoned for all their days. Perhaps some actually liked that life, of prayers and bells and downcast eyes all day, she hoped they did, for their sake. But it was not for her. He offered her no choice at all, only one form of imprisonment or another.

No, she had needed a plan and she had come up with one and it would do. She felt her spirits return as she paced, and her body warmed. She would make it work. She must. It was an adventure after all. Think of what she'd see. She'd always imagined a sea voyage, but this trip through unfamiliar forests was a journey also. She looked around her with new interest, deliberately examining the ancient elm tree, its trunk encrusted with lichen, and the rain-soaked pine beside it. And the king's court would certainly be impressive and fascinating. She felt herself beginning to smile. She'd crossed a threshold, leaving her home. Launched something new. To turn around now would mean she was a coward and a failure. She had to go on. And truth be told, it had grown dull at Caerwyn, or she had grown dull. Since Niall died, nothing had been the same. She needed to be out in the world and seeing something new.

Ailsa rubbed her icy hands together. Still, a fire would be comforting. Jamie had warned her not to light one, for fear of robbers. But surely none were out in these damp and dismal woods today. She gathered dead branches, sweeping aside the frosty leaves to find dry twigs underneath. She piled the sticks, took out her flint, and kindled a flame. Orange licks of color climbed into the wood slowly, but eventually broke into flames and smoke curled up through the branches and mingled with the mist. Ailsa dragged over a log and sat with her wet garments as close to the flames as she dared. The fire caught and she threw on more wood and soon it blazed.

She forgot the dismal woods and began to plan her meeting with the king. She would be poised and calmly logical, convincing the king of her right to rule her lands. David, impressed by her arguments, would nod and his lords would murmur with approval. She would return home and see that all the lands were returned to proper order, the men returned from the towns, the fields planted, and the gardens verdant and the orchards ripe and heavy with fruit. She would do it. The king must let her. It seemed she had never appreciated Caerwyn properly until the threat of losing it forever appeared.

A log fell, scattering orange sparks. She beat them off her cloak. Crows cawed to each other in the branches overhead, disturbing the quiet.

"Lady!" Jamie swept into the clearing, pulling up his snorting horse. He looked so small on the big horse's back, but he did ride well. He slid off, a frown on his normally cheerful face.

She jumped to her feet. "I'm glad to see you."

"Lady, I said 'twas not safe to build a fire." Without asking permission, he swept the logs apart, scraping moss and earth over the flames. Her bright fire became a smoking heap of charred logs.

"It will do no harm, surely."

"It's a danger. We are only two. Best to take no chances."

Ailsa frowned. "I was enjoying it."

"Time we ride now anyway," said Jamie, his face flushed. "Be you ready?"

"Aye," said Ailsa. "Let us start if we're not to freeze here. I am anxious to reach the king. Where do we find him? Had the people here any news?"

"None, other than the march on Carlisle," said Jamie, covering the charred logs with wet leaves. "They saw the soldiers pass by some miles from here on the old Roman road, a fortnight past. The king could be in Carlisle now." Jamie paused and then rushed on, "Think you it might be wiser to return home and bide there until we have news the king has triumphed? Then we can arrange a proper visit with a stronger escort for these roads."

"No!" Ailsa said. "I'll not turn back. The king rides for Carlisle, and so will we."

"But we need a plan, Lady. And another man."

His face was so serious. "Where would we get another man?"

Jamie examined the ground, then looked up again. "I found a cousin of mine at the village we passed. I told him he could come along." He whistled and there was a rustle from the woods. A boy emerged from a stand of willow, of about Jamie's age, but already tall and husky. He gave her a shy grin. "He's very strong, and knows these woods," said Jamie.

Ailsa assessed the boy, his brown hair tangled and hacked off at his shoulders, hat squashed in big hands. "What is your name?"

"Trefor, Lady." He gave her a wide smile, missing one front tooth.

"Well, why not." Ailsa felt cheered, despite herself, at the thought of a larger escort. "Let us go on then, to Carlisle."

"One more thing," said Jamie.

"Another surprise?"

He thrust a bundle into her hands.

"What is this?"

"Some clothes. Men's clothes." Jamie wouldn't meet her eyes.

"Why would I need these?"

"It will be safer," mumbled Trefor.

Ailsa hesitated and then grinned. "Why not?" She walked off to the far side of a wide oak and covered her homespun gown with the overlarge tunic. It came down to her ankles, but she wound the leggings on anyway, stuffing the top of her gown into the leggings. She wasn't sure it would hold too well, but from a distance it would serve the purpose.

"You'd best cover your hair too, begging your pardon," said Trefor.

She twined her hair up and thrust the hat down to keep it in place. "There." Feeling awkward in the layers of clothes, but much warmer, she climbed onto Nia. "Have you any more surprises for me?"

"Only that I asked Trefor's father and uncle to come along too."

"What!"

"They wanted to see the excitement in Carlisle, and they'll be of help to us. We don't know what we'll find on the road after all."

She frowned. "They haven't told anyone where we're going?" She had the feeling grown men might feel somewhat differently about her plan than Jamie or Trefor.

"No, no. And they'll be good for hunting up meat along the way too," said Jamie.

She considered him with her eyes narrowed. It seemed he hid some surprising qualities. "Well, they can come then." She looked around. "Are they hidden in the woods as well?"

Jamie laughed. "They'll catch us up on the road. They had to chop some fire wood first and I wanted to get back here to you," he explained. "They'll be meeting us at the cross on the Roman road, if not before." At that Jamie mounted his horse, and Trefor vaulted up behind.

Ailsa thought a moment, then shrugged. She didn't think they needed anyone else, but as long as the men didn't slow her down, she didn't mind their company.

Robert and his men rode south toward his new lands. The grey sky promised hard rain toward evening and the wind was raw. As he rode, Robert tried to picture the hall at Caerwyn; would it be warm and welcoming, or grand and imposing, or dusty and in disrepair? And what of his wife to be? She would be young, he thought, but not, he hoped, a child. How could a girl, even one of marriageable age, understand anything of the life he'd led?

He shook his head and focused on the road. He'd sent a scout ahead, down the twisting path. He wanted no more trouble of the sort they'd had yesterday. He glanced back at Will, who acknowledged his look with his characteristic wide grin, though his wrist was sprained, and he'd bound his left arm in a sling to rest it. Robert frowned. They'd come off lightly, despite all the blood, but two men had been wounded, and Nevin, badly. He'd left plenty of food and a hot fire, though it was risky. He'd send help, horses and medicine and a healer, if one could be found, just as soon as they reached Caerwyn. He hoped it would be in time.

They were all trained for surprise attacks, and they'd certainly weathered many. Still, he always felt angry at the waste. Odd for a soldier, but he'd not been able to get over it. The woods were a tight mass of twisting oak branches here, and under the grey skies so dark it was nearly night under the trees. He'd stayed awake long last night, pondering who might be behind the attack. One of his new neighbors perhaps. But there was also fitz John's man back in Edinburgh. Could he be involved, or was he letting animosity cloud his judgment? He dug his fingers into Tanet's mane against the wind. The old urge for revenge bit at him. For a moment, he dreamed of leaving Scotia and racing Tanet down to the Welsh borders and his old home to confront the bastard. He shook his head. He was one man and fitz John had thirty knights or more.

They rounded a corner in the path, wet leaves flying up from the horses' pounding hoofs. A figure rode toward them, waving his arm. "It's Nick," Will called out.

Nick's horse was lathered from hard riding and the sound of harsh breathing cut through the still air. "Riders ahead," he gasped out.

"How many?"

"Three together, and another two behind." There was a stir among the men.

Just the number who had escaped them yesterday. Robert twisted in his saddle to face his men. "No honest men ride in this foul weather. It could be those we seek. But I want them alive." The clang of metal sounded in the damp air as his men loosened their swords and pulled out knives. "We'll leave the path. Cut west and take them at the Roman road."

The men nodded. "The wind is in our favor," Robert said, and added, "alive, remember. I have questions for them." He turned Tanet, and they headed single file into the forest.

Ailsa hummed under her breath, a happy tune more appropriate to May Day than the cold wind circling about her. Besides, she hardly noticed the wind, her men's clothing keeping her warm. They'd be on the main road to Carlisle in no time. She patted Nia's warm neck and murmured to the mare. Brown leaves skittered across the path, and clouds of mist wove in ghostly swirls through the trees, but Nia ignored them and trotted on. She was a certainly a competent mount, thought Ailsa complacently, as she'd had the training of the mare. She turned round and smiled to Jamie and Trefor riding just behind her. Jamie grinned, pleased to be approaching the Roman road too. Always worrying, was Jamie.

They mounted a rise, and up ahead, she could see the cross, and with a joyful yell she urged Nia on. The mare leaped ahead. Ailsa heard Jamie call out to her, but she bent down over Nia's neck and urged her faster. The wind tugged at her hair and her eyes blurred with tears. Jamie's horse, big-boned and double-loaded, was left behind. Ailsa galloped into the empty crossroads, swinging around to await Jamie and Trefor who were now well behind. When they approached, their horse snorting, for Trefor clearly had ridden little and was leaning first to one side and then the other, Ailsa shouted, "We're nearly to Carlisle!"

Jamie shook his head, but he was laughing. He pulled the horse up. "We'd best give this one a rest. We can eat while Trefor's father and uncle catch us up, and then move on."

Ailsa stifled her frustration at having to wait and nodded. But when had Jamie taken charge of her trip? He was just a horse boy, after all.

Trefor stared back down the road, his eyes squinting in the mist, which was fast turning to something more like rain. "There they are," he said and waved. Two men trotted toward them on sturdy ponies, shaggy with winter coats, their long manes flapping.

Ailsa greeted the men as they dismounted, holding in her impatience, hoping there would be no more delay. Just as she extended her hand, the pound of horses' hoofs sounded from behind. She turned, hearing a yelp from Jamie. Mounted men streamed into the crossroads from all sides, whirling like devils out from the shadows under the oaks. Jamie's horse sidled and reared and Trefor tumbled to the ground. Jamie yelled, "Ride! Ride!"

Ailsa hesitated, then rode Nia toward Jamie, her hand out to grab him as he tried to control his panicked horse. But a man dressed all in brown rode between her and the boy. "Ride," Jamie yelled to her again.

Her hands seemed to belong to someone else, but she gathered up the reins. Nia danced sideways as the men advanced. She twisted around and saw Jamie pulled from his horse, his arms drawn tight behind his back by a burly man who held the boy easily as he struggled. "Ride!" Jamie yelled once more, frustration clear in his high voice. She whirled the mare and dug her heels into Nia's sides. The mare leaped forward. Caught unprepared, the man in front of her fell back.

A tall man stepped into the road just ahead of the mare's path. Nia shied and reared. The man grabbed for the reins and yanked them from her hands. The mare whirled around him in a tight circle. Ailsa clung to Nia's mane, thrown half off her seat. He grasped Nia's bridle, quieting the mare with a word.

Ailsa heard shouts and the ominous scrape of swords. A chill ran through her, as more men crowded into the clearing. They separated Jamie and Trefor and bound their arms with thick cord. The thieves wore hoods pulled tight over the faces, and their shouts were muffled by the thick wool. She stared, frozen, until Jamie called again, "Save yourself!"

The burly man holding the boy knocked him to the ground. She grabbed her reins back and whipped the tall man holding her horse. The leather struck his neck and drew a bloody welt. He cursed and a powerful arm pulled her to the ground.

She struggled and yelled, and the frightened mare jumped away. She felt the man's grip on her waist loosen. But before she could slip out, he caught her again, and spun her around to face him. She could smell leather, iron, and sweat. She watched a drop of blood on his neck, where his pulse leaped. He glared down at her a long moment, his eyes unreadable. Then he yanked the hat from her head. Her hair tumbled down over her shoulders.

Ailsa glared into the masked face, but her heart was racing, and she couldn't catch a breath.

"So." The voice was low, menacing. Holding her with one arm, he picked up a strand of dark hair and rubbed it between long gloved fingers. "Don't scream, it will only serve to alarm your men."

Ailsa bit her tongue hard and swallowed, tasting blood, knowing he was right. Jamie would try to rush to her aid and be wounded or even slain. The thief was holding her tight; her hip ground into his hard thigh. Her heart pounded and skipped, and she saw now that his eyes were grey and cold as the winter sky.

"A woman," he said in a quiet voice, "wandering out here in the winter forest. Unusual."

Ailsa swallowed and said, "We have food, if that's what you seek, but no coin."

The grey eyes narrowed, and Ailsa sucked in a breath at their expression, shrinking back. He whirled her around, and shouted, "Will." A tall fellow appeared at his side. "Take this woman to a spot of safety." She was handed off.

"Wait," she called to his back, "you cannot treat me this way, what are you doing to Jamie?" But the grey-eyed leader did not turn around.

"Come, miss," said the man beside her, "best do as he says."

Ailsa frowned at his hand on her wrist. "Unhand me this minute, I am the ..." She caught herself and stopped.

The man waited, but when she fell silent, he said again, "Come miss," and pulled her to a nearby thicket, where a horse was tethered. He swung her up as easily as if she were a sack of barley, though he was injured and had one arm bound by his side. He jumped up behind her and they trotted off. The clamor of men's voices and sounds of struggle faded and there were only the sounds of the forest and the rhythmic thud of the horse's hoofs.

Ailsa bit her lip to keep from crying.

"Are you cold, miss," said the man behind her.

She straightened her back, "No, and I demand you unhand me and my men too."

"Well," said the man, "I can hardly do that when my master left me instructions to keep you safe by me here, now can I?"

Ailsa felt anger flare at the man's amused tone. But beyond clench-ing her fist, there was nothing to do. She thought of trying to push him from the horse, but he was big, and his one arm wrapped around her waist firmly. They rode for some time through the grey forest, with Ailsa too miserable to feel the cold, then he pulled the horse to a stop and slid off. He pulled his hood off then and she stared into laughing blue eyes under tousled brown hair.

"As you heard, my name is Will," he offered, "and who might you be?"

Ailsa glared down at him. "That is none of your concern. Unhand me and we will be on our way."

Will continued to smile and said, "I think we'll bide here till my master returns."

Ailsa clenched her teeth, fear and frustration warring in her. Surely, she had a better chance to convince this seemingly amiable stranger than to attempt to argue with the grey eyed leader. Biting back more words, she decided to wait. Slowly, she slid off the horse.

She must help Jamie and Trefor. There would be an opportunity. This man was favoring his arm. There'd be a chance for them all to escape. She suppressed a shiver.

What was happening to Jamie even now? Her stomach felt sick inside at the thought. And to Trefor and his father and uncle? Faithful worrying Jamie, he was right. The roads were dangerous, and she had led them all into trouble. It was an uncomfortable thought and made her want to cry. She took a deep breath. She wouldn't cry. This was all her fault. She must set it right.

Will finished tethering the horse. "I'll just get a fire going, and things will warm right up. The rain is sure enough pelting down."

He kindled a fire in the center of the clearing with no trouble, despite the wet. This must be the robber's camp. The story teller who came to Caerwyn each winter told terrible tales of thieves on the road, men who lived all the year in the forest, hard men who lived by preying on merchants and travelers, murdering with no mercy and all for a coin or a trinket or some bit of food. She looked around, desperate to see any sign of help, but she could see no smoke or light from any village or hut. Only grey trees and mist under a grey sky met her gaze.

Will turned from her then to pick up a heavy log, and she saw a chance. She whirled and ran. Hide, I must hide, she thought as she flung herself through the brush, careless of stones or logs, surely, I can find a spot. She crouched behind an oak and slid back into some bushy undergrowth. I can wait, and then come out and save Jamie later, tonight, in the dark. She heard Will shouting curses back in the clearing and felt a small moment of satisfaction. Then she heard him crashing into the brush right behind her. She jumped up and ran, looking for somewhere to duck out of sight. But the woods opened here, tall oaks with little underbrush. Will darted out, shockingly close and grabbed her from behind, scooped her up with his one strong arm and carried her, struggling, back to the fire. She was breathing hard, from exertion and fear, but he was not.

"Now miss, that was not a good idea. Where will you go to anyway, out in those woods, it's no kind of place for a woman alone deep in winter." He held her with one arm against an oak and pulled a length of cloth from inside his sleeve. "I must have you here when my master returns," he said, apparently by way of apology, and bound her wrists and tied the ends about the tree.

Ailsa sank to the ground, heart pounding. She blinked back angry tears. She would think of a plan. She would. She thought of the tall leader, face grim, eyes stormy. She must.

His back to the cross marking the Roman road, Robert surveyed the men with a frown. He felt a cold anger roiling inside when he thought of young Nevin, lying wounded and white, alive he must hope. He thrust it down. He must decide what to do with these men. Common thieves? Or the ambushers? He suspected some connection to the latter more troubling possibility.

"Fan into the woods; see if there are others." The men stood, their hands bound, staring at the ground.

"We found these two trying to hide in the woods. And these boys here were with the woman." One of his men pushed two youths, hands bound with ropes behind their backs, before him. One was a tall lad, but they couldn't be more than twelve or thirteen. Robert frowned into their young faces. They were pale but trying to seem unafraid.

"Where have you taken the lady?" said the smaller one.

"All in good time," he answered, noting the word lady. The boy looked as though he would say more but didn't.

"Bind them on two of the pack horses," he called out and strode over to Tanet. Two men, two boys, and a woman, disguised as a man. Were there others? Where was the big man he'd fought with? He mounted Tanet and rode into the woods, calling an order to bring the men along behind, thinking as he rode. No one would be out on the road in this winter season, in this raw wind and rain, for an innocent reason. It was too coincidental to think they had no connection to the men who'd ambushed them yesterday. And the woman, what was she doing out here? That was even more strange. He would get to the bottom of this, he assured himself, and urged Tanet to a faster pace, following the track Will had laid behind.

When Robert reached the clearing, he watched Will hovering over the campfire, stirring a pot, and the woman, sitting on the ground, her back straight, tied to a small tree. She must have tried to escape, he thought with a twinge of amusement.

But this was no game. The Western coast must remain untroubled while David marched on Carlisle and maneuvered in the uncertain world of England's battles over Stephen and Matilda. He had been entrusted with the task and he would see it done. It was his duty as the new lord of Caerwyn. And his honor required it for he owed all to the king. But even more, he'd protect his own men no matter what. He thought of Nevin again and anger flared in his throat.

He swung down from his horse. Will gave him a wink, but the woman had her back to him. She did not seem to hear his silent approach over the heavy mosses. "Good day," he said, and watched her start; she turned, her eyes wide, greenish in the shadowy light, and dark against the pallor of her skin. Her hair was dark too and fell tangled and unkempt to her waist. He pushed that distracting thought away. She was an enemy, sent to entice, or perhaps she was the coin behind the entire ambush. "I trust you have met with every comfort here under Will's care, Lady." He saw her frown. "Who are you and who has sent you here?"

She lifted her chin and said nothing.

"You will answer as I require."

She regarded him steadily. He frowned and saw a shadow cross her face in response. "Who are you?" he repeated.

"That I will not say. You have no right to the information. You must unhand me and my men. What have you done with them?" Her voice quavered.

He shifted from one foot to the other. This business of grilling a woman, he did not particularly like. "I will ask your men, then."

"You have not killed them." Her voice was full of relief.

"Of course, I have not," he said, irritated. "I don't go about killing boys."

"You set upon us without cause," she answered. "How do I know what you might do?"

"Why do you disguise yourself as a man, and why wander with servants rather than men at arms in the forest? Hardly usual for a lady, even in Scotia." Robert waited.

"I cannot see that as your concern. We are simply wayfarers."

"Wayfarers," said Robert, "and where do you intend to go?"

"Nowhere," said the woman too quickly, and she clenched her hands at her mistake. "I will tell you nothing. You must let us all go immediately."

"That is not likely," said Robert. She was very pale, but the eyes met his. They held just a sheen of tears. He felt sympathy rise but thrust it down. She was hiding the truth, and she was a certainly a dissembler, to raise false tears and face him this way.

Just then his men rode in, leading the packhorses with the two boys and two men tied on. She jumped to her feet. "Let me go, I must see to them."

Robert pulled his sword from its sheath and sliced the cloth tying her to the tree. The woman stared at his sword, then ran to the boys, now standing awkwardly at the edge of the clearing, hands bound.

"Are you all right," she cried. She assured herself that they were fine, then she turned to Robert. "You must untie them too."

Robert raised his eyebrows. "I don't think so." She turned away, her back stiff. He watched her greet the older men with obvious relief but with formality and noted the quick hug she gave the smaller boy.

The smell of venison and onions swirled through the air, interrupting his observation. Time enough to figure this puzzle out. "I'm starved," he said, and settled himself with a sigh by the fire. Will handed him a bowl filled with hot stew and ladled more out to the other men.

"Come to the fire, there is food here to eat," called Robert to the woman. She looked undecided, then walked over.

"You must feed my men. They have not eaten since last night."

"You were in a hurry, it appears."

She frowned, her hands twisting together.

"I plan to feed them in due course. I have no need of weaklings keeling over on the way." He gestured to Will.

"You must let us go on our way, this very evening. We are expected."

Robert crumpled a dry leaf in his fingers and said nothing. Will approached and held out a bowl of the steaming stew. She hesitated, then took the bowl, favoring Will with a small smile. Will walked over to the prisoners and tied the feet of the boys and men with some stout rope. He unbound their arms and fetched them some food as well. They fell to with enthusiasm.

The woman watched, then, apparently satisfied, began to eat herself.

Robert studied her. Her cloak was of fine thick wool, but the tunic and leggings she'd donned were of rough stuff, suitable for a peasant or woodcutter. He got to his feet. They'd wasted more than enough time. He didn't forget that Nevin waited for aid.

The woman jumped up too.

"Stay by the fire."

"But, said the woman, "what do you intend with my men?" Her voice was faint, but she stood her ground.

"I intend a conversation. Now return to the fire or it will go the worse with them." She backed off, her bowl of stew forgotten in the grass. She looked forlorn, the wind stirring tangled hair, her nose reddened with the cold.

Robert turned toward the men, sitting at the edge of the darkening woods, their cloaks beaded with moisture, their bowls empty on their laps. Time for some answers.

Ailsa watched the leader go. She no longer felt hungry. This day had gone dreadfully wrong. A drizzle was falling off and on, and she pulled her hood up over her hair. The winter woods were full of shadows; night had come on early. How could they all get free? Her thoughts whirled, but she had no answers.

The thieves laughed as they ate their stew. They seemed a normal, if rough, group of men, not much like thieves should be. Though after all, what did she know of thieves, apart from the old tales? Their clothes were serviceable, dark green or brown in color, blending well into the woods and mosses. Their weapons were well-kept, silver swords and spears. They had enviable horses. Of course, they could have stolen them.

The leader had untied Jamie and was leading him away from the others. His hand rested on Jamie's shoulder, and he was talking low into his ear. She tensed, but there was nothing she could do. She saw Jamie cast a glance her way. She clenched and unclenched her fingers.

"Why don't you eat, miss, 'twill be a long night and day without. We do not stop for breakfast, but eat as we ride in the morning," cautioned Will.

Ailsa thought of refusing, then forced herself to eat some more of the stew. It had cooled, but it was good and she found herself finishing the bowl. Will sat himself down opposite her and stretched out long legs in thick leather boots. "Where do we ride to?" she asked, thinking perhaps she could get some information from him now.

Will just chuckled. "He'll let you know that in his own time, I imagine."

"Do you also ride with us William?"

Will laughed out loud at this. "Call me Will and it will do fine."

"And what shall I call him?" Ailsa gestured toward the leader.

"I guess it can't hurt to tell you that," answered Will, poking at the fire with a long stick. "Robert, that be his name, though his few friends do call him Robb."

William, Robert. Her mind raced. English names. It was true then, these English were nothing but adventurers and thieves. Setting on her men in the open daylight in the public crossroads. Robert. The disturbing thought floated into her mind and lodged. But Robert was a very common name among the English. Extremely common. Ailsa tried to sound only mildly interested, "Which Robert would that be?"

"Why," said Will, lazily pulling grass and shredding it in his big hands, "him as lately come to Scotia from Normandy to serve King David and settle. He's been given lands direct from the king. So I guess you could call him Robert of Caerwyn now. It's near here, you know it perhaps."

Ailsa stifled her indrawn breath. Will was staring at her. She tried to school her face. She could not be so unfortunate. She thought she might be sick.

"Miss?" Will, his face creased with concern, bent toward her.

Just then Robert strode back into the firelight. "Sleep. We ride early on the morrow," the leader called out.

Will jumped to his feet.

She watched him go with relief, her stomach tight. She must be very careful, give nothing away. She saw with a sinking heart how the men doused the fire, settled the horses, and gathered up the supplies into neat piles ready for an early start in the morning. Clearly, they were used to obeying their leader's orders. They were organized and disciplined. They had swords. This was no robber band. Of course it was not. She looked at the leader, his tall straight back. At Sir Robert, she forced herself to realize. An English knight.

She surprised herself by addressing his stern back. "Where is Jamie?" Her voice sounded sharp with worry, even to her own ears. "He is but a boy."

Robert turned, his black brows drawn together. His beard, she saw now, was of several days growth only. So he was usually clean shaven, like all the English. "I do not war on boys or women." He added, "Yet, I will find out who you are and why you have harmed my men."

She sighed in relief. Jamie was not harmed. And apparently, he had told this stern man nothing. She felt a glow of pride. "We have not harmed your men. You must let us go on our way as soon as there is light."

"I will know who you are. Why not tell me now, and be done with it?"

She almost found herself wanting to answer, but she said nothing. After a moment he turned from her. Alarm prickled cold across her skin. How could the king even think to marry her to this man?

CHAPTER SEVEN

AILSA WAS MOUNTED ON A STURDY PONY, his fur matted and dark. Rain streamed down his neck, but he plodded on patiently. She wasn't patient, more wild with uncertainty and worry and the miserable knowledge that this was all her fault.

Will, sitting easily on a chestnut horse, rode beside her, holding her pony's reins. Nia had been relegated to the back of the line. Ailsa twisted around, but couldn't see her, for the path they followed bent and turned, following a ridge studded with scrubby pines. She'd hoped they'd let her ride the fast mare. Given half a chance, she could have made a break for it. Only the leader's massive grey stallion could possibly have kept up, and even then he might not have been able to catch her. But Sir Robert had cast a casual glance at Nia, as they set off in the half-dark of dawn, and turned immediately to say a word to Will. Ailsa had found herself off the mare and remounted in short order.

They had been riding since early morning, with only a short break once. They'd eaten their meal, if you could call it that, as they rode. The clammy bannocks had crumbled in her fingers. Ailsa flexed her stiff hands, tired from clenching the pony's wiry mane. They were headed west. Back to where she'd come from. Headed for the coast and Caerwyn. And once they neared Caerwyn, there would be no hope of keeping her identity from him.

Should she tell him now? What would he do to her? But if she didn't tell him, and he found out, it would go the worse with her. She was deceiving him, every moment now.

She bit her lip. She had started down this road and she wouldn't waver. She would get away, somehow. She would get to the king and persuade him, demand, that he give her land back. She straightened her back and tried to ignore the rainwater dripping down her neck.

At the front, she glimpsed Sir Robert's back, clad in black leather mail. He showed no signs of cold or fatigue. Indeed, he seemed quite jovial, joking with his men, his distinctive voice with its odd accent carrying easily back to her. Jamie and Trefor, double mounted on a fat pony, were riding along beside him, clearly awed by this paragon. She'd have to do something about that.

Trefor's father and uncle were behind her somewhere in the straggling line of wet riders. From the looks they'd shot her way this morning, and their cold silence, she felt sure they were regretting their rash promise to accompany her to Carlisle. Still, they'd kept their silence so far, with the wary caution of woodsmen who lived far from villages and communal life. Hopefully, they'd stay silent. But what if Robert coerced them with more than words, or offered them coin or other reward?

They slogged on through the gathering shadows, grey clouds darkening the winter sky. Ailsa retreated under her wool hood and tried to calculate. She had at best this afternoon, before they might meet some traveler who could identify her. If the rains continued, that is, and most folks stayed dry indoors.

"Will," she turned abruptly in the saddle. "How much longer do we ride?" She tried to sound plaintive. "It's so cold and wet. My servant, he is just a boy, surely we should stop for the night and soon."

"Well…" Will hesitated, glancing up the line of riders to Robert, who showed no signs whatsoever of stopping. "I don't know. Robb, Robert that is, likes to put in a good number of miles in a day, and we've been riding somewhat slow." He glanced at her apologetically.

"With me along, you mean," she said.

"Well, yes." Will shrugged and grinned at her.

She rode for a time in frustrated silence. Could she slow them down further? She hated to even pretend she needed help. She felt she could ride all day and into the darkest night if need be. But if she could persuade them she was exhausted and needed rest, it could buy time.

The trees passed slowly by, their bark wet and glistening in the afternoon's fading light. Indeed it was getting hard to tell tree from man, everything shrouded in cold rain. "Give me the reins, Will," she demanded.

"I can't do that." His bushy brows arched up and he stumbled over the words.

She leaned over and grabbed the reins from his hands. Before he thought to stop her, she urged the reluctant pony to a jolting canter. She rode up to Robert at the front.

Will was beside her in an instant. "The reins," he said, reproach in his voice.

Robert had pulled up his horse. "Perhaps you have decided this would be a good moment to tell me your name and your business wandering in these woods," he suggested, without offering a greeting.

"My name is no concern of yours."

Robert blinked at her sharp reply but said nothing.

She clenched her teeth. "We must stop for the night. It is wet and cold." She tried to look woebegone. But her voice, she knew, sounded defiant. "The horses are tired if you are not. And the boys. It is not right to drive them so." Robert glanced at Jamie, who was indeed beginning to look bedraggled, but he held himself firmly up in the saddle.

"I am just fine, Lord," said Jamie.

Ailsa frowned at him. Jamie looked abashed and turned his eyes to the ground.

"We'll stop when I am ready and not before," Robert announced, then turned his horse and rode on. The men followed and Will took the reins from her hands.

She fumed as the pony slogged on through the winter rain. By the time they pulled up to make camp, Ailsa was too tired to do more than slip from her pony's back and plod toward the fire the men had efficiently kindled. They all looked rested, as if such a sodden ride were nothing out of the ordinary. Indeed, it probably was not.

Despite Robert's rude behavior, it appeared they'd stopped much earlier than the men had expected. Still, at this pace, there was no doubt they'd reach her lands first thing on the morrow. She sank down on an icy log.

Soon the cook had a stew of onions and oats cooking, and apples and some white cheese appeared. Despite herself, Ailsa felt her stomach rumbling.

Will approached. "Will you have some food?"

Ailsa nodded mutely and took the offered meal. She tried to preserve some dignity and not bolt the hot stew down. But she was starving, and it was very good stew. Will brought her a mug of ale as well, and some more oat cakes. Robert was nowhere to be seen.

Warmed by the food and fire, Ailsa ventured a question. "Where do we ride to, Will?" Though she knew the answer full well.

To Robb's new estates on the coast," he answered, between mouthfuls of stew. "He has been given land by the king himself." He grinned. "But I told you that already."

Ailsa frowned. "And what has this Englishman done to deserve these lands?"

Will laughed and ladled more hot stew in her bowl. "He deserves them, never fear."

"And you, why do you follow him? You have an English name, but I think by your speech you are not English."

"I am not. I hail from Gwynnedd in Wales, though I've ridden with the English for a long time, so long I barely remember my old home." He chewed a mouthful of stew slowly, staring at the fire. Then he grinned. "And Robb is a poor sort of Englishman as well."

"What do you mean?" asked Ailsa. "He seems…"

"I seem what," said a voice behind her.

Ailsa blushed, annoyed at being caught in her questioning.

"Will, I feel sure you have duties to attend to," said Robert.

Will grinned and clambered to his feet. "I think I'll see to the horses," he agreed, taking a last swig of ale.

"Do you always order everyone about so?" asked Ailsa.

"Of course," said Robert, "that is my duty, after all."

She shifted her gaze back to the fire. "You have brought us many miles out of our way. In the morning, you must let us continue on our journey."

"Three of your men have gone already," said Robert, and sat down beside her on the log.

"What!" Ailsa twisted around, searching the clearing. There was Jamie, standing by Will, each holding a steaming bowl of stew in their hands. But she couldn't see Trefor, his father or his uncle. "Where have they gone?" she asked reluctantly.

"Home, I expect."

Ailsa's mind raced. What had he learned from them? She recalled the dark looks from Trefor's father. To be honest, she couldn't blame them. They'd not expected this kind of complication. She stared at Robert, his face shadowed by the flickering fire. She could read nothing there. "What did they tell you?" she asked finally.

"I could see well enough they were not the brains of this plan." He shrugged. "They'll be watched, of course, to see who they go to with a message." He continued to stare at her, obviously expecting something.

Ailsa turned away, uncomfortable under that gaze. "Then you must let Jamie and me go free in the morning." She tried to sound commanding.

"I don't believe so," said Robert. "After all, I have still not discovered who you are, and more important, why you seek to harm me and my men."

Ailsa frowned at the ice in his voice. "What harm have we done to you or your men?"

"Until I know exactly what your part is, you will remain my guest." He moved away.

"Guest," called Ailsa after him, stung by his tone. "Is this English hospitality? We treat our guests differently here."

"Is the stew not to your liking?" He looked pointedly at her empty bowl. "You'd best sleep. We ride again early." He walked away.

The trees ringing the fire were black with night shadows and far off she heard the howl of a wolf. She shivered. 'Till morning, she had little choice, it seemed. She had best sleep, aggravating as it was to take his advice. She'd be ready, then, for tomorrow's chance. For tomorrow, early, she must find a way. It was a piece of luck, she realized as she lay down, that now there were only two of them to get away. They could do it. They must, for after that, it would be too late. If they entered Caerwyn, or even neared its gate, he would know who she was. He would know she had deceived him. She did not think he'd take that lightly. She shivered again, curled up in a ball, and wrapped her arms around her knees, against the cold and her dark thoughts.

Ailsa woke to the smell of smoke from the morning fire and the welcome scent of meat sizzling in an iron pan. A thick wool blanket, woven in four colors and embroidered with interlacing fanciful animals was keeping her warm. Had the kind Will put it over her in the night?

The cook looked over. "You're awakening, I see. My fine cooking, no doubt."

"Aye, the food smells good."

He chuckled. "We have you to thank, for the chief doesn't often stop for hot food in the morning."

"Whose blanket is this," she asked, as she folded it neatly.

Fergus looked up from stirring the pot, his face shiny and red from the heat. "Why, that's his, the chief's."

Ailsa stiffened. Her hand touched the intricate embroidery, tracing the swirls of colored wool. Had Sir Robert placed it on her in the night? Surely not, she couldn't imagine that. It was a Gaelic pattern, though not one she'd seen before. Odd that an English knight had such a fine piece of Gaelic thread work. What woman had sewed the fine stitches? She frowned. But it was not her concern, after all.

She tried to straighten her clothes, an impossible task. She'd kept the man's tunic and leggings on, for warmth. They were damp and smelled of earthy leaves and mildew. She looked around for Jamie, as she raked her fingers through her hair, trying to work out the worst tangles. It seemed years since she had sunk into a tub of warm water. Dirt was caked under her fingernails.

Robert entered the clearing, and the men finished their food and readied the horses. Today he wore a silver hauberk, glinting in the early half light. He had dressed in his finery, she understood, for entering and claiming her home. Feeling sick, she swallowed and looked away.

An hour passed, their steady riding eating up the miles. Ailsa barely saw the passing oaks, but when they passed a circle of ancient stones on a bare hilltop, she realized she was recognizing landmarks. She was on the sturdy pony again. Could she snatch the reins away and ride? She'd get no further than a few feet on this old fellow. And how would Jamie get away?

They halted in a high clearing not far from the stones. The lands spread out below, forest mostly and some strips of cultivated land and to the west an area of marsh. Ailsa noted Robert's caution. From here he could survey the area around for miles. Yet little untoward was to be seen. No smoke from campfires darkened the sky. Did he know, as she did, that the sea itself lay beyond the next line of hills?

Before they'd set out, she'd whispered to Jamie her intention to get away this very morning. She'd told him to be ready to ride at her signal, a high whistle. He had nodded his understanding. But now she saw him deep in conversation with Robert, who was apparently showing him how to read direction from the tree growth. Jamie's rapt look made her uneasy.

Ailsa looked around cautiously, trying to attract no attention, but she'd get nowhere when they had this vantage point. They could track her every move. She'd have to wait till they descended into the valley once more and take her chances there. Sighing, she unlaced the soggy leggings. At least she could dry them by the fire.

She felt her eyes drag over to Robert again. Engaged with Jamie, this was the first chance she'd had to really examine him. Here was the man the king intended her to marry. He was very tall and had the lean body of a fighter. As she watched, he pulled a Welsh bow from his horse's pack, and bent to string it with ease. Then he unstrung the bow and handed it to Jamie, who struggled unsuccessfully to bend the long weapon. Robert laughed and took it from the boy, stringing it again with no apparent effort. Then he bent over to show him the way to sight the bow. His dark hair was uncovered and fell in uneven waves to his shoulders. As if feeling her attention, Robert looked up and their eyes met. He said something to Jamie and started across the field toward her. Ailsa felt a moment of panic, but quashed it down, rising to her feet.

He walked up to her, but said nothing, just stood and looked at her. Ailsa felt herself blush. After a moment, she said awkwardly, "You are kind to the boy. I thank you."

He nodded.

"Why do you stare so," she stammered.

"I wonder who you are, and why you would seek to harm me and mine."

"It is you who have harmed me, taking us far from our intended path."

He took a step closer and suddenly she could smell him, leather, damp air, horse. She felt her breath come faster. "It is unjust of you to pluck us from the woods. You must release us now. I have important business to complete."

Unexpectedly, Robert reached out and caught a fistful of her tangled hair. He wound it around his hand and silently drew her to him.

Ailsa swallowed and stared up into his grey eyes, trying not to show her surprise. She tried to glare at him, but found his face too close, swimming before her eyes. His hair was rimmed in bright light from the sun emerging from the clouds. She broke his gaze to look down at his fist closed around her dark hair.

"Robb." Will's call split the air enveloping them.

Robert dropped her hair and stepped back. The air around her was suddenly cold. She frowned, not meeting his eyes.

"Robb." Will ran up the hill, panting. "The scouts have returned. They've word of the king. He has reached Carlisle and taken it. She's in Scots hands again."

"Good news." Robert looked out over the hills. "We depart after the horses have been watered. By mid morn we'll enter Caerwyn."

Ailsa stopped Will as he turned away. "How went the battle? Is the king now ensconced truly at Carlisle?"

"I believe it so. It's said David won the castle back handily, and waits now to negotiate with Stephen of England, and sends missives to Matilda, still in Normandy." Will smiled, then loped back across the field to the men and the horses.

They were left facing each other once again.

"Let us stop this useless sparring. You are no servant girl, and I would know your business in these winter hills now. What is your interest, for example, in the king's progress?"

"I have nothing to reveal to you, save that my servant and I journey on our own business. We are not involved in any plot against you. How could we, a boy and a woman, harm you?

"Yet we were set upon, and one of my best men lies wounded even now, with a sword slash to his gut."

Ailsa chilled at his words. Surely, he could not blame her? How could she have been involved in such evil happenings?

He turned toward the west, the wind blowing his dark hair back from his face, newly shaved this morning in the English way. "If you will not reveal your identity, then you must continue on with me, to the manor at Caerwyn, where someone is sure to know you." He did not wait for an answer.

She stared after him and shivered. Unless she could contrive an escape, his answer would come this very morning.

They slogged down the hills and into the wooded valley beneath. Granite boulders littered the path and it was hard traveling, the horses picking their way between the rocks and tree roots. Ailsa knew there was a better path, but apparently Robert wished to avoid the traveled routes, or perhaps, he did not know of it. She was not going to inform him.

Clouds gathered in long streaks of purple, blotting out the pale sun. Ailsa rode beside Jamie, hoping there'd be a moment when they could break free. But how? The thought of Robert's anger when he discovered her name was sobering. She hadn't lied to him outright, not exactly. But nearly. He was unlikely to forgive or forget that. If only she had Nia. The idea of leaving the mare saddened her further.

Deep in the valley, stunted trees grew close together and boggy ground blocked their way. Robert called a halt and sent scouts to find the best path to the high ground where he hoped to make the final descent to the sea and Caerwyn. Ailsa slid from her pony. "Be ready," she hissed to Jamie, as she walked past. His blue eyes widened, but he nodded.

Ailsa stumbled to the stream, gulped a drink of the icy water, and gazed down at her dark reflection. She could see little but a cloud of tangled dark hair and huge staring dark eyes. She felt so tired. How could they ever hope to get away? No wonder Jamie seemed surprised. The forests looked ominous and a wind had blustered up. She wondered if there were wolves close by even in the day.

On the far side of the stream, on a patch of dry land, Robert and Will bent over a parchment map spread on the ground before them. Her gaze shifted at a movement in the woods. It was the grey stallion, tethered loosely in the trees opposite her, not with the other horses. If only, she thought. A shiver of hope ran through her. No one rode the grey but Robert, she'd noticed. He might not accept her. But what if she could? Surely it was no worse than staying here. He believed she was involved somehow in this assault on his men. He could charge her and sentence her for such a crime. Or simply marry her, take her lands, throw her in Caerwyn's dark dungeon caves, unused for so long. He would be furious, once he knew who she was, there was no doubt. An English knight would not suffer such an insult to his men or his own honor.

She glanced about, biting her lip, still kneeling by the stream. No one was watching her. There was little hope of her going anywhere, after all, and the men were occupied, their vigilance relaxed. She was very good with horses. And truly, she could hardly make things worse than they were.

She sucked in a deep breath and let it out slowly. She must be calm and quiet and deliberate. She gave a high whistle and made a small sign to Jamie, who stiffened in reply. She looked pointedly over at the grey, and catching her idea, he nodded. She watched him wade across the stream, then fade into the woods. Will and Robert stayed glued to their map, pointing and looking up at the sky from time to time. It was true the wind was whipping up sudden and strong.

Ailsa stood up and straightened her gown and leggings, thinking furiously, but trying to look nonchalant. She crossed the stream on a path of rocks, then walked to the edge of the trees and sank down on a boulder. The men were busy, engaged with the horses and shifting the loads for the trek uphill. Robert glanced up, looked for her at the stream, and located her. She nodded to him, frowning. Unexpectedly, he grinned at her. His stern face looked quite different, carefree for a moment. Then Will drew his attention back to the map and their discussion. Planning how to steal her lands.

Ailsa shifted her weight off the rock and eased into the shadows behind a large oak tree. She saw Jamie creep toward the big grey. The horse raised his head. Jamie had been helping Robert care for the horses, so the stallion merely snuffed and pawed the ground, then returned to his grazing. Jamie whispered some words, then put his hand to the horse's neck and slid a rope loop over his head and ears. He fed the horse a handful of grass. Then he led the grey into the forest. Ailsa drew a deep shuddering breath and cast a last look at Robert and Will. Then she faded silently into the trees as well.

Ahead of her, Jamie stopped, and she approached slowly, whispering Gaelic words to the horse. He snorted at her. She murmured, a stream of melodic words, desperate that he make no noise. The horse sidled back, but she approached, talking all the time, touched his neck and fondled his ears. She took the rope from Jamie and taking one last desperate glance around, she motioned to Jamie and he stuck out his hands to help her up. She jumped onto the grey's back. He danced about, unsure at her light weight, but she talked to him, hoping they hadn't roused Robert's too capable men, and miraculously, the grey pricked his ears to hear her words and calmed. Bending over, she pulled Jamie up behind her. The stallion settled with the double weight. She turned the horse north, using her knees to guide him. They rode at a walk first, worried about noise, then at a fast trot, winding their way through oak and birch.

Tanet was jumpy and it was all she could do to hold him in, especially with the makeshift reins. Jamie clung to her waist. She hoped he could hang on. She was jumpy too, thinking each crack of a stick beneath Tanet's hoofs was Robert or one of his men. They came to a small stream and she urged the horse along its bed, heading west and then north. She hoped Robert's trackers might be confused, though it was a common ruse. She hoped the horse wouldn't stumble or break a leg on the stones. She wanted to get on a reasonable path and urge the horse to a gallop. His speed was their main advantage. Why didn't she hear the men coming after her? It was quiet in the woods, but for the gusty wind, whipping the smaller branches and sending the last dry oak leaves spinning off the trees. She kept to the stream for as long as she could bear it. If she could mislead his men, get them to think she'd headed north, they'd be far safer. Finally, she pulled Tanet to a stop, then urged him up the stream bank, steep and covered with low brambles which tore at her legs and boots. She turned the horse and headed south, riding along a wooded ridge crossed with deer trails.

They rode on through the stands of firs until they picked up the path she had hoped to find. If it was the right path, it headed south, straight toward the Roman Road and then on to Carlisle. It was not the main road and she hoped it did not appear on the map that Will and Robert had been studying with such care. Now they had a firm surface, she urged the horse to a canter, still listening for sounds of pursuit. He had no horses to match the grey's speed or endurance, not even Nia, she thought with a pang.

If they could put some miles between them, she had a chance, she might get away. And he would not seek her for long, she was sure, though she did have his horse. He had another stallion with him, and besides he was anxious to reach his new lands, and his new wife, she thought, with a sudden wild grin.

They flew along, wind whipping her face, and Jamie clinging behind. She kept wondering if she heard the pounding of hoofs behind her, but when she turned to look, the path was always empty. Early winter shadows lengthened into full dusk, and still they rode on, the grey untiring, until they reached a river running perpendicular to the path. She cajoled the horse down a narrow trail that ran along the water. This was the shortcut to the Roman road, she was fairly sure, for she'd been here once before with her father. If she had it right. They traveled slower now, as the light failed.

Jamie tugged at her gown. He'd said nothing so far, but now he said, "We must stop."

Ailsa ignored him at first, but she knew he was right. The light was gone and the horse could be lamed. She pulled the stallion to a halt, and they slid down his warm sides. "How wonderful you are," she crooned to the stallion, who snorted and searched about for some grass. There was little enough. She ripped cloth from her tunic and wiped him down, but he was hardly hot, and clearly used to long rides with heavier weight.

Jamie pulled some cheese and oatcakes from his pack. "Thought they might come in handy," he grinned. "I stuffed some in with each meal. We've enough here for a few days if we're careful."

"You're wonderful too," said Ailsa, biting into the cold food. She rolled it on her tongue. It tasted marvelous despite the crunch of a few grains of sand. They rested, in the dark, and Ailsa thought about wolves, and their howling, and mouths full of sharp teeth, but she did not dare build a fire. Robert would be annoyed they had escaped and angry that they had his horse. Even now, he was certainly searching. Ailsa wrapped her arms tight around her knees and tried to calm her breathing. When he reached Caerwyn, he would be even more furious, when he discovered who she was.

Sometime during the long night, the wind shifted, and it began to rain, softly at first, then harder. Ailsa moved next to Jamie and held her cloak over them both, hardly minding the icy downpour, optimistic for the first time that they might actually get away. Their tracks would be gone.

At the first hint of light, she woke the boy. They rode on, ears straining for any sound out of place in the forest, but she heard no sounds of pursuit, only the winter winds in the tree boughs, rushing small animals busy with their own lives, and the wonderful patter and splash of rain and more rain.

CHAPTER EIGHT

Robert sent men out in each direction, despite the boggy ground and the driving rain, but all returned at full dark without the woman.

Only Will approached. "She's just a girl. She can do us no real harm."

"She has Tanet."

"True," agreed Will. "It's a puzzle how she got that horse to go with her and no mistake."

"The horse is dangerous. He'll harm her or the boy." Robert frowned into the smoking fire, running a hand through his hair. "And she's not a girl." The winds shifted and a cold trickle of rain slid down his neck.

The next morning, two of his best scouts rode in, horses lathered. "They head south," shouted the scout as he slid from the saddle. "Both are riding the stallion, and at a hard gallop."

Robert turned to Will. "Toward de Morville's lands. Perhaps the lady has people to meet at Irvine."

Will sighed. "Fine neighbors."

"She'll outrun us, on Tanet," Robert said, "even my chestnut can't catch her. And perhaps that's what she intends. Have us chase her, lead us away." He thought for a moment. "We'll go on to Caerwyn, but once we arrive I count on you to find the woman and what she intends."

Will nodded. They rode on, as rain continued to drive down, and arrived at the outskirts of Caerwyn's lands at dusk, soaked and mud covered to their thighs. Robert winced at the dull pain in his head.

He'd intended to arrive in the morning, arrayed in the new clothes in his pack, but all that was abandoned now.

Will pulled up beside him. "No matter the mud and rain," he said quietly, "you've finally got your own lands."

Robert nodded. "It's not every day a man rides into holdings he's never seen. I certainly hope the king's charter made it here first."

Will laughed. "It would be awkward." He added, "You deserve these lands, Robb. Don't let any worries mar this day."

Robert put a hand on his friend's shoulder. "I count on you to find out what's afoot. Who that woman is and where she's gone. Whether she's connected to that ambush. I fear there's more here than that attack, something that threatens my lands and Walter's too."

"Think only of your success this day." Will turned his horse and melted into the woods.

The forests thinned and fell away; the meadows stretched wide and brown in winter's grasp. Robert hardly saw the fields, for he was thinking about Will. How long would it take him to overtake the woman? He shook his head impatiently. Here he was riding across his new lands, the fulfillment of his long dream. The de Morvilles, fitz John, or whoever it was, devil take them, they could wait. He would deal with them in good time.

He tried to conjure up an image of the Lady Ailsa, who awaited him in the manor, but failed. He was nervous, he realized, and took a deep breath. Far ahead, he saw a strip of grey, the sea. Soon he caught the smell of salt. Perhaps, someday, he'd have a son or daughter who'd play on the beaches here. A strange new thought.

But what was he thinking? Caerwyn would not be his home. It was a means only. A source of coin to fund his true dream, a return to his real home lost to him long ago. Caerwyn would provide the coin for revenge, against all those who had stolen his land and life away.

He spurred his stallion on, and galloped across the meadows, his men flying the banners of the king. They passed a cluster of long houses, and children pointed and shouted as they passed. They flew on, the horses' hoofs pounding, and finally reached the outskirts of the manor house itself. They slowed and approached the gates. Robert signaled to one of his men, who sped ahead to warn the gatekeeper to open for his new lord.

This proved unnecessary for the gate stood propped wide open. Perhaps they'd seen him approaching. But invaders could arrive in any guise and it was best to be cautious. Scotia would be no different that Normandy in that, as the last days proved. They clattered into the wide courtyard paved with granite stones, dragged, no doubt, from the beaches. A few servants clustered already by the kitchen, and children darted around, eyes wide at the display. Horses, colored banners, the men's armor, their gleaming armbands, and showy winter furs.

Robert dismounted and looked around with appreciation. The manor house, half built of granite and timbered on the upper floor, rose above him. It looked in good repair, though the walls and the gate needed fixing immediately. His rudimentary survey done, he checked the small crowd gathered in the courtyard. But he could see no one who looked anything like his future wife. Three serving girls clustered by one of the outbuildings, and several stable lads were hurrying to do the bidding of his men. A group of farm workers stood by the barns. Several milkmaids ducked back into the kitchens when he glanced their way.

Evidently his lady was one to stand on ceremony, or perhaps she was shy. Perhaps she waited in the hall. He entered through the main door, and one of the kitchen girls ran ahead, curtsied, and opened a second door for him. He gave her a wide smile and passed inside.

All was dark, the tall windows covered for the winter with hides, and no candles lit. No fire burned at the large central hearth. Indeed, the room smelled distinctly musty, and dust coated the long table set to one side of the large chamber. He turned to the servant girl, who still stood by the open door. "What is your name?"

"I be Osla, if it please your lordship." She gave an unpracticed curtsy.

"Osla, then, where is your mistress, and why is the hall so unkempt? Is she ill?"

"My mistress, Ailsa you mean, sir." Osla blinked, then forced out, "She is not here."

Robert narrowed his eyes and said nothing for a long moment. Then, quietly, he repeated, "Not here. What do you mean? Where would she be?"

Osla was silent, her blue eyes wide.

"Where is the lady? Did she not receive the king's messenger?"

Mention of the messenger seemed to revive Osla's wits. "Oh aye, he came indeed, wearing such a wonderful cloak, and covered in fur, more than a few weeks past…" Her voice trailed away.

"And what did your lady then," demanded Robert.

"Sir," stammered Osla, and burst into tears.

Robert cursed under his breath and controlling his voice, he said, "Now, now, Osla, it's not so bad as that, what did the lady say and where is she now?"

"Why she's biding at the neighboring manor, sir. And Meriel has gone off with Dugald to visit with friends at Renfrew, as Ailsa was not to home and she was lonely and sad having lost the child."

Robert frowned. This was not the welcome he'd imagined. He ran his hand through his hair. He must be fair; she'd not known, after all, when he'd arrive. He tossed away the daydream of a woman awaiting him at the door, a cautious smile in her eyes, soft arms folded that would soon learn to twine around him. He sighed. This was a marriage of convenience. For him and for her. He turned abruptly. "And where might this neighboring manor be?"

"Oh easy it is to find sir, not more than a half day's ride. The boys in the stables can easily guide you," said Osla, seeming relieved to have something concrete to relate.

Robert glanced about the dingy hall. "See you scour this place and ready it for a meal tonight," he ordered.

Outside, he counted off five men and ordered them into the saddle again. They brought a sixth horse, saddled but riderless, as well. The rest he tersely instructed to close and bar the gates and organize the kitchens. He sent another three men, with horses and a pallet, linen for bandages, and more provisions, to pick up the injured Nevin.

After questioning the cooks, he discovered there was no healer here, only an old woman who knew her herbs and a Father Gille, who had evidently journeyed off on a religious quest of some sort and was not expected back for some time. He sent for the old woman to come to the manor. At least she could care for Nevin once they got him into the hall. Then he swung into the saddle, and with an old man from the stables pointing out the way, headed off to the neighbor's manor.

As they rode, Robert gave silent vent to his irritation. What could his future wife mean by this disrespect? She had been ordered by the king to await him. He cursed himself for waiting so long. Why hadn't he ridden directly from Edinburgh, as Will had suggested? This thought annoyed him even more and he urged the chestnut stallion on. The fields stretched before him, brown with winter, but he could see them green and growing. A chance like this came only once. She'd come home with him, and this night. It was late for a long ride, and already shadows approached, but he couldn't stand the idea of waiting another whole day.

Could it mean she did not welcome the marriage? This was an uncomfortable thought, and he pushed it away. It wouldn't stay out of his head though. His mother had loved his father well, and she had not welcomed the king's decree that she marry again. This girl, or woman, he realized he still didn't know her age or her history or anything of her, did she welcome the king's wishes?

The horses pounded down the narrow pathway, edged by dark forests. The men's fine cloaks, donned for their arrival at Caerwyn, flew like bright banners in the wind. Robert rode fast, trying to escape his thoughts. She needed a husband, a capable man to protect her manor and people. Surely she knew that. And he had a need for these lands. He bent closer to the horse's neck and they pushed on. There had better be a good explanation for her behavior. If she thought to evade him, or rob him of these lands, she'd not find him easy to deter.

After several hours, they swept into the meadowland on a cliff above the sea. Sleet had been falling, but they'd been sheltered by trees. Now the icy sea wind flung sharp pellets in their faces. Robert took a great lungful of the salty air and pushed on.

Soon the manor rose before them, grim and tall. He could just see the guards moving around the gates, watching their approach. Robert raised the banner of the king, and they rode forward, slowly. They halted before the gate and he called out in a loud voice. "I am Robert of Caerwyn, and seek entrance. I wish to speak with your master and with the Lady Ailsa."

There was apparent confusion and whispered conversation among the guards, then one left the others clustered by the gate and ran toward the great hall. A young man soon appeared, followed closely by a large woman with stiff black skirts and a billowing cloak.

"Who are you, and who do you seek," called the man in a reedy voice.

"Open your gates for the king's man and we'll speak," answered Robert.

The man stared down at him for a long moment, then signaled to the guards. The heavy gates swung open and they rode in at a walk, the men on both sides keeping a cautious eye on each other.

Robert swung off his stallion. "I seek the Lady Ailsa of Caerwyn, my betrothed by the king's writ. I understand her to be visiting with you here." The man's eyes widened and the tall woman beside him frowned, her heavy brows creasing together. There was a whispered conversation between them, and Robert felt his fingers fiddling with his sword hilt. He moved his hand away from his belt and said, unable to keep the edge from his voice, "I have word that the lady is here on a prolonged visit. Pray tell her I have arrived."

Thomas said, "Do enter my hall, sir, and we can discuss this within, as is more fitting."

"I thank you, but it's not the time for visiting," said Robert, glancing at the sky, which was darkening, "we must return to Caerwyn before nightfall."

Thomas looked at the older woman, who shrugged her shoulders, then he said, "Lady Ailsa is not here."

"Do not dissemble," said Robert. "I am the lady's future husband by King David's own hand. Have her brought out to me and we'll speak no more of this."

Thomas raised his eyebrows and looked even more worried. "Ailsa would not deceive you. 'Twould be most unlike her. I'm sure there is some explanation for this confusion." He took a step back as Robert advanced.

"You will inform her I am here. She should come down immediately. Her bag can follow on the morrow."

At that moment, a woman slipped into the courtyard, a most beautiful woman, wearing soft leather slippers despite the icy sleet congealing into brown puddles around the slates. She came and stood by Thomas, slipping her hand in his, saying nothing. Her long blonde hair was woven in braids that fell to her hips and her blue gown highlighted her pale blue eyes.

Robert's hand went to his sword. "Stand away, Lady," he said. "You shall not evade the king's order or my will so easily."

Thomas frowned and stepped in front of the woman. He stared at Robert with a puzzled expression, but he was angered now as well, a new glint in his eyes. "This is my wife. We are new married, by the grace of the King's own Constable, who I owe fealty to for these lands and this manor."

"The King's Constable, de Morville?" Robert demanded.

"Aye, Hugh de Morville," said Thomas. "The Constable's wife is cousin to my mother." He indicated the tall woman with the black skirts. She raised her brows at him, her face haughty. "And Lady Elinor…"

"Then this is not Lady Ailsa." Robert felt a moment of regret, looking at the beautiful woman before him.

"No," spoke up the lady. "I am Elinor, but I have met your betrothed, for she favored us by attending our wedding feast. Do come inside the hall, where we can offer you proper refreshments and see to your comforts. And your men as well," she gestured to the men standing about them, faces grim.

"But Ailsa returned to her own manor after the feast," broke in Thomas, looking concerned. "Are you saying she is not returned to Caerwyn? I begin to worry for her safety."

"Oh, Ailsa is fine," broke in the older woman in an impatient voice.

"She is always gadding about. 'Tis nothing unusual. Come Thomas, bring our guest into the hall. He comes from the king himself." She smiled at Robert, though the smile did nothing to warm her black eyes, and she offered him her arm. "I am Jocelin."

There was nothing to do but accompany her into the hall. Inside, Robert scanned the room, which was large and furnished with heavy oak tables and benches. He turned to Thomas, "How many men did she have with her?"

Thomas sent the maid off to the kitchens for refreshments and then said slowly, "Actually she had none of her men with her."

"You must have sent your men with her, to deliver her home after your feast."

Thomas' face creased. "Actually, Ailsa left quite early and rode off alone."

"You let her ride off unaccompanied?" Robert was unable to keep the astonishment from his voice.

Thomas looked pained. "She did not ask. We were busy with the wedding guests, and she left a message with the maid, conveying her congratulations and saying she'd returned to her home. Ailsa is very self-reliant," concluded Thomas. "I never thought to check on her."

Robert stared at him as he tried to stay calm. Surely it was safer here, in this backwater, then in the contested lands of Normandy or the Welsh borders, where women went nowhere without strong guards to ensure their safety. He must not overreact. "When exactly did she go?"

Jocelin broke in, a triumphant note in her voice. "Ailsa did seem more than a little distraught, to tell truth. She was not best pleased to find my son wedding another, I'll wager."

Robert felt his face harden. Noxious woman. He should pity this Thomas for such a mother.

"She left here near a week ago." Thomas frowned at the table. Elinor again took his hand in hers.

Not at Caerwyn and not here either.

A maid entered the hall and set a tray of refreshments on a small table by the fire. Jocelin gave the maid a cold glance and commenced a monologue in her deep, grating voice. She described the feast in excruciating detail, naming all the important guests and describing their clothes and jewels and the gifts for the couple. Robert knew he should pay attention to the names, but all he could think of was Ailsa. Where was she? Suddenly his ear picked out a disturbing note from Lady Jocelin's stream of comments. "What did you say?" he demanded.

"I said," Jocelin gave him a severe look, "that Ailsa did have the most curious clothes, a sort of brown homespun, not at all the thing to wear to a wedding gathering; indeed I had to lend her my second best gown."

Robert's eyes narrowed at a disturbing memory. "Does Ailsa have long dark hair pulled into a braid?" The words choked him.

"It's rather a lovely chestnut, I would call it," said Elinor, her cheeks rosy from the warm fire. "I do hope we'll come to be friends, for she is my nearest neighbor." She stopped as Robert got to his feet.

"I believe I know where to find the lady after all," he said in a tight voice.

"Won't you stay for the night," offered Elinor. "It grows late and the weather is harsh."

"My thanks to you. Another time. Now, I must fetch my betrothed, it seems." He did not explain, though he saw the questions in their eyes. "We shall meet in better days, as is fitting for close neighbors." He wrenched open the door before they could answer.

Robert and his men pounded back down the path they had traced only a short time before, their tracks icy puddles of dark water across the endless grey fields. They rode without halting, past the long meadows, and into the forests, down the narrow, winding path through the pines. Robert rode fast, too fast, and the shadows made it hard to see the way. The stallion was surefooted but stumbled more than once. When they reached a clearing, he pulled the horse to a stop and leaped off.

Ignoring the cold and the dark shadows and the sleet, he paced back and forth. His men rode into the clearing after him, but did not interrupt, seeing full well he'd not appreciate their comments.

She had fooled him, he fumed, incredulous and furious. He kicked at a tree trunk. He was furious with her, and more furious at himself. He strode up and down, muttering under his breath. And worse, he realized, coming to a halt in his pacing, she could have been with the band who'd ambushed his men, the timing was right. But why? Who were the ambushers and what did they seek?

He ran his hand roughly through his wet hair. Ice tipped the straggling ends. She was a target for thieves and wastrels wandering about in these woods, especially riding a horse like Tanet. Or, she could be thrown from the horse, hit her head on a rock or a tree. Anything could happen.

Unless Will had caught up with her. He stopped pacing. Surely, he must have, by now. One woman and a young boy couldn't evade an experienced tracker like Will for long. Yes, he convinced himself, Will had found her already.

He sent his men back to Caerwyn, with a message to prepare for their return. He'd ride on alone, intercept Will and his lady, and bring her back.

After a cold slow ride of several hours in the dark, his stallion picking his way by the light of a pale moon that had emerged as the clouds slid away, Robert spied Will coming over a rise. He could see the distinctive set of Will's shoulders. His eyes searched as his friend approached, but he saw no lady, not even one dressed in men's clothes. He spurred his horse up and grabbed Will's arm. "Where is she?"

Will rubbed his forehead. "I did not find her, Robb, nor her boy, and I went even to the de Morvilles at Irvine. They had no word of a lost woman or a robber band either, or so they said."

Robert drew in a ragged breath.

"What's wrong," asked Will. "Why aren't you at Caerwyn with your lady? I told you I'd bring word soon as I had any."

"My lady," said Robert bitterly. "She has seen fit to trick me well."

Will frowned. "What do you mean?"

"It seems the lady was in our hands and slipped through like water, and on my own horse as well."

"What!" said Will. "You can't mean the girl? She was your lady, the girl we found in the forest!"

Robert said fiercely, "The very one. It seems she had planned her escape."

"Escape," said Will, his kind face troubled. "From what? What can she hope to gain? Where does she go?"

"I know not, save if she has a lover. She has no mother, nor father either, remember. Perhaps she has been misled."

"But," Will was saying, in his slow and careful way, "where can she be now? We must find her soon. The roads are unsafe this dark time of year."

"I thought to find her with you," said Robert flatly. He looked out across the wintry clearing, brown stubble poking through the snow patches. A raven flew overhead, cawing loudly. Where would she go? Perhaps to a convent. There was one at Sanquehar, several days ride into the forests. He thought of Ailsa's defiant eyes. She was not one for a nunnery, he'd wager. To a friend somewhere? She'd gone to Thomas, her neighbor, already, it seemed. He stared into the dark woods, where water dripped from the ghostly grey trees under a dim moon in a dark sky. Forests were full of dangers; he knew that well enough. She must be found and quickly.

A seabird, far from home, winged overhead, flying south and as he watched another joined and the two winged on together. "No," he said out loud. "She'd not dare." But he knew as soon as he said it that she would.

"What?" asked Will.

She would dare. He'd seen it in the direct look in those hazel eyes. So impatient she'd been to be on her way. And headed south. Not to Irvine, but to Carlisle. "She has gone to the king."

Will looked amazed. "The king!" he echoed, "whatever for?" His brows drew together in worry. "What can she be thinking?"

Robert wheeled his horse, his blue cloak cracked in the wind. "We ride after her. Now. The moon will last another hour yet. We'll catch her by noon tomorrow."

CHAPTER NINE

AILSA HUMMED A LITTLE DITTY as they trotted along. The sun was shining, though the breezes were cold, and she turned her face up and shut her eyes, welcoming the gold on her eyelids and the illusion of warmth. She had escaped the invincible Sir Robert, she thought with some glee. Clear away and no mistake. And it was fair enough she had his stallion, compensation for her troubles. Besides, she'd send him back with Jamie once she was safely at Carlisle, and none the worse for this bit of a ride. She was not a thief, after all. And she wanted Nia back too.

They passed huge oaks with heavy leaning branches, interspersed with spindly birches and clumps of holly, for they were deep in the borderlands forest. The road was wide enough for them to ride two abreast or would be had they two horses. This was the major route south into England, used for trading most days and occasionally for marching bands of men. Used too by the English, riding north to raid or worse. But nothing to disturb their peace today, only the rhythmic thud of Tanet's hoofs, a steady comfortable sound.

"When will we reach Carlisle?" asked Jamie, seated behind her.

"I expect something close to a week."

Jamie was silent.

Ailsa twisted about to look at his face. "Or sooner, if we make good time. What's wrong, Jamie, you're not homesick already," she teased, "we've barely started our adventure." She turned back again as Tanet skittered sideways across the path. A hawk glowered at them from a branch overhead. "Never mind," she murmured to the horse.

"I'm just wondering, is this venture, truly…wise?" Jamie stopped.

"There's many dangers on the road, and Sir Robert seems a good master."

Ailsa pulled up the stallion. She felt hot color race to her cheeks. "Whatever Sir Robert may or may not be, I won't have my husband picked for me by the king and my lands stolen away."

Jamie shifted uncomfortably. "Yet he is the king," he mumbled.

Ailsa urged the horse forward again with an angry jerk, making Tanet toss his head. "I have no wish to hear more of your opinions," she said.

Jamie said no more, but the day now seemed colder and she noticed clouds gathering. She pushed her doubts down and focused on that word, master. She would not let that stand. She remembered Robert, bending over to help Jamie learn to shoot the bow. He might be kinder than most English, still it was no reason for the king to sell her off like a cow or a sheep.

Besides, once Sir Robert reached Caerwyn, and discovered she was gone. She paused in her thoughts, her stomach tightening. She had as good as lied to him. And stolen his horse. Perhaps he was at Caerwyn already. He might have ridden in last night, depending on how long he'd searched for her.

This wouldn't do. She straightened her back and looked about resolutely. Home would never be the same again, not if that Englishman were in charge. He'd change everything, turn it into a castle for the king, meant for fighting and dominating. He'd invite his fellow soldiers to drink with him in her hall. He'd be in her hall, and in her bed. No, they were going to Carlisle, new acquisition of David, King of Scotia. She would present her case to him. And take Caerwyn back.

That evening they pulled up early. Ailsa felt exhausted, for she'd slept little the night before. She told herself she wanted to make sure Tanet didn't tire. A wide stream crossed the road, flowing under a bridge of green logs. No doubt the king's men had built or at least repaired it as they came through. If they followed the stream, they'd surely find a good clearing in which to camp for the night.

She slid off Tanet, who nickered and nudged her. Ailsa laughed.

She rubbed his soft ears and ran her fingers down his neck. "Come on," she called to Jamie, "let's find a good spot. I think we can even have a little fire tonight. Surely they've abandoned the search by now." Jamie followed her silently; she could feel his disapproval.

They walked along the stream, the ground crusty with cold beneath their boots. Ravens cawed to each other in the trees, but otherwise the winter woods were quiet. They'd not seen a soul all day on the road. January wasn't the month most people picked for long travel. Perhaps that was for the best. Ailsa glanced down at her gown, mud streaked and wrinkled. Still it was good to be out of those awful leggings.

She helped Jamie gather dead branches and watched him start a fire. Small licks of orange ate into the twigs, gathering strength. She pulled oatcakes and cheese from her sack. "This is nearly the last of the food."

Jamie shrugged. "Don't worry, I'll set a snare tonight." They gulped their food down and warmed themselves by the fire. Ailsa stared into the flames, fingers outstretched, stomach comfortably full. She was definitely beginning to enjoy this adventure, now that they were finally on their way. Above the stark branches, stars shone, clear points of light in the cold air. She had never slept outside in weather such as this, but summer nights, they had often camped out by a small loch on their lands.

Jamie got out some string and fashioned several snares. Without a backward look, he disappeared into the brush near the stream to set them and returned just as she began to get anxious. "Perhaps we'll have meat for breakfast," he said.

She smiled at him and got stiffly to her feet, wishing she had more than one warm blanket to pull from the pack. She was so tired she hardly noticed the dark shadows in the trees beyond the ring of firelight but fell fast asleep in moments. In the morning, she woke early, and saw Jamie, curled up in a tight ball. He'd obviously tried to stay awake and keep watch, for he held a knife in his hand.

The pattern of their days was a delightful novelty to her. They'd rise early, with the winter birds clustering all puffed out in their brown and grey feathers, twittering in the brush. After a hurried cold breakfast, they'd mount and ride till last light in the afternoon. Sometimes Jamie would walk, to stretch his legs and give Tanet a break, though the stallion seemed hardly strained by their progress. Ailsa thought she was tough, but all this air and exercise made her exhausted by nightfall. She tried to help Jamie, but was glad to let him do the hunting, the gathering of wood, and the cooking. He seemed to know how to do many things she did not, and that was good, but also frustrating.

They saw few people, and those mostly men, trudging into the woods to sneak firewood, or perhaps poach a hare. They were anxious not to be seen as well, and melted into the trees as they approached, or passed with a simple nod and a long curious look at the stallion ridden by a woman and young boy. At night, Ailsa slept, without a thought and few dreams.

When Sir Robert came into her mind unbidden, she dismissed him. She tried to think of what she would say to the king instead. What arguments could she marshal that would convince him, but not offend? The more she pondered, the trickier it seemed. For one thing, the king had many English relations and advisors. He'd been raised in the court of Henry of England, so what could be expected? He was very pious, she had heard, but she had no desire to retire to a religious life. He was said to be fair and a dispenser of justice. Well, justice, that was all she wanted.

One afternoon, the fair weather they'd been traveling under threatened to turn. A cold wind blustered and blew under her cloak, making her shiver. The unfamiliar smell of snow was in the air. They were far from the sea now, climbing into the high hills; snow patches could be glimpsed in the woods. "What think you," Ailsa asked Jamie anxiously. "Should we seek cover?"

"I think we must find a hamlet," answered Jamie. "This snow might last several days. We must have shelter."

"We are getting so close," said Ailsa. "Do we truly need to stop?"

Jamie studied the flat clouds piling on the horizon. "It would be safer."

They rode on, looking for shelter, ideally a house but more likely an abandoned hut or even a cave. The wind whistled in the treetops and limbs creaked and groaned. Tanet became skittish, not liking the wind ruffling his mane and all the strange sharp noises. Ailsa tried to calm him with Gaelic words and songs. "Don't worry, we'll find you a warm byre. Will you like that?" They'd spotted smoke in the woods from time to time, doubtless the site of small villages, families clustered together in the woods. They'd avoided them so far, not wishing to explain themselves. Now Ailsa searched the sky eagerly, hopeful of seeing a thin stream of grey smoke rising. The skies remained bare though, save for the scudding clouds, and dry oak leaves torn from their branches and thrown up tossing.

Midafternoon it began to snow. Cold flakes settled on her nose and brows. All around them the land and sky were muted to various shades of grey. Ailsa began to worry they might lose the path. She unclenched her hands, stiff with clutching the reins. The wind blustered and billowed her cloak. She wrapped it tighter. It felt like the wind tore the heat right out of her body. Snow fell thicker and faster, the large flakes gave way to small stinging pellets cold and hard against her face. She peered out from her hood, trying to see any sign of habitation. There must be houses somewhere.

Jamie nudged her from behind. "Look!" He pointed to their right. Ailsa saw an endless meadow of driving snow edged by dismal trees. Puzzled, she shook her head. Jamie nudged her again. "It's a field, see the hedges growing at the ends. There will be houses somewhere near."

Ailsa pulled Tanet to a stop and they twisted around, seeking the smoke. The snow was falling so thick now, blowing near horizontal, and the shadows so deep, it was nearly impossible to see. Tanet pulled at her hands, and Ailsa tried to quiet him.

"Let him go. He knows the way," said Jamie.

Ailsa released the reins and the stallion jumped forward. He began to pick his way across the frozen field, rutted from planting. Ailsa tried to imagine the field green with oats or barley in the summer sun but failed. She huddled down in her cloak, leaving the reins loose on Tanet's neck, letting him take them where he would. They crossed the field, then threaded through a wood of tall beeches, white bark ghostly in the snow. At least it was partly sheltered from the wind here, but the trees groaned in an alarming, nearly human way. Ailsa shivered. They were far from the road; how would they ever get back? She had no sense of what direction they'd come from. Jamie was silent and stiff behind her.

An hour wore on and they clung to Tanet's back, both of them coated with sleet and near frozen to the saddle. Suddenly Tanet lifted his head and began to trot. Ailsa nearly toppled from him in surprise, but gathered her cold muscles, trying to make her knees and hands do her bidding. The horse plunged on through a stand of birches and they broke out of the trees into a clearing. Three huts clustered together, candlelight shining through the cracks around the doorway of the central home.

"Thanks be to the Lady," muttered Ailsa, and slid from Tanet. "Good boy," she whispered, leaning her head against his neck. She handed the reins to Jamie. Then she straightened her cloak and marched up to the door. Once there, she stopped, suddenly nervous. But the creaking of the wind driven trees urged her on. She knocked on the door. There was a shuffle and silence within. She pounded again. The door was flung open by a bearded man, who gaped at the sight of her. Behind him clustered a plump woman and several small children. Warmth poured from the cabin doorway.

"Please," stammered Ailsa, "we are caught by the storm, can we shelter with you for the night?"

The man seemed stunned, and said nothing, but his wife recovered from her surprise and bustled forward. She drew Ailsa in. "A terrible night for anyone to be about. How came you to be out there, are ye lost?"

Her words seemed garbled to Ailsa's ears, spoken as they were in another dialect. But when the woman repeated herself, she caught the meaning. "My horse and boy are with me," she said, speaking slow, too cold to explain further. Without a word, the man pulled a wool blanket around his shoulders and marched out into the night.

Ailsa looked around her. The packed earth floor of the hut seemed to sway and tilt before her, she was that tired. She counted four pairs of eyes, staring back at her, round in the firelight. She let the children's mother pull her sodden cloak off and lead her to a stool by the hearth. The woman kept up a stream of soft conversation, seeming glad to have someone to talk to, even though Ailsa only caught one word in seven.

She brought a cloth and helped Ailsa dry her hair and hands, all the while pointing to each of her children in turn and saying something, which Ailsa assumed was the children's names and ages. "And I am Mairead," she concluded, gesturing to Ailsa to pull her soaked boots and sodden hose off. She took the wet clothing and hung all to dry on a rack by the fire.

Ailsa smiled at the children, who stared back, unsmiling, but soon they pulled out their toys to show her, a wooden horse and cart, and a doll and several small animals, all cleverly carved from wood. Ailsa held a small cow in her hand, marveling at the calm expression on its face.

"Ivor, he is good with the knife, and makes many fine things for the children." Mairead pulled out a beautifully carved spoon, with a handle of entwining ivy leaves and flowers, wonderfully intricate.

Jamie and Ivor came in, accompanied by a blast of wind that tossed the children's hair and made Ailsa shiver. As soon as they entered, Ivor pulled Mairead into a corner by her elbow and whispered urgently in her ear, glancing their way from time to time. Mairead flushed and avoided Ailsa's gaze.

Jamie approached the fire and distracted the children by pretending the small carved animals could speak. "They don't want us here," he whispered to Ailsa.

Ailsa looked over at Ivor, but Jamie put his hand on hers. "Don't draw attention." Ailsa withdrew her hand and kept her eyes on the fire. Surely, they wouldn't toss them out into the storm. Outside the wind was howling in the treetops and the branches creaked and cracked.

Ivor came back to the fire. He handed a blanket to Ailsa. "You sleep in the barn, only until the snow stops."

"The barn," said Ailsa, incredulous, but Jamie grabbed her elbow and squeezed.

"We thank you," he said, and in a moment they were outside the door and Ailsa heard the wooden bolt falling down.

"We can't sleep in the barn," she said to Jamie. "Why did you agree to that?"

"It's better," he said, "in case they decide we have seen too much." He pulled her along and they struggled with the barn door in the wind.

Inside, it was colder than outside it seemed, but at least snow didn't drive into her face.

"It will be warmest here," Jamie said, entering one of the pens, "with the sheep." Ailsa followed him, hardly believing.

"I will stay awake the first half of the night," he said, "and you must take the second. I'm too tired to stay awake the entire night."

Ailsa looked around. "We're safe here. We can both sleep."

Jamie sighed. "They are runaways, cannot you see? If they think we'll turn them in, who knows what they might do."

Ailsa sat down, annoyed at Jamie's tone and unsure what he meant. Jamie piled straw into a heap and draped the blanket over her shoulders. The sheep glared at her with their strange eyes and chewed. The barn shuddered in the wind gusts and she hoped it wouldn't tumble on their heads. She would never sleep. "What kind of runaway?" she said.

Jamie looked away. "From one of the estates, no doubt. Some head for the cities, but some hide out in the forests, at least until they're sure they're not searched for. Or they may stay here always."

Ailsa thought of the men who had slipped away from Caerwyn the last few years, so they'd had to abandon fields, cutting the harvest and endangering everyone. "They are better off on the land where they've always been," she said.

Jamie looked like he would argue, but he turned away. "You should sleep," he said.

"But what about the woman, his wife?" asked Ailsa.

Jamie just looked at her for a long moment. Then he shrugged. "I suppose a woman might want to be free as well."

Ailsa covered her confusion by adjusting the blanket. She lay awake a long time, listening to the wind roaring in the treetops and thinking about what it would be like to run into the forest and never surface again. A person could be lost here, for all time. She thought of the old stories, where children wandered into the woods hand in hand, or a young woman ventured in and though many searched for her, she did not return. She thought about that word, free.

To her surprise, she slept and only awoke with Jamie shaking her shoulder. Outside branches still creaked as the wind blasted. Jamie fell asleep immediately and she watched him dream and stared into the dark, hoping not to hear a step out in the snow.

The next morning, the children could be heard shouting and crying, and the smell of breakfast porridge seemed to float across the yard. Ailsa straightened her wrinkled gown as best she could and tried to ignore her rumbling stomach. Outside, the snow still fell, but softly now, falling silent and straight in giant clumping flakes to the ground. The drifts were deep and rose in swells like ocean waves. Jamie stared at the snow and said, "We'll have to chance staying a day or two, else we'll just be buried in the forest."

Ivor swept the snow from the door and made a path to the barn. Silently, he fed the animals and left. At least he did not say they must go. They spent the day silently too and Ailsa went to the door each hour, hoping the weather had shifted, but snow still sifted down from a low grey sky. Her stomach ached and she thought she'd never be warm again.

The next morning, Ivor took the oldest child and disappeared into the woods, lugging a sled.

"Getting more wood," said Jamie. "He'll likely be gone all day."

Ailsa waited for an hour, but then she slipped out and made her way through the thick snow back to the house. Mairead looked nervous and peered into the woods, but put a finger to her lips and gestured her in. She spent that day playing with the children, giving Mairead a break and time to catch up on other chores. As twilight approached, Mairead sent her back to the barn with two bannocks, an apple, and a pitcher of milk.

Mairead's calm smile reminded Ailsa with a pang of Meriel. Where was Meriel, she wondered, feeling guilty for not thinking of her cousin's wife before. Did she still wait at Caerwyn, or had she gone back to Arran with Dugald? It could be lonely when the men were gone, and Meriel loved companionship. She would be big now, with the baby, if she had been with child as she hoped. If all had gone well. She thought about Mairead too; surely it was lonely here in the forest, with only the children and Ivor for company, and no other women about. Did Mairead want this freedom from the land as much as Ivor, or had she come just for him? The language difficulty was too great to ask such a complicated question.

The next day, the pattern repeated. But as the afternoon turned to dusk, Ailsa felt more and more uneasy. It felt wrong to make Mairead deceive her husband. She pulled on her cloak and patted the children, who ignored her as they played with their carved farmyard. "Thank you Mairead, for your kindness," she said and swallowed. "And you need have no worries, for I won't reveal your hiding place here, nor will Jamie. And we will leave at first light."

"What can be so important that you risk everything?" Mairead asked. "The snow is yet dangerous. You could easily lose your way, or the horse be lamed. Stay the winter. I can convince Ivor."

Ailsa wasn't sure that was true, yet she almost wished she could stay. It was easy to believe here under the oak trees buried deep in the forest that the whole world outside had faded away and that Robert and the King of Scotia were simply villainous characters in a bard's tale. But she couldn't let her home fall into English hands, and this story was not hers or Jamie's.

Jamie nodded when she told him she wanted to leave in the morning. They led the big horse out of the barn when the dark was just breaking, the air crackling with cold. Ailsa didn't need to urge Tanet, who seemed pleased to be moving again. But the field they had to cross was deep with drifts and the footing uneven. The going was dreadfully slow and Ailsa fretted that Tanet would break a leg. When they finally reached the path, even then the going was chancy, for it was piled high with snow in places, and swept clean by the winds in others. Sometimes she and Jamie had to get off and wade through deep drifts. After hours, they found the road south again deep in unmarked snow.

Their progress was slow. Their clothes were caked with snow and dragged heavy when they had to walk. Tanet's hoofs collected slush and Jamie had to dig the ice out with a pointed rock. Ailsa said nothing, but she was frantic at their creeping progress. She tried to take comfort in the unmarked road, for certainly no one had passed here since the snow fell. But the forest seemed so empty and lonely and far too quiet. And her thoughts circled around and around one idea. She had to get to the king.

Jamie sat across from Ailsa, cross-legged, chewing methodically to make his oatcake last. He seemed always to be hungry, so Ailsa silently handed him the rest of hers.

He grinned and stuffed it in his mouth.

Cheered by his smile, Ailsa felt her lips twist too. The sun was just lifting over the treetops, sending golden rays down in long shafts to the snow-covered ground. The world was so bright her eyes watered. "Let's go," she suggested, getting to her feet. "I'm hoping we'll join with the main road to Annan today."

Jamie got to his feet, still chewing.

"There will be more food there, perhaps a market, and the road will be trampled down and the going easier."

"Maybe so." Jamie scraped up some snow to dump over their small fire.

By afternoon, Ailsa was even more hungry. But they had made better time, for the sun was warmer, softening the snow, making it easier for the grey stallion to plod through. The winds had certainly shifted. If the snow would melt, they could double the ground they covered in a day. They might even reach Carlisle the day after tomorrow. With new energy, she urged them on.

Still, it was afternoon, with long shadows reaching across the path, when they finally reached the cross that marked the way through Annandale, estate of the powerful de Brus family. Ailsa wasn't sorry to leave their snowy track behind and enter the well-trampled road. They even passed a few houses, with smoke issuing from chimney holes in the thatched roofs. A toddler stopped to stare at them. Ailsa waved and called, "Hello," but the child just turned and ran. The sun was sinking into an orange sky when they began to pass some fellow travelers. Jamie stopped the first group they encountered and queried the way toward Carlisle.

"It's a far piece yet, but you have a fine horse," said one, looking enviously at the grey charger. Ailsa tightened her hands on the reins, but the men were just farmers returning from the market, held, so the men told them, each fortnight on a Tuesday. As they'd just missed it, one agreed to sell some cheese, oats, and apples to them. At the sight of Ailsa's silver, they became friendlier, and left them with cheery shouted advice.

Watch the road when it crossed the marshlands, they'd counseled, for it was too easy to lose the path there, and more so in winter. And the boggy ground was treacherous. "We'd best look out for a good place to stay," Ailsa said to Jamie. "We can't push on in the dark. Wouldn't it be lovely if there was an inn in Annan; I'm so tired of sleeping in the cold."

Jamie looked at her askance. "Inns are no place for a lady."

Ailsa sighed, for it was true, but there was no abbey or even a rude church nearby. "I can dream of hot baths and warm suppers," she grumbled.

Jamie just nodded, then climbed up behind her, and they continued, looking for a place to camp for the night. Just before full dark, they found a brook, frozen solid and snow covered, but offering a path into the woods. They followed it to a clearing a short way off the road.

"This will do," said Ailsa shortly. She ached all over and was disinclined to venture further off the road into the dark woods tonight. Somehow the sight of people had made her long for her own warm hall and hearth and the company of Meriel and all the others at home.

"Shouldn't we go further in?"

Ailsa frowned. Nearly every traveler they'd met so far had been kind. Despite her housemaid Osla's frequent tales of horrible murders and thefts, traveling didn't seem nearly so dangerous or adventurous as she'd thought it would be. The biggest danger seemed to be boredom and cold. "This will do for tonight," she said in a firm voice. "We'll be back on the road before anyone else is even up."

"Perhaps so," said Jamie. He hesitated, but then jumped down. He lit a fire, then tramped down the snow around the small circle of orange flames without a word. He disappeared into the woods, his back stiff, and returned with pine boughs, which he used to make a windbreak. Ailsa stretched in the warmth; it felt so good to be off the horse. Jamie was certainly priceless, she thought, whatever would she have done if he hadn't agreed to come with her? But he was so cautious, reminding her of Dugald.

They ate a quick supper, roasting the apples on long sticks to eat last, then Jamie pulled the heavy blanket out of the pack to place over her. Ailsa felt her eyes growing heavy with the food and the warmth, and she watched the leaping flames of the fire through her lowered lashes. She was just about to drop into sleep when she heard the jangle of bells, and a loud voice bellowed, "Hallo there, fellow travelers."

Jamie leaped up, grabbing his long knife.

Ailsa stumbled on her skirts as she tried to get up. A man mounted on a shaggy pony and a woman on a donkey rode into the circle of light round the fire. Ailsa tried to see the man clearly. He was big and wrapped in a cloak of sheep wool; the smell indicated it was none too clean. His black beard and long hair curled in disarray round a thick neck.

"Hallo," he called again. "May we share your fire, fellow travelers, for we've journeyed long today and my wife is fair tired with it."

Ailsa glanced at the wife, huddled on the donkey behind him. Her thin cloak was frayed on one edge and billowed in the night wind. She looked tired indeed, and stared at the ground, silent. "Well," she began, uncertain, and glanced at Jamie.

The man's eyes glittered as he swung down off his horse. "I knew a fine lady as you would never refuse hospitality to a fellow human in need." He pulled his wife off the donkey and seated her by the fire.

"Let's just build this back up," he said, and pulling an axe from his saddlebags, he quickly chopped some large branches and dumped them on the flames. "Roger is my name and I'm a farmer by trade," he commented in his loud voice, "and my wife here is Una. We came from the market at Annan, but Una here is feeling poorly and we've not made good time. We're still a far piece from home. So when I saw your fire here, I thought to myself, why not meet some fellow travelers and let Una rest a bit, and carry on in the morning."

The man spoke quickly, leaving Ailsa no space to interject.

"Aye," he continued, as he stretched out by their fire, "I think it's a fine plan and I thank you for letting us share your fire. Where are you folks headed?"

"To Annan," said Ailsa quickly, not sure why she didn't like to say Carlisle to this man.

"A fine town, and the de Brus castle is a wonder to see." He peered at Ailsa. "And what is your business in Annan, if I may be so bold."

"My cousins expect us there on the morrow," said Ailsa, deciding a white lie was better than telling this man the true story, that she was meeting no one at all, and traveling alone on this dark road except for a boy servant of twelve.

The man droned on, his heavy voice penetrating the night while his wife continued to sit silently by the fire, her head bowed. Ailsa tried to address a question or two to her, but always Roger answered for her and she merely sat, her face hidden by her brown hood and the shadows of the firelight.

Finally, as Ailsa stifled a yawn, Roger said, "Now I can see I've kept you awake with all this talk. I was just that glad to have someone interesting to speak with. Let's sleep now, and morning will come soon enough." Immediately he unrolled two blankets, and he and his wife huddled down near their donkey on the other side of the fire.

Ailsa glanced at Jamie, who was looking at her with dismay evident on his face. She shrugged her shoulders, for what could they do? The woman was certainly exhausted and perhaps ill. She could hardly force them to move on.

Jamie motioned to her to go to sleep. "I'll stay awake," he mouthed.

Ailsa glanced at the big man. He made her uneasy, but the farmer and his wife were already breathing deeply. Uneven snores, she noted with distaste, erupted from his large mouth. She huddled under her blanket. I'd best sleep too, she thought, and then I'll wake and give Jamie a chance to sleep as well.

She was so tired she fell into a fitful sleep despite her distrust. She awoke for no reason, in the middle of the night, and saw the stars stretching clear overhead. The big man was still snoring away, and Ailsa sat up and shifted her blanket around her shoulders.

She winked at Jamie, motioning to him to sleep while she kept watch. He fell into the deep sleep of a child, and indeed, although he was already her height, he was still a boy, and looked so in his sleep. She stared up again at the stars, bright overhead. The night was clear and the air chill, but perhaps with a tinge of spring? She thought about Carlisle. Would she be able to convince the king? He must have received some very bad advice from one of his lords, for he was rumored to be just. It was so difficult not to worry and chafe at every delay.

The night was silent, except for the rustle of coals falling as the fire shifted and fell. She settled herself more comfortably for the wait until dawn, drawing her knees up under her chin, and stared into the fire, her head on her arms. What was the best way to say her piece to the king? What would win him to her side? Her thoughts went round and round, and her eyes felt so heavy.

Suddenly Ailsa felt a strong hand clamp over her mouth. She struggled, smelling garlic and musty clothing. She realized, too late, the snoring had stopped.

"Won't do you no good at all, little lady, so high and mighty," muttered the big man, his face next to hers and his breath reeking of sour ale. He held her tight with one large hand, the other searching through her clothes. "You've got coin and maybe jewels somewhere here I'll wager, and I'll find them." Then he chuckled, "Aye, I'll find them, though I strip you bare to do it."

Ailsa froze. She could see nothing, for the man's thick, greasy hair fell over her face and she couldn't breathe, much less scream, with his huge hand clapped over her mouth. She must have fallen asleep. And he'd been waiting for that moment! And Jamie! Where was Jamie? She struggled again and managed to free her face for a gulp of air. She tried to scream, but he was on her again, smothering her face in his greasy tunic.

"No sense trying that," he muttered, "and no one to hear you."

What had happened to Jamie? thought Ailsa, what if this evil wretch had killed him! And what about the wife? She kicked, trying to wrest an arm away.

"Ah," said the man, satisfaction in his voice as he found the pouch hidden at her waist. He ripped it from her and tossed it aside onto the cold snow. "And now for a little taste of you."

Ailsa felt her stomach heave and she struggled, but the man just laughed and ran a rough hand down the length of her body, his other arm pinning her against the icy ground.

"Not much of a lady now," he snarled. His filthy hand fumbled with her laces and then he gave that up and ripped at her bodice. Struggling, Ailsa freed her mouth and yelled into the night. He slammed his hand against her mouth, but she managed to grab a chunk of ice in her grasping hand. Swinging wildly, she hit him full in the face.

The man stumbled up, away from her. "You're naught but a slut," he snarled. Ailsa tried to get to her feet, but he slapped her with the back of his hand, knocking her down. "Naught but a slut," he repeated. He picked up her pouch from the snow, then stood still a moment, swaying. He must be very drunk, Ailsa realized, or perhaps she'd hit him harder than she thought. She scrabbled in the snow and found another chunk of ice.

"Get the horse," he called out suddenly. The silent wife appeared, leading the pony and donkey.

"Nay, you foolish woman. The horse," bellowed the man.

Ailsa tried to get to her feet, but she was too dizzy. They couldn't take the grey, Robert's stallion! She had to give him back! But the sky above, so full of stars, seemed to be spinning.

Ailsa woke with sun glaring into her clenched eyes. Her head ached and she felt shaky all over, as though she'd be sick. She groaned and struggled to open her eyes, and saw Jamie peering down at her. His boyish face relaxed into a wide grin. "You've awakened."

"You're not dead," she muttered, her voice coming out as a low croaking.

"Nay, God be praised, that old bastard clouted me on the head right good, but I awoke after he'd gone. He was so lazy he'd not even bothered to bind me. Probably thought he'd done me in." He looked at her, blue eyes clouded. "Are you all right, Lady? Did he harm you?"

"No," she said, trying to sit up, "other than a blow to the head. He was after the silver, and he got it too."

"Well," Jamie said philosophically, "at least we're still here, no thanks to that bastard."

Despite her pounding head, Ailsa managed to sit up. The sky swung wildly but then settled into its proper place.

"Can you stand?" Jamie asked in a worried voice. "It would be best if we moved on."

"I think so," she said, then remembered about the grey stallion. "Did they get the grey?" she asked, as she got slowly to her feet.

Jamie laughed. "No. He has a mind of his own, that horse."

Grinning weakly back at him, Ailsa walked to the brook and painfully knelt and scooped a handful of cold sand. She scrubbed her hands and face until her skin felt raw and rinsed off with the icy water.

Jamie had the horse ready and was looking at her with concern. "If you can," he suggested, without looking at her, "we should ride now. He may return for the horse. Or to quiet us."

"I wish I'd listened to you last night." She limped over to the stallion.

"It do pay to take care. The stories be true."

The big horse seemed to sense she was hurt and stood quietly as Jamie helped her climb on. "I'm amazed he left the stallion."

"I found his reins ripped from the bush where I tethered him. I think he didn't let himself be taken. And perhaps they knew he'd make them easy to track."

Ailsa patted the grey's neck. "I hope you gave him a good kick," she whispered, and the horse pricked his ears.

They rode out and the bright sun felt good on her face, but Ailsa had to close her eyes to still the throbbing in her head. We might have been murdered, she thought. She felt the man's rough hands on her still. She hoped she'd marked him well with that chunk of ice. Now she realized the difference between her own well patrolled lands and these desolate forests. And Jamie! She'd thought him dead, killed by that dreadful man. And it would be my fault, all my fault, she thought, if Jamie were killed. She shivered at a dreadful image of the boy, lying prone in the trampled snow. "I'm so glad you're not hurt," she said to him in a rush.

"Oh, I'm fine enough." He grinned at her, but his eyes were troubled and a dark bruise was rising on his cheek. "I should have kept you safe."

"He was a big man," said Ailsa, "and caught us by surprise. Besides you don't have your full growth yet."

"'Tis my duty," he said. "It won't happen again."

"I hope not," agreed Ailsa, thinking it was her fault for falling asleep.

They rounded a bend in the road, and saw in the distance, far ahead, a group of farmers with a loaded cart. Ailsa pulled the grey to a halt. "We must skirt the village and not go straight on through." She turned the horse into the woods and let the farmers pass on out of sight.

We must reach Carlisle, she thought, as soon as possible. She needed to reach the king. And she needed to get Jamie and herself to safety.

CHAPTER TEN

The Eastern Forests

ROBERT AND WILL LOLLED BY THE FIRE, comfortable after their meal of roasted apples and venison. The flames flickered and leaped in front of them, and the sun was just setting over the hills. Streamers of gold light lit the snow-covered valley and made the burn running through sparkle and glint.

Will settled himself against the log serving as his backrest. "There's nothing like a good meal cooked out of doors to make a body feel pleased." He grunted as he tried to get comfortable. "Still, these old bones aren't loving this weather."

"If you stayed home, you'd likely grow slow and fat." Robert grinned and poked at the fire.

"I'm fat already, just as the ladies like it," said Will, laughing.

Robert didn't answer but gazed off into the forests. His own younger legs and back ached, for they'd traveled hard today. But for four full days before that, they'd been holed up and impatient, for the snows had made travel impossible. Now, with the weather cracked, they'd covered many miles and if their luck held, they'd certainly reach Carlisle on the morrow. "I'm just wondering what was in her mind," Robert said slowly.

"I've ever found women difficult to comprehend. Your lady isn't likely to be any different from the rest." They were both silent, watching the night shadows creeping over the valley, with the fire crackling and the wind sighing through the bare branches.

"But why would she run off," persisted Robert, a frown creasing his brow. "I hope she is not flighty, or unstable somehow. It's hard to know what she could be thinking. Doesn't she know her duty? What kind of a wife and mother will she be, I'm wondering." He paused. "And what does she hope to get by running off to the king anyway? It's dangerous and makes no sense. He's the one who handed her wardship to me."

Will was silent. "We'll know in time," he said finally.

Robert grunted and got up to add a few logs to the fire. "I'll see to the horses."

Walking downhill toward the stand of birch trees where they had tethered the horses for the night, he continued to think of Ailsa. She thought to confound him by going to the court. If she wanted to play out their differences in front of an audience of the highest nobles, he had no objection. He cared not who watched or what they thought. But one worry burrowed in the back of his mind. He thought of his mother, forced to marry when his father had been barely cold. Forced to watch her son driven away. He needed Caerwyn and the coin he could raise from her lands, he must have it, to fund his return, to reclaim his own home. For revenge in truth. But what if it meant this woman was being forced to marry him? The thought was disturbing.

Yet he'd vowed long ago to revenge his father and his mother and regain their home. He would be a poor son if he backed away from that.

He reached the horses and ran a hand along the chestnut's neck. And he needed Tanet back as well. Tanet was special. He'd had the horse since he first landed back in England, finally a man, set on his plan of recovering his home.

"Well, my fine fellow," he said to the chestnut charger, running his hand along his sleek neck, "you're wondering where your friend is. Never fear. We'll have him back soon, and he'd better be none the worse for the traveling." Tanet was strong and fast, too fast. He'd hoped they'd catch up with Ailsa on the road, before reaching the court.

His eye caught a movement in the brush on the hillside. He narrowed his eyes to see better in the gloom. Only the rhythmic sway of dark branches in the winds. The hills had turned an inky blue in the twilight. He was about to turn away, telling himself it was nothing, when he saw something, a movement out there, again. He swung up onto the horse, grabbing a fist of mane as bridle, and urged him up the hill. "Will," he shouted, as they galloped up to the fire. He flung himself off the horse and sent him into the brush with a slap on his flank.

Will emerged from the shadows near the brook. "What …"

"There!" Robert gestured, as he tossed a sword toward him and kicked out the fire. The light doused, they faded into the brush, swords and daggers in hand.

The ambushers had seen their defensive actions and ran toward them openly now, yelling curses into the night air as they climbed the hill. Robert felt his breath quicken, his hands tense, and his mind clear. This kind of problem he could deal with.

His sword heavy and warm in his hand, familiar, and he waited as the men combed the hill, yelling and beating the brush. He had no need to caution Will to stay still. They crouched, letting the men come closer and closer. When he felt the swish of air as a sword sliced the branch in front of him, he roared and leaped to confront the raiders. He heard Will shouting and crashing through the bushes at his side. He swung, the sword balanced in his hands, and felt the blade clang against the hauberk of his assailant. Beside him Will grunted and thrust and one man sank down with a groan. The smell of blood and sweat filled the air. Robert fought his way forward, but the men melted back into the woods.

He darted behind a cluster of evergreens. He saw a man, well behind the others, shouting directions. The leader. Tall, protected by fine mail that gleamed with recent polishing. Robert burst from his hiding spot, racing toward the man, counting on surprise, but the leader saw him and wheeled his horse and raced away. His men watched him go, then turned back toward Robert and advanced.

The first to reach him laughed and swung his sword in a huge arc. Robert countered, sword clanging against sword. He swung his dagger up with his left hand, catching the man by surprise. He sank down, blood seeping from his side. The other two hesitated, then turned and ran back into the forest, escaping into the darkness.

Will staggered up. "There's another, down by the brook, I think that's the last of them."

Robert raked the now silent woods with his eyes. He walked over to the brook and stuck his sword into the ground next to the wounded man. "Who sent you?"

The man's face twisted, but he said nothing.

"Who sent you after us, and to what purpose?" Robert repeated.

But the man was past talking and only sighed once, long and deep.

Will swore. "Whoever they are, they meant to finish you off, no question."

Robert crouched beside the man, looking for something, any evidence that would leave a clue. But there was no sign on the body telling who the man served.

He ran a hand through his hair. Two ambushes in but two weeks. He wondered, what did the king know of all this? Did he know something about this Caerwyn he hadn't mentioned? Were the lands contested? Perhaps David had been less generous than he'd thought. He got to his feet. It was always best to be wary around monarchs, who played by their own rules and seldom thought about the consequences for ordinary men. His experiences in Normandy had taught him that. Why had he thought Scotia would be different? And his lady, soon to be wife? Would Ailsa stoop so low to keep her land? Have him killed? "Check the others," he said to Will, "see if any can talk. We need to know who's behind this."

Will headed down the hill, and then called, "Over here, Robb."

Robert knelt by the injured man. He was very young, his beard still fair and sparse, his face white. Robert felt a twist of pity. God's blood! Again, they sent mere youths against him. "Why?"

The young man's brown eyes slowly focused on him. "Will I die?"

Robert looked at Will, who was probing the youth's wounded arm. There was a lot of blood.

"You will not, this time at least," said Will after a long moment. "'Tis bloody and deep, but just a wound to the skin." He cupped his hands in the stream, then poured the cold water on the arm and shoulder, washing away the blood and dirt ground in the wound. He ripped the man's linen shirt and bound the arm with moss. "You must keep it clean, you hear."

"What is your name?" asked Robert.

"Peter," said the young man, color beginning to return to his face.

"How come you to ride with these ruffians, and why do you seek to harm us?"

"'Tis a long tale," said the youth uneasily, shifting to ease the pain.

"We have time," said Robert.

The youth sighed and turned back, looking him in the eyes. "Well enough," he said in a low voice, "I joined with them because my father lost his lands and I needed someone to serve. I had a mother and sister to support, you understand."

Robert nodded; he understood only too well. "Who is your lord?"

The man hesitated.

"Out with it," said Robert. "'Twill do you, nor him, little good to hesitate. I will find out anyway and it will go the worse for you and yours." He paused. "A chief who sends you after peaceful men, for underhanded reasons, is he one you would willingly serve?"

The youth looked unhappy, his face strained with the pain of his wound and the decision he must make. Finally, he said, "'Tis the Constable, de Morville, that I serve."

Robert's face hardened. "He ordered this attack," he demanded.

"No, no!" said Peter, "Not so, for indeed, he's off on the borders attending King David. I thought to be with him, but he left me here on the estate, told me I was too young, to wait for the next round."

"Who then?" said Robert, annoyed by the meandering tale.

"Why, 'twas the lady."

"Lady?" said Will sharply, looking up.

"Aye, de Morville's wife," answered Peter, and Robert felt his breath ease from his lungs. Not Ailsa. Though she could still be part of all this, he reminded himself.

"How did she come to order you to this? Her husband is surely aware of what she does."

"I do not know," said Peter. "But she bade me follow her orders strictly before she left for Carlisle, to join her husband."

Robert shifted his weight, trying to quell his impatience.

"De Morville told me to obey his lady when he left, but I admit, I am uneasy that he may not approve when he returns." His face crumpled with unhappiness.

Robert frowned at the young man, thinking hard. Indeed, the Constable was likely to be most displeased at this violation of the king's peace, and this young lad more likely than the lady to pay the price too. "And what of him?" He pointed to the body on the slope below them."

Peter swallowed. "He's dead?"

"Yes," said Robert. "Did he serve de Morville too?"

"I know not," said Peter. "He came to Irvine a few days past and met with the lady there. She told me to go with him and follow the tall man's orders."

"The one in the fine armor? That took off? What is his name?"

"He gave no name. We were just told to do as he said."

"Will, hoist this lad onto your horse." He turned to Peter. "You'll ride with us."

"Just leave me here."

"Things seem dark now," said Will, "but sleep will turn you around."

The youth shrugged and then winced with the pain.

Robert hoisted the young man to his feet. "We'll speak more on this, later, now we ride. Save your strength." He whistled for his horse.

The boy's eyes sparked with sudden hope. "Yes, Lord."

"We'll sleep a few hours before dawn," said Robert, as he mounted, "but for now we can get some miles in."

As they rode, picking their way by the light of a torch Will held, Robert thought on this second attack and who might be responsible. But nothing could be ascertained until they reached the king's court. They must get there as soon as possible.

CHAPTER ELEVEN

The King's Court at Carlisle

AILSA FELT EXCITEMENT SPARKLE THROUGH HER as they entered the king's town, now the journey was ending safely. Her spirits bounded up, welcoming the noisy energy of the crowds. She examined the sturdy houses of two stories and the colorful stalls with apples and pears piled high. Bread loaves filled deep baskets and round cheeses dipped in wax hung from cords. She twisted to see the glass windows of the rich homes and the dark twisting lanes that beckoned until Jamie, behind her, protested. Laughing, she said, "Isn't it grand? Can you believe we'll soon enter the king's own castle!"

Jamie grunted in reply.

A group of soldiers lined the crowded road ahead, signaling that they approached the northern gate. And in good time, for the late winter afternoon was drawing to a close and shadows lay across the rough cobbles. A cold wind blustered, making Ailsa's cape billow, and causing the big stallion to prance despite the crowded street. Ailsa held him in with some difficulty, but they reached the iron gate without incident. They found it firmly barred. Three guards with swords belted at their sides stood watching the crowds. They stared at Ailsa as she rode up, eyes cold, and offered no answer when she greeted them.

Ailsa was surprised but thought they must not have heard her in the tumult of the crowds. It was noisy, with hawkers selling sausages, cheese pies, and all manner of trinkets near the twin stone towers guarding the entrance. She walked her horse up to the friendliest looking guard in the center and said in a loud voice to cover her nervousness, "I am Ailsa of Caerwyn and I come to see the king."

"Where'd you come by that horse, missy?" the soldier asked.

Ailsa disliked his tone but forced herself to be polite. She did look disreputable; her gown was streaked and crumpled, and only brown homespun to begin with. Her long hair had not been washed, nor her hands and face, in a fortnight, except at the icy streams they'd passed.

She straightened her back. "I am the Lady of Caerwyn," she repeated, "and I ask you to open the gate, for we are tired from long traveling and seek audience with the king."

At this the guard turned to his fellows, who were staring at Ailsa in a bemused fashion. She followed their gaze and noticed that the hem of her gown was torn and her boots caked in slush. She raised her chin in the air and fixed the three with an intent stare.

They ignored her and joked among themselves. Finally, one said, "Be off with you, lassie, and take that horse away fast, wherever you got it. Else you're bound to lose it here."

Ailsa flushed and clenched her hand over the grey's reins. "I tell you I am the Lady of Caerwyn, and I demand you open these gates at once."

"She demands," laughed the one with sandy hair and a dripping nose.

"I'll show you a demand, my fine lady," said the other, and he stepped forward and grabbed her leg.

Ailsa pulled away. "Do not dare to touch me."

Jamie tugged at her sleeve. "We'd best come back tomorrow," he whispered.

Tomorrow, thought Ailsa, visions of a hot bath and audience with the king evaporating. With all her worrying thoughts of Carlisle, she'd never anticipated having trouble entering the castle. She turned with fresh determination to the guards. "You will listen to me," she said. "My father was Griffith of Caerwyn, and he'd not take kindly to anyone disparaging me so. Now open that gate."

At this one of the three peered at her more closely. "She could be right about that," he said to his fellows after a moment. "I knew old Griffith, and he was a fine man, and not one to fool with either, and she does have somewhat the look of him." They all stared at her now, indecision clear on their faces. Then the one who had spoken of her father said, "Forgive us, Lady," and turning, threw open the gate. Relieved, Ailsa rode through.

Men and women bustled from one building to another, carrying loaded baskets of flat bread and rolling barrels of ale. Large banners, burgundy and green, flew from the doors and outbuildings. And the noise! After days in the quiet forests, it was wonderful to hear the clatter of hoofs and shouted commands and the screeches of children playing. A groom approached, and she slid down from the stallion.

"Go along and make sure he's well cared for," she murmured to Jamie, who looked relieved at not having to enter the huge door to the great hall. He quickly disappeared.

Suddenly uncertain, and feeling very alone, Ailsa looked about the busy courtyard, where everyone seemed to be on an important errand, and wished she hadn't sent Jamie to the stables. She tried to brush her skirt off, but it was hopeless. So she marched up to what appeared to be the main door into the hall. The guard, garbed in dark red and standing erect at the entrance, looked her over, and asked her business in a disdainful voice.

"I have business with the king." She wished her voice sounded more commanding.

The guard disappeared behind the door. He was gone some time, and the cold began to chill Ailsa's toes. The wind was freezing, and now she was so close to her goal, her feet were icy and she felt wet and alone; it was hard to wait. It seemed all was formality here, not like the warm hospitality she knew from her home and the coasts. She blinked several times, determined that she would not cry, not here on the king's very doorstep.

She was beginning to wonder if the guard intended to return at all, when a small window opened in the wall above her head. A man peered out, his eyes squinting to see in the dusk, then he slammed the wooden shutter. But the oak door creaked open in front of her, and she heard someone instructing the guards to open the inner doors.

They complied, and Ailsa walked through into the hall, a grand room heated by twin fire pits and lit with torches, but empty now of all but a few servants. She paused, wondering what to do next.

A wiry man with black hair and dark eyes approached. "Lady," he said. "What a terrible mistake, please forgive the insult, I will have these oafs whipped."

"Oh no," she answered, startled. "I am perhaps difficult to recognize." She looked down at her gown.

"'Tis no excuse," he said sternly and taking her arm, as though she were gowned in the finest silks, he directed her through the hall and up a dark stairway. Unsure what to do in this strange place, she let the man, talking away, lead her along. He described the rooms they passed, and named the various high personages gathered to celebrate with the king his victory at Carlisle. It was all a blur to Ailsa, who knew she'd never remember.

Soon he pulled her down a dark passage, lit only by a smoky torch, and into a chamber with a pallet on a wooden frame and a huge chest crowding the space. A tiny window was shuttered tight against the winter air. On a stool, embroidering a silken material by the fire, sat a very large woman.

"Lady," said the dark man, bowing, "I have brought you a guest, a visitor in need, she is the Lady Ailsa. Of Caerwyn." His voice seemed to linger over her manor's name.

The large woman put down her sewing and surveyed her with black eyes under bristling grey brows. "I am most pleased to make your acquaintance. I am Beatrice, wife of the king's Constable."

Ailsa had never met Beatrice, though she knew her to be the great cousin to her neighbor Thomas's mother. Remembering her manners, she curtsied and murmured, "I am most honored to meet you." Beatrice gestured to the fire, so Ailsa approached, though the room was stuffy and overheated. "I seek audience with the king. Know you where I would find his apartments?"

The woman started and a slight smile came and went from her lips. She glanced at the man still hovering in the doorway. "Gilbert, be useful. Go and get my maid." The wiry man, who must be a servant, though so finely dressed, disappeared into the dark hall. Turning back to Ailsa, Beatrice said, "We must certainly get you bathed and properly clothed."

Ailsa started to protest, then silenced her tongue, for the great lady was correct, no doubt. She was a sight and could hardly go before the king himself so. She must be patient a short while longer.

The maid entered, and Beatrice briskly ordered a bath drawn and refreshment brought. "Bring her to me when she's ready," she said, and swept out of the room before Ailsa could question her further or even thank her.

She warmed her hands before the fire and looked around the chamber with curiosity, welcoming a quiet moment. Soon the maid returned, accompanied by two men lugging a heavy tub and buckets of boiling and cold water. The men placed the tub by the fire and withdrew. The maid, chattering all the while, drew off Ailsa's clothes and set them aside with cries of dismay and promises to wash and mend them immediately. Ailsa stepped into the tub. The hot water felt lovely and she began to relax, but it was all so new and strange, and she felt quite unusually shy. She realized she was lucky to have someone take her in hand and help her out.

"What lovely hair you have miss." The maid interrupted her thoughts. "So long and a beautiful color." She untangled the chestnut strands and lathered Ailsa's hair thoroughly with a soap fragranced with roses.

Ailsa smiled at the maid. "I thank you, but I know it is too dark for fashion."

The maid, of her own age, smiled back. "Oh, never think so! Men do not all like the pale ladies with colorless hair, you know."

Ailsa laughed in disbelief, and then sighed with bliss, for it felt so good to relax in safety and be clean. At home she bathed every week, though in a tub near the kitchens to lessen the work. The court would be different about that, and much else besides.

The door opened and Beatrice walked in. Ignoring Ailsa's embarrassment, she bustled about in her wooden chest, ranged against the whitewashed stone wall, and eventually drew out a linen shift and green gown. "This will do," she said, holding out the gown. "Make haste, Annie, for we'll need to take them in for her."

"Shall I see the king now?" asked Ailsa eagerly, as she stepped from the tub onto towels laid on the floor.

"The king," echoed Annie, looking surprised, "why…the king…"

"The king is very busy at all times," broke in Beatrice, "but I will do my best to get you the first possible audience."

"You are most kind," said Ailsa meekly, and she let Annie pull the linen shift over her damp skin.

Annie sat down by the fire, concentrating on marking the green gown to fit, for there was plenty of cloth to be taken in and not wasted. When she had it marked for stitching to her satisfaction, she combed out Ailsa's hair and toweled it dry by the fire. Wine and cheese had arrived, and they tasted like ambrosia. She was certainly getting sleepy; it was so warm in this room, and she was so very tired after her long journey. In truth, she had not slept well at all since the night with that man in the woods.

Beatrice watched her solicitously. "You are tired, my dear. Take Annie's pallet for tonight," and she shooed Annie from the room with whispered orders to finish the gown by morning.

The king, Ailsa thought, I must see him, and she must have said it aloud for the large woman answered, "Don't worry, my chick, you'll see him soon as can be, perhaps in a bit, for now just rest."

She agreed to lie down on the pallet for a few minutes while she waited. She put her head on the lumpy pillow and it passed through her mind that she must check on Jamie and how he fared in the stables, but as she thought it, she fell asleep.

Ailsa woke, confused about where she was. A slit between the shutters over the narrow window showed a sliver of pearly grey sky. She had slept through the night. She sighed with aggravation, now she'd certainly have to wait till later in the morning to see the king. No doubt he'd be occupied with important matters with his councilors in the hours after breaking his fast.

Beside her, on another much thicker pallet, the huge body of

Beatrice, covered with a fur robe, jiggled as she snored. Ailsa tiptoed across the floor, and found the green gown folded neatly and placed on a stool by the hearth. She slipped it over her shift and walked on bare feet to the door, wondering where poor Annie had found a pallet for the night. With a last glance at the large sleeping lady, she slipped out.

The corridor was empty and dark, so she felt her way along and soon found herself in a large empty chamber. Finding stairs at its far corner, she descended into the great hall, lit to a dim light by its many large windows. Hearing voices, she followed them, and found herself, after a few twists and turns, by the kitchens. Quickly she tied the side laces of her gown and smoothed her hair. She had no boots, but she would do. She walked in and found three cooks sitting at the large oak table having a companionable mug of herb tea before starting the breakfast tasks. They stared at her, astonished.

"Good morning," she said. "I am newly arrived last night. Do you know where I might purchase a pair of boots, and could you show me how I might locate the king's apartments?"

At this oddly paired request, the three women glanced at each other and the youngest giggled. "Well, I know the way to the king's chambers, if that's what you mean, dearie," said the woman in the middle, with a smile on her round face.

"Sit right down here and have a bite with us," said the other cook, pulling down a thick mug from a shelf and slicing a big chunk of white bread for her. "You'll have plenty of time for the king anyways," she continued, "after all he's off in Durham for the time."

"Off!" said Ailsa.

"Why yes," said the first, "with the Prince, young Henry that is, treating with the English at Durham."

Ailsa sank down on the offered stool. Her knees felt wobbly.

"He may be back by Lent but 'tis hard to know with all the legal talk and such. So difficult to plan the cooking and provisioning here you know. They expect us to do it with no warning at all." The other cooks agreed and murmured among themselves.

"I suppose so," Ailsa said bleakly and looked down at the muddy tea in her mug.

"What business has a young miss like you with the king," asked the third, silent until now. Her blue eyes stared with open curiosity.

"I have matters to discuss regarding my lands."

"Hmm," said the first cook. "It will have to wait, won't it, no way to hurry things that won't be hurried, I always say." She plunked a plate of oat biscuits with currents and butter in front of Ailsa and poured her a bowl of milk. Ailsa realized she was starved and concentrated on the food. After eating, she felt much better. She thanked the cooks for their kindness and the information, and as they started to bustle about, readying breakfast for the great ones in the castle, she retreated.

"Ye can buy the boots in the streets outside, no doubt," one called after her.

"What now?" Ailsa said aloud to herself as she stood in the dark hallway outside the kitchens. The cooks had been kind, but she felt terribly homesick and confused. She'd never considered that the king might be gone away. She'd best find Beatrice, and ask her advice, and also thank her for her hospitality. Though it was odd the lady hadn't mentioned the king's absence last night. Probably she'd just thought that I was too tired to deal with the news, Ailsa thought. Then she'd find Jamie and see what they must do next.

Feeling better for having something of a plan, she headed back down the corridors, and reaching the right chamber with some difficulty, knocked on the door. It was quickly thrown open.

"Ah, there you are, naughty child, you had me worried."

"I ventured to the kitchens after awaking early and they fed me breakfast."

"Of course, you were surely hungry," said Beatrice. Annie, the maid, winked at Ailsa from behind the lady, where she pulled at her laces, her face red with exertion.

"I understand the king is away, and 'tis not known exactly when he returns," said Ailsa unhappily.

Beatrice looked up at her, black eyes sharp. "The king wants these lands of Northumberland for Scotia. Yet I'll wager he returns for Lent, which comes in only a few days, my dear. The king is a pious man and will not miss the Ash Wednesday masses done with full ceremony here in his own castle. Not after so long a time with Carlisle in English hands."

"Truly," said Ailsa, brightening, for Lent was only a sennight away.

"Yes, my dear," said the lady, "and you can just stay right here with me till he returns and perhaps, if you'll let me in your confidence, I can be of some help to you in approaching the king."

"You are indeed most kind," said Ailsa, for, now that she was here, the king's castle seemed a formidable place, and it was comforting to have someone to help her find her way about. Though the lady was not exactly comforting in her person. She couldn't quite put a finger on it, but there was something about her dark eyes that missed nothing. Perhaps she just associated her with her overbearing cousin, Jocelin, and that was unfair. She resolved to be more friendly.

"Let us descend to the hall," said Beatrice, "and I'll introduce you to the other ladies assembled here for the king's great triumph." She turned with a frown to Annie. "Fix her hair decently and find her some boots."

Annie scurried from the room and returned in only moments with a pair of black leather boots, close in size to her feet. Ailsa pulled them on with a grateful smile to the maid, who smiled back as the lady searched in her chest with her back turned.

If only the king arrives back before Sir Robert, Ailsa thought, as they descended the stairs. Yet, surely Robert would stay a time at Caerwyn to ensure all was in order, before seeking her out, if he sought her out at all. Indeed, he'd hardly follow her himself, he'd send some underling. One of his men. Perhaps Will. And he could hardly know she'd come here to the king. She might be anywhere. She shrugged. She had some time, no doubt. Days, she thought more cheerfully, weeks even. By then, the king would be back and Robert definitely too late.

The next afternoon, Ailsa sat at a long trestle table in Carlisle's great hall. The table was clothed in heavy linen and covered with an array of savory dishes and silver goblets of red wine. She too was finely arrayed in borrowed, but elegant dress. She felt the soft wool as she smoothed her gown over her lap. It clung to her waist and hips, before sweeping into a wide skirt. Her shift was of the finest linen and delicately pleated, her laces emerald silk ribbons. Even her hair had been entwined by clever Annie with sprigs of evergreens in her two braids. She felt more beautiful and sophisticated than she had ever thought possible, but also awkward. She wasn't used to such finery. Beatrice had certainly been wonderful to her, but she wondered what the cost would be for all these favors.

"Why do you sigh?" asked the young woman seated at her right. She had just been introduced to Ailsa as Lady de Senlis. "Call me Effie," she had said, with a friendly smile showing a gap between her front teeth, and Ailsa immediately thought she might like her very much.

"Only because I'm happy," responded Ailsa. "Everyone is so beautifully dressed. And I've never seen so many candles. Or so many people gathered, in one place."

"Yes," agreed Effie, "we must be especially gay for in a few days we enter Lent, and then the foods and entertainments all vanish."

Ailsa tried to keep the dismay she felt from her face. "Not all surely."

"Well, nearly all," said Effie, picking up a pastry in her fingers. "For the king is very pious indeed. There'd be no dinner like this, so near to Ash Wednesday, were it not that he is still en route to Carlisle. The earls do not disdain a fine feast or agree so much with his austerity."

Ailsa's pleasure dimmed. She'd come so far; she'd love to see more of this court's worldly pleasures. "Well, we have tonight at least," she said, resolved to be philosophical.

Effie smiled. "And after the feasting, I've heard there will be music and story telling."

Soon she and Effie were eating spicy swan meat and tiny fried fishes in strange sauces, and Ailsa sipped, cautiously at first, at the unfamiliar but deliciously bitter red wine. Her cheeks felt warm with the heat of the room, and Effie's conversation was so entertaining.

How wonderful that I decided to come here, she thought, congratulating herself. She took another sip of the delicious wine. Robert might be at her Caerwyn now, but not for long. She'd have her lands back within the fortnight. The journey had been difficult. She had to work hard each night to push the unpleasant memory of the frightening thief and his silent wife from her mind and the feel of his hands on her body still made her feel sick. But now everything would work out.

Though she wondered sometimes about the runaways they'd encountered in the forest, and the life they were building, somewhere new, unchained to the land or to the past. It seemed a sad sort of life, to be pitied. But they had not seemed sad at all, worried at times, and cautious, but also joyful. What would it be like to have one's life ahead uncharted?

Effie jostled her elbow and she shook her head to banish her serious thoughts. This was a moment to be savored.

When the feasters finished their lengthy meal, serving boys rushed in and carried off the platters, and returned with even more foods, sweetened conserves of fruits and nuts, honeyed pastries, and almond wafers. Ailsa sampled the desserts, which tasted marvelous, but she was already full, and she wondered when the tales would start. The hall was packed, and the din grew louder as goblets were handed about and men laughed over bawdy riddles.

Effie leaned over. "I must go to the privy, I'll be back soon," she whispered, and slipped from her place on the bench.

Ailsa started at a man's voice at her elbow. "May I join you?" A handsome man draped his long body on the bench beside her before she could answer. He was most elegantly clothed in black with touches of gold embroidery.

He took her hand and bowed over it. "You must be Ailsa, newly come to court, I have heard. I am indeed pleased that you have arrived."

Ailsa felt herself blush as she thanked him for his welcome. Although many guests had come to her father's table, the elegant manners at this court were strange. She supposed they were the customs of the English or the French from the continent.

"Do you enjoy music?"

"Oh aye," she said, "Though I am most eager to hear the stories the bards will tell here." She was wondering who he was but thought it might be impertinent to ask; perhaps he was so well known he just assumed she knew. She shifted slightly on her seat.

Immediately he said, "Are you uncomfortable? Here, let me find you a better seat, and a cushion." He drew her away before she had time to respond, to a seat in a corner much closer to the high table. He settled her there and signaled a boy, who appeared quickly with a large silver goblet and a wineskin. "Bring sweets for the lady."

"Yes, Lord." The boy scurried away.

"I must introduce myself. You have met my mother," he said.

"You are Lady Beatrice's son?"

"Yes, I am Hugh," he replied. "My father is also Hugh, the king's Constable. I make my home in England, but I thought to spend some time with family." He sat down on the bench beside her, too close, but she didn't dare to offend him by moving away.

She nodded, curious, as this elegant man did not fit her picture of land-grabbing English brutes. She wanted to ask him many questions, but he began to discuss the music they'd be hearing, for even now lute players entered the hall. One carried a harp and the second was an old woman, with long grey hair unbound. Hugh was telling her all about the songs they'd play and the skillful manner of their renderings, but she hardly could concentrate on what he was saying, for he seemed to have moved closer to her on the bench and his long thigh pressed from time to time against her leg. He poured more wine into the goblet they shared. His handsome face was animated as he told her stories about various personages scattered about the hall. He certainly seemed to know everyone, and he had a humorous way of describing their foibles.

The musicians had drawn their instruments out, and now the plunking of harp strings filled the hall. Ailsa was drawn into the unfamiliar haunting melody. Hugh offered the goblet to her and insisted she sip, as it was a fine example of French wines, so she politely drank. When the last notes of the sad tune died away she gave a contented sigh and leaned back, noticing only then that Hugh's arm had slipped about her waist. He gave her no time to think of it, for he launched into another story and handed her the goblet again after drinking deeply himself.

Here she was at the King of Scotia's court, with a handsome man beside her and strange music flowing and filling the air. Surely, she thought with a tinge of triumph, I was right to come to the king and see something of the great world. Dugald wouldn't take me with him to the Irish, but I have come to a king and a new world myself. The music slid over and around her, and she felt Hugh's long fingers brush the lobe of her ear, slipping down to linger for a moment at the bare skin on the back of her neck.

The next morning, Ailsa found a maid who was able to help her locate Effie's pallet. Effie was just rising, in a room crowded with a dozen pallets, and smiled to see her. They laughed over the events of the night before, whispering to avoid waking the others. "Whatever happened to you," asked Ailsa, "I never saw you return."

Effie grinned. "I'll tell you a secret," she said mysteriously, "but not now, let's go to the kitchens and get something for breakfast and then we can go out to the gardens. I know a spot that's private and out of the wind. We can talk there."

The two gathered wheat bread, cheese, and apples from the kitchens and Effie grabbed a small skin of ale when the cook's back was turned. Ailsa chased after Effie, just ahead, and surprisingly fleet considering her plumpness. They entered a stone-walled garden lined with cedar trees trimmed into square hedges. In summer it would be a beautiful place. Even in winter it had a graceful symmetry. The bushes offered a comfortable backdrop and they sat on their woolen cloaks in a sunny corner, well out of the light winds.

Effie spread out the food with great care. Ailsa thought she was still full from yesterday's feast, but after one bite, she found herself enjoying the unfamiliar salty cheese; the apple was stale, but good and she ate it, then tossed the tiny core into the bushes. "Now, tell me," begged Ailsa. "Where did you go off to last night?"

Effie lay down on her back despite the damp grass. "When I was coming back down the hallway, it was very dark in one spot as the torch had burned out. I was edging along so as not to stub my toes for I had my new slippers on. When I just reached the light of the next torch, I heard someone coming, and it was…" She paused dramatically.

"It was who?" prompted Ailsa.

"Will you keep this completely confidential, for it's a deepest secret until we're ready."

"Aye, of course," breathed Ailsa.

"It was David."

"David?" said Ailsa. "The king?"

Effie sighed. "Oh, I do forget you know no one here, no one at all. Not the king of course. Sir David of Liddesdale."

Ailsa shook her head, not recognizing the name.

"The youngest son of Lord John, who has an estate in Normandy and another here in Northumberland," explained Effie.

"Oh," said Ailsa, not sure of what else to say.

"He has the thickest brown hair."

Ailsa nodded. "What kind of man is he?"

"Oh, so wonderful, always telling a joke. He is cheerful and carefree, nothing like his father," concluded Effie, her happy face clouding over, "for he is so serious and always talking about heiresses and lands and sheep. But, I have a bit of income coming with me, and we can make that do, there are many opportunities for younger sons these days, and I know Davy will do well."

Ailsa thought about that, for her sense was that the younger sons of these English families were indeed ambitious land grabbers. Robert was likely one of these younger sons looking about for opportunity. The sky seemed to cloud over and the wind blow colder at the thought.

Effie didn't notice her silence. "He was at the hall last night, and he followed me out to the corridor. And Ailsa," she paused and put her finger to her lips, "here is the really secret part. He kissed me."

Ailsa smiled, though Effie's news made her think of Niall. "And how did that seem to you?"

"Wonderful, like nothing else," said Effie. "I would let him kiss me anytime." She laughed. "Ailsa, you look so serious. We are going to marry, that's the secret and you must tell no one."

That night, Ailsa found herself placed at a different table, off in the corner, for more people had arrived and the seating arrangements reflected the status of all in attendance. She did not mind, though it did mean she was not sitting with Effie, for she had a wonderful view of the crowded hall, though it was smoky with the huge hearth fires at each end and so many burning torches. The savory smells of roasted venison and pork mingled with the smoke and the spicy perfumes worn by men and women alike. She had only the lavender water she prepared at home, and though she'd brought a tiny vial with her, it seemed homespun compared to these exotic scents. She was dressed again in the green wool gown, for she had no other, but Effie had found her a looking glass and she'd been pleased with the impression she'd glimpsed in its murky depths. Tonight, she wore her hair in one long braid down her back, with a band of twisted gilt wire, borrowed from the generous Effie, around her brow.

Though she had been shocked when she first heard the king and his army were away at Durham, still it was rather fortunate, she thought now, for she had this chance to truly experience the wondrous feasts the bards were always telling stories about. And she would have Caerwyn back well before Sir Robert ever found her.

Her eyes fastened on the high table. She knew she was looking for Hugh de Morville's light hair, but she could not find him. She had thought to see him again tonight, but perhaps he'd just been polite to someone new to court. She conversed with her neighbor, an elderly landowner from Shropshire who was most interested in eating his way through the many dishes being set forth on the long table. Effie was far across the hall, and much occupied with a young man who must be this Davy. She wondered if Effie would be able to marry as she wished. And that made her think of Niall again. What would her life have been, had he lived? They'd had such a short time together. He'd been cheerful too, and carefree. But life offered many challenges and cheerfulness did not meet them all.

She shook the dark thoughts away and tried to concentrate on the elderly lord's remarks, but they were hard to understand, for he tended to speak with his mouth full of beef and gravy. She turned to her other side and found two men conversing in serious tones. One was fairly old, his grey hair neatly combed for the fine occasion and the other looked as though he might be his son. He wore fine but sober clothes and his brown hair was cut at his chin. Both were neatly shaved in the French fashion. They were talking of the king, she realized after a few moments, and she listened harder. She needed to know all she could of this monarch if she were to make her case.

"He couldn't take Bamborough, for it was well fortified," said the older man.

"'Tis further south as well, and perhaps none of his true purpose," answered the younger man, spearing a chunk of charred venison. "He had little enough trouble to take Carlisle, and all Cumbria."

"England is weak now, with all the nobles occupied with this question of Stephen or Matilda," answered the elder. "I fear our lands will see much unrest with this trouble."

"Perhaps," shrugged the younger, "but there's much opportunity with a weak England, 'Tis fine to be out from under Henry's iron hand."

"The king's made the Prince Earl of Northumberland. That won't sit well in either Stephen or Matilda's craw. I'd as soon see less chaos."

The younger man laughed. "First you predict dire happenings from Henry's greed and iron fist, and now he's dead and gone, you see worse from the infighting. I for one am glad to see Scotia's king back in these parts, it's been too long since Ranulf lost it to Henry."

"Yes. These be Scotia's lands proper," agreed the older man.

"When think you the king will return?" broke in Ailsa. "Will his negotiations go on long?"

The two men turned to her, surprise on their faces. "Well, dearie," said the older man kindly, "it is hard to say what a king will do, but

I'd surmise he'll be back for Lent despite the treaties, for David's a fine one for holding to the religious seasons."

"What's your interest in the king's doings?" teased the son, spearing another chunk of meat.

"I mean to get the charter for my lands back," said Ailsa. They seemed honest men and she had need of advice on approaching the king. The two looked at her with increased interest, for land always seemed to fascinate these English.

"And where might these lands be?" asked the older man. Ailsa began to regret her confidence. She hoped the younger man had a wife at home, else she'd be sure to rue her slip. She managed to turn the conversation, for the servants entered at that moment with more French wine. She chattered on about her impressions of the court until they were well bored.

Finally, the dinner was over, and the minstrels arranged themselves, after lugging their instruments around the chamber, and tuning them, adjusting the strings to the heat of the hall. The servant boys ran by, carrying the heavy platters up over their heads. Ailsa thought for a moment she glimpsed Jamie and realized with a guilty shock she'd hardly even thought of him since she'd arrived. She had checked on him once, and he'd seemed well enough off in the stables, but she had not returned. She decided she'd look for him first thing the very next morning to make sure he was adjusting to life in the castle. He was her responsibility, after all.

The minstrels struck up a dance tune, and Ailsa forgot her distress as she found her feet tapping. Servants were dragging the heavy benches to the sides of the hall and lifting away the long boards of the trestle tables, clearing a space for dancing. Ailsa looked on, unsure how to join in. She felt a hand on her elbow and turned, thinking to see the old man and his son, but instead, it was Hugh de Morville, bowing over her hand. Not all Englishmen were alike, she was beginning to realize, for the old man and his son were rough thanes compared to Hugh with his graceful ways.

"Lady," he said, "please join us in the dancing."

Ailsa put her hand in his, and they moved to the dance floor, where the rushes had been cleared away. She wondered where he had been during the dinner, but soon forgot all else in the pleasure of moving to the music. They stood in two rounds, men on the outside, women inside, and circled in alternate directions, then crisscrossed in an intricate pattern. Ailsa found she followed the steps, for they were similar to the circle dances she'd learned at home. The room whirled and her cheeks felt hot and her breath came fast. The minstrels struck up another tune and another. Finally, they called a halt and stood to drink the bowl of ale sent to them, and the dancers dispersed to partake of honeyed almonds and wine.

Ailsa found herself steered to a bench along the wall. It was a dark corner, for the torch had burned itself down, and cooler away from the big hearths. She sank down gratefully and then started for Hugh sat down right beside her and put his long arm about her shoulder, pulling her closer. "Please," she said, and inched away.

He only laughed and started a long story, talking softly into her ear. Ailsa found herself unable to follow what he was saying, but she hardly like to interrupt. And no one seemed to be paying them any undue attention, for most of the dancers were gathered in groups chatting in the middle of the floor or seated like themselves on the long benches along the walls. One tall man leaned over and begin kissing a woman in the far corner. She turned her eyes away, feeling her face get hot. Perhaps this was acceptable behavior at court, one of those French customs King David had brought. She realized Hugh had concluded his story, for he was staring at her, an enigmatic smile on his face, his blue eyes shaded to black by the dark shadows. "I'm sorry," she said, "I did not hear all you said."

"No matter." She could feel his breath on her ear. She shivered and shifted away from him. Hugh was so different from most of the men she knew, like Dugald or her father. They were gruff and hearty, big men, full-bearded and quick to frank laughter or anger. This man was lithe and elegant, like a cat, his blonde hair silky and almost silver in the dim light. He leaned back, perhaps sensing her confusion. Letting her hand go, he began to tell another long tale.

Grateful for the reprieve, Ailsa tried to attend to his story, but her mind wandered. Everything was complicated here at the king's court. Yet Hugh seemed to be expecting nothing more from her, but just went on with his tale, a story of two friends and a hunting expedition. She must remember she wasn't at home, and things bound to be different, and that was what she wanted, after all. To get away, see new people and new customs. She rubbed her forehead, which ached.

"Shall we dance some more," he asked, and gestured to the musicians, who had returned to their makeshift stage.

"Oh aye." She stood up too quickly, her long gown wrapping around her ankles. He smiled, and clasped her hand, and pulled her gently but firmly back down beside him.

"You're so beautiful," he said, so softly she wondered if she'd heard him right. "Call me Hugh," he murmured, and leaned closer.

She half tried to lean away from him, but it had been so long, since Niall, and for the first time in so long, she found she was curious. She felt the warmth from his lips near, so near to hers.

A grim voice interrupted. "We meet again."

She pushed Hugh away. The light flickered over a tall man, silhouetted against the gold-lit hall, his eyes nearly black. Her face flamed as she got to her feet. It could not be. But it was. Sir Robert loomed over her. She pulled her hand from Hugh's grasp.

"Have you naught to say to me? Let me say you look in good health and indeed quite lovely tonight. The gown is much an improvement."

And indeed she did look beautiful, Robert thought, and this made him even more angry. Her wool gown clung to her body in moss green folds. In the flickering light, tendrils of chestnut hair gleamed and curled as they escaped her long braid. He wanted to pull her to him with that hair. Her breath was fast and her color high. She was nervous, and well she might be, for she'd not evade him a second time. "My fair betrothed," he said firmly. "Won't you come with me now?" He stretched out his hand.

She frowned and took a step back. He cursed under his breath. He wanted to get her away, without a scene. People were casting looks their way. It would be far better for her. As for making a scene, he cared not for himself, as she'd soon find out. He gave her a look designed to chill.

"It would seem the lady prefers my company, sir," said the young man, still seated in the shadows.

Robert ignored him and said to Ailsa in a fierce whisper. "We have far to ride and we start early in the morn."

She whispered back. "I am going nowhere. I wait upon the king who returns any day."

Robert felt his control slip. "Come," he said, more loudly.

Hugh clasped Ailsa's hand and pulled her down beside him on the bench. "She prefers me, as I've said." He stretched out his long legs and crossed them at the ankle. Light gleamed off his polished boots.

Robert reached out a hand. "The lady is my betrothed and she would prefer to come with me, now, rather than make a scene, I am sure."

Ailsa tugged her hand from Hugh's grasp and stood up. People were indeed glancing their way. "Sir Robert." Such an awkward and embarrassing moment for him to arrive, but what did that matter. "It is a great pleasure to see you once again." She paused, biting her lip, remembering that the last time she'd seen him she'd been dressed as a boy and occupied in stealing his stallion. She turned to Hugh. "Please give us a few moments for private conversation."

"As you wish, of course." Hugh glanced once at Robert, then picked up her hand and gave it a lingering kiss. Ailsa looked at Robert in some dismay, but she could see no change in his stern expression.

Ailsa watched Hugh walk off, having no idea what to say next. Her face felt like it was burning up. She turned to Robert. What would he do now? And what would she do? But he said nothing, only stared at her with those grey eyes. "Why do you examine me so?" she stumbled out.

"I am wondering what manner of woman you are, my future wife."

"I am not your wife, nor like to be."

"I see we must remedy that immediately."

"I do not wish to marry you."

He frowned at that. "The king has said we will marry."

"It is not his right," she said, feeling her eyes fill suddenly with tears. She must not let them drop.

There was a long silence. Then he grabbed her hand. "Come." He hurried her along, through the hot crowded hall, then pulled her out the huge door into the cold night. Undoing the cloak at his neck, he wrapped it round her. The fur lining was warm and smelled of leather and his body. He pulled her across the courtyard, and up a steep stone stairway cut into the castle wall. Did he mean to throw her over and take her lands, thought Ailsa as he pulled her along, her thoughts tumbling over in confusion? Would he ravish her and then insist they marry?

He halted, finally, in a dark corner, out of the winds. He dropped her arm and she backed away, ready to flee. But he stood still now, seeming unaware of her. He was looking up, head tilted to the sky. She followed his gaze. And it was beautiful. She caught her breath at the stars scattered wildly overhead, huge sweeps of white specks against the blue-black sky and the scent of the distant sea in the cold air. He stood, a few foot from her, just watching the sky, face lifted up.

"This," he said abruptly, still looking at the stars. "This is real. What is in that hall is all foolishness." He hesitated a moment. "You are a woman. You've been protected. You have not seen what I have seen. I don't mean that badly, it just is. I don't know your thoughts, nor even what manner of woman you are, but I think you must have a reason for fleeing me and this marriage. Tell me, for if your reason be good, I would not force you to a marriage you do not wish."

Confused by this sudden reversal, she was silent. Was this Englishman asking her why she wished to keep her lands? Was he actually saying he would release her? He was watching her carefully.

She turned away from his intent gaze. "I have no wish to marry," she stumbled out.

He shrugged and ran a hand through his hair. "So you have said. But you have lands, lands that rest insecure for the king's peace when held by a woman. They must go to someone able to hold them for the king. You know this. You must marry. And with the king moving ever south, in these uncertain times, his western borders are even more at risk. Your lands and people are at risk. Therefore, you must marry soon."

She made no answer.

"Is there no other reason, no other…"

"No other man?" she said, catching his meaning.

He stared at her, silent.

"There is no other man," she said, and blinked suddenly, thinking for a second time this night of Niall. She closed her eyes and squeezed them tight.

He relaxed slightly. "Not that pup inside? I wondered at your taste."

"Hugh de Morville has been delightful to me," she said, "as has his mother." She stopped, for his face had tightened.

"De Morville!" The young de Morville, the Constable's son, the one who had made a scene at the king's table at Edinburgh. No wonder he'd hidden his face in the shadows rather than stepping forward like a man. He'd been much too occupied looking at his future wife. He should have recognized the man. He was not usually so careless.

"If you are to be my wife, you must not plot with others. Tell me all, and all shall yet be made good. Do not be afraid." He looked back toward her, his face stark in the starlight.

"What plot? There is no plot."

His grey eyes hardened. "This is your chance," he said. "Tell me now and I will hold naught against you. We start anew. Indeed, you could not be the one to instigate all this."

"I don't know what you mean," she said.

"As you wish." He moved back a few paces. She could no longer see his face. "Tomorrow morn, we will marry, and then immediately return to Caerwyn, so you had best retire to your bed early and be prepared for a long day." He bowed and walked away, quick and silent on the stones.

The winds gusted cold around her, whipping at her skirts. Her hands shook as she pulled his cloak tighter. She smelled horse and leather and hay. She wanted to throw it off, but it was bitterly cold. She sat down in the corner, wrapped in his fur and contemplated the far-off stars.

Tonight had been most confusing. She rubbed her forehead with both hands. How simple everything had been with Niall. How she had wanted him, and he her. How complicated her life had become now. Her head ached with it.

She must run away. Again.

But it was here at Carlisle the king would come. She must be here when he arrived, it was her only chance to regain her lands. Cold wind swept over her and the stars shone on. Now they seemed to mock her.

But perhaps, she thought with a sudden gleam of excitement. Perhaps there was a way.

Could she hide?

Of course, she could hide, somewhere, in this enormous castle.

And if only she hid on the morrow, the day after was Ash Wednesday. With the beginning of Lent, no marriages could be celebrated. She'd have the full forty days until Easter and no one, not even Robert, nor even the king himself, could alter that.

CHAPTER TWELVE

THE KING'S CROWDED HALL STANK of sweaty men, musty rushes, and old grease. What would it be like to have a well-kept hall of his own, Robert wondered, with the sweet scent of new clover mixed in clean rushes? He left the snoring and smells behind and walked out into a dark morning. The clouds hung so low they seemed to drape over the castle walls. It would certainly rain or even snow before nightfall. They should get this marriage accomplished and get on the road back to Caerwyn.

He found Will asleep with their horses, both the chestnut and his beautiful Tanet. "You have the sweeter smelling bed," he said.

Will yawned and sat up. "You have a plan, I can see that."

Robert grinned. "You're right, as always. I'm planning a wedding, as soon as we can yank the priest from his pallet."

"And that would be my job, I see." Will pulled a strand of hay from his hair. "He'll not be best pleased. You owe me, Robb."

Robert ran a hand over Tanet's muzzle. The horse nudged him, and he laughed. "I'm glad to have this one back."

"I'll get that priest and feed him some breakfast. Sweeten him into a short ceremony," said Will.

Robert gave Tanet a final slap and headed back to the hall. He'd send one of the servant girls to wake Ailsa and gather witnesses and then he'd be the new lord of Caerwyn. What would it be like, to finally close in on his longest held dream?

Though it was a dark dream, woven with nightmares.

But no, he must remember that this was a dream to end nightmares. With Caerwyn's coin, he would return to his true home and finally, after many hard years, mete out justice. He sent one of the kitchen maids to find his future wife, slipping a silver coin in her hand for added luck. Thrilled with her good fortune, the girl raced up the stairs.

Ailsa crept from her hiding spot in a deep storage closet, chiseled into the thick stone walls, in the dark end of the corridor near Effie's chamber. She felt stiff all over, and filthy from the grime and cobwebs which had long been gathering in the recesses of the closet, stuffed with old bed hangings and clattering stacks of pottery. But, she thought triumphantly, I have succeeded! Two long days and nights she'd spent crushed in there, but now it was Lent, and no one could force her to marry. She stretched her stiff arms. It had not been very pleasant in that dark closet, though Effie had been wonderful. She'd brought bread and cheese and a flask of water, and even taken her chamber pot to empty. The few moments of whispered conversation had kept her spirits up. She had brought no news of Robert though. Effie whispered that she'd not seen him anywhere and she had not dared to ask.

Ailsa bit her lip. Then she shrugged. Probably he was on a pallet in the hall, sleeping deeply after the drinking customary on the last night before Lent. Or if not, he was in the stables, with his horse. After all, it wasn't that he really wanted to marry her, he just wanted her lands. Once he accustomed himself to the thought that he wasn't going to get them, he'd move on, find someone else to marry and somebody's else's lands to acquire. Until then, she'd avoid him.

She ventured down the dark corridor, feeling the way with her hands on the rough walls until she came to a lighted passage. Then she ran along till she came to Beatrice's chamber. She paused, remembering Beatrice hated to be wakened early. Maybe she'd go to the kitchens instead. She could put some peat on the fire and warm herself. Then she'd find Effie, though Effie liked to sleep late also and certainly deserved a reward for her help.

Her feeling of triumph was draining away. She needed to find someone to distract her. It had been uncomfortable certainly, in that closet. But even more uncomfortable had been her thoughts, especially the thought that she, Ailsa, Lady of Caerwyn, was reduced to hiding herself away, that her life had shrunk to the domain of a storage closet. Hidden and constrained.

This was not what she'd imagined when she'd set out to assert her rights to the king. She shook her head, willing herself to forget, and hurried out the door.

In the kitchen, Ailsa found a bustle of activity, the trestle table piled with apples and the entire room lit bright with torches set in the walls. "What's happening?" she asked, as Cook rushed past her, her face red and her hands piled with mixing bowls.

"The king has come," Cook called over her shoulder. "I've no time to chat today." She rushed off, shouting out orders to the serving maids to run to the larder and pantry for supplies.

Ailsa blinked and put her hands out to the cooking fire, burning with cheerful ignorance. The king was back. Her breath caught in her throat. Her plan was working. She must just pull together her thoughts, for when she faced him, she must be convincing and eloquent, she had to be, to save Caerwyn. She had a responsibility, to her father, to her mother, to Caerwyn's people. And, of course, to herself. She certainly didn't wish to be tied to this grim adventurer. She swallowed, seeing him again staring up at the stars. He wasn't entirely what she had expected.

A manservant swept into the room. All activity stopped as the cooks and serving maids looked to him. "Good morrow to all," he said. "I seek a lady. If any of you see her, send her to me in the king's waiting chamber, for he wishes to see her immediately."

"Who?" said Cook, though her arms did not stop mixing the pudding in her bowl.

"The Lady Ailsa of Caerwyn." Ailsa shrank down in her corner, for all eyes turned to her.

"Why here she is," said Cook, in a surprised voice.

Ailsa stood up as the king's messenger turned his gaze on her. His face altered as he tried to hide amusement, or was it scorn? He was dressed in fine clean clothing, his tunic a deep blue with the king's badge embroidered with black threads. She drew herself up to her full height, but she was covered with cobwebs and dressed in her old brown homespun.

"Follow me, Lady," he said, and swept out of the room.

Ailsa stood rooted to the floor, until Cook said, "Run after him now, don't you be keeping the king waiting."

"But my gown."

"No help for that now, my girl," said Cook. Then, more kindly, she added, "Run along with you," and gave Ailsa a push.

Ailsa followed the king's man, who moved quickly indeed. The king must be in a hurry to demand her presence at this early hour. But how did he even know about her at all? Her mind was in a whirl. But this was her chance. She must not fail. As she walked, she clicked through the arguments she'd prepared on the long trip to Carlisle. Home suddenly seemed so far away, and she felt her heart racing. She must calm down enough to make sense. She tried to dust off her skirts as she hurried along, and straighten her hair, escaping its long braid.

The king's man stopped before a double oak door, barred with iron straps and flanked by two guards with drawn swords. He gestured to one who opened the door wide and they swept in, the heavy door banging shut behind them. Inside it was very bright with the light of many candles, and the scent of beeswax filled the air. The man swept forward, but Ailsa hung back, desperately nervous, now that she was finally here.

The room was long and narrow, lined with tall windows looking west, out over long flat fields, and in the distance, she glimpsed the grey of the sea marshes. Beautifully colored hangings lined the other walls. Normally, she would long to examine them, but now her eyes were drawn to the end of the room, where several men clustered on benches before the hearth. Behind them, she saw with dismay, stood the tall figure of Sir Robert. He stared not at her, but into the fire. He wore long leather leggings, as though for hard riding. She took a deep breath.

The king's man beckoned. "Come forward, Lady."

She forced her feet to move down the long length of the room.

Her eyes watered with the brightness after the dark corridors, and she felt all their eyes upon her. They stopped talking as she approached.

Which was the king, she wondered desperately, for none wore bright or especially elegant dress.

"Come forward, lass," said one then, extending his hand, adorned with a single silver ring. "I am David."

She curtsied low to him, then came forward slowly. "Your grace," she said, and stopped, unsure even how to address him.

He was looking at her intently, and she thought his serious brown eyes looked kind. His face was lined and tired, his hair streaked with grey. His clothing was simple, but of fine wools, and all in brown. "My son Henry," he said indicating with his hand a younger man, quite handsome, with an open face, and dark blond hair.

She curtsied to him as well.

"And my steward, Walter," continued the king, introducing the other man on his left, a chunky man with hair the color of sand. She looked at him with curiosity, wondering why the king had given this man huge tracts of land surrounding her estate. He was appraising her as well, and his eyes were shrewd, at odds with his freckles and the smile lines around his mouth.

"I believe you have met Sir Robert," added the king. Ailsa dared a quick glance at Robert but could read nothing on his face.

"Now," said the king. "You are my ward, by virtue of your orphan status, and you and your lands are my responsibility. Pray sit." He waved her to a stool. She sat, and looked down at her hands, which were, she noticed with exasperation, extremely grubby. Her heart sank.

"In my writ to you, which I trust you received…" He paused and glanced at her.

She nodded.

"I have indicated my willingness to offer you a choice. You need not marry if you do not wish."

Ailsa looked up eagerly, ready to speak, but he signaled her to silence.

"If you wish to seek the religious life, I certainly will not stop you, indeed I will use the income from part of your lands to fund your living in a suitable nunnery, say at Sanquehar. A most peaceful spot. I have stayed there some few years back. They have a pleasant garden overlooking the river, and a small orchard of apple trees." The king paused, seeming to savor his reverie, then rose from his chair. "Or you could journey to England, to the nunnery at Barkeley, if you prefer a more active life, for they are skilled at artwork there and also much occupied with copying and translating texts."

Ailsa swallowed, horror growing in her chest at the idea of becoming a nun, imprisoned forever, exactly like being buried alive. She glanced again at Robert, but there was no help there, he merely stared at the fire, as though he had no interest at all in her answer.

The king waited, so she stammered, "Your grace is kind, so kind to think of my wishes. But," she paused, "I have no vocation at all for the contemplative life."

The king frowned, and she remembered too late he was counted a most pious man.

"I mean, your grace, I mean that…" She floundered and stopped. There was a long silence in the room. She drew a long breath, then raised her chin and addressed the king in a firm voice. "I mean that I have no wish to marry at this time. Indeed, it is not that I have any particular animosity to Sir Robert, who indeed I hardly know, it is that I have been responsible for my estates for the years since my father died and the lands are doing well indeed, for I have always done the books and been my father's steward while he was off on his long summer voyaging. I have much experience with it and," she paused again, then rushed on, "and I do not wish any man to simply come in and take my lands from me. It is the Gaelic way of my people by long custom that I, as my father's daughter and only child, may inherit these estates and marry as I please. And I have not yet chosen." She stopped and now there was a deeper silence in the room.

She stared at the floor, then dared to look up at their faces. The king's was a careful mask revealing nothing; he stared out one of the long windows at the grey sky. His advisors and the prince murmured among themselves, surprise or shock clear in their voices. But Robert's face caught her attention, for he alone stared at her, and his eyes held something odd, amusement certainly, and something else? It almost seemed like admiration, though that could not be. He must be furious.

David spoke and all eyes turned to him. "This will require further consideration, and by the fact that you were apparently unavailable," he said, "yesterday, for your wedding, 'tis true that we must delay your marriage for the duration of the Lenten season. We will pray God gives us guidance during this holy season to reason wisely as to the outcome of this matter."

She hesitated, thinking to speak again, but the king turned away; she was dismissed. She curtsied and dared a final glance at Robert, but he had turned and was staring out to the marshes, where wind bent the grasses in long sweeping waves.

"Wench! What impertinence!" cried one of the advisors when the door closed behind Ailsa. Robert barely heard him, but then the king spoke, drawing his attention.

"I have many subjects in my western lands, who by birth and inclination follow more the Gaelic ways of the Isles than the ways of England or the Continent. It will take time to bring them all into the fold of the new Scotia. Time and good strategy," he paused, his brow wrinkled. "Force is not always best. I must think on this further."

"But," Prince Henry interrupted, "recall father, that Robert has served you well, for indeed he saved your life and I am truly in his debt."

David smiled at his son, then spoke directly to Robert. "I do not forget. Nor do I cede her point that the Gaelic ways take precedence. She is my ward and under my direction. It is a matter of timing only. I must have a man under my direction seeing to the estate's defense." He frowned at the floor. "Stephen met me in Durham with a large army of mercenaries; this information I have relayed to no one here in Carlisle as of yet. I could not fight him, so I have given him Newcastle back, for he needs the funds and thinks the burgh a fair enough exchange. He goes back to London to keep the holy days and plan his next moves against Matilda, no doubt. At least we are free of him on the borders for some time." The king sighed deeply. "Yet I have not done him homage for these lands, though Prince Henry took the oath and did homage for his. He has been granted Huntingdon in his own right for this concession. Still, I'm wary that Stephen will march north again, and I must have peace on my western borders to deal with this chaos in England as is best."

Robert nodded.

"I intend you to hold those lands on my western coasts, but I would prefer the woman come willingly, rather than give you a determined opponent. As I would have the western coasts come into the realm of Scotia willingly, not forced into our midst. Time is often a companion for success." He paused, a deep frown creasing his brow. "This is a season for holy prayer and fasting, and a good time for you to serve your king further, if you will."

"I am at your service."

"I require you to journey to the Isle of Arran and speak with the peoples there, find out who the leading families are, ascertain the temper of the merchants, on Arran and on the coast. For there is word of unrest about in the Isles, of a religious fellow calling himself Wimond, who disrupts and raises feeling against our new order. Find out the nature and extent of this threat and report to us at Eastertide. You will learn much that will be of use to you as Lord of Caerwyn, and no doubt the woman will come to see the matter differently over these holy weeks, with the proper instruction. Time will serve you and me both well."

Robert glanced at Walter, who smiled ruefully. Outside the door, he stopped and stared at the granite floor. Then he walked slowly down the long corridor and headed outside. He climbed to the western outlook and stood, looking out over the grey fields, to the grayer sea far beyond. All would not go quickly and decisively as he'd planned. Could it be true that this matter of Gaelic custom was the reason she rejected him? That she was not involved in any plot against him? He wished it so. But why hadn't she spoken freely, when he'd asked her, the other night on the castle walls? Instead, she'd been defiant and silent by turns, and then she'd hidden away from him. His fingers drummed on the stone wall.

He heard a slide of pebbles behind him and turned, his hand on his dagger. Ailsa stood at the top of the stairs. This woman kept surprising him. "You are an eloquent advocate," he said.

"I followed you here, but I have no wish to intrude on your thoughts for long," she said, "only I tried to speak the truth, in the king's presence below. But I wanted you to know that I do not seek to be your enemy, for I do not even know you. I only seek to keep what is rightfully mine."

She seemed sincere, but she had fooled him well enough in the woods; he feared she could deceive and lie at will. "And what of the de Morvilles, how do they come into this?"

She frowned but answered in a patient voice. "They come into it not at all. Why are you always questioning me about them?"

"Hugh de Morville," he demanded, and winced inwardly at how petty he sounded.

She flushed. "He has been gracious. But I have made him, or no man, any commitment."

"I suspect de Morville's hand in these attempts against me and my men."

"There has been more than one?"

She raised a hand to brush the hair from her face, looking troubled. But how could he trust that?

"It's hard to believe the son of the king's Constable would be enmeshed in any plots against an ally," she said. When he didn't answer, she walked a few steps away, and looked out over the walls toward the grey strip of sea. "I do not wish to be married off like chattel. But I have not sought to harm you, nor would I."

He wanted to believe her, but men and women both, he'd found, often looked and sounded sincere, even as they plotted against you. And he wondered if young Nevin had recovered or even now lay ill with wound fever.

A sudden clanking of metal on the stairs startled them both. Robert yanked his dagger from his belt. A guard mounted the last stair and peered at them. Recognizing Robert, he mumbled, "Good day," and shambled off to his position.

"The king has ordered me to Arran."

"Arran," she repeated. "Why?"

"I am instructed to discover what the rebels are planning."

She lifted her chin. "We are not rebels in the Isles. We simply have our different laws and customs, and we will keep them."

He stared at her. "Nonetheless, I will be away for a time, until Easter or beyond." He stepped forward and his fingers wrapped tightly around her wrist. "Then, I will return." He paused, staring at his fingers encircling her wrist. "There are dangers, more than you know. Go nowhere. Wait for me, here. Promise me that."

She hesitated, frowning. "I promise," she said finally and shook him off.

CHAPTER THIRTEEN

AILSA TRIED TO STIFLE HER YAWN. Impossible. Yet an hour until dawn and the sky had been black and starless when she left her cold bedchamber and hurried to the chapel. Mass was chanted thrice daily for Lent at David's court. She tried to wiggle her stiff toes in her thick boots, without appearing to fidget. The priest's voice droned on. She attempted to lose herself in the rhythms of the Latin words, but it was just too early. Her mind moved irresistibly to thoughts of a bowl of warmed milk with cinnamon sprinkled on top. There would be nothing like that this morning of course. Nothing at all until nones, when they could eat the one sparse meal of the day. It was hard to school her mind when thoughts of her precarious future crowded in, making her wonder and question, so restless that at night she tossed on her pallet until her roommates snarled at her to be silent.

Beatrice was seated on a bench two rows ahead of her, wrapped in grey furs that gave off a pungent odor. Beside her was a stranger. She had arrived at court only yesterday and come late to the hall for the austere meal. Beatrice seemed to be her friend or relation, for they'd spent the evening huddled by the fire in close conversation.

The priest concluded his lengthy chant and the worshippers filed silently out into the grey dawn. A cold wind was whipping up. As she passed the stairway to the castle walls, Ailsa thought of Robert. There had been a brief moment of something between them; it was hard to give it a name.

With Lent upon them, the days were long and wearisome, filled with grey skies and pricked fingers, embroidering cloths for the chapel with the other women. Ailsa often found her mind wandering. What was happening at Caerwyn right now? Where was Robert? Perhaps in her own manor, or on the sea heading to Arran, investigating rebellion for the king. He was certainly having the more exciting time.

She stomped up the uneven stone walkway. She found Effie alone, hunched in front of the fire in the deserted great hall. Many had removed to their own manors for Lent, where, she suspected, they held the season with far less austerity. Beatrice remained at Carlisle, but her son had disappeared. She'd not asked, but Beatrice had volunteered that he was off seeing to his extensive estates in Lauderdale. She was half glad, for he made her uneasy, but she couldn't deny he was exciting too. "'Tis so very dull," she said, dropping onto the bench beside her friend.

Effie paused in her embroidery. "It is always so during Lent. The king goes to mass three times daily and so must we all. And the weather is so bad, one cannot walk in the gardens, or hunt."

"Let's go out anyway."

"Into this wind?"

Ailsa was already on her feet. She tossed Effie's embroidery down on the stool.

Effie rose reluctantly. They found their cloaks in the hall by the kitchens and pulled on stiff boots.

"We'll explore," suggested Ailsa, when Effie hesitated at the gusts of wind which hit them as they left the building. "Let's go right out the gates and find a path and see the surrounding area. I've not had a glimpse of the meadows yet, or the river."

"I suppose it would be possible," said Effie.

Ailsa was beginning to enjoy herself. "It will be fun," she said. They wandered out the gate, nodding to the sleepy guard, for an attack during the holy season was most unlikely and especially so as David had just made a firm truce with Stephen. Prince Henry was even now traveling to London to spend Easter with the English king as a sign of the new alliance.

They crossed the River Eden on the narrow bridge, pausing to watch the brown water flow beneath them, wending around ice-glazed rocks and frozen sandbars, then they struck out on a path heading west.

"Do you know where we're going?" asked Effie.

"Of course," said Ailsa, though that wasn't precisely true.

Just then, they heard footsteps behind them, someone running, heavy boots thudding against the frozen track. It was Jamie, his brown hair flying as he ran toward them. "Where do you go?" he called out.

"We're just wandering," Ailsa answered. "How are you faring?"

"Fine," said Jamie. "Though the food is far less plenty, the work is light enough." He was employed in the king's stables and thrilled to have the care of the expensive chargers. He no longer had Tanet, however, for Robert had taken the stallion. "I'll come along with you then."

Ailsa smiled at his casual tone. "As you wish, though we hardly need protection, you know." She looked pointedly at the deserted road and fields.

Jamie grinned. "I know, but for sure Sir Robert will have my hide if I don't come."

Ailsa made a face. Jamie had been sticking to her like a leech these last two weeks. It seemed Robert had charged him with her care, and Jamie idolized the tall knight. He'd also left a small bag of silver, which Jamie delivered to her the day after he left. She was chagrined Jamie had told Robert of the robbery on the road, but she couldn't deny the coins were useful here at court. She'd pay him back, of course, when she returned to Caerwyn, every silver penny. "Let's be off then."

As they trudged along the frost hardened path, Effie began to cheer up, for the sky was clearing and the sun peeping out for the first time in some days. "This is better than sitting in that old hall," she said. "Let's go by the village. Perhaps the market is on this morning."

Ailsa agreed and they walked on, the wind sweeping her hair into a tangle. Her hands and toes warmed. The clouds scattered and soon the sky stretched blue overhead. They entered the village, a prosperous place of timbered houses painted in deep reds and blues and golden yellow and found the market square by the noise of the milling crowds. The shouts of vendors selling salted bread made her stomach growl and Ailsa pulled a piece of silver from her sleeve. She purchased three slices from an old man with a grey hat pulled down over his forehead and they munched as they walked from stall to stall examining the wares. They shouldn't be eating now, in the middle of the morning, of course, but everyone around them seemed to be ignoring that and Ailsa licked her lips, getting the last crumbs of the salty crust. It tasted wonderful after the bland afternoon meals of plain brown bread and salt cod at court.

They spent an amusing time watching the merchants hawking cloth, shoes, metalwork, and livestock. Effie was entranced by the cloth stall and fingered the fuzzy wools in shades of blue, green, and brown. There was a beautiful dark red wool too, very fine, the color of the wines the French brought with them to the king's table. By noon, though, the merchants began packing their things for the trip home.

"We should return to the castle, I suppose," said Effie.

"Not yet! Let's buy more bread and walk along to the sea," suggested Ailsa, reluctant to end their holiday.

"I'm starved," agreed Effie, "but don't you think we should be getting back? Surely it's a good way yet to the sea."

"We'll be there soon enough." Ailsa purchased a loaf from a vendor packing up his wares. She sent Jamie after some watered ale. Provisioned, they headed down a promising path toward the sea, which they could just glimpse glinting in the distance. The sun was high overhead, and the air felt soft, almost warm, with a hint of spring. Ailsa loosened her hood and let it fall down over her shoulders.

It was longer than it looked to the sea, but Ailsa encouraged Effie with thoughts of the delightful picnic to come. "We can't turn back now," she said, "and admit defeat!" Jamie trudged along tirelessly and without comment. Finally, they reached the beach, which was more a marshy area of sand dunes and grasses blowing flat in the wind, much stronger here. Still, Ailsa sucked in the familiar smell of cold and salt and thought of her home.

Effie held up a beautiful shell, its mother of pearl gleaming. "Let's gather some to make jewelry back at the castle. It will help pass these winter days."

They gathered limpet shells, finding the most enticing and placing them into neat piles by size and color on the sand. Jamie ignored this pastime, and sat on a high spot overlooking the beach, keeping guard no doubt. When they had gathered all they could carry, Ailsa sat down on the warm sand, and piled the shells in the folds of her gown, fingering their soft curves and feeling the sun on her face.

Effie came, with her hands full, and sat beside her, brushing sand from her arms and fingers. "Let's eat," she said.

"Aye, let's." Jamie agreed to come down from his guard post long enough for food. They ate everything they'd bought, and after, Ailsa lay down on the sand, scattered with rounded white pebbles, her face in the sun, her eyes closed and gleaming red from the bright light. She let her mind drift, half listening to the occasional cry of a sea bird. She could hear Effie's rhythmic breathing beside her; she'd fallen asleep. Jamie had wandered off down the beach, apparently content no dangers lurked.

She didn't want to sleep but stay awake to enjoy this day of freedom. Her thoughts drifted, from the beach, to the boats skimming on the sea, and to Dugald and Meriel and home. It was wonderful to be at the king's court, but how she missed Caerwyn. So much more than she'd thought possible. It was very strange, wishing to be home one moment and away the next. It seemed both desires sat in her chest, making her always discontented. It would perhaps be somewhat dull when she returned home. That was an uncomfortable thought. Would it have been dull after a time, even if Niall had lived? An even more disturbing idea.

She heard the slide of pebbles shifting behind her. She looked around, surprised that Jamie would appear from that direction, and glimpsed a dark hood ducking behind a boulder above them on the dune. "Show yourself!" she called out.

The stranger ignored her and instead ran back toward the path, sliding out of view behind another boulder.

She scrambled to her feet. "Jamie!"

Effie stirred. "What is it?" she muttered.

"Get up!" said Ailsa, pulling her to her feet. She ran toward the boulder. "Show yourself I say!" she shouted. She started to climb up the steep dune, but the sand was slippery, and it was hard to get a footing. A rock whirled by her head and she ducked.

Jamie ran up, panting, and pulled at her skirts. "No, Lady, 'tis not safe!"

The dark clad figure peered out, threw another rock, hitting Jamie in the shoulder, then ran, dodging between the boulders and tall grass until he disappeared.

Ailsa climbed the dune, Jamie behind her, still protesting, but when they reached the summit, all was still and empty except for wind moving across the grasses. They checked behind the boulders, piled haphazardly at the top of the dune by some ancient storm, but could find no one, and only the tracks of the one man they'd glimpsed, leading back toward the road and the village. Impossible to find one man there. It could be anybody.

Ailsa gazed back across the fields toward the village, disturbed. Who had been spying on them? It was no farmer nor merchant she'd glimpsed, nor a common thief; the man wore fine clothes, she was sure, and he had been hooded. "Come Effie," she said, sliding down the sand dune and grabbing her friend's hand, for Effie was still crouched on the beach below, looking terrified. "It was just someone watching us for fun," she said and forced herself to smile. "It's getting late anyway, time to be going back."

The path back seemed long, for the weak sun began to sink and the wind blustered in their faces. Ailsa tried to distract Effie with chatter, but she was disturbed herself, remembering again the awful man that night on their journey to Carlisle. The path seemed lonely now and she longed to reach the castle. When they arrived, she sent Effie to her room with a cup of hot milk from the kitchen and she took Jamie aside. "Let me see that shoulder."

He argued, but she made him pull his tunic aside. The skin was unbroken but already bruised and purple. She didn't think a bone was broken but it would be sore. She found him a salve from the healer who resided behind the kitchen in a hut filled with dry herbs and sent him to sleep early.

That night, Ailsa thought long about the spying man in black. Who would be interested in following her, watching her, or harming her, other than a thief? Yet no thief wore such fine wool. She had no answer. She thought about Robert's warning. *There are more dangers than you know.*

After the incident with the black-clothed man, Ailsa's days faded into a dull sameness. The king departed for Durham again, the urgency of England's troubles making him travel, though it was Lent.

Ailsa walked with Effie in the gardens most mornings, but she couldn't persuade her to venture past the castle gates again. She walked by herself to the village once or twice, with Jamie doggedly following her, but she felt guilty for dragging him from his duties in the stables just because she was bored, and uneasy despite herself about the man in black. So she warmed herself by the hearth with the other women and tried to think of iron arguments to persuade the king to hand her lands back when he returned.

She also thought of Hugh. She wondered what his estates were like and how it would seem to live so far from the sea. She thought of Robert, perhaps lording it at her own estate in Caerwyn, while his servants took the dangerous winter passage to Arran to gain infor-mation for the king. It was so unfair that he could go to her manor and she must wait here on the king's pleasure. She thought of Meriel and wondered what it would be like to grow a child within. She had thought of her cousin's wife as young, but now she seemed embarked on a journey that was more exciting than her own adventure.

She wanted to think Robert was the cause of all her problems, but now she'd seen the king's court, she had to admit that was untrue. For some reason the king was interested in her, or rather in her lands. If not Robert, some other husband would certainly be found for her. The king was all powerful and here at the center of his power, she was pinned right under his gaze. Maybe she'd made a mistake in coming, she reflected uneasily. But something told her the king would not forget her, or Caerwyn, even if she were far away.

Worry about the king's attention led always to worry about Robert himself. He confused her; he didn't fit her assumptions of a grasping younger son or violent tourney knight. There had been something about the look in his eyes when he told her to wait. Something she had no word for. And wait for what?

The sad truth was that she sat at an almost English court waiting on the judgment of an almost English king. She heard the rumors, when men talked. That David was too closely allied with the English court, that he was near English himself, that he'd stolen the Scottish crown even, from a more rightful heir. And where did that leave her, and Caerwyn? The English now ruled Scotia, being at court, she saw that now too clearly. She saw also that the coast and Isles were a troublesome frontier for the king, one he sought to control. Caerwyn sat right in the midst of this trouble. It could not be hers alone much longer.

Worse, there was no husband she could find among her own people, for such a man the king would never trust or approve. They would insist she marry soon, and insist her husband be loyal and English. How could she secure a Gaelic Caerwyn and ensure her own security and even some freedom? It seemed, in the dark end of winter, impossible.

The one bright spot, as she waited for the king, was a new friend. Through Beatrice, she had met Alice, the stranger she had watched covertly in chapel. Like herself, a widow in straightened circumstances, Alice told her she had been comfortably married to a good man, a minor baron, with sufficient lands adjacent to the estates of the great de Brus, the king's longtime advisor. The lands had kept them, though not in luxury. One day, her husband had been set upon by robbers in the woods while hunting and died when his wounds festered. She had been left with little, for moneylenders revealed her husband had mortgaged their properties, trying to help his brother who had spent his fortune on ill-fated border raids. She had fallen under the protection of the king and he brought her to court while deciding on a husband for her. She had no lands of her own and little enough to offer in a marriage bargain, except her exceedingly lovely face.

Here she looked so piteous that Ailsa took her hand. "Please. You are so kind. I know someone will fall in love with you and will not care at all that you have no estates."

"I wish it were so, but in marriage, men seek land and fortune above all."

Was that true? It seemed so of these English certainly. But surely the lady would have many suitors once Lent was over. Meanwhile Ailsa tried to coax her to laugh more often. As the early days of March passed, grey skies and even flakes of snow lengthened the days, Ailsa spent more and more of her time with Alice, who didn't like to sit in the smelly bustle of the great hall. She tried to enlist Effie to join her in cheering up the widow. But Effie, normally so sociable, had taken a quite unreasonable dislike to Alice. "There are some that are no better than they might be," she sniffed mysteriously. "You be cautious, Ailsa."

Ailsa decided Effie might be jealous and indeed the widow was so beautiful it was hard not to feel envy. She had the vivid blue eyes and very white skin the bards extolled in their songs. Only her nose was perhaps somewhat long. Giving up on getting her two friends together, Ailsa divided her time between them, visiting with Effie in the solar most mornings, working on the cloths for the church or walking in the gardens, and spending her afternoons with the widow.

"Surely the king just awaits the end of the holy season to settle your future. But," Ailsa hesitated, "don't you wish to choose your own husband?"

"Not at all," sighed Alice. "I know the king will choose wisely for me."

"But do you not wish to hold onto your own lands?"

Alice shrugged. "Why should I wish that care? That will be my husband's responsibility."

Ailsa puzzled over this but decided that, as always, the ways of the English were hard to comprehend. These people, some of them, could be kind, but she often felt she dwelled among strangers.

A week before the end of Lent, Ailsa wandered by the river, on her own for once, as Jamie was occupied with a new foal in the stables. She glanced behind her often, still troubled by the hooded figure who had spied on them, but she refused to be cowed into staying forever in the castle. She needed to think, and to think she must be out of doors. The king would return any day, as would Robert, and life would pick up its threads and weave a new pattern.

She followed a path, pushing the twiggy underbrush aside and ducking around a holly bush, sharp with pointed leaves. The river was free of ice, and flowing fast, rushing white over the smoothed rocks. The day was dark with low clouds, but the twittering of the wrens told her spring was near upon them. A soft breeze lifted the hair at the nape of her neck. At home, the fields would be prepared, ready for planting. She knelt and picked up a handful of sandy gravel and rolled it on her palm, thinking of the rich soil in the fields at home.

Suddenly, she felt she was not alone. She stood quickly, and before her, in a brown gown that blended right into the willow brush, was a tall woman. So quietly she must have come, she hadn't heard a crunch on the gravel or a twig snap. They stared at each other. The woman had unusual eyes, like the teardrop stone from the North forests her father had brought home once from his voyaging.

"Who are you?" said Ailsa, surprise making her rude.

"I could ask you the same," said the woman.

Ailsa felt her face heat, with anger or embarrassment she wasn't sure.

The woman touched her neck, where a silver amulet hung and smiled, though the smile did not reach her eyes. "I am Eachna."

"Do you stay at the castle? I have not seen you there before."

"For a time."

Ailsa waited, but the woman added nothing more and asked her no questions. Feeling awkward, like an intruder, though that was strange, she turned to go.

The woman did not call after her, nor stop her.

When she reached the bridge once more, Ailsa looked down and she could just make out the woman, her brown dress and copper hair blending into the leaves as though she were a part of the forest; she was sitting cross legged on the cold ground at a bend in the river. She seemed to be speaking, her lips forming words, her hands moving, though no one else was there. As though she spoke to the river itself, flowing on, or perhaps to the soft spring air.

The woman seemed to feel her gaze and looked up and their eyes met.

Ailsa broke their gaze first. She hurried away, feeling flustered, yet also strangely excited and pleased.

CHAPTER FOURTEEN

ROBERT CLIMBED THE STAIRS, his sword clanging once on the rough timber wall. Behind him clambered the housekeeper, Agnes, keeping up a stream of nervous chatter. Hearing her puffing behind him, Robert slowed his steps, stifling a sigh.

"We'll be over the hall now, Lord, and there be three chambers up here, one was always for Griffith, Ailsa's father," said Agnes.

They reached the landing at the top of the stairs and Agnes sorted through the ring of heavy keys attached to her girdle. "'Twas his and his lady's, though she liked the view over the meadows, coming from country people you know. She wasn't really one for the sea and he humored her, he always humored her, except that he never would give up the sea even for her and she was always saying it would be the end of him and so it was. Though she never lived to see it poor lady, for she was in the grave when Ailsa was just a little mite and a terrible sad time it was too."

Robert frowned, disturbed at this vision of the defiant and independent seeming Ailsa as a sobbing child.

Agnes glanced at him. "Let me show you," and plunged ahead down the short corridor, shoving open the heavy oak door at the end. It swung back on leather hinges and revealed a chamber of medium size, with early morning light streaming in two large windows.

Robert walked in, suddenly uncomfortable, as though he intruded on someone's home. Which he had not, he reminded himself, for all this was now his own. The room smelled of fresh air. "Who stays here now?"

"Why, no one, 'tis empty these years since…" She stopped and stared at the ground, her hands twisting together. "Since Lady Ailsa's husband died," she said in a low voice.

Robert went to one of the windows. Looking out, he surveyed the fields and distant evergreen forest. His fingers drummed on the oak sill. He hadn't known Ailsa had been married before. "Why did she leave, when she knew I was coming here? Did she seek to evade me?"

The housekeeper stuttered and turned red, wringing her hands. "She's always a most responsible girl, truly you must not judge her harshly."

"I do not," said Robert. "I expect she will return with me after Eastertide."

Agnes smiled at that, her round face crinkling into lines of pleasure. "Oh indeed, that is welcome news."

"You have kept the rooms in good order," said Robert, and she beamed even wider, twisting her plump hands in her linen apron.

"'Tis Ailsa always insisting all be just right," she said. "Still, I was away with my sick uncle when you came before. I'm that ashamed the hall was in a state."

"We'll speak no more of it," he said.

"Will you see the other chambers?"

Robert was impatient to be outside and ride the borders of his lands, but he answered yes, for she clearly wished to show him more of her handiwork.

Agnes swung open a second heavy door. "This room was used as a sitting area in winter," she began. From downstairs came the distinct sound of a wailing baby, "Mercy," cried Agnes, yanking the keys from her girdle and thrusting them into his hands, "'tis the cook's new daughter, excuse me, I must see to her." She dashed off, disappearing down the stairs.

Robert was left alone, and he entered the chamber, which was small but had a window and a window seat. His hand touched the linen cushion. An embroidered hanging hung on one wall. It depicted the manor, with men and women laboring in the fields in one scene, and men heading out to sea on small ships in another, women and children gathered on a headland waving farewell. He wondered who had embroidered the piece, for the work was very fine.

He must get to the fields. Will would be waiting. From the sound of wailing spiraling up the stairs from the kitchen, Agnes wasn't likely to come back soon.

He started down the stairs, then stopped. He unlocked the third door with the housekeeper's keys and entered. A tall, narrow window took up most of the outside wall. He threw open the shutter. The ocean spread before him, green fading into misty horizon, with rock bound islands in the distance. The smell of salt swirled in. There was a bed, narrow and surrounded with green hangings of soft wool. A carved chest of the style they made in Ireland, ornamented with swirling designs, sat against the inside wall. Ailsa's chamber. The thought made him feel awkward. He started to leave, but his eyes were drawn to the chest with its fine carvings. He ran a finger along the polished oak. He wondered what was inside, but instead of opening it, he walked to the bed and sat down.

He sighed, thinking of the tangle they were in. What had her husband and their marriage been like? Was she planning with de Morville even now to push him from these lands, or even to kill him? There were no answers here in the silent rooms and no use thinking of her until he finished the king's business and returned to Carlisle. Hopefully, she'd see reason then, and hopefully too the king would be pleased with what information he could bring, pleased enough to agree to their marriage. As always, the king held their lives in his hands. How careful David would be with that trust, he found he wasn't sure.

Uncomfortable with that thought, he walked to the window and saw Will down on the beach, calling to the men. He stopped for one more quick glance around, then opened the pouch at his belt, and fumbled inside, finally pulling out the tattered packet of lavender and emerald silk ribbons he'd purchased long ago. He placed it on the chest, beside an engraved wooden comb. He picked up the comb; A for Ailsa, and N. He put the comb down quickly, as though it burned him. Embarrassed suddenly, though there was no one around, he left, slamming the door in his haste.

He found the hall empty, so he strode out to the courtyard, intending to go to the stables and meet Will down on the beach with the horses. Outside, he nearly collided with a pair of his men, waiting for him, faces somber. "What it is?"

The older of the two frowned, his bushy eyebrows drawn together. "Young Nevin."

"How does he fare?" asked Robert quickly. "Is the healer needed again?"

"Nay," broke in the younger. He was silenced with a fierce look from the other.

"Tell me the whole," said Robert.

"The old woman seemed to know her business. The sword cut healed up fine. But Nevin would be impatient. He rose from his bed too soon and went out hunting two days past. Not for long. It should have been all right." The man paused and distress chased across his gruff face. "Got caught in that weather we had. Soaked to the skin and exhausted when he came back. He got fever again that very night."

Robert stared at him, saying nothing.

The man's jaw twitched. "The priest here does most of the healing as is necessary, but he has not returned from his journey. The old woman did her best, stayed with him all the day and on into the night. But his wound festered and the fever rose and wouldn't come down, whatever she tried. Young Nevin died, yesterday morn."

Robert shifted his gaze beyond the two men, to the sea, emerald and calm and uncaring. Yesterday morn. He wished he'd been here, at least, to tell him he'd been full of courage. The two men shifted uncomfortably, staring at the ground. "Has he been buried properly?" asked Robert, his voice hoarse.

"Yes, he has of course," replied the older soldier. "The ground be less solid here by the sea, though it do be winter. We buried him this morning, not knowing you were coming, and said some words over him."

"Where?" asked Robert.

The soldier pointed, across the fields to a small rise that overlooked the sea.

Robert passed through the manor gates and climbed the hill. At the top he found a dozen graves in a place of long grasses and wind and a few twisting apple trees, the whole ringed with piled stones. The fresh disturbed ground above one was all too obvious. Someone had placed a wreath of evergreen boughs on the earth and there was a wooden marker, Nevin's name chiseled in rough letters. Nothing, nothing he could do now. His man, his responsibility.

Four days later, Will and Robert finally had a chance to talk. In the hall, there was never a chance for private conversation, so despite the wind, they sat on a cliff overlooking the sea. "There seems little likelihood of treason at Caerwyn, though 'tis true the king and his English ways seem far away when here," said Will.

Robert sat, long legs stretched out on the grass, feeling the feeble winter sun playing across his face. "We haven't found out much here, though it doesn't mean there's nothing to be found." Afternoon sun played on the waters far below them, turning them violet blue. White caps slashed the waters, and the rhythmic splash and roar of the small breakers running up the pebbled beach accompanied their talk.

"This manor does seem exceptionally well run," ventured Will.

"Yes," agreed Robert. He lapsed into silence, considering this fact. Compared to the other manors of Walter's they'd assessed as they rode through, Caerwyn was a virtual model. The account books were written in an angular hand with ink on bound pages of parchment, neatly tied and placed well wrapped in a greased sack in a chest in the great hall. There were no mistakes that he could find. The fields were productive, though he thought their yield could be increased with the new methods he'd learned in Shropshire. But the key problem here as everywhere was a shortage of labor, for more and more men left to seek out the towns. How many had left Caerwyn in recent times was a hard number to discover, for no one was anxious to give him that information. But the labor issue would have to be solved. He frowned. The idea of forcing people to stay on the land was troubling. But how else to extract the coin he needed?

"The lady has done well," said Will. "You have to admit it, Robb."

"But too few men to till even the ground they've broken." Faced with the uncertainty of rains and winds and rotting crops or twisted parsnips and wizened apples, many had taken the chance and slipped away in the night. Seeking more interesting work in the towns or markets. And seeking there the freedom they'd find, if they could bide for a year and a day. Robert sighed. The week they'd spent in Caerwyn was adding to his confusion. "And the productivity of the lands can only be secured if Caerwyn can be held against a possible attack. You know that as do I." Robert got to his feet and began to pace. Was his future wife the competent lady of the manor or the darker woman, who plotted against him. He rubbed his hands through his hair. Nevin was dead. That alone was certain. He looked out across the waters, squinting at the glare. "I'll not let the king off of his promise to grant me these lands."

"You're still set on using them, to fund your revenge," said Will.

"Of course. My plan to return home has never wavered."

Will suppressed a sigh. "It's possible to reset your future. You have a chance here, Robb. A chance for a good future."

"We go to Arran on the morrow," Robert said. "There's work to be done there for the king. Distasteful work, I've no liking for spying. But that's his price for all this." He swung an arm about to encompass all of Caerwyn. "With kings, there's always a price. And I will have justice." He gave a bitter laugh.

"I'd say we need two days to travel, one day on land and one to sail," responded Will after a time, flipping a small grey rock from one hand to the other, "what with these spring winds."

"We'll find this cousin of Ailsa's, and from him we'll ascertain more about this matter of Wimond the fighting bishop. For the king. But I intend to also learn somewhat of Dugald's loyalties. And perhaps hers as well."

"Think you there is aught to reveal?" asked Will, bending to toss the stone over the headland to the deeps below.

"I know not." Robert searched the brilliant waters to the west. "They are open enough, here, about their adherence to their Gaelic and even Norse ways, but I see no obvious evidence of treason."

"There are these culdees in the forest," said Will, "but they seem holy men of God, not the sorcerers the priests name them, though strange in their clothing and staring eyes."

"I understand them to be healers with much knowledge. If only they'd been here for Nevin."

"This Wimond fellow is not even of the Isles, I hear," said Will. "He voyaged from Ireland, and an abbey in England before that. He claims to be the son of Moray now and but a year ago, he said he was son of the Norwegian king."

"Whatever he says, he draws men. That's a danger. And there must be grievances if he can draw them. We must find out what those grievances are." Robert got to his feet. "Find five or six men. We need a solid boat and provisions. Choose well, for we must trust these men. Our own haven't the knowledge of this sea, and besides, I'll need to leave some here to hold the place firm for our return."

"I'm not too sure of the seas myself," said Will, grinning, and falling in with him as they walked back down the hill.

Robert laughed, remembering Will hanging over the rails on the voyage from Normandy back to England. He left him near the stables, saying, "I have one task more to complete."

Some hours later, Robert clattered into the neighbor Thomas' courtyard, shouting up to the guard to let him enter. The ride had been long and chill, and full of too much thinking. Everything about his proposed wife was a mystery. It was time for some clarity.

He threw himself off the horse, not waiting for the startled groom, and banged on the door. It swung open, and a housemaid with mussed hair only half hidden by a wrinkled linen cloth peered out.

"I am Robert of Caerwyn," he said slowly, for she looked so startled, he feared she would not understand.

Her brown eyes opened wider, and she backed away into the dark corridor.

He waited, but there was no further sign of the maid. He entered and shut the door behind him. He let his eyes adjust to the sudden dimness and awaited the maid's return. No one appeared, so he made his way into the hall. He noticed the cold central hearth and nearby a tidy pile of wood and charcoal. He quickly kindled a fire. When the blaze was well started, the housemaid had still not returned.

Then a door in the paneled wall swung open and Thomas entered the room. "You have our hospitality. Forgive our slow response, but we are unused to winter visitors in these parts. Perhaps you'd like some refreshments."

Robert agreed and sat on the offered stool.

"Well," said Thomas with a calm smile, "we are hearing much said of you, our new neighbor, even in the depths of winter." Thomas spoke to the maid, who hovered in the doorway. She hurried away, and returned with haste, carrying a platter of dried apples and watered ale, which she arranged for them.

"A poor meal," said Thomas. "My apologies. The maid is new and not yet trained, I fear."

"I thank you for it," answered Robert and they consumed the food, saving their conversation for after, as was proper.

"Now," said Thomas, "it is good of you to ride here, but we did not expect to see you again so soon. I thank you for sending word that Ailsa is well. We were worried when she left here. But I think you have another purpose, venturing here just as the spring winds blow?"

"Two matters," answered Robert. "I seek knowledge of this one who calls himself Wimond the bishop. I must know of his intentions in these parts. And the intentions of the landholders of this coastline. I seek this for the king, who wishes his subjects to live in harmony, under his rule."

Thomas nodded. He did not seem disturbed by Robert's direct approach, but he paused for a long moment before speaking. "We have heard here of the king's great success in Carlisle and celebrate with him the return of Arthur's castle to her proper people. Yet the king is far from here, and his worries far from the people's worries here."

"David is a good king. He seeks great things for Scotia, and with

Henry dead and England under Stephen's sway." Robert shrugged and emptied his cup of watered ale. "Stephen is weak, and even now 'tis said the empress Matilda gathers her forces across the water. Impossible to know who will reign in England, but it will be long before peaceful days can be lived there. With much consequence to Scotia's favor, if played right." He paused, then said, "I have come to these parts to seek peace. I would not see the ramblings of a confused priest destroy that peace I see here, on your lands and mine. What say you?"

Thomas stared at the rafters of his hall. "Yet the ramblings you speak of contain some truths that must be acknowledged if our lands are to remain stable. English ways of religion are sometimes strange to people here, and other customs strange and distasteful even." He lifted an eyebrow. "Such as the question of women's inheritance. We do not hold that a woman should be kept a minor all her life and deeded over with her lands by any lord who calls her ward. Even though that lord may be a king."

"English ways with women can be over hard," Robert said, "and I have had ample cause in my own life to know they are not always just. Yet the estates on the coast are vital to David. He must build a buffer against the turmoil that roils Ireland and demands of the Norse earls in the Isles. Surely Ailsa knew she'd be declared the king's ward and a husband picked out for her."

"Perhaps, yet I think not," said Thomas slowly. "You do not know Ailsa. Or the ways of the west lands."

"Forgive my direct speech, but I find myself surprised that you speak so eloquently for the Gaelic ways. Are you not related to the king's Constable, and married into an English family?" Thomas nodded. "I am. But living here, in the middle of two worlds, I have come to see good in both. Yet people cling to what they know. I fear troubled times are coming." He tapped his finger on the wooden bench.

"Nonetheless," said Robert, "Gaelic customs must mesh with English ways, for all Scotia is in a time of ferment and change. I fear too many men leave the fields for the villages and burghs. None are left but the old to work the land."

"That is a problem we have in common," agreed Thomas. "I am working to keep them here, as it's surely in their own best interests to stay on the land they and their fathers have always worked."

Robert frowned. "Forcing them to stay on the land is a change, and one that binds them and weighs on them more than in their fathers' time."

Thomas shrugged now. "True perhaps, but unavoidable for the greater good."

Robert got to his feet. "David is a just king, but like all kings, he wants his way and he has the power to make his wishes real. You are my closest neighbor now, and I would have you on my side if there be troubles in this region. With this troublesome bishop, or any other."

"Let us join hands on that much, at least," answered Thomas. "And now, let us demonstrate some of our famed hospitality. Let me take you into the garden room and you can visit with my wife, who will be greatly angered if I keep you all to myself here, for visitors are rare enough." Thomas led him, chatting amiably, into a large square room adjoining the hall, with long windows facing to the east. The shutters were open and sunlight streamed in. They found his lady bundled in a deep blue cloak trimmed with white fox fur. The sunlight silvered her blonde hair twined in a crown of braids, and her blue eyes smiled at him as they approached.

Robert bowed and the lady raised a pale hand for him to kiss in the fashion of the English women.

"I hope you will be able to stay with us for some days," she said. "I remember your lady well from her brief visit to us, and I wish you very happy in your marriage."

Robert frowned. "The lady and I are yet to be married."

Elinor raised her brows and turned to her husband.

Thomas took a step forward. "Why have you not married her; 'tis not right to dishonor her in her own home. Ailsa deserves better of you."

"Yes," broke in his lady, "you must marry her immediately, or bring her here to me and she can stay with us until…" She stopped and began again, "I long to get to know my husband's childhood friend." Her lovely face was anxious, and she glanced from Thomas's angry face to Robert and back again.

Robert sighed. "The lady is not at Caerwyn, and we are not married at her behest, not mine. I hold the lady's honor as my own, for she will be my wife."

Elinor glanced at Thomas, clearly puzzled. "Not at Caerwyn," she echoed, "where is she then?"

"She is at the king's court, at Carlisle," said Robert.

"Oh, how lovely," smiled Elinor, her face clearing. "So you will be married at Carlisle then, in the presence of the king, a great honor indeed, and worth waiting for. Thomas, isn't it fine!"

Later, when Robert rode in to Caerwyn, he shrugged off the shouts of the men greeting him and mounted the stairs to Ailsa's room. The chamber seemed cold in the dim light of the dying day. He looked at the bed, arranged so the sleeper could see the ocean on awakening, and the simple green coverings, planked floor, and wood chest. He picked up the comb, ran his finger along the carving, then placed it down. He threw the shutter open; violet skies arched over the ocean and the first few stars were shining. He stared at the water, a frown furrowing his brow and his head beginning to ache.

He wanted the lands here, for the coin they could bring for his long-held intention of revenge, in truth he must admit no less. But buried inside, he had discovered something surprising. A need or perhaps only a wisp of a dream, for a home and a wife. The quiet contentment of Elinor and Thomas had sparked something unfamiliar and unsettling. Or set flame to something he'd buried deep inside.

He stared out the window, turning this new thought over in his mind. But even as he tried to examine it, it seemed to melt away in his hand like a snowflake, beautiful but too fragile and ephemeral to withstand scrutiny. What of his long-held vow? Who would he be if he abandoned his promise to deliver justice for his father and mother?

He must drive fitz John from his family lands and for that, he must have Caerwyn to fund the assault. Anything else was unthinkable.

CHAPTER FIFTEEN

Carlisle

AILSA TWIRLED, WIDE SKIRTS FLYING in a circle.

"You look wonderful," cried Effie. "Look!" She held up her precious mirror, in its carved wooden frame, and Ailsa peered at her reflection, though the king's priest said looking glasses were a sin. Her skin showed pink through the translucent linen of her shift, and her gown was a deep green fall of heavy silk, laced tight at her sides with gold ribbons.

"'Tis by far the finest gown I have ever worn, or even seen," said Ailsa, fingering the folds of alternating greens, so like the sea. "But Effie, surely you can use such a gown!"

"You must have it," said Effie. She resumed threading yellow ribbons into her own blue gown, which lay across her lap. "It was my cousin's, but she is grown big with childbearing to wear such now, and she has plenty. When we went to London last year, she gave me several. Can you imagine? I have this blue to wear and you must have something for the Easter celebrations too." She looked up at Ailsa with a smile. "The color is made for you."

Ailsa nodded uncertainly, uncomfortable with such a costly gift. She peered at herself again in the mirror. Her hair did actually seem the russet of oak leaves against the green. She bent over to hug her friend.

Effie blushed. "I am glad you are pleased," she answered. "Now, pull that off so I may take down the hem, for my cousin was shorter than you."

The room was quiet as they sat in a companionable silence. Now that the widow Alice had returned to her old estate for the Easter feast, Ailsa had been spending more time with Effie. "It's good to have you all to myself," said Effie. "Tell me another of your stories."

Ailsa gladly put down her sewing and related one of the old tales. She'd discovered the stories she'd grown up with, tales of the forest and strange elvish beings who lived there, capricious and vain and mischievous, were not known to Effie. She'd been glad to retell them, finding a kind of comfort in them, though they all told of strange adventures and not all ended happily for the human beings caught in the faery world. They reminded her of childhood and home and she needed that comfort now.

Watching the sun creep along the floor, Ailsa wondered what sort of day it was at Caerwyn. She pictured Meriel in the kitchen putting together one of her fruit pastries and sighed, quietly as she could. That she was homesick was one of the surprises of this journey. She crossed to the narrow window and peered out across the meadows as she'd done so often during these long days of Lent. As usual, they were empty; brown stubble still covered the fields. No men plowing or planting, nor animals. Easter would come before the spring this year.

"Don't fret," said Effie.

"I cannot be at peace. Not until this matter of my lands is settled. I do wish the king would return."

"He will be here for Easter, only a few days now," said Effie with certainty. She looked up from her sewing. "Yet I think you are waiting for more than King David's return."

Ailsa put her head down on her arms, feeling the wind play with her hair as it swept in the open window. "Beatrice has been so good to me. I feel in her debt. I believe she hopes for an agreement, between Hugh and myself. She presses me."

"And what do you wish? Would you marry Hugh, if you could," asked Effie.

"I should want that, it would be logical for Caerwyn, and perhaps I do." She stared out the window. "Yet I think it is not the match my father would have wished for me." She pulled her wool wrap tighter.

"He would have wished a man from a Gaelic family." Yet her father had not figured on the power these English had gained in the West, and in such a short time. It seemed the past could not help her. What was the right thing to do now? For Caerwyn and its peoples? And for herself? She rubbed her forehead. "I have been down to the town again, did you know it?"

"I knew you went out, but I wasn't sure where. It is dangerous, are you careful? What were you doing there?"

"I saw someone I thought I knew. And it was true, I found him. One of the men who works our fields. He's even brought his wife and children here." Ailsa shook her head. "He doesn't mean to return to Caerwyn. Not next planting season. Never."

Effie continued to sew. "I suppose," she said, "you'll have to get your new husband to drag him back, once you've decided who that husband is."

"I suppose," said Ailsa. "That's what I must do, if Caerwyn is to thrive. We need to grow enough food to live. But, if they want to leave, if they can have a better life here?"

Effie put down her sewing. "The king means to tie the workers to the land, as is done on the big estates in England and in France. He would back you, if you seek to return them." She sewed again, picking out a daisy in yellow thread. "It's why you must think with care about who you'll choose. The de Morvilles certainly have power, and Hugh's father is the king's closest advisor. They have lands and wealth and an honorable name."

"Lands and wealth and a name are much, but surely not all," said Ailsa quietly. She turned to the window to cool her hot cheeks. "He has not said anything to me anyway." Hugh had returned from his estates several days earlier. He had been her constant companion these last few days, and it had been well noted by all the ladies at the court. He was witty and handsome, she admitted, and she felt flattered he had apparently chosen her. Yet he kept her off balance somehow.

And what of Robert and his urgent voice saying, wait, promise me you will wait.

Hugh was much the better match in every way, if she must marry an Englishman. She listed off the reasons in her head. He was from one of the highest placed English families, his father loved and trusted by the king. He was handsome and courteous. He was wealthy and held estates in his own right and did not need hers. And though English, at least he would be her choice. Caerwyn would be well protected.

And yet with a marriage all would be so changed. And she had not told Hugh about her workers. Instead, she had given them all the coin in her purse and wished them well.

The king had returned, so the dinner tables were crowded again, and though Lent continued, Ailsa noticed the fish and breads and fruits were heaped in plenty on the platters. Though she was impatient, she knew she must wait on the king's pleasure. He had much business to conduct, and she would have to wait some days, even weeks, to hear his decision. She found her seat and greeted her neighbors, then sat, twisting one of her blue hair ribbons around her finger.

Robert had not yet returned from Arran. Could she hope he'd be delayed until she'd had a chance to speak again to the king? Behind her, above the din of voices and clattering tableware, she heard a familiar voice.

"You are looking most enchanting."

Hugh, clothed in the black silks he favored, bent over her hand and kissed it, lingering a moment overlong. Then he straddled the bench she sat on.

"Do you not need to sit at the high table?" she asked.

"I will sit nowhere but here." He took his jeweled knife and carved slices from the platter of fish nearby and added onions and a dried pear. He ate little, just watched her, and refilled his goblet of wine. A dog slunk up to their feet, whining for scraps. "Be off, cur." Hugh booted it away.

Ailsa cast about in her mind for a topic of conversation. "How did you find your estates?" she began, for though he had talked much of the hunting he'd done in the eastern forests since he returned to the court, she'd learned little else concerning his time away.

"What?" he asked, frowning. "Oh fine, to be sure." He launched into a monologue about the bad weather, boring villagers, and lack of entertainments at Lauderdale.

She puzzled over this as he talked, for it had been dull here at court too; it was Lent, after all. She wondered uneasily what he would think of Caerwyn. It was not much compared to Irvine, his father's grand castle. Hugh went back to drinking steadily from his goblet. "Is anything wrong," she asked finally, uncertain if she should intrude.

"I long for this dinner to be over." He straightened up, pushing his wine away. "I long to be alone with you."

His eyes were reddened by the wine. When he placed a possessive hand on the small of her back, she felt herself stiffen.

"Come," he said, "it is stuffy in here." Though the dinner had not ended, and she did not wish to go, she also did not wish to call attention, so she followed Hugh through the crowded hall and out the door.

It was clear, but chill, and Hugh placed his cloak around her neck with much ceremony, his hands lingering as they pinned the brooch at her neck. The cloak was of black silk, and not very warm. He grasped her hand and pulled her along, toward the castle gardens, through the gate, and on into the far gardens, where the wildflowers and grasses would grow come summer. Now it was dark and the ground still hard with late winter, but there was a scent of green things in the air. She sniffed appreciatively and walked along, wondering where he was taking her.

Hugh stopped near a stand of oak trees, still bare of leaves. Stars shone through the interlacing branches, reminding her suddenly of a similar stand of trees at home. "I wonder that you did not enjoy your time at your estates," she said looking up. "I am missing mine, though the court is wonderful." She turned to look at him, smiling at the thought of home, and was surprised by the grim look on his face. "What is it?"

"Ailsa, you must listen to me, for I must declare my feelings."

She tried to take a step back, but he grasped her waist, and thrust his face close to hers. His blue eyes were black in the night.

"I wish to marry. We are well matched and I find you entrancing."

She drew in a breath.

"I should speak to your kinsman first, but," he said, "I thought you an independent woman and I wanted to know your own heart and mind."

"I hardly know," she stumbled out. Feeling awkward, and annoyed at herself for letting this conversation happen, she tried to pull her hands away.

Hugh pulled her closer.

"Lord de Morville, please," she stammered, trying to push him away, but gently.

"Call me Hugh." He frowned. "You have let me think you welcomed me."

"I do." Her voice sounded shaky even to her own ears. "At least I think so. I must have some time to decide."

He hesitated, then laughed suddenly and released her. "Of course. I have thought long on this, but you will need time. You must think," he agreed, in his usual charming voice. "Please forgive me, I am but so anxious for your answer."

She regarded him silently, relieved by his return to his normal courtly manners, but puzzled by his manner.

"But not for too long," he said, and placed a possessive hand around the back of her neck, under her hair, drawing her toward him. He let his lips brush over hers. "Not for long, Ailsa, for I cannot stand to wait. Say yes to me, you have but to tell the king of your wishes…" He held out a hand. "Let us return to the dinner, for I have heard there will be tales told, though it is Lent."

Her mind whirling, she walked back with him to the hot and noisy hall. Not long echoing in her head.

Hours later, Ailsa left the great hall, her head crowded with a jostle of new thoughts. She wished she could wake Effie, but her friend had disappeared with Davy earlier in the evening.

Something so new and so important and no one to tell.

She slipped out the door and walked through the deserted kitchen garden, her skirts brushing over the dead rosemary and onion tops.

After the king's dinner, there had been three storytellers and the tales they told were entirely new to her, brought, she expected, from somewhere far, perhaps the Continent. That had been exciting, but the unexpected part had been the third storyteller. A woman! Women told their tales around the peat fires in their villages or in their own homes of course, but never had she heard a woman tell tales in a great hall, in front of everyone, much less in front of the king.

And the woman, who had spoken last and longest, had been so compelling. Her eyes grew wide and dark as she spoke and her face seemed to change and alter and hold every emotion. Her voice, low and haunting, seemed to seek out every corner of the huge hall and silence every sound and draw everyone leaning in closer and closer to hear.

And it had been the woman, the very same mysterious woman she had seen by the River Eden speaking into the air that day. Eachna, that was her name.

Ailsa couldn't think of sleep at all. She waited, walking about the kitchen garden to keep warm, until dawn approached, a few hours only as the days were lengthening already. She walked out the unguarded gate, using the dim light to guide her way, and followed along the twisting path until she found the old bridge with the flowing water of the river moving ceaselessly below. And there she found Eachna, washing her long dark hair in the cold water.

She approached, and Eachna nodded to her, seeming unsurprised to see her, and continued rinsing her hair. Then she dried it with a linen cloth and left it loose to curl in the mist. "I dislike the smell of grease and smoke," she said. "A sad thing for one of my profession. I must duck my head in cold water near every morning."

Ailsa sat opposite her. "Will you teach me?"

The woman paused in unsnarling her hair. "And why should I do that?"

"I want to learn. I want to tell a story as you do."

"Many think that, but it's not the work of one or two days to learn such."

"I know how to work hard and turn up day after day," said Ailsa.

"But I will not be here day after day," said the woman, standing up and picking up her basket.

"What can I offer you? What do you want?"

The woman laughed. "What I want cannot be delivered by you."

"But you can give me what I want, what I need." Ailsa hesitated, wondering what she could say to persuade this woman. "Perhaps it would give you pleasure to pass it on, this ability of yours."

The woman stared down at her, seeming to truly see her for the first time. Then she smiled, with a flash of even white teeth. "If you are sure, come tomorrow, at this hour in the morning, and we will see." She walked away, her back straight and her long hair curling at her waist.

Ailsa watched her go. Would she grow as confident and sure as this woman? As free?

"But you must come alone and you must tell no one," said the woman, over her shoulder. "No one."

CHAPTER SIXTEEN

At Sea Near Arran

R OBERT LAUGHED ALOUD as the saltwater sprayed over his face.
"Good to be alive on a day like this."

"Yes," said Will dubiously, and he edged over to Robert's side.
"You take to the sea like a selkie." His normally genial voice emerged
grumpy.

Robert grinned. They'd been on the water all day, the wind working for them. Arran was near but he regretted having to land at all.
He loved the sail snapping and the rushing sound of white-capped
waves as they parted at the bow.

They sailed into a perfect harbor, ringed with purple hills, just
as the sun set behind Arran's hills. Dories piled with nets and two
larger fishing boats dotted the quiet waters. There were also four
bright painted galleys pulled up on the beach. Those could do serious
damage in a raid on the mainland, each holding some twenty men
and built for speed. Shallow-drafted, they could be hauled ashore on
any beach for easy landing.

They put a coracle over the side and climbed in. Robert left two
men on the boat with strict orders to stay at the port, ready for
immediate departure when they were through with their task for the
king. The beach was still, though peat smoke rose from the trees; no
doubt the village sat there, safe from the winter winds that would
beat this shore.

They set off, weapons loosed but not in hand. Robert had the
feeling they were watched, though he could see no one. Arran was

a big island, he knew, for he had a rough map the king's clerk had provided him. Already he could see the good earth and plentiful streams that would make a prosperous settlement. People lived here, many people, but the woods appeared empty.

Suddenly there was a grunt and a shout. "Halt."

Ahead of him, Will stopped short. Armed men surrounded them, silent, but with raised weapons. Robert gestured to his sheathed sword. "We seek your lord," he said. "MacLaughlin of Arran."

"Who speaks?"

"Robert of Caerwyn. I come with word from the king."

There was silence at that. "What king?" called out one of the men finally, his tone belligerent, but he was silenced with a sharp look from his leader.

"I come with word from David, King of all Scotia," said Robert.

There was silence again, then the leader said, "Follow." He led them off the path straight into the woods, and they stumbled after, for he set a fast pace and they did not know the land.

They walked for some four miles, Robert estimated, skirting the hills the whole time, crossing fields and boggy meadows and clambering over granite. They arrived finally to a settlement situated under large chestnut trees and well hidden from the port and transient visitors like themselves. It was full dark and a brisk wind blowing when they were finally ushered into one of the huts. Inside was a hearth, cold now, but with wood and peat stacked nearby. And a pile of straw sufficient for pallets.

"You'll bide here," said the leader and banged the door shut. Robert shrugged as he met Will's anxious eyes.

The next morning, grey light filtered through chinks in the thatched roof. Before long, the door was flung open, letting in a blast of cold wind. A religious man, dressed in a brown tunic and hood, entered, along with their guard of last night. "I am brother Gille," he said, his accent tinged with a sound of Normandy. "Welcome to Arran. I understand you wish to see my brother?"

A younger son, thought Robert. He got to his feet. "We must see MacLaughlin on the king's business."

Gille nodded. "Then follow me, if you would."

They donned their cloaks and followed, walking again through forest, deep and pathless. Yet the monk seemed to have little difficulty finding his way. Twigs snapped under their feet, and a red squirrel scurried out of their way. Once, Robert saw a fox, staring and still by a granite boulder. In the distance, he began to hear a dull roar, which he realized was the sea, wind carrying the sound. They walked most of the morning, climbing gradually, but ever uphill.

Midday, they reached a sun-dappled clearing. In the center rose a manor house built of timber and beaten earth. Narrow windows looked from a tower over the firs and oaks. "From here," Robert said quietly to Will, "you could see the whole island and the sea beyond in all directions." His host was indeed a cautious man. They were ushered into a hall, decorated in the Gaelic style with interlacing carvings of fantastic animals. Robert noted the fangs of a giant serpent twined around an ancient oak tree. They were made to sit and fed bannocks and apples.

As they finished, the door was flung open and a guard appeared. "Which of you is Sir Robert?"

"I am."

"Come," said the guard, gesturing with his leather-bound arm. Robert ignored Will's quick frown and followed, hearing the heavy door bolted behind him. They climbed a steep stair and he was ushered into a chamber with rough walls and a narrow window looking west. The man left him there, shutting the solid door behind him. There were two benches and a small table, built of the same oak. Having inspected the room, Robert waited, watching the sea, the waves wrinkles on a grey cloth from this height. Clouds were gathering overhead, and the sea was soon patterned with rain drops.

Boots clumped up the stairs and the door opened. Three men crowded in. The first was dressed in simple clothes of excellent deep blue wool. He wore no weapons but an eating knife at his heavy belt. His face was grey-bearded, and shaggy brows topped his eyes. He did not speak but stood off to the side and stared. Robert returned the look, turning only when one of the others finally spoke.

"I am Dugald," said the man. "Cousin to the Lady Ailsa of Caerwyn."

Robert inspected the man, sandy haired, bearded, and strongly muscled. Ailsa's cousin. She had not spoken of him at all. But then, they'd hardly had the time or proper chance to speak of much.

"And I am Torquil," said the third man.

"He hails from this Isle," said Dugald, "as do I. Thus we have an interest."

"And I am MacLaughlin," said the man by the window. "You seek me," he said. "What have you to say?"

"I bring you cordial greetings from the king."

MacLaughlin nodded, but his face conveyed nothing.

"The king sends me to discover what I may about rumors of rebellion. Perhaps from the Dubliners, or the Galwegians, or this warrior bishop naming himself Wimond. David would know the hearts of his subjects in these Isles," he said.

A smile appeared on MacLaughlin's face. "You do not beat about with the small talk of the court, I see."

Robert shrugged. "I do the king's bidding. He seeks to build some bridges, meld the ways of Gael, Norse, and English in these parts."

"Does he now," said MacLaughlin. "Be those your words, or the king's?"

Robert shrugged again.

"Why come now?"

"The why is of no consequence. The king orders it, so I am here. With a task to complete."

MacLaughlin laughed again. "We welcome you. Learn what you will, we have naught to hide here, and meantime be honored as our guest."

"We may move freely?" said Robert, not yet taking his extended hands.

"Come, we are about to have our meal and we can talk."

Over a dinner of fresh caught fish, stewed apples, and watered ale, Robert learned that his host was lord of the entire island as his father had been before him. They traded with Ireland, sending sheep wool and hides in exchange for silver work and jewelry, which they sold on the mainland. Business was good, what with the new-found taste of the court for such luxuries. No quiet backwater, thought Robert, for where the merchants and traders came, news would flow. Indeed, the room in which they ate was richly furnished with carvings, embroidered hangings, and jeweled silverwork. Close to the fine surroundings of a prince. These islands were a law unto themselves, he surmised. No wonder David was concerned about the Isles and their loyalty.

"Is there a market held on the island?" he asked.

"Aye, on Wednesdays," answered his host, "even through the winter months. Dugald and Torquil go there tomorrow to sell wool. They can take you, if you like."

Robert saw Dugald grimace at the offer, but as quickly mask his disapproval. Interesting. But he said only, "I'll be ready."

Next day, they walked down a path wide enough for a cart, the first he'd seen on the island. He yawned as he walked, for despite MacLaughlin's apparent geniality, he'd been returned to the uncomfortable hut for the night. They reached a generously sized clearing. The morning was cool, soft clouds puffing high in a blue sky. Merchants were setting up. Robert observed the arrival of a stream of carts and horses from the south and the west. There must be small roads connecting with ports in those directions. A man could learn much in a gathering place like this.

"Come along then," said Dugald, his voice abrupt.

Robert trailed after Ailsa's cousin, skirting a cart loaded with squawking chickens, and another piled with barrels of ale. The sound of merchants hawking fish pies and roasted nuts filled his ears. He sniffed appreciatively. There'd been no time for food before they left.

Dugald did not stop though, so he followed as they threaded their way to the far side of the clearing where two wagons were settled under an oiled canvas. Here Dugald stopped and lifted the heavy canvas aside, grunting when Robert bent to help. Underneath, wool was piled in curling heaps of brown and grey. Dugald started sorting the wools by color and quality. He ignored Robert, who went to sit on a granite ledge and surveyed the crowds gathering. There were villagers, obviously farmers, and many women with children, so there must be other small settlements nearby, hidden in the woods and backed against the hills out of the winds. There were rough looking men, their tunics short, who must be seafarers. Near the cloth wagons, he saw a tall and slender woman, dressed in deepest blue. Her hair shone gold even at this distance.

Robert glanced at Dugald who was staring at him with an unreadable expression. "She lives here?"

"At times," said Dugald, his voice unfriendly. "When she wills. She is the half-sister of MacLaughlin's wife and widow of an Irish lord who traded often in these parts."

Ailsa's cousin was a puzzle. What side was he on in these troubled times? Dugald had returned to his work, but his eyes had been dark with anger.

After midday, the merchants drew their carts into a rough circle on the outskirts of the clearing. Families consumed their meals, while babies napped, and small children played noisy games under the trees. Dugald had sorted his wool and bargained long with several merchants. Now he placed his heavy pouch in his leather pack, and strode off, calling, "Let's go," over his shoulder. Robert followed him to the edge of the clearing where a group gathered around a man stringing a bow.

Men called out encouragement and jokes and then fell silent. The target was placed. The man, his bow near as tall as he, aimed, and the arrow flew, arching into the blue sky and down, into the center of the target. Men yelled their approval and the small man waved, blushing, and gathered up his arrows. Robert tried to gauge the distance they were shooting. Far, but not as far as he'd shot at home. Though he had no bow here with him. Several more men took their turns, and some came close to the target, but none hit it as the small man had. Robert felt the gaze of Dugald's eyes on him before he heard the shouted challenge. "And you Sir Robert, will you try our little game?" Dugald's loud voice carried over the field, as he intended, silencing the crowd.

Curse him, thought Robert, moving to the center of the field. So much for staying inconspicuous. "Yet I have no bow," he called.

"Give the English fellow a bow," called a man. "Aye, let him try it." The crowd shouted approval and a bow was retrieved from the small man, who handed it, unstrung, with a wry smile on his face. Robert thanked him. He walked to the end of the field and turned to assess the target. It was very far away, surely near to the bow's range. He lifted the weapon in his hand. It was a beauty, polished and perfectly weighted. He strung it and heard the crowd hush. He raised the bow and sighted the arrow. He watched it fly, heard the crowd sigh as it stabbed right into the target's center.

The small man walked with Dugald to the target and they examined the two arrows. Dugald, frowning, raised an arm. There were a few cheers from the crowd, but most shifted uneasily and drifted away.

Dugald returned. "You're good with the bow to equal Malcolm. Where did you learn?"

Robert handed the bow back to the small man, who seemed to hold no grudge for he grinned at him as he turned to go. "At home as a boy." He knew Dugald wondered how an Englishman knew how to shoot a Welsh bow, but he said nothing more.

Dugald glared at him and then sighed. "My cousin is a difficult woman, but she is my cousin," he said. He hesitated, then clapped Robert on the back. "A whiskey for all," he called, and a keg was wheeled out. The fiddler struck up a tune. Robert found himself being twirled about by a hefty apple seller, and then by a comely miss from the village, but the woman in the deep blue gown had disappeared.

Several days later, Robert woke late, head heavy with ale. He and Will had been moved to the MacLaughlin manor, and while that signaled he'd passed a test of some sort, it came with the discomfort of late nights. He walked to the window and shoved open the wooden shutter. Bright sunlight streamed in, making him wince.

It was past time to make progress on the king's business. But how? His experience was all with direct fighting. With strategy for besieging and taking a castle, or by preference, with designing defenses and building. This matter of discovering information called for different skills. MacLaughlin was clever. Was it coincidence that led to so many pre-Easter festivities timed with his arrival, so many relatives over from Ireland to be entertained, or was he being diverted from his purpose?

Dugald and Torquil had been friendly enough companions over the past few days, but he had discovered little from them on the subject of loyalties or rebellion in the Isles. Were people here truly ignorant of the bishop Wimond's treasonous claims? Did they support David and his plans for a united Scotia? Rumor was Wimond was in Galloway now, far from his home base of Man, and if he knew that so did Dugald, yet nothing was said. And what did Ailsa's cousin think about her impending marriage to him?

Robert threw on his clothes and went out, ignoring the pounding in his head and the puddles scattered over the courtyard. A dozen landowners probably gathered on Arran this day, here for the spring trading and Easter, and perhaps for some other purpose of MacLaughlin's? He'd begin with them.

By nightfall, Robert was tired but pleased. He'd shaken off his shadows, Torquil and Dugald, with a ruse about a repair to his boat, necessitating a day back at the port. They weren't fools, but he thought they were glad enough to take the hint and head off to their own business. Perhaps they thought he'd find little information. He'd sent the gregarious Will to seek out villagers and servants who might be willing to talk. Then he'd taken a horse and struck out on a south bound path.

It had been easy enough to locate the manors of the local landholders, for each was surrounded by cleared fields, empty of grain and activity this time of year. He'd found three at home. Impatient with the diplomacy of the courts, he'd been direct. He'd found Olaf, a big man who looked clumsy but proved to be quick on his feet, practicing arms with a few of his men. Invited to join in, first, they'd arm wrestled, then they'd had a session of swordplay in the small timbered courtyard. He'd been invited to the midday meal, and after, he'd said simply. "I am here on the king's business."

A loud grunt was Olaf's response.

"I am now lord of Caerwyn, and as such, one of you, but as you know I'm also of David's court. English and French though I am by training and birth, I am also of Welsh blood on my mother's side and I was raised in the Welsh countryside well into my youth. I see both sides." He stopped, unused to unburdening himself so.

Olaf peered at him with narrowed eyes, brow furrowed.

"So I ask you," continued Robert, "what think you of this Wimond and his complaints against the king. Is he justified?"

Olaf had laughed and settled his big frame back in his carved chair. "This Wimond is an ambitious fool and a charlatan, but that doesna stop him from seeing people's needs and desires. We of the Isles are traders first. We see the good of different ways. We're a sea faring people, and well used to taking a custom here or another from there and melding them. But this David, he must not lose sight that it's our choice to make the calls, what we take and what we don't."

Thinking over Olaf's blunt words, Robert realized they made sense. This island outpost was far from Scotia's centers of power, and it was none too sure that David could keep invaders out, even if it were one of his priorities. The people here needed to be self-reliant and along with that came a fair bit of independence.

But he wasn't sure how David would take this. A good king and a pious man. But raised in Henry's court all the same. Brother to Henry's queen, he'd been the privileged court favorite as a youth, and English ways were close to his heart. To David, a kingdom meant united territories, under his feudal power, with lords paying homage to him and owing him service for the lands, and it meant workers tied to the fields, producing wealth for those lords.

Robert got to his feet. The glimpse of community he'd seen at the market was something different entirely. Free men, trading, laughing, living. He sighed. He hadn't thought much about these matters, not for many years, and it was painful. His duty here was just to relay the message. Not to take sides.

Restless, he walked out into the cold evening air, and took a deep breath. The scent of fir and sea met him. He passed through the gates, when the guards back was turned, and found a well-trodden path, heading along the fields. A good walk would clear his mind. He wasn't sure Dugald and Torquil would give him a second whole day so easily.

He walked for a time, deliberately emptying his mind, appreciating the smells of spring approaching. Wet earth, wild garlic, green ferns. Suddenly, he stopped. Yes, there it was again, a sound out of keeping with the woods all around, a metallic clanking. He stepped into the trees at the road's edge, loosening his dagger.

A man appeared, walking stealthily, peering ahead in the darkening pathway, looking for his prey. Silently, Robert moved behind the man and held his dagger to the back of his neck. "Who do you seek and why?" The man tried to stammer out a reply. Robert could feel him shaking.

"I'm sent to ask you to meet my lady," he got out.

Robert gripped his shoulder and swung him around. "Why sneak up on me?"

"She said to come upon you silently, to let no one else know."

"Who is your lady?"

"I cannot say sir, but I am supposed to bring you to her. She has important news for you about the bishop Wimond."

It could be a trap, but he had put the word out that he was seeking information and would pay for it. He let the man's shoulder go. "Where?"

"This way," said the man, clearly relieved to be out of his grasp. Immediately he started off at a fast pace down a winding route through the woods, barely more than a deer path. Robert followed, his ears straining for sounds of ambush. The woods were silent but for the crackling of their boots on dried sticks. After perhaps two miles, they turned off the path and followed a route downhill toward the sea.

"Here." The servant stopped before a clearing, and then faded into the woods before Robert could question him further. A timber house of two stories rose in the clearing. Small windows on the upper level showed the glow of candlelight; below all was dark.

Robert approached the silent house, skirting around in a circle, but there were no guards on any side. As he reached the front again, the sturdy door swung open on well oiled hinges. He could see nothing in the darkness within but he caught the scent of a spicy perfume.

"Enter," a woman's voice said, "and be at home in my house."

He moved forward, cautious, but he was pulled over the doorstep by a soft hand on his sleeve. He saw a lady, dressed in a dark gown of some rustling material, a veil drawn over her face. "Please, follow me to a more comfortable chamber where we can talk," she said, and mounted the stairs, spiraling up in the dark. He shrugged and followed her.

They entered a circular room, brightened by a fire in a stone hearth and by two heavy silver candelabra on a wooden table. As his eyes accustomed themselves to the light, he noticed the walls were covered in jewel-toned hangings of wool and silk. The room smelled pleasantly of beeswax. A sumptuous chamber.

His hostess drew off her veil, flinging it down on the floor. "I hate these things, but it was necessary."

He drew in a breath. It was the lady he'd seen at the market earlier that week. Her bright hair, outlined by the firelight, glowed. Her gown of some midnight colored shining cloth clung to her body and whispered when she moved. She reached out a hand, her full sleeve falling back to show a white arm. "Come, sit by me, for I have much to tell you."

He shut the door against the cold air from the stairs and tried not to stare. "A welcome surprise." She motioned to the bench beside her and he smiled, but continued to stand. "What have you to tell me, that requires me to come to you in the deep of night?"

She assessed him a moment, then turned her face so it was shadowed from him. She gestured to the table drawn up to the fire. "Surely you will have some refreshment before we speak." She poured red wine from a silver pitcher into a chased goblet, drank a sip from it, then handed it to him.

He took a sip, wondering what she wanted. It was quiet in the manor. There should be the sounds of servants and guards. A companion of some sort.

The woman smiled, seeming to read his thoughts. She strolled across the room, creaked open a chest, and returned with a box of carved wood. "In this box," she said, "is proof of my sister's husband, MacLaughlin of Arran's, loyalties." She held it out.

He did not move. "Why give it to me?"

She did not answer but put the box on the bench beside him and turned her back to him. "Look if you wish, or not. I care little for the affairs of men." Her gold hair looked soft as it fell over her white shoulders, and though she clearly knew it, still she was stunningly beautiful. She leaned toward him. "I asked you here for another reason."

"And what would that be?" He smelled her perfume of exotic flowers, such as the women in Normandy were wont to wear, and as she lifted her dark lashes he noticed her eyes were the blue of gentian flowers.

"Will you not have some more wine?" she asked, "my brother-in-law imports it and shares it with me when the mood strikes."

He agreed and sipped, thinking hard. Her brother-in-law could not know she was here, inviting a man such as he to visit her in the night. He doubted the lord of Arran would be well pleased. Or, had he planned it?

She took the cup from him and placed it on the table. Around them, the house was still and the night winds in the trees outside the only sound.

She touched him on the cheek with her white hand, with a small smile of triumph. "Do you find me beautiful," she said, her voice low, clearly knowing the answer. She let her silvery shawl drop down around her waist. The bodice of her midnight gown was cut low and wide across white breasts. This one was a practiced seductress, he thought, but found his hand reaching for her bared shoulder. She tipped her head back, letting him see her long white throat. She was like the many ladies of Normandy, practiced in pleasing a man, but she was exceptional too, most unusually lovely.

"Stay with me," she murmured, "'tis so lonely since my husband died, and there are no interesting men here. I am alone." Her fingers reached for his tunic laces and she slipped her hands inside onto his bare chest.

The sudden loud call of a bird outside made him start. "And this box," he found himself saying, leaning away from her. He picked it up and she laughed and took it from him. "Later."

He put his goblet down on the table and bowed, and backed away. The woman froze for a moment, an odd look in her eyes. Then she reached out her hand, "Come," she said, "there is no need to fear MacLaughlin, or any other. Tonight, I am only Alice." She opened a curtain and gestured to a wide bed, covered in furs. "Come," she murmured, "you are not one to be worried about the Lord of Arran's wrath, I would wager." She untied the laces up her bodice side, looking into his eyes.

He saw triumph again, and something else. He moved to the door.

"You do not want me?" she said, her voice no longer melodious, but harsh and incredulous.

"Forgive me, you are enchantment indeed." He evaded her hands. "Please understand, I have one who waits for me." Even as he said this, he wondered at his own words.

Alice smiled, confident again. "I can teach you many things your lady will never know."

"No doubt," he said, and his fingers found the door latch and swung the door open. A chill wind rushed in and fluttered her skirts.

"Men talk," she said, pulling her shawl up over her bare shoulders, her eyes snapping. "I can tell you what you want to know, about this fool bishop Wimond. And of another. More dangerous even." She laughed harshly. She pointed across the room to the carved wooden box. "I could tell you much, if I chose."

He considered her silently. "It is not my way," he said at last.

Robert and Will rode abreast, the sturdy small horses of the island plodding along. Will told him what he'd learned from a farmer willing to talk, for he had a grievance against MacLaughlin. According to this farmer, Fergus, the second biggest landholder on the isle and

MacLaughlin's rival, was gathering men at his manor in the south of Arran.

"We must find out what these rebels against the king are after. Why would men follow this Wimond anyway, what does he offer?" Robert frowned and stared off into the trees, where the buds on the overhanging branches were just beginning to swell with the coming of spring. He'd told Will of his strange encounter with Alice the night before. Will had laughed at first, but then scrunched up his forehead and said it was best if they left Arran sooner rather than later. Robert agreed. Something wasn't right here. He clucked to his horse, who would not be hurried. "I begin to wonder. They keep throwing this Wimond in our face. It seems too obvious. Could he be a distraction? Is it true the real threat lies elsewhere?"

"Maybe so," said Will slowly. "It's true that Wimond has only the strength to harry David and not to overcome him."

"He claims royal descent, a powerful elixir to those with grievances," said Robert. "Still, I think we must look beyond this Wimond. To someone else guiding events. To this Somerled we've heard mention of perhaps."

"They say he's powerful and crafty, though young yet. But he has made a treaty with David, has he not? David gave him Bute to seal their peace. Though it's rumored he has gathered galleys enough to challenge anyone since."

"Even the king?" mused Robert. "I wonder if he would dare."

By midafternoon they approached Fergus' manor.

Fergus had a stomach that stuck out in front but he was solid with muscles and his shrewd eyes narrowed as they stared at Robert and Will, in the courtyard of his manor. "Join us for a meal," he grated out, and left them to the servants. They brushed the mud from their clothes and then waited, Will lying on a bench and Robert pacing.

Will opened his eyes finally. "What's got into you?"

"I just want to finish with this business for the king." He stopped pacing. "And I'm wishing I'd looked in that carved box of hers."

"It does make you wonder what was inside," agreed Will, getting up and pouring some water from a pitcher. "Could be anything from a comb to a jewel to a letter. Some sort of writ. But no help for it now."

At dinner, twelve men, all having holdings on the southern part of Arran, were gathered for the meal and a day of hunting on the morrow. The mood was boisterous, and all were drinking mead served in silver goblets chased with Gaelic designs. Fergus related a story of chasing a red deer with magical speed. He was a good tale teller and his listeners laughed uproariously and groaned at all the appropriate moments. He launched into a new tale fast upon finishing the first, and Robert saw no way to turn the conversation closer to his interests. He wondered if the tales were supposed to tell him something, or just served to avoid any serious talk. On Fergus' heavy wooden chair, intricately carved animals writhed under his thick arms, and his fingers traced the long tail of a ferocious dragon.

Will caught his eye; someone new had entered the room. A big man swung off his heavy cloak, handing it to a servant. Dugald. He greeted their host with loud voice and hearty handclaps on back and shoulders, and then turned to the other guests. He nodded to Robert, not looking surprised to see him. Then he swung back to Fergus and said, "I bring news."

"Ah? Out with it then," Fergus commanded.

Dugald took a goblet from the hovering servant. He took a long swig, seeming to savor both the drink and the attention. "Interesting news," he said, "for all of us here on the Isles," and his eyes rested on Robert. "Wimond, he's made a formal claim."

"What sort of claim," said Fergus. "The man seems loud mouthed enough for a bishop, and not with praying either."

"He's saying he's a natural son to Angus of Moray. In line to be king himself."

"'Tis not news, he's been claiming royal descent all these months."

"Others have said it. But now he claims it himself, and publicly," Dugald said and took another swig from the goblet. "And, he's spilled blood over it, in Galloway."

"And what if he is a true son to Angus?" asked a young man, jumping up from his bench.

Fergus abruptly gestured the youth silent. The room fell quiet, save for the snapping of the fire. Fergus said, as though to himself. "What is he after?"

"My man brought this news with the load of ironwork shipped in today and I have brought it to you all, as befits our common purpose," said Dugald.

Robert looked up and saw Dugald's eyes on him.

Fergus stood up, shoving his big chair back from the table. "We'll speak no more of this tonight," he commanded. He pounded on the table with his goblet and servants rushed in with more mead, while he launched into another hunting tale.

Had Fergus been surprised along with the rest tonight? Or was it all an elaborate ruse to fool the strangers? Later, Robert and Will spoke of it. "Dugald wishes us to know, telling us in public like that. This Wimond must feel sure of support to go beyond vague rumor and make a formal claim, and back it with arms. Does he not fear the charge of treason? Perhaps Dugald hopes to encourage us to rush off to the king with the news, leaving them free to plan and act as they will?"

Will nodded.

"Yet, if I do not take the news, I could be branded traitor. It could seem I've withheld this important information." Robert sighed. "They have boxed us in."

"We should return to Carlisle first thing," said Will.

"But we still don't know who leads in this. Is it Wimond the bishop, or is he just a decoy and the real threat is this Somerled, whom David has made a treaty with and who he trusts?" Robert was quiet for several minutes, listening to the fire crackle. Then he said, "Yet strangely, I find I am with these Islesmen on much."

Will tossed a stick on the fire.

"This way of life," Robert said, "was much like mine before Henry wrested it away from my family, exiling me from my home and sending me off to Normandy. Still, the quarreling of the Gaelic and Norse princes must stop. Peace for crops and families is important, and David can bring that. Perhaps." He peered out the window into the dark night. A brisk wind brought the smell of salt. "I'll leave tomorrow morning, on the early tide, and tell the king what we've learned. I must, or be open to charges of traitor myself. I'll wager Fergus will be sending a ship on the same tide for further news. So you'll stay here, Will. Finish our task. Gather what further information you can. On Wimond and Somerled both."

Will's face screwed up into a knot of wrinkles. "If you are too honest with the king, you may lose all. Lands and lady. Are you prepared for that?"

Robert sighed. "I just hope to avoid the hangman now."

"You'll think of something. You always do." Will was quiet a moment. "Do you still think to strip the lands of Caerwyn and use the coin to ride against fitz John in Wales?"

"What would you have me do? I made a vow."

Will sighed. "And the lady?"

"It is time to see Ailsa and speak openly with her as well."

"Her cousin plays a complicated game here," Will observed. "You're wondering still what part she plays in these plots?"

"I must know. I do not forget young Nevin."

"She might be innocent of that, or any plotting."

Robert shook his head.

"Times change. People change. The world changes," said Will. "It can't be wise to dwell always in one's past, vow or no vow."

CHAPTER SEVENTEEN

Carlisle

Ailsa left the castle when the guards were distracted by a keg of ale wheeled over by the kitchen maids. She walked along slowly, despite the shadows and the wind, lost in her thinking, waiting for the sun to rise enough to see her way. When she reached the River Eden, coiling dark and slow under the bridge, she stopped and stared at the moving water, the patterns formed by deep currents as water rolled over stones and circled sandbars. It was very quiet and for a few moments she felt afraid. She thought with longing of her warm pallet and wool blankets and Effie's comforting snuffles nearby.

Then she straightened her back and took a long breath. Each morning this month, well before dawn she had come, and she never knew what she would find, or if Eachna would even still be camped beside the river. Each morning, she was afraid, of the shadows, of the wind, or her own inability. But each morning she came. She had to do this.

She crossed over the bridge and took the path along the river, down into the tall grasses and the birches and finally along into the deeper forest.

When the servants had called for silence at the close of the Easter week feasting, and the three storytellers stood up to begin, up on the dais, nearly as high as the king, this time it had been Eachna who had begun the tales. Her low pitched voice carried with strange ease throughout the room and as she spoke the revelers fell quiet and quieter, shuffles and joking and coughing fading, until nothing could be heard but her words. She described a castle and the land about it, the sea marshes, the flowing green river, the elm trees, and the cloud-topped hills. She spoke of strange folk who lived within the hills, a people of the forest, and of their queen. All the creatures who lived with this queen, loved her, fought with her, crowded into the story. The pictures she painted made the king's hall fall away and a deep forest and fantastical castle seemed to swirl around them all. Even the smell of green moss seemed to fill the air.

After the tale finished, a second storyteller stepped forward and picked up the thread and Ailsa found herself breathing again. Even with the many tale tellers who had come to her father's hall, she had never seen or heard one who could make a story live as she did.

Eachna made it seem effortless. Ailsa knew now that was illusion. She'd met with the tale teller every dawn for an hour or for the entire morning, and always out in the forest somewhere by the flowing water. Eachna said sun and rain and mist would make her tales more true. She wasn't sure how that would be so, but she had decided to trust all she said and learn all she could. The lessons differed each day. Perhaps how to breathe so the voice came out resonant and rich. Perhaps how to weave in fantastical details and the rich and real smells and sounds of nature. Perhaps how to memorize long involved tales and how to invent and improvise within the basic familiar structure. She asked questions too. Sometimes she got answers.

On the third day, she'd asked, "I have never seen a woman story-teller. Is it common in other parts? In England or the Continent?"

Eachna laughed. "Not common, but there are some. As you see."

"How? How did you do it?"

"I wanted it. I listened, I practiced by myself in the woods, and one day I just stood up." She shrugged. "It wasn't smooth or easy, but it you want it, you do it. You must."

"I want it."

Eachna shrugged. "We shall see. If you truly want it, you must listen and learn the tales, but more, you must listen to your own life and the nearly silent voice behind your thoughts. Follow your own questions. Dare to wonder where they will lead. Weave your own stories in your head, and then aloud to your birch trees and the tall oaks, and then one day, you'll tell a tale that will mean something to you and also to someone else."

A brisk wind from the window tossed Ailsa's unbraided hair. Outside, cold rain poured down. The fields were greening under its steady fall, but the world looked downtrodden and ugly. She was trapped inside.

Ailsa turned from the window with a sigh. Eachna was gone. She'd searched for her every morning this week, but the horses, the three tale tellers, and all their magic were gone, as though they'd never been. How would she learn more?

Before she'd gone, Eachna had taken her on a trek through the forest after their lesson. They'd crossed through a stand of birches, their branches pink and tipped with pale green buds. They'd crossed a ridge crowned with hemlocks, thick and sprouting new green shoots on all their branches. They'd crossed a meadow, hidden between three hills and covered with white flowers that smelled sweet and had no name she knew. In the very center of the field, Eachna had stopped and sat down, cross legged.

She had smiled, then pointed to a spot in the tall grass and Ailsa had seen him, nearly hidden, as though alive and peering out at her. A little man. A carved granite man half the size of a true man. Puzzled, she'd looked to Eachna, but her teacher just ignored her and lay down on the grass and closed her eyes.

She'd circled the statue, who was, she could see on closer inspection, wearing a tunic with the cross and the shaved tonsure of a priest. When she walked around him, she was startled, for on the far side the Christian cleric disappeared and the carvings, she saw when she looked closer, were the same as those the druids of the forest carved into the huge old oaks, symbols of life ongoing, birthing and dying in an endless chain.

She looked to Eachna for guidance, but her teacher just laughed and said they must return to the castle. And the next morning, Eachna had been gone. If that was a way to say good bye, it was certainly annoying.

Effie sat by the hearth, chatting about Davy, for the couple had made an agreement last night to marry, no matter who disapproved. They had good hopes of achieving their end, for Davy's father was coming around. Ailsa listened to Effie's plans and tried to make the appropriate comments and feel joy for her friend. But though she did feel glad for her friend, it was hard to concentrate; her heart felt heavy.

By midmorning Ailsa had to escape. She made a weak excuse and left, ignoring the surprise on Effie's face. Miserable that she couldn't put aside her own concerns, she scolded herself as she walked out to the stables. When she entered the horse barn, she peeled off her dripping cloak and used it to wipe her face and dry her hair. She spent a quiet hour currying Nia, grateful that Robert had returned the mare to her when he took Tanet back. Though she'd been hard pressed to thank him.

She thought about Eachna and the strange message of the little man. What was she supposed to learn? It was frustrating to have to puzzle everything out for herself. She'd been learning so much, but now her teacher was simply gone. And the message she'd left was so confusing. A man facing one way and the other, toward the past of the druids and the present of the Christians. The problem with symbols was they were so ambiguous, just like all of life.

It was warm in the barn with the heat of the horses, and quiet save the drumming of rain on the timber roof and the occasional knock of a hoof against the wooden stalls. The scent of hay and horses reminded her of home. She thought of the salt smell of the sea, sweeping over her as she lay in her bed above the hall. Robert had not returned for the Easter feast or in the fortnight after. She patted Nia's soft neck. "And what do I care where he is anyway," she said aloud.

Nia whickered and put her soft muzzle in her hands. It must be the weather and the late hours and the unaccustomed wine. She hadn't slept well. It was noisy, the court full, and she woke each morning with her muscles stiff, as though she'd tightened them all night long. Yet, she must try to think, make some decisions. Hugh was pressing her more each night.

Caerwyn must be secured, at all costs. And to keep Caerwyn safe, she must marry. She could see that now. The king would not let her lands sit; he intended to marry her off to someone and soon. For the news from England was all of turmoil, and the king must be sure of his Western lands if he meant to wrest territory in Northumbria. And that was his prime ambition. So, if she wanted to be part of the decision, have some influence on who she would marry, she must make a choice, and there was little time.

She had ample reason to ask for a new audience. And the king would likely favor Hugh de Morville as her husband. Indeed, she considered, chewing on her lip, seeing those stern and cold grey eyes in her mind, perhaps it was best Robert had not returned from Arran. She should seek a meeting with the king; it was much better not to wait.

She wound a piece of straw tightly around her finger. She'd made Robert no promises. He'd asked her to wait, that strange day on the stairs, but for what? She must secure Caerwyn if she could, make it a safe place where people wished to stay and farm and live. With the English Hugh as her husband, Caerwyn would be protected from these other Englishmen.

She sat down in the hay and then curled up in a ball. How strange. She'd left Caerwyn so sure she could secure her people's safety and her own freedom, but duty had locked her further into an unlooked-for marriage. She'd started out with such hopes and daring, and found herself hiding in a dark closet and pursued like a deer in a hunt. She had not escaped at all.

Ailsa sat outside the king's chamber, clothed in her best linen dress. An unaccustomed headdress of white linen covered her hair and she pressed her hands together in her lap to avoid fiddling with it. She was nervous, but this audience with the king would go much differently from the last, she would make certain.

She waited, watching various lords and churchmen being ushered into the king's presence and ushered out again. When the king's squire passed her by yet another time, she rose to her feet. "Surely my turn to see the king must have come. I know that I arrived before those priests you ushered in."

"All churchmen proceed first according to the king's wishes."

Ailsa felt herself color under his haughty stare. "I must see the king now," she said, abandoning all attempt at sophistication.

"Many have urgent business."

She sank down on the bench with a sigh of frustration. The door to the outside corridor banged open. Three men rushed in, dressed all in moss green, spattered with mud. "Urgent news for the king," the largest shouted as he passed her. They were hustled into the king's chamber, and the door shut in the faces of the gathering knot of petitioners wondering what the news could be, all whispering, their red faces clustered together.

Ailsa waited with the rest, wondering what this latest intrusion would do for her chances at admittance. There was silence from the chamber and then the sound of raised voices. The door banged open again, knocking an elderly nun on the elbow. David himself, with a tremendous frown, strode from the hall with never a glance at the people waiting there. He was followed by a rush of courtiers and clerks all grabbing their belongings and hurrying after.

Silenced for a moment as they all flew by, the excited crowd began to speculate. A nun sitting next to Ailsa, said kindly, "They'll be no seeing the king this day, best run along now. He'll no be back today, nor likely for several days 'till whatever this is blows over."

At the dinner tables the talk was all of the news. The king himself did not attend, but rumors flew. Ailsa heard from the priest at her table that the prince had been most mortally insulted by the English. He'd been visiting King Stephen, she knew, for the Easter celebrations. The priest, chewing his venison with enthusiasm, said, "Yes, the nobles absolutely refused to allow him the status of prince, they wanted him to sit below the salt at table. The English king, Stephen that is, protested, 'tis said, but he's no strength any more against his own barons. England is in sad straits."

"'Tis too bad they insulted the prince," agreed Ailsa, for she liked the freckle faced Henry. He was full of harmless fun and generous.

"'Twill set the king's mind on Northumberland again, no doubt," said another man at the table.

"What do you mean?" asked Ailsa.

"Why, he sees the English barons weak and quarreling among themselves, and then they insult our prince. 'Tis an opportunity, mark my words. Northumbria is wide open. He'll be marching within the month. Yes, no doubt at all, mark my words."

"I hope not," said Ailsa.

"Ah, well, the maids never like the fighting, but I'm not opposed to it myself. I'll march along with him, I will."

Ailsa felt cold in the pit of her stomach. I must see the king before he goes, she thought. But how?

She felt a hand on her arm, and turned to see Hugh, his light hair gleaming in the candlelight. "Come," he said in a low voice, "let us walk in the gardens."

"It is uncommon chill."

He looked like he wished to object but led her to a secluded window seat. He stood over her. "I wait for an answer. You are hard to make me wait so long."

Ailsa looked away. She felt cornered, but to be honest, he was right. "You've honored me with your request."

"And," he prompted, placing a hand on her arm.

She said nothing, staring down at the three gold rings on his fingers. One had a large black stone, polished to gleam darkly in the candlelight. She had thought to have her discussion with the king accomplished by the time she saw Hugh again. She must know for certain if the king would grant her the lands and manor of Caerwyn. In her own name. Otherwise, she could never be certain if her estate and people would be secure. She looked at Hugh, studying his face.

He put his hands on her shoulders. "Ailsa, just say yes."

Abruptly she turned away and opened the shutter and looked away out the window over the marshlands toward the sea, hidden now in the dark. Cold wind blew in and made her shiver.

Hugh took the shutter and closed it.

Reluctantly, she faced him.

He raised his hand to her chin and cupped it. "The time approaches when decisions must be made."

Ailsa haunted the king's chambers the next few mornings, though it was obvious the king was busy and seeing no petitioners at all. She avoided the hall at dinnertime, pleading an indisposition. Indeed she felt ill, her stomach tense and tight. She especially avoided Hugh, and even his mother. She even went to the king's chapel and tried to pray for guidance. But she felt only cold stones beneath her knees.

One afternoon, she asked a maidservant for the boots she'd worn when she arrived.

"The soles are too thin," said the maid. "And they are not the fashion."

"They keep the wet out."

"Yes, miss," responded the maid, her face dubious.

Ailsa pulled on her cloak and went out into the late afternoon shadows. She swung open the heavy gate to the gardens. It was quiet there, a soft rain falling, and plants were beginning to push shoots out into the chill air. Small brown birds were busy building their nests and the garden was full of their soft twitters and calls. Ailsa crunched along the graveled path, then turned down one of the grassy paths through the meadows that led to the far reaches of the king's estate. She sat down on the damp grass under a budding apple tree, ignoring the mud and enjoying the swooping flight and sounds of the finches, imagining she could hear the crocus and jonquils grow. It was so different from the crowded castle. It was never quiet there; always people chattering in corners, whispering, snorting with suppressed laughter. I will be glad to get home, she thought, no longer surprised at her change of heart.

But what would home mean, if she herself belonged to someone else and no longer could be free. Each day, subject to another's orders or rules, and the dream of far travel just that, a dream never to be realized. She closed her eyes and felt the mist gather and trickle down her cheeks like tears.

Suddenly, she heard a sharp metallic sound, like spurs, on the graveled path. She pulled herself behind a nearby cedar, its evergreen branches strong scented in the rain. A moment later, a man and a woman appeared, walking slowly and conversing. Now she felt foolish. She hoped they'd pass by quickly. They'd think she was spying on them, for heaven's sake. Why hadn't she just stayed out in the open?

There was something familiar about the voice. It was Hugh, she realized, peering out. He bent over the head of Alice, just returned to court from visiting with her friends. The widow's bright blue gown swept by, trailing over the grassy pathway, gathering twigs. They were engrossed and did not see her as they passed by. Ailsa stared at their backs from her hiding spot. Hugh had a possessive hand at the widow's hip.

She brushed wet grass strands from her skirts, ducked under the bushes and emerged on the other side, spattered with drops she'd knocked from the branches. She ran toward the garden entrance, turned a corner and blundered into another couple, arms linked. "Excuse me," she said, having run right into the woman.

"Ailsa." It was Effie, a flushed and smiling Effie, walking arm and arm with her Davy. "Is something wrong?"

"No, no," stammered Ailsa, "I've just remembered something I must do right away."

They let her go, clearly anxious to return to their private walk.

Ailsa spent a long afternoon in her tiny chamber, pacing and worrying and trying to think. About her duty to Caerwyn, about Caerwyn's future in a changing world, about her own future. Her damp clothes made her sneeze, but she ignored that. Finally, as dinner approached, she called for the maid and dressed. She put on the sea-green gown she'd worn for the Easter feast. It was too elegant for tonight, but she needed the courage. The gown fell in heavy folds that dragged at her waist. Her face looked pale and remote when the maid held up the mirror. She looked like a court lady, she realized, and felt a pang.

In the hall, the now familiar smells and sounds assailed her. She was late, and she looked about for a place to sit at her regular table. The seats were all taken. Then she saw a place near Beatrice. She shrugged and walked in. The lady was busy eating, for she loved her dinner, but welcomed Ailsa.

Ailsa picked at the bread and fowl covered with plum sauce before her. "I must speak with you," she said finally, as Beatrice tasted another meat pasty.

"Of course," answered Beatrice, "do have some of this, it is superb."

Ailsa bit her lip. "About Hugh," she said in a rush.

"He does seem most attentive to you."

Ailsa stared at her plate. "I thought so, but this afternoon I saw him in the gardens with Alice." She stared down at the meat platter in the center of the table, where bits of meat and gravy congealed.

Beatrice paused, chicken wing in her large hand. "Ah," she said, resuming eating.

Ailsa fiddled with the linen tablecloth, but Beatrice said no more. "I was surprised to see them there," she stumbled out finally, "together."

"She is an old friend of the family, my dear. Hugh is generous, always trying to help out. I am sure he was just speaking with her, trying to fix her situation, which is delicate, the finances you know." She stabbed another chunk of goose with her knife. "Though widow or not, she is quite beautiful." She stared at Ailsa, eyes glittering in the flickering torchlight. "He offers you marriage. Yet, you keep him waiting."

Ailsa hesitated, but felt she was expected to say something. "I find myself homesick these days."

"Spring is coming on, an unsettling time when one is young." Beatrice's hand hovered over the pastries. "He is a very good prospect for you, indeed a most excellent prospect, for all I am his mother, and more than you've a right to expect. You've no father to settle matters for you, and that's a pity. Still, you have a head on your shoulders, do you not? He will not wait forever, for he has his pride, as well he should." She waved the pasty in the air to emphasize her words."

Morning sun warmed Ailsa's head as she bent over some tiny shoots of green. She ran her fingers over the delicate sprouts, searching for dandelions and chicory for a salad of spring greens. She had left her stuffy chamber early, restless with the bright morning. The breezes in the open meadow carried the scent of new turned earth and growing things. Her hands were dirty from foraging and she rubbed them on her skirt and sighed with contentment. By winter's end even a king's hall was a musty place, smelling of wood smoke, dirty rushes, and cooped up hounds.

She tipped her head to let the sun shine full on her face. She listened to the sparrows, chirping as they swooped, her eyes closed. She had learned much at court. Caerwyn had seemed a far-off bastion, isolated and safe. The changes that filtered in to them had seemed as fairy tales, of no moment to their everyday lives. Now she knew different. She must prepare her lands and people for the changes that had come, and those coming. Englishmen and their new ways were everywhere and Caerwyn could not escape. Feeling a rock under her shoulder, she shifted uneasily. But surely with the right choices, she could ease the way for the families. It was her responsibility.

She squinted at the sun. And there lay the difficulty. For she could not seem to decide what to do about Hugh's proposal. At first she thought she'd been comparing him with Niall, which was unfair, for that had been a marriage for love and she hadn't been thinking of Caerwyn at all, only of her own desire. She wondered what it would have been like, had Niall lived. Would Dugald have grown to accept him? Would they have continued to be consumed by each other, or would they have grown less passionate or even distant? Impossible to know now. She felt like the Ailsa who had loved and lost Niall was another person. Death surrounded them, even on a day such as this. Life moved on. She sighed and tried to return to the problem at hand.

It should help to be linked to the powerful de Morvilles. But Hugh himself seemed so uninterested in his own estates, she wondered how much attention he'd be willing to pay to hers. From Jamie, she'd heard that three more men had left Caerwyn, heading for one of the burghs, and they'd taken their families with them. Did they think she'd abandoned them, or were they enticed by the coin and freedom of the towns? Should she try to send them back or just let them go? Hugh would force them back to the land, she was sure. Was that right? She had no one she could talk to about such questions.

The meadow stretched out below her, for she sat on a small rise. The trees showed pale green, their buds swelling into tiny new leaves, as branches danced against a clear washed blue sky. She smiled ruefully. It was not a day for dismay. She got to her feet and picked up her basket. She'd walk, wander as she would and not return till dark fell. Have a whole day of peace and sunshine. But by tonight she'd have to make a decision.

Robert rubbed his forehead, which ached from lack of sleep. He'd arrived at Carlisle late last night and immediately requested an audience with the king. David had received him, late though it was, dressed in a linen nightgown covered with a purple woolen robe, near the hearth in his private chamber, which although warm, was nowhere near as sumptuous as the public hall and council chambers.

Robert stretched his stiff back and sat up. Where was Jamie this morning? He wanted to give him Tanet to exercise. And check on how the boy got along. He got up from the thin pallet in the great hall, which had served for a brief time as a bed and headed for the kitchen. But the boy was not by the fire, though the head groom was there, a drink of hot cider in his hands and a smile on his face. He was chatting with a kitchen maid with plump arms and a cheery smile. Robert left him to flirt. He found a mug and poured himself some cider, then made a meal of cheese and coarse rye bread.

Feeling better for the food, he lingered at the table, musing over his conversation with the king last night. Perhaps it had been the lateness of the hour, he'd certainly been frank. Dangerously so. He'd told the king of Wimond, the little he'd learned. But the formal claim to royal blood seemed news to David. And he'd told him of the rumors Somerled was behind the unrest circulating in the Isles. He'd told David of the lords of Arran, their comfortable life of trade and sea faring. Their far-reaching contacts. Their swift galleys and fortified manors. He'd spoken of their apparent will for peace to prolong this trade, but also of their loyalty to their own way of life and their own customs. When he'd fallen silent, David had asked a few questions. Then he too had fallen silent. The two men sat by the fire staring into the flames.

After a time, David asked, "And you, what do you think is wise?"

"I hold my lands and title by your grace," Robert replied. "But though I came north with the Normans in the retinue of fitz Alain, and though Walter is my good comrade and friend, I am no Norman or Englishman by birth. I was raised in Wales. My lands were lost when Henry invaded." He paused, then with a deep breath, plunged on, "Thus I find I share many customs with these Islesmen." He began to pace up and down in front of the fire. "I find them right about their fears of English conquest, not of political conquest, but of a conquest of culture and customs. They value their way of life and fear to lose it." Stopping in front of David, he ran a hand through his hair. "I think each group must be allowed to hold to his own ways, yet a path must be found to live together in mutual peace. I would follow and support such a plan. But I cannot support forced change of long held ways." The room was silent, but for the creak of the walls in the wind, and the fire's gentle hiss.

David said, "You speak openly. Most unusual at court. And sometimes valuable."

And sometimes not, thought Robert, feeling a shiver.

The king leaned back in his armchair. "So you find this Wimond charismatic, and even convincing."

Robert started to speak but the king stopped him with a wave of his hand.

"You will delay the date of your wedding, and formal overlordship of Caerwyn, till early summer," David said. "In July I journey to Glasgow, to dedicate the new cathedral. You will attend with Walter fitz Alain. And it will serve as a good time for a wedding, if I so decide." The king waved a hand again and Robert had found himself ushered out.

The kitchen boy dropped an iron pan on the stone floor with a mighty clatter. Robert remembered he sat in the kitchen, an uneaten piece of bread in his hand. He shook the king's warning from his thoughts and finished off his breakfast and still thinking went out to the barns. Was the king sincere, did he truly value open speech? Or was he about to be seized and charged with treason? Impossible to know a king's true mind.

Jamie ran up, his long legs bare and spattered with mud.

He gave the boy a friendly slap on the back. "Ye've grown a foot since I left."

Jamie grinned. "Do you seek the lady? She has gone walking, gathering greens by the burn. Shall I take you to her?" he asked eagerly.

Robert hesitated, but then said, "No. See to Tanet, he needs to stretch his legs, will you?"

He had much to tell Ailsa, and much to ask of her. But first he had to know the king's mind. He played with fire, and the safety of Caerwyn, and even Ailsa's own life, might depend on the king's decision or whims. He couldn't risk involving her further.

CHAPTER EIGHTEEN

ROBERT RAN HIS HAND over the stallion's neck, feeling the warm body quiver. Tanet was dancing, anxious to go after several days cooped up in the stables. He was anxious to ride as well, for he had a message to deliver for the king and he wanted to be done with it and back early. They headed north, toward the de Brus holdings at Annandale. But when he was sure none watched or followed, he halted Tanet, then led the horse through the woods until they found the narrow path leading south.

They had a long ride to deliver the king's message to Ralph of Greystoke, and a long way home before any watchers noticed he was away. The king meant to switch sides in the great battle shaping up between Matilda and Stephen and wanted it secret as long as possible. Perhaps it had been David's plan all along, for Matilda was family, and the daughter of his great mentor, Henry. Stephen was but a cousin, and now he'd let his wayward barons so insult the prince, it took no great insight to see the Scots king would be looking after his own best interests.

When Robert reached Greystoke, he gave the message over to Ralph's son, for the father was out hunting, and not expected for several days. He would not tarry. The king had said he'd not expect a message in return. This was a warning, of shifting winds and alliances. Not yet a call to action.

Late that evening, back in the stables at Carlisle, Robert made sure Tanet was carefully groomed and watered as he thought on what the king's shifting alliances might mean for him. It hadn't escaped him that de Morville showed an interest in Ailsa, but it was odd, for she was not the largest heiress at court by any means, and in truth, de Morville could look higher. He continued to ponder as he left the stables, thinking back on Hugh's anger at the king's table back in Edinburgh. Did Hugh have some prior claim to Caerwyn? Was there something important about the small estate, something he was missing?

Will should be back soon from Arran and glad he'd be to see him. Perhaps he'd have more information about this rebellion and the possible involvement of Ailsa's kin. He hoped so, for there was a missing piece to the puzzles here. Could this Somerled of the Isles be at the root? The king had not seemed rattled at the rumors of Somerled's power, for he thought him loyal and they'd made a treaty only a few months past, but it would be a great danger if he chose to make trouble now, just as David contemplated shifting sides in his dealings with the English.

Robert stopped by the door to the hall, reluctant to leave the quiet evening, the spring air fresh on his face. He had an uneasy feeling that something linked the incipient rebellion in the Isles and de Morville's anger over his grant of Caerwyn. He ran his hand through his thick hair. In his mind flashed the barren earth sodden with rain over Nevin's grave. If only he could be certain Ailsa was not involved.

A commotion across the courtyard caught his eye. Two men rode in. "Will!" he shouted. He waited while Will picked up his bag and gave Jamie some instructions about his horse.

"That boy has a way with the horses and he's eager to learn more," said Will, as they walked together toward the hall.

"Well?"

Will grinned. "I know you be anxious for news, so yes, I can wait for my dinner."

"Let's find a spot away from curious ears." They climbed the steep stairs of the castle wall two at a time and found a corner well away from the young guard watching the eastern meadows. The fields were already darkening and the forests beyond loomed black against a purple sky.

"My story is quickly told," said Will. "I followed Dugald, but he's a canny one and whether he knew I followed him or no, he did nothing unusual. Stayed on and hunted for two days with Fergus and the rest. They got the red deer and did some hawking for rabbits. The evenings were as you saw, full of song and story, but little else. If they talked about Wimond and whether to give him aid, they did it out of my sight and hearing." He frowned. "Perhaps they only waited until I left to gather and hold council, so I pretended to depart on the third day, then circled back and entered the castle."

"How did you do that?"

Will laughed and sat down on one of the rough stones provided for the archers. "Well, that's a story in itself, for I found a most amiable lady among the servers and 'tis easy to slip into a castle when the door is open to you."

"And so you entered…" prodded Robert.

"Yes," answered Will, looking like he enjoyed spinning out his tale. "I entered, during the dinner, while all in the hall were occupied with the minstrels and she led me to a storeroom, packed with old cloth and household items, and packed me in among them. At first I thought she meant to store me away to use later as well, but she shifted some of the cloth, and sure I could hear the music from the hall. She shut the door on me and it was dark as hell may be, but I could hear. After a long evening of music and tales, there was much shuffling of feet and I figured all were heading to bed. Disappointed, I was about to slip out, when I heard voices again. Of a few men only."

Robert leaned forward, drawn into Will's tale. "What said they?" He could hardly see the expression on Will's face in the dim light. "Was Dugald there?

"He was, for his deep and rumbly voice is easy to tell. And Fergus, that old codger, he was there too. As for the others, I think there were two, but I know not who they might be, though it seems likely they were of the guests invited. They talked only a short time, and Fergus it was who did most of the talking. They spoke low, so I had a hard time to hear, though sitting in the dark like that, it sharpens your senses and it seemed I could hear more than normal."

Robert gestured impatiently, and Will smiled. He could see his teeth gleam in the dusky light.

"Fergus said they must be on the lookout for ships from Man, for there could be trouble there and soon. He told the others to send him word if any ships were sighted. One of the men asked him if he expected trouble on Arran and he said nay, but he'd not be caught unawares. He counseled them to ready their defenses and then he spoke of David."

Robert leaned forward.

"He said the king was nervous and 'twas a good time to achieve some of their long-held aims, for Godfrey is occupied trying to control this bishop he's set up in Man, and David has extended himself into England's woes."

"What aims?" asked Robert.

Will shrugged. "They all seemed to know well enough what he spoke of, but he did mention one name."

"Wimond? MacHeth?" said Robert.

"No, he said Somerled," said Will, "and all went quiet after he spoke. Then Dugald, for I know his voice, asked what he knew of Somerled, sounding angry, and Fergus said not much, but he did know the king's Constable spoke from both sides of his mouth. Then he scraped back his chair and the meeting was over." Will tossed a pebble over the wall. "There it is, and what you'll make of it all I don't know."

Robert was silent. It was clear the Islesmen thought to take advantage of David's preoccupation with England to press their own goals. But was the Constable involved somehow or just speaking the ever ambiguous language of the court advisor? "Where does Dugald stand in all this?"

Will hesitated. "I overheard him in the stables, talking to Fergus' groom. He was giving instructions for the care of his horses, saying he'd likely not be back for some three weeks or more."

Robert frowned. "That sounds like a sea voyage. But why leave the horses with Fergus, why not on his own lands?"

"That's the question, unless he meant to keep his going secret.

And indeed he did so, for I watched him go, taking only Torquil with him and dressed plain. They had one of those galleys, with but four men aboard and they sailed with the tide that very morning."

"And meanwhile the king is off to Durham again, leaving the coast abandoned. I must send him a message, though he will not be glad of it."

"I can go, though I'd prefer to get my dinner first."

Robert laughed, and drew his friend to the stairs. "Past time," he agreed. "But I need you here," he said, "events are drawing to some crisis, though I can't puzzle it all together yet."

Will nodded. "Perhaps young Peter?"

"A good idea. It would put the boy in a safer position, I've been wishing for a way to get him out of here. Can you arrange it with Lady Beatrice?"

"Yes," answered Will. They crossed the empty courtyard and approached the hall. "And your lady?"

Robert shrugged and walked ahead of Will into the crowded hall. He scanned the crowd and spotted Ailsa seated at a long table on the dais, talking once again to Hugh de Morville.

Will followed his gaze and caught at his arm, speaking low. "One thing more Dugald said at Fergus' council. He mentioned de Morville had been there, on Arran, said he'd seen him at the market. In disguise."

"Hugh, the Constable's son? How could he be sure?"

"He seemed sure and Fergus seemed unsurprised."

Prince Henry, still smarting from the insults of Stephen's barons, called the men of the court together after dinner. He stood on a crate above the throng and announced a tourney, to be held in two days time. His excited men pounded on their shields and clapped each other on the back. Tourneys were popular in Normandy, but infrequent yet in these parts. A melee promised fighting and the chance of rich prizes. Besides, all knew they were preparing for possible battle against the English over Northumberland.

Robert's eyes roamed the crowd and he beckoned to one of his men. He pointed out Hugh de Morville, surrounded by excited men dressed in gaudy silks. His man nodded and faded into the crowd. He would be Robert's eyes and ears, for he meant to keep Hugh de Morville under strict surveillance. Threats to him, and to his men, and now a possible link to rebellion against the king. He meant to find out what the de Morville family sought with these strange maneuvers. Yet it was dangerous, for they were close to the king, and he an outsider, for all he'd been granted Caerwyn.

A figure in the crowd drew his attention. A man, short and burly, dressed simply in grey. The man surveyed the crowd with apparent casual interest, but he was looking for someone. For a moment, the man turned his way and sun struck his face. Robert drew in a breath and felt his fist tighten. Fitz John's man. Again. The same he'd seen in Edinburgh, the day someone shot an arrow at the king. He felt the old anger surge up, crowding out thought.

The prince finished his speech and the crowd of cheering men began to disperse. De Morville waved to his friends and took off toward the stables. Fitz John's man followed, edging around the fringes of the excited throng. Robert drew in a deep breath and resisted chasing after them himself. He watched his man edge closer. De Morville and fitz John somehow linked? And Ailsa? There was no avoiding the bleak fact that she spent considerable time with de Morville.

He stared at the empty courtyard, then shook his head. He was no longer a boy who Payn fitz John could manipulate or frighten away. This time he'd be ready. If there was a plot, he'd find it. A sweet revenge for past injury.

Still, he'd best stay away from Ailsa. Until he knew her loyalties, and knew exactly what she might do to keep her Caerwyn.

CHAPTER NINETEEN

AILSA SMILED AS EFFIE RAN into the chamber. She was scrunched up on the rather hard window seat in Effie's room, embroidering a wedding gift for Effie with sky blue silk, trying to see by the fading afternoon light. She thrust the present under her skirt, but Effie was much too taken with her news to notice.

"Ailsa, you'll never guess! A tourney, just like in Normandy, isn't it wonderful? And Davy is going to join in the melee." She spun around, twirling her skirts in the tiny space. "I must think, what do you think I should wear, my green gown, or the blue?"

Ailsa looked at her friend with affection. "You'll look wonderful in either, and Davy will be the most handsome and brave knight there, I'm sure."

Effie stopped spinning to give her a hug, then dropped onto a stool and chattered on, telling Ailsa how Prince Henry had ordered the melee and how even now men clustered in the courtyard, polishing their lances to a sheen of silver.

Ailsa peered out the window, but she couldn't see the courtyard, so she pushed Effie's present under a pillow, then smoothed her gown. "Are all the men out there?" she asked, trying to sound casual.

"I suppose, how could they stay away?" said Effie. She had pulled several gowns out of her chest and was studying their hems. "I did see Hugh de Morville. He was quite the center of attention. Except for the prince, of course."

Ailsa turned to the window to escape Effie's knowing look. She looked out over barren fields, the crops planted but not yet sprouting, and in the distance, a green line of sea.

A knock sounded at the door. Effie opened it and uttered a polite welcome in a toneless voice.

Beatrice followed by Alice entered, filling the chamber with their rustling gowns and the heavy smell of their perfumes. Effie wrinkled her nose when the ladies turned toward Ailsa, but she offered them refreshment. Ailsa had to admit Beatrice and Alice were overdressed. Still, they'd been kind to her. Though of late, she'd found Effie's undemanding and cheerful company much more to her taste.

Beatrice took the offered stool and lowered herself. The stool creaked but held. The widow ignored the offer of a seat and continued to stand, carefully arranging her laces and seeming to ignore the proceedings. Her golden hair hung in long braids from under the ruffles of her tiny white headdress and surely her cheeks were rouged a rosy pink.

"You've heard the news," said Beatrice.

"Of the melee, you mean? Aye," said Ailsa.

"Of course, my son will be competing."

Ailsa nodded, unsure what this was leading to. Effie, standing behind Beatrice widened her eyes and gestured toward the door.

"A melee and the attendant festivities would be a lovely time for a betrothal announcement."

Ailsa stiffened, but tried to keep her face neutral. So the visit was to her, and not to Effie at all. There was an awkward silence. Ailsa bit her lip, wondering what she could say to stop what seemed to be coming.

The widow stopped fiddling with her hair. "Come now," she said, her voice higher pitched than usual. "Let us not be coy; you cannot keep Hugh waiting on a string forever. You must offer him your colors to wear, a token of some sort, and if he does well on the field, it would not be amiss to offer a kiss as a symbol of your promise." Just then Effie's maid entered the room with a loaded tray. Alice reached out for a mug of wine, and took a sip, then sunk her white teeth into a piece of cheese.

"What promise?" said Ailsa, irritated by Alice's words.

"Indeed," Beatrice was saying, as she helped herself to a large chunk of wheat bread. "It is the English custom. You must offer a kiss and then a suitable third party, myself in this case, can announce the betrothal. You have no parents," she continued, "so I'm offering to help arrange things for you myself, though it is unusual for the man's mother to take on this role, still it is hardly without precedent." She rattled on, citing cases when mothers became involved in the matchmaking, and emphasizing the honorable state of the families involved.

"You are most kind," Ailsa said, as Beatrice wound down.

Effie, her face a careful blank, turned to Beatrice. "As it happens, Ailsa, though well aware of the honor you do her in seeking to welcome her to your family, is not ready to make such a decision, so momentous for her future, and certainly not without her relatives and kin present. She may be an orphan, but she is hardly without kin."

Beatrice's color deepened. "I urge no improprieties, but people are talking; 'tis past time to announce this betrothal."

"There has been no talk," said Effie firmly, her blue eyes beginning to spark. "Perhaps you are mistaken, Lady Beatrice."

Ailsa drew her breath in, surprised at the usually gentle Effie.

Beatrice turned to Ailsa. "And what say you?"

"I do need time to think on this important decision," she said, "you have been so kind, Lady Beatrice, but..." her voice trailed away. There was a brief silence.

Alice flicked some dust from her ivory skirts and moved impatiently to the door. "Do not think overlong," she tossed out over her shoulder and swept out.

"I know you'll see things more clearly soon," announced Beatrice. She too swept from the room. The door banged back into place.

Effie put a comforting arm around her shoulders. "They are two witches to my way of thinking. You will make up your own mind."

Ailsa went to the window and leaned out, taking deep breaths of the dusky air, and the faint salt scent made her eyes tear. "I do not wish to be rushed into marriage, not with anyone. I know I will have to marry, and sadly I will have to settle for one of these Englishmen." She shrugged.

"It is a burden, having lands," said Effie. "I am fortunate to be without and so fortunate, I know, to love and be loved. It is most unusual in our world."

Ailsa smiled. "I had no idea you could be so forceful!"

Effie grinned. "I am known at home for having a bit of a temper. But truly Ailsa, I urge you to wait until you are sure."

"I have been married before."

"You have never said!" Effie hesitated. "What happened?"

Ailsa shrugged. "He died." She turned back to the window. "He died. And I carried on. As one must. But though I was young and thoughtless then, I did love him. And now, I hope for some sort of sign, but I fear I will just have to choose and hope I have chosen wisely. The future of so many families rests on what I decide and I find myself so unsure."

"Like the heroine in one of your stories," said Effie, wrapping her in a hug. "Tell me one of your tales now. Perhaps it will make you feel better. There are truths in the old tales."

"In a story one can be free and do anything one wishes, but it seems real life is not that way."

The morning of the melee dawned bright and blue. A crisp wind snapped the colored pennants and made the horses stamp their hoofs. Ailsa came in from the courtyard, her cheeks flushed with the brisk air. Cooks and serving boys were bustling about the crowded kitchens. Her stomach was growling.

She had come down early and walked the grounds, where men readied the field for the early events, set to begin mid-morning. Servants joked as they erected a linen tent as shelter for the women of the court, with benches of long planks. The linen billowed alarmingly in the wind, but it was brightly striped in gold and red. Ailsa wondered what the men were feeling, waiting for the action to begin, wondering how they would acquit themselves. She wandered to the stables, munching an apple, but the grooms were sorting bridles and tethering skittish horses and the atmosphere tense. Even Jamie was too busy to talk. On an impulse, she climbed the stairs to the castle walls.

When she reached the top, the noisy scene down in the courtyard faded to distant shouts and she watched the people, gaily dressed in reds and blues, hurrying around on their various errands. She walked past the guards, their eyes trained over the far meadows and to the sea, her skirts sliding over the wet stones and turned down a passage to a quiet corner, facing east toward the forests. It would be sunny and warm at this hour, and a good place to observe the activity.

She rounded the corner and stopped. A man stood, his back to her, outlined against the pale blue of the sky. He stood very still, looking beyond the bustling courtyard, to the distant hills, where the sun was just clearing, edging the rounded forms with gold and sending gleaming rays over the mist shrouded fields. She thought to back away, but she must have made some sound.

He turned, hand already drawing his dagger.

"Sir Robert," she said awkwardly. Her plan for the day did not include an encounter with him. He narrowed his grey eyes and she took a step back, then stopped.

He folded his arms. "Robb," he said. "Remember?"

"Aye… Robb."

He said nothing more, just stood, observing her, his eyes impossible to read. She felt the sun break full over the hills and shine down onto her shoulders, and she remembered a day last spring in the fields at home, the sun shining on her as she worked at the planting. This man thought to take those lands from her. She must remember that.

"I have much to say to you, Lady Ailsa." She had the disconcerting feeling he could tell something of what she'd been thinking. "Much that I did not have a chance to say or ask the last time we met."

She focused her eyes on the intricate metal work of his hauberk. It was very finely worked, with an unusual curving and twining pattern of leaves and strange looking beasts.

When she did not respond, he stepped back, and returned to examining the hills. Apparently satisfied that whatever he searched for wasn't there, he looked back at her. "You have not asked me what I found at Caerwyn or on Arran, where I went for the king."

"And have you found something?" she asked reluctantly. She could feel him examining her with those piercing eyes.

"Whispers and rumors, some perhaps of importance." His eyebrows drew together in a frown. "This bishop Wimond calls himself royal; he thinks to take the crown."

Ailsa started, despite his quiet voice. If the bishop intended treason, even to speak of it was dangerous.

"I went to Arran," he continued, "to MacLaughlin and another lesser landholder named Fergus. There I met many who play a dangerous game, hovering between this Wimond and the king. One who I met there was your cousin Dugald."

"Dugald! He would not betray the king, if that is what you imply." But Dugald could be foolish, she knew too well, and he was far too trusting. She felt a cold clutch of fear in her chest. Robert had the king's trust, and she was less naive than a few short months ago. Even a hint of treason could be dangerous for Dugald, and poor Meriel, and all of Caerwyn's defenseless tenants.

"I do not know him well enough yet to tell." He paused. "Though you do."

"My cousin is not a traitor."

He stared at her with those grey eyes, but she could not read in them whether he believed her or not.

"Yet there is some justice to their cause, some grievances that need hearing. It is difficult to see which way even good men might go." He said this softly, meditatively almost, then turned back to the forests.

"There is a great deal of right in their complaints, for you English have come, lawless men in swarms, stealing our lands and denying our ways, as though by right."

"Is that what you see before you? Yet I am not English. And I wonder just what you would do to keep those lands of yours. One of my good men lies buried at your Caerwyn." He looked away from her, out over the grey fields for a long moment. "No wonder you seek to avoid our marriage. Do not trouble yourself further. I have no need of you or your lands, but will make my way on my own, as I always have." His voice was even, but his eyes were dark. "From this time forward, consider yourself completely free. I will make all due arrangements with the king." He bowed over her hand and was gone.

Ailsa gazed after him, her mouth open. It was very silent, but for the brisk winds snapping her cloak. She wandered over to the wall, and stared out at the hills, rubbing her fingers back and forth on the rough granite. She had what she had come for. She was free of him. She lifted her chin, but strangely, she felt confusion and dismay, and some regret, but no triumph.

The ladies of the court, despite their brilliant gowns, jostled each other for the best view. Men gathered on the two ends of the great meadow, having chosen lots for the opposing sides. Their hauberks glinted, and the wind carried the clang of metal, the neighing of skittish horses, and the shouts of impatient knights. Young boys scurried back and forth, doing the bidding of the older men, and, no doubt, wishing for the moment when they might join in the mock battle themselves. Though this would be rough enough. Ailsa had never seen a melee herself, but she'd heard the stories.

Effie chattered about the different knights and their chances in the coming struggle. Davy hoped for a chance at the reward monies, for he was a big man, and few could best him with club on foot, though he was less solid on a horse. The silver would be welcome indeed to the young couple.

Ailsa tried to force her face into the appropriate signs of pleasure and interest. But she saw Robert's eyes and heard his icy voice informing her she was free. She shifted on the bench. The new cut wood was rough.

Her eyes searched the throngs of men. Hugh, garbed in black, flourished his shield painted with blue, red and gold in the new style of the Normans. He sat a big black stallion with easy grace.

Absently winding her laces around her fingers, Ailsa stared at the men on the meadow below, thinking. She must find Robert, after the melee, and explain. Explain what? It was quite possible her cousin was scheming with the Islesmen against the king. But she had nothing to do with that, nor with the death of this Nevin. Why did he doubt her? And what did he mean by legitimate grievances? It almost sounded like he sympathized with the Islesmen, but how could that be?

She swept the throng of men again with her eyes. What if he'd left suddenly, what if he weren't going to fight in the melee at all? What if he just went back to Normandy? Angry tears pricked the back of her eyes. That was her aim, was it not? He did not want her explanations. He wanted her lands.

Effie poked her. "Look!" She pointed to the field, where Prince Henry rode at a ceremonious walk on a splendid white horse with gold bridle and crimson draped silk. Ailsa's eyes swept over the knights massed at the far end of the field, a daunting sight. These English were so powerful; how could she return to Caerwyn, with her people still unprotected?

The prince laid out the rules of the fight. The crowd cheered and the prince pivoted his horse and rode back to the stands. He would not participate but judge the melee instead. The men mounted and the chargers, excited by the crowds, pranced and jostled their riders. Ailsa saw Robert, on his grey stallion. His hauberk was covered by a midnight blue tunic with a panel of gold silk stitched with swirling green leaves. Her stomach tightened and she clutched Effie's hand without thinking. Effie asked her something, but she couldn't hear for the blaring music of horns. The men gathered at each end of the field and Ailsa could feel their tension; it seemed to float on the shimmering air above their heads.

The prince raised the banner and then swept it to the ground. A thundering rush of horses and men flung themselves toward the inevitable collision in the center. Appalled and fascinated, she could not tear her eyes from the spectacle. The horses pounded toward each other, throwing clods of mud and grass behind their heavy hooves. A clash of metal. Men flew from horses, rolling with heavy thuds on the ground. Cries of pain and the frantic neighing of horses mixed with the clang of metal on metal. Impossible to see who had survived that onslaught. At a shout from the prince, mounted guards rushed in and moved among the men, separating them and calling for the second charge.

The men hurled insults, maddened by the struggle. Gradually they gathered again on the two sides of the field, as the guards dragged the wounded off. Ailsa shifted uneasily on her hard seat, moving closer to Effie's plump comforting body.

Effie whispered, "There," into her ear.

She looked and saw Robert, still astride the grey.

Ailsa found Hugh still astride as well, exchanging his shield. She could see him yelling to his squire, though the sounds of the crowds and shouts of the men made it impossible to hear. "What of Davy?" she remembered to ask.

"'Tis fine he is." Effie pointed out her tall betrothed, still astride his bony chestnut.

The prince dropped the flag. The horses charged. The clash was more furious, each man determined to stay in the running for the foot battle. Horses reared in fear and pain, and one went down with blood glistening red on its neck. Ailsa stared, fascinated and horrified. She saw Hugh wheeling triumphantly and waving to the roaring crowd. Finally, she found Robert, sitting his grey nonchalantly, as though on a ride through the meadows, cantering back to the field's edge. He jumped down from Tanet, clapped the horse on the neck affectionately, and surrendered him to his man, with a few words in his ear. Or boy, she thought, for he looked young. Staring harder, she realized it was Jamie. She saw Robert toss an instruction over his shoulder and grin. Jamie straightened proudly and walked off tall as he could, the grey following peaceably behind.

Again, the wounded were being lugged from the field, and as the men were carried away, merchants came through the throngs, taking advantage of the break in the action to sell trinkets, ribbons, and meat pasties. Effie, satisfied that Davy had survived the second round of the bout, called out to the nearest merchant. He approached, anxious to make a sale, and Effie bought two pasties and deliberated over a blue ribbon.

"Do get it," urged Ailsa, seeing her friend wished for the wide ribbon, "it will exactly match your eyes and Davy will be pleased to see it."

Effie purchased the silk ribbon and wrapped it in her sleeve. She ate the pie with concentration, clearly enjoying every crumb. The men were assembling into two lines, facing each other. Those left were the experienced knights, hard and confident. Each had a blunted sword and a shield, and they glared at each other under the noon sun, while the crowd roared advice.

The prince signaled, and the men rushed at each other. Though a mock battle, cries of pain and howls of anger floated on the wind. Ailsa watched the confusing mass of men, brooches glinting in the sun and gaudy tunics creating a colorful weaving line. The clash of metal and clunk of shields was deafening. Suddenly Effie stood beside her, shouting and gesturing and she stood up too, to see. It was Davy, with three smaller men ganging up to bring him down. But the big man calmly swung with his broad club and one fell to the ground. Another backed off, looking for easier prey, and Davy thumped the last on the head. He dropped.

Effie sat down in a flurry of skirts and put her head on Ailsa's shoulder. "I can hardly bear to watch," she cried, but she continued to stare at the jostling crowd of men, hammering at each other with fists and swords. Only some six or seven still battled. They swung at each other, but with skill, experienced fighters all. There'd be no more easy gains.

Ailsa saw Robert, still standing. He struck one man a tremendous blow with the flat of the sword, and the man fell heavily. He groaned and rolled over awkwardly. Robert turned to another, a smaller wiry fellow who leaped about, avoiding his blade. Yet when the man tired, he felled him with a blow on the side his head.

Ailsa caught her breath. For now, Robert faced de Morville. Hugh was smaller and lighter; he moved with ease, well trained to dance away from dangerous swings. Robert, taller and heavier, hardly looking winded, swinging the heavy sword as though it were light wood. They battled, moving gradually apart from the few others, who wore themselves out, and were dropped to the ground by big Davy.

Effie's fiancé waved his sword in the air, for he was one of three left and sure of a prize. The crowd laughed and clapped, and Davy headed toward Robert and de Morville, for he was on de Morville's side and duty bound to enter the final battle.

Ailsa caught her breath, for how could Robert hold against these two. The crowds were roaring with delight, for the end approached. Davy moved in, methodically swinging. Effie clutched her elbow.

"'Tis his duty," Ailsa said but her nails bit into her palms. Robert was being beaten back to the line and beyond that he could not go or lose his prize by forfeit. Ailsa looked at the prince. He should stop this; it was usual to save good fighters by ending the bout, but the prince was joking with a friend, watching the struggle with casual interest. She forced herself to swallow and look back, clutching her gown in both fists. Davy was beating Robert back with heavy blows toward the line, and now de Morville darted around to the side and as Robert parried one of Davy's heavy swings, de Morville swung in and gave him a blow to the shoulder. Robert staggered and almost fell, but tripped Davy as he tried to give another huge blow. Davy fell and could not stumble to his feet quickly enough. He shook his big head, rolled over, then rose and trotted off the field. The crowd screamed and shouted.

Now Robert closed with de Morville. Surely the prince would halt the battle now. But no halt came. De Morville, his black tunic ripped and rippling in the wind, shouted something. Robert's face darkened and he rushed at de Morville. Ailsa drew in a long breath, sensing an entirely different battle. The onlookers quieted. The prince looked up and frowned. It seemed he didn't wish his best fighters to kill each other after all; he dropped the flag, and guards rushed in and pulled the men apart.

Robert yanked his arm out of the guard's grasp. He walked to the stands, where the prince stood, ready to hand out the prizes. Davy was there already, joking with the prince's men. Robert bowed to the prince, then nodded to Davy. De Morville approached, having taken the time to don a new black tunic, and waved his sword to the yelling crowds. Henry handed a wooden box to each. Ailsa knew the boxes held silver daggers, set with a precious gem in the hilt, rich prizes indeed. Davy waved gleefully to the crowds. Effie was hopping up and down beside her, bursting with pride.

Ailsa hugged her friend. Just as she turned back, de Morville shouted something to Robert, then laughed.

Robert turned and his eyes raked across the women's pavilion, searching, and locked with hers. They stared at each other a long moment, across the crowds. Then he turned his back on her.

Ailsa watched Robert bow to the prince. She started to rise from her seat. De Morville shouted something to Robert's back. Robert swung around and de Morville pulled a dagger from his belt and thrust. Robert twisted at the last moment but the dagger sank into his shoulder. Blood poured down his arm. Jamie and Will ran from the sidelines. The prince shouted, his arm sweeping in a wide arc. Guards rushed to the winner's circle and de Morville was hustled away by the prince's men. Robert was helped off the field.

Ailsa pulled away from Effie. "I must go to him."

"Hush, you must not make a scene here. Many are watching."

"I don't care." Ailsa shoved her way through the crowd of chattering ladies. But when she reached the edge of the field, it was already emptied.

Effie appeared beside her. "They've taken him there."

She looked where Effie pointed. A group of men gathered near a tent on the far edge of the field. She lifted her gown and ran after them.

A strong arm encircled her waist, whirling her to a stop. "But Effie," she cried, twisting around. It was Davy who held her.

"You cannot follow there," said Effie, running up, panting, and Davy nodded, still gripping her arms.

"I will find out how matters stand," he said, his eyes kind. Ailsa swallowed, but he was right. She nodded and he dropped her arms and left, threading through the dispersing crowds.

Effie pulled her back into the swirl of ladies, chattering about the brave moves of various men and the feast to come in the king's hall. Ailsa realized the unfair blow was of little concern to most. She watched as the king's physician hurried in the direction of the tent.

Effie shook her elbow. "Ailsa," she said, alarm in her voice. Hugh de Morville sat astride his black stallion, gathering in admiring comments. "Lady Ailsa," he called out, "favor me with a token of your esteem." She felt all eyes upon her. With a sick feeling in her stomach, she realized the son of the king's closest advisor could do no wrong. Robert was the outsider.

Effie poked her in the ribs. "You cannot embarrass him here, in front of all. They are too powerful." When Ailsa didn't move, Effie pulled the pale silk scarf off Ailsa's head, and handed it to the ladies in front who handed it up to the hero.

Hugh knotted the scarf to his sword and raising it aloft, stared at her, but his eyes were cold.

Her eyes felt dry and hard as she stared into his confident face. She did not lift her arm in the ritual wave. He cantered off to the prince, the silk streaming behind.

Ailsa tore her hand from Effie and pushed through the crowd of women, ignoring their titters and attempts to congratulate her. She needed air; she could not breathe. Surely she would choke here at this English court.

CHAPTER TWENTY

THE KING RETURNED to Carlisle several days after the melee. He called his son into an audience immediately after his arrival. When the prince emerged, he looked subdued, it was whispered, and it was whispered further that the king was angered, for he did not hold with tourneys. He thought them a waste of men and a vainglorious show, not in keeping with God's wishes. The castle was silent for several days, for no one sought to aggravate a king.

Even Hugh was out of favor, said the tellers of gossip among the ladies in the solar, and he'd gone off to his estates to leave the king time to cool. But Sir Robert was only wounded, not dead. Men were always injured, if not killed, in these tourneys, which was part of the Church's quarrel with the lords who held them. And Hugh was son of the king's Constable, and no man more trusted and valued by David, especially now, with matters so grave on the border with England and rumors of trouble in the West. Robert's misfortune was discussed much for a day, but no one seemed to know exactly what had happened, or why. Ailsa found herself the subject of curious comments and some spiteful jibes. But in the end, there was little to keep the court's interest, save it concerned the son of one high in the king's favor. Still, even that was not enough to keep the court chattering and the talk died away.

Ailsa heard from the kitchen maids that Robert was expected to recover, though she could not discover how serious his wounds might be. In the hall, which she entered once in desperation, she found little reliable news and the ladies' speculations about her upcoming marriage to Hugh quite trying.

No more news of Robert came to her ears as the week wore on. Her first fear that he might die now seemed extreme. Twisting her embroidery in her fingers she stared out the narrow slit of a window. What if the wound festered? And what was she to do about de Morville, who apparently regarded her as his betrothed? The thought of him now made her angry, but he was powerful indeed. And his castle at Irvine, so near to Caerwyn, now loomed as a serious threat. Caerwyn's safety must be her first concern. The laborers and farmers and their children must be protected somehow. It was all her responsibility, but she found no answers to her questions, and there was no one she could ask.

One late afternoon, Effie swished into the room with a container of hot wine. She busied herself pouring out the hot drink and preparing slices of cheese and apple on bread. All the while, she chattered on. Ailsa knew she should enjoy the story of the prize-giving Effie was relating. Davy had received a small holding near Annan, and a bag of silver coins, newly minted at Carlisle, with King David's seal upon them. The silver, from the king's new mines, gleamed. Ailsa fingered the coin and thought this king grows ever more powerful.

Effie continued with more news. "David is angry with the prince, though he agreed to honor the prizes and a good thing too." Effie smoothed the skirt of her gown, brushing away the bits of cheese.

Ailsa grasped her elbow. "Have you heard anything of Robert and his wounds?"

Effie gave her a sharp glance. "He hasn't been seen at court, but stays in his tent. De Morville drew considerable blood and the king's physician took more."

Ailsa received this news silently, though she felt her stomach turn over.

"Yet the physician says he'll recover. If it does not fester."

"I should not care so much."

"Yet somehow you do." Effie touched her shoulder and went away, promising to check in on her later.

Ailsa went to the narrow window and peered out. How she missed home right now. Soft gold light slanted across the courtyard. But this was a king's castle, and the courtyard was crowded with armored men, servants rushing back and forth, and courtiers in knots, gossiping, laughter and shouts mingling on the fresh breezes. Ailsa sighed. She longed to walk down her secluded garden pathway or ride into her forest and swim in her pond; she imagined how it would look on such an afternoon. The light would send long shafts through the clear water. It would be cold on her bare skin and the only the sound the calls of swallows overhead.

And yet, even in that sanctuary, she'd been surprised by armed strangers. The entire world was changing, and try as she would to hold onto the past, she could not halt it.

I'll send Robert a message, she thought, and immediately a weight seemed to lift off her chest. Of course, how simple. But who could she send? She decided to write her message, it was more likely he would get it. She found a maid sweeping the stairs, who returned in a short time with a quill and some ink and a small piece of paper. She penned her words, then rolled the note in a piece of linen cloth. Finding a boy downstairs, she whispered her directions, pressing a coin in his palm.

This done, Ailsa smoothed her hair and gown, and entered the hall. Effie waved to her with a glad smile. She moved over to give her room on the window seat, where she was embroidering leaves on a gauzy length of cloth as an edging for her wedding gown. Ailsa turned the work over in her hands, admiring her skill, and said in a low voice, "I have sent a message to Sir Robert."

"And what said you," asked Effie, putting down the sewing work.

"I asked after his health, of course."

"Of course," agreed Effie. "And what else?"

"Need there be anything else," said Ailsa, with a small frown.

Effie shrugged.

"I asked him to meet me."

"Ah," said Effie. "And what will you say to him then?"

Ailsa pressed her lips together. "I am not entirely sure, but I must know his wound improves, and I must make him understand."

"So," said Effie, "you fear he has misunderstood?"

Ailsa twisted Effie's fine work in her fingers.

Effie gently pried the fragile embroidery from her hands. "I wish you to be as happy as I am," she whispered. Then in a normal voice, she said, "There is your boy now."

The boy handed her the rolled linen. Ailsa turned it over in her hands. It was unopened. "Sir Robert sends regrets, but he cannot accept your letter," the boy said, "given your betrothal to Lord Hugh de Morville, it would not be proper." He nodded and pleased to have recalled the long message, skipped away.

Ailsa felt her face flame. She ignored Effie's sympathetic look. "If that is how he sees it, I'll not send another message." She made for the door. She wanted to be away. She wanted to go home.

Instead, she blundered into Beatrice, her servants clustered around her. "Ailsa, I've been looking for you."

Ailsa struggled to rearrange her face.

"About the Midsummer celebration," said the lady, "I've just received word from Hugh. He will return in time to accompany you. It will be an auspicious time, do you not think, for the formal announcement."

Ailsa could not choke out a response, and she felt tears burning, so she nodded and pushed past Beatrice and hurried down the path. Apparently, everyone thought they would marry. And whatever her feelings, she had learned this much at the court. Caerwyn needed a protector. And one would be found for her, whether she willed it or not.

It was the quiet time of day when servants prepared the afternoon meal and courtiers idled time away in the great hall. A cold wind blew into Ailsa's face. She pulled her hood up over her hair. Rain slanted down in a steady pouring. She ran across the courtyard to the stables. The warm smell of hay and horses was comforting. She paused and listened to the contented chewing of the horses and felt her tight shoulders relax. She found Jamie where she expected, grooming Robert's Tanet, crooning to the big stallion as he worked. Tanet pricked his ears, seeming to understand, and let Jamie pick up his massive hoof for cleaning. "Jamie," said Ailsa softly. The big horse shifted and swished his tail.

"Easy, easy," said Jamie, coming out of the stall.

He had learned a good deal about caring for such a horse. From Robert himself, no doubt. She yanked off her hood. "I must see Sir Robert. You know it has been another full week and he still has not reappeared at court."

Jamie's eyes clouded over. After a pause, he said, "I will try." He put down the rag he'd been using on the horse, measured out some oats, and dumped them in a bucket for the stallion. Then he grabbed an oiled cloak and started walking, so she followed him. They walked across the courtyard, emptied in the pelting rain, and then on to the farthest edge of the field, still pitted from the melee, to where two tents were erected beside the stockade fences that surrounded the castle. Ailsa was soaked, her wool cloak heavy and her hem covered in mud, but she ignored that, and waited while Jamie spoke with a man standing outside the tent.

The man disappeared inside the tent. Jamie returned and said, "I'm not sure he'll see you, but he said he will try."

Ailsa swallowed, then thanked Jamie. He headed back across the field without a word. When had he become Robert's man and not hers?

Water streamed down the oiled sides of the tent and into ditches which overflowed in a torrent rather than channeling the water away; it seemed a terrible place for a wounded man. The guard did not reappear. Finally, she drew a deep breath and called out, her voice sounding unnaturally loud in the rain-sodden field, "May I enter?"

Her query met with a long silence. Then she heard the rumble of voices, pitched low. The guard emerged and behind him, another man. It was Will, his face drawn and pale. He stared at Ailsa. "Come," he said finally.

She ducked her head and entered, then stood uncertainly just inside, dripping water onto the earthen floor. The tent was dark and crowded, for three of Robert's men sat on upturned crates around his cot. They looked up at her but offered no greeting. At Will's signal they donned leather cloaks and slipped outside. Finally, Ailsa dared look at the man on the cot. They'd made him comfortable as they could; his straw mattress was deep and dry despite the rains. He had a rough wool blanket pulled over him and a flask of water and another of a darker liquid rested on the upturned box beside the bed. He was asleep, his strong arms unnaturally still.

Ailsa frowned and moved forward, forgetting her prepared speeches. "What have you done for him?" she asked, placing a hand on his brow. It was fiery and damp with beaded sweat.

"All that I know," said Will. "Comfrey and marigold for the fever. I dressed the wound with onions and honey." He touched Robert's limp hand. "He was doing fine as could be wished, even stood up and walked outside the tent yesterday. The fever came on sudden, last night, and gone higher all this day." His face was haggard. "He's in God's hands now."

Ailsa yanked off her sodden cloak and dropped it on the straw. She drew the blanket down and revealed the shoulder, swollen and streaked with red. She caught her breath. "This must be drained surely," she said, looking up at Will.

"So it has been," he said heavily. "Three times. And still fills again. It is beyond my skill." His face quivered, and he was quiet for a long moment. "The king's physician counsels more bloodletting, but the surgeon bled him twice already and each time he seems no better. Perhaps worse. I judged it best to halt." He shifted his weight from one foot to another. "I sent them away."

Ailsa nodded. She touched the shoulder gently. It was hot and tight. Robert stirred, as though her touch pained him.

"We have been together twelve years. Since Normandy. I never thought to see worse than some of our times there. This was supposed to be our new beginning." Will sat down on a straw bale and put his head in his hand. "I have done all I know."

"You're exhausted yourself," said Ailsa. "You'll take ill." She hesitated. "I know little of healing, yet I learned somewhat from our culdee. This must be drained again, surely."

Will shook his head. "It causes him pain. I thought it best to let him rest now." He turned away from her gaze.

She touched Robert's shoulder. The man on the bed stirred but did not waken. "No. We must do it together, try one more time. We cannot give up."

Will got to his feet, swaying with lack of sleep and worry.

"We need boiling water and clean rags and that light green moss that grows just at the edge of the birch trees where the forest meets the meadow."

Will sighed, but then went out and spoke to one of the men. The man returned within an hour, sodden to the skin, with a wad of wet moss wrapped in his cloak.

"Your culdee, he follows the old religion?" asked Will.

"He does. But he is a good man. I trust him. I saw him use this moss many times." She took a deep breath. "It did not always work. But sometimes it did."

Will nodded. "Well then." He handed her a knife.

Ailsa took the heavy knife and closed her eyes and focused, drawing back into her memories. She took three long deep breaths, harking back in her mind, hoping that what she found was truth and reliable.

She opened her eyes. Robert's face was white but for his brilliantly flushed cheeks. She breathed a few words of a blessing, long unspoken, that she'd learned from the old women who lived in the forest above the pond. She had died some years back, before Niall even. But she had been very old and very wise.

"You must hold him," she said to Will. She touched the shoulder, looking for the spot to pierce, the spot of greatest heat. One must slice open the area, a full two or three inches wide and cleanse it well with wine. She had watched the culdee do this, for a child with a deep and angry wound from a scythe. But she had never done it herself. Did she have the skill or the courage? She heard Robert's men behind her, whispering.

"Do it," said Will. He grasped Robert's shoulders.

She plunged the knife into the swollen flesh half a finger deep. Pus spurted from the opened wound. Robert twisted on the bed and blood began to flow out. She motioned to Will to hold him again, and swallowing hard, she steadied her hand. She sliced the wound open wide in a cross and peeled back the corners of flesh. She poured wine into the wound and used the cloths to press the corruption out. Blood, so much blood, ran and ran out too, staining the sheet beneath him. Robert groaned, then seemed to fall into a far deeper sleep. His face was grey. She packed the wound with the moss. Then she bandaged it all in the linen cloths.

When it was done, she rinsed her hands and feeling suddenly faint, she sat on a crate near Robert's head.

Will stood at the foot of pallet, watching Robert's still face, his own face creased in lines of distress.

"Go to the kitchens, and get some hot food, and then sleep an hour or two. He will need you when he wakes. I will call you if there is any change at all. You are exhausted, you must eat and rest," she said, "if you are to help him."

Will rubbed his face with both hands and stumbled out of the tent. The heavy flap closed behind him. She heard him speak to the men outside, the words drowned by the rain.

Rain drummed down and Robert's uneven breathing seem to expand to fill the tent. Wind gusts tore at the cloth and water seeped on her arm. She brushed it away and blinked. Though she had spoken brave words to Will, she did not feel brave or sure. She waited for each breath. His face, brows starkly outlined, eyes closed to her, was so very pale.

She sat until the chapel bells rang and all sounds in the courtyard stilled except for the bursts of rain on the tent walls and still he slept. His face was splotched with crimson patches, his forehead even hotter than before. She thought of the embers of November bonfires, when they slaughtered the cattle for winter meat. November, the dark month leading into cold and hunger. She'd held that off, at Caerwyn, since her father died, but each year it grew harder. So many men gone. And who could blame them, though it made winter all the tougher for those who stayed behind. There was no answer to that swirl of thoughts so she turned her mind away.

She thought of Eachna, proclaiming her stories out loud to the river. She thought of her own small stories and how she held them close. She must send them out into the world. Time could be short. Time was always short. She thought how lovely it would be to escape all this, to be far away, and free. She imagined her pond or some distant sea water bay and herself in the cold water swimming and strong. Her finger reached out and she touched his face with fingers dripping cool water.

Soon, the fever would turn, for better or for worse. She had tried to reassure Will, but she had no idea if their efforts would be enough. It was in the hands of God, or the gods that lived in the streams and the forests, or Robert's own strength.

The night hours passed. Once, Will came in to check, his eyes reddened and his hair streaming water. She shook her head and he stared for a long time at Robert, his lined face so sad she couldn't bear to watch and hid her face in her arms, then he left again. Night moved slowly by and gradually the rain lifted, becoming a soft patter. The gusty winds slowed, and the world grew very quiet.

Will appeared again, with a bowl of hot soup. She wondered if she should attempt to feed Robert, but he slept on, so soundly, it seemed wrong to try to wake him.

"You eat," said Will, "else we'll be nursing you. I had some at the kitchen." She grimaced but forced down half of the hot soup. "I'll sit with him now," said Will. "You must go back to the castle, else they'll be missing you. Day is breaking."

She wanted to say no. But he was Robert's good friend, and she was only a stranger, after all. Tied up with him by the king's plans only. She walked back to the castle, her mind empty save for a grateful sense of the pale milky beauty of a new day.

CHAPTER TWENTY-ONE

Midsummer

THE SUMMER SOLSTICE WAS INTENDED this year to be greater than ever, lasting a full three days, for King Arthur's court had finally returned to Scottish hands and Carlisle was in full festivities to mark the event.

Effie was at her chamber door, waiting, a finger to her lips to stop her greeting. "Where have you been?" she demanded. "I've been looking for you everywhere."

"I've not felt well," murmured Ailsa. She didn't like to fib, but she wasn't ready to discuss the strange events of the night with anyone yet, even Effie.

Effie pursed her lips but accepted her answer. She pulled Ailsa down the corridor, toward her own chamber. In her arms, she had the two gowns they'd worn to the Easter feast, blue and green. "We'll finish making them over today. It will be the best Midsummer ever, and Davy and I will dance." She twirled around the small room, holding her skirts high.

Ailsa smiled as Effie turned to her. Such a strange day and night she had spent. Back in the castle, surrounded by Effie's normal chatter, it seemed unreal. Perhaps Will would let her know how Robert fared. Or perhaps he would not.

"Let's try on your dress now," said Effie. She pulled the silk over her Ailsa's head. "I knew it would look just right, though you are pale today."

"Effie." Ailsa turned to her friend, startled to feel tears filling her eyes. She blinked them back. "I am so tired and confused."

Effie put an arm around her shoulder. "They are saying you are betrothed to Hugh."

"No, not yet. In truth I have no wish to marry him. But perhaps I must for Caerwyn's sake. I have agreed to attend the festivities with him. His mother insisted."

Effie's face creased into unfamiliar frown lines. "I have heard odd things about that family."

"What things?"

Effie swallowed. "I have wanted to tell you for a long while, but I thought you wished to marry him. I didn't want to trouble you. And I could not believe the stories true." Effie's gown slipped off her lap and she did not notice. "Beatrice, perhaps, is not such a lady and certainly not kind." Her round face flushed. "Some years ago, when she was younger and beautiful, she had a lover. At the king's estate near Ayr."

Ailsa frowned. "Effie, I . . ."

"Let me finish," said Effie. "She had a lover, a man much younger than she, and impetuous. 'Tis said she loved him well. But after a time, Lithulf, for that was his name, he abandoned her for another woman, young as he and marriageable." Effie took a deep breath. "'Tis said she was furious and vowed revenge to all who would listen. One night, when her husband was back from court, she tricked him into drawing his sword in her husband's presence, and he was immediately seized and taken away to prison."

"An unpleasant story."

"He was boiled to death."

Ailsa blinked and said nothing, seeing Beatrice's face. It could be true. The woman had always made her uneasy. But no, it could not. "That is a dreadful rumor."

"I did not believe it either, when first I heard it. I thought it was spite, for they are powerful, and she a domineering woman. But then Davy's uncle, he knew the young man and his family, and he says the story is true. There is something about her, about that whole family. They frighten me."

Ailsa wanted to reject Effie's words outright, but hadn't there always been something unpleasant in those observant eyes? She smoothed the soft material of the gown over her hips. "Thank you, Effie," she said finally. "I will think on it."

Midsummer dawned brilliant and a soft breeze tossed the new leaves. Ailsa breathed the fresh air at the window, then plaited her hair, weaving in buttercups a servant girl brought round in a basket, still fresh with dew drops.

Effie woke and pulled on her shift; even today she was a late riser. "Ailsa," she cried, "you look beautiful."

"So do you," said Ailsa, as a maid tugged Effie's gown over her head and arranged the folds about her hips. "Do you join in the celebrations too?" Ailsa asked the young maid.

"Oh, yes," she answered with a shy smile, "my only task today is to gather these flowers and bring them round to the ladies as they dress, and that's no task at all!"

Ailsa and Effie went out to the meadow beside the castle, where a throng gathered and musicians were picking out a gay tune. Servants circulated with trays laden with watered ale and wheat bread. Davy hastened over, and talked politely to both, but his eyes were on Effie.

Ailsa whispered, "Go, go, I'm fine, go along." With a grateful smile, Effie went. They wandered off into the crowd, oblivious to all but each other. Ailsa looked after them wistfully. Around her people laughed and joked, drinking the copious ale. For a moment, she thought of Niall. She'd never had the chance to spend Midsummer with him. He was gone before they'd ever had the time. Feeling out of place and out of sorts, Ailsa slipped away from the knots of laughing and boisterous people, heading toward the woods bordering the meadow.

As she entered the forest, bird song replaced the shouts of revelers. She walked along a wide path, her mind turning back to last year's Midsummer, and the bonfire back at her home, high on the knoll above the sea. A year had passed and so much had happened, she hardly knew what to wish for now. Her thoughts turned to Robert and she wondered how he fared and then she wondered why she bothered to think of him at all. She yanked at a branch, ripping the tender green leaves from the stem and tossed it to the ground. Yet it was time to think, a decision must be made, one that would have consequences all her life, for her and for everyone at Caerwyn. Hugh waited for her, even now, back in the meadow.

She followed the loop of the path deeper into a grove of birches and up a hill into tall beeches, their leaves new and brilliant green. Gradually the spell of the woods and the open air and the puffs of cloud overhead worked their magic. How restrictive life at David's court was. She pictured her own courtyard, and her special sitting place, an oak bench in a sunny spot out of the wind, up on the timbered walls, where she could see meadows in one direction and sea in the other. I want to go home, she thought. And why shouldn't I?

She sat right down, on a grassy spot in dappled sunlight, and considered the idea. She had achieved her original purpose after all. She was freed from Sir Robert now. He would, no doubt, be true to his word once he recovered, and he would speak with the king and arrange any details. She need not stay around for that.

But for how long could she remain free? Now she'd been at court, she realized how a woman's fate was mere politics here. David was a pious man, but stern and self-righteous, and she was just a token to be given away as a reward to ensure or sway loyalty. He'd offered her the chance of a religious life and that was the most freedom she could hope from him.

He would simply find another man to give her to. Maybe Hugh. Maybe some other stranger. She shivered and jumped to her feet, rubbing goosebumps from her arms. How hard it was just to be free.

"What are you doing here?" A stern voice interrupted her reverie.

Sir Robert, dressed in a blue tunic, his shoulder bound in linen, stood before her. "Thinking," she stumbled out.

"A strange place to do it."

She shrugged. "Did you follow me here? It is too far, how is your wound?" She stopped, afraid she was babbling, but she was glad to see him out of that bed, standing before her. "You should not be up and walking about yet, it is too soon." She stepped toward him.

"I thank you for your care. My men, Will that is, informed me of your aid when I was fevered. But I am quite well now."

She stopped at his clipped words. "I am glad." But he did not look fully well yet. He was pale, his brows a dark slash and his jaw tight. She blurted out, "You refused my message." And felt heat rush to her cheeks and neck.

"You are betrothed to de Morville."

"I am not."

She saw the flash in his eyes, before he turned away. She had startled him. "Sir Robert . . . Robb." She swallowed, words caught in her throat.

He hesitated and raised a hand, as though he would touch her. But he did not.

She felt her cheeks grow warm. "It is Midsummer," she said and blushed even more. She broke away from his gaze and examined the ground. An acorn cup lay tipped on a bed of moss.

He moved closer; she could feel the heat from his body and for a moment she thought of Niall and closed her eyes. "I wrote to you as I wanted to see you," she said in a rush, "to explain to you. I'm sorry about what I said. What I thought. Calling you a land grabber. I did not know you. I did not want a husband, any husband," she stopped. This was so difficult.

It was very quiet in the woods, even the breeze had fallen away.

She pressed her lips together.

Soft wind ruffled the long strand falling out of her braid and she went to thrust it from her face.

His hand reached out and bumped hers.

She did not back away.

He'd been angry, when she'd called him an adventurer, and angrier still, when de Morville taunted him on the field, claiming he'd had her. I should tell her now, Robert thought, about my conversation with the king. About the danger. What it would mean for her Caerwyn, for us, if there could be an us. I must tell her now.

Instead he put his good hand on her waist and drew her, slowly, to him.

For a moment, she let him, her eyes looking deep into his. Then she stepped back, shaking her head. "We come from different worlds entirely. I do not belong here, at a place like this court. In the world of the Normans and the English. Nor at any court. I am longing for my home."

"Then go home," said Robert in a burst. It would be the best thing. It would give them time. She was not marrying de Morville. His heart felt buoyant and free. He would be going on another mission for the king, a last dangerous mission, and if she went home, she would out of it; she would be safe. Though she could be involved, a nagging voice whispered inside. He brushed it aside. But if she would just go home, he need not broach his suspicions and on Arran, this time, he would search out the truth. "Yes, go home," he said. "It would be best. Take Jamie."

A twig cracked and they whirled around, separating. Will stepped into the path. Robert's hand relaxed from his dagger.

They were jumpy, thought Ailsa, but then Robert had just been stabbed. Will smiled at her, a big open smile that filled his whole face and Robert, seeing it, frowned. He spoke sternly, "What?"

Will gestured to him, and the two men moved aside and spoke together, their voices urgent but the words indistinguishable.

Ailsa took a deep breath, trying to regain her composure. Men always sought to keep women out of their calculations but, of course, she was not really involved; there could be many matters they'd speak of that were none of her concern.

They approached and Will, despite worry lines etched in his forehead, smiled again, and said, "I'm glad you go home now, Lady Ailsa."

Ailsa tried to return his smile. They were so very glad to get rid of her. She scraped her blowing hair back from her forehead. "I must return to the celebrations. I may be missed."

They watched her leave.

"How did you convince her to go home?" asked Will.

"I didn't have to," answered Robert, "she had already decided, which was fortunate, for she'd not be easy to convince otherwise."

"Does she know of our suspicions, about de Morville or fitz John?"

"I'd not see her worried for no reason."

"Rebellion and treason are hardly no reason. Wouldn't she be safer if she were on her guard? And what if that cousin of hers is involved…"

"She'll have the best of guards," said Robert smiling.

Will raised a brow.

"You," said Robert. "I'm sending you home with her." He frowned again. "Payn fitz John is ruthless. He will stop at nothing. I know this full well. I must find out what he is doing here in Scotia." He ran a hand through his hair and winced at the pain in his shoulder. "And I don't trust these de Morvilles. Yet I still don't know what they're after. If they're tied to this rebellion somehow." He sighed. "Or how Ailsa and Caerwyn figure in their schemes."

"I'm sure she is not involved," said Will.

Robert's lips tightened; he did not answer.

Will slashed at a branch with his dagger. "You cannot still believe it of her."

"I want you to leave as soon as possible." Robert glared across the field filled with a noisy crowd. "Cursed celebration. I'd have her go today."

Will squinted into the afternoon sun. But Ailsa was lost among the revelers. "I'll have her away on the morrow." He paused. "And when do you go?"

"The king awaits a messenger, then I must go straightaway. We may not talk again." He frowned. "I'll take boat to Arran, with more word from the king to MacLaughlin and Fergus."

"And will they want to hear it?"

"They will not." He paused. "But I can't afford to anger the king further. I return in a few weeks. The king journeys to the new cathedral at Glasgow for the dedication ceremony."

Will turned to him with a thoughtful look. "So de Morville spoke too soon, of wishes not facts." A smile brightened his face. "The lady has agreed then?"

Robert frowned. "You assume too much."

Will just grinned, slapped him hard on the back, and disappeared into the crowd. Robert found himself searching the revelers again. Searching for Ailsa in the mass of dancing people. He sighed. Nothing could go right until this intrigue with fitz John and the de Morvilles was cleared up. And this last mission for the king accomplished. Then he could come to her and explain all. He would break free. He had not come to Scotia to be in thrall to anyone, even a king.

Ailsa, in the throng by the dancers, turned to search the edge of the woods, but Will and Robert were gone. Taking a deep breath, she turned back to the dancers. Soon she'd be home, and all this a distant, if distressing, memory. She'd find Jamie and let him know they'd be leaving. They'd have to get provisions but it would be light nearly all night and travel easy.

Hugh de Morville, dressed in his usual black, but edged with green for the holiday, broke away from the knot of young men surrounding him and came toward her. She waited, feeling it was ridiculous to keep evading him. "Let us find something to drink at the tables," she said. "Then I want to dance all afternoon."

He laughed. She could smell the wine he'd been drinking. "Dance with me. Midsummer. The time for dancing and coupling. I want you, for my wife. Does that mean nothing to you?"

She tried to step back, but he gripped her arms and pulled her with him into the fringe of leaves at the edge of the woods. His voice dropped to a smooth whisper in her ear. "I will cherish you."

"I am not ready."

His frown gave way to a confident smile. "You are more than ready." He ran a finger from her chin down to the edge of her bodice.

She tried to step back, but he grasped her tight.

"Soon we shall be man and wife."

"We will not." But even as she said it, she thought, perhaps it is my duty. To Caerwyn, to my people.

Hugh hovered over her, as though he sensed her indecision, and moved a finger gently to her chin. When she did not back away, he traced three soft kisses down her cheek and neck. "Now," he said. He gestured to a bed of moss, sure of her, his grip loosening on her arm. "And after, we will announce our betrothal."

She yanked her arm away and ran, toward the noisy milling crowds, across the hot sunlit field. And felt his gaze in the center of her back.

CHAPTER TWENTY-TWO

A KNOCK SOUNDED AT THE DOOR. Before she could turn, it opened with a bang against the stone wall. Effie burst in, a flurry of blue ribbons and lace. "Ailsa!" she cried, "have you heard? Tonight they will commence the Arthur tales."

Ailsa stared up at her friend.

"You know the ones," prompted Effie, "Geoffrey of Monmouth has just written them up. 'Tis said they're wonderfully entertaining. The king's minstrel will read after the meal."

Her smile faded, as she took in Ailsa's pale face and the heap of gowns and shifts on the floor. "What are you doing?"

"Sorting through my things," said Ailsa, looking down at the gown in her hands and then standing up to shake out its folds.

"You are leaving."

Ailsa nodded.

"For home?"

"Aye, home."

Effie was quiet a moment. "Now? I will miss you. I hoped you could stay for my wedding. 'Tis but a month away."

"I know," said Ailsa, feeling wretched, "and I want to."

Effie crossed the room and gave Ailsa a hug and stared into her eyes. "Never mind, I will come to your Caerwyn and visit you. You must be prepared for a lengthy stay. And then, we will talk. Truly talk. As sisters would."

"I'm not practiced in sharing my thoughts," said Ailsa. "Yet, I would like that." After a moment she added, "You will not tell anyone where I go or when?"

Effie's expression was troubled. "Will you not have Davy escort you?"

"He must see to his lands before you wed."

"Surely someone…"

"I'll take Jamie."

Effie frowned. "He is only a boy. Still, I will not tell. Though some will discover soon enough. Is there nothing I can do?"

Ailsa shook her head. "I hope in my home to think more clearly."

Effie sighed, then she looked at the chest, and turning to the practical, said, "We must pack up these extra things and I'll put them in my chest and bring them along when I visit you."

Ailsa gave her friend a hug. Effie felt warm and solid under the lace of her dress. "I'll miss you too."

Effie sniffed, and turned to folding up the linen shifts. "It will seem strange if you are not at this dinner; everyone will be there, on account of the tales."

"True." She'd been raised on the Arthur tales, storytellers coming to her father's table many winter nights. Now some Englishman had written them down on paper, as though he'd invented them himself. "I'll have to leave after then. Though it will be late, still it will be light all through the night."

"I wish you'd change your mind."

Ailsa felt the breeze swirl in the window. It carried a smell of sea salt. She felt her courage rise. She grinned at Effie. "Don't worry, it will be an easy canter through the woods, now it's summer.

The hall was certainly crowded. It was hard to push her way to her customary seat on the long bench at the middle dais. Already the room was overheated and the smell of too many people mingled with the smoke from the tapers.

Ailsa sat and smoothed her gown again, fiddling with the cloth. She must not appear nervous. No one knew her plan but Effie, who would never tell. At least on purpose. She had only to get through this dinner and wade through the crowds celebrating Midsummer out in the courtyard. They'd be about their own amusements and well soaked in ale in the hours past midnight so that would be little difficulty. And she would not be alone; she'd have Jamie and they'd be on her fleet Nia.

But she must avoid Hugh. She looked around the crowded room, splashed with the colors of women's gowns and men's best tunics. He'd question her and press her. It might be best for Caerwyn to marry him. It might be her duty. It might be her only option. He had a violent side, but men's quarrels were inexplicable and brutal. She needed more time, and the comfort of home, to decide. She would not hide again, as she'd hidden from Robert in a closet. But she would not be forced either. She would make up her own mind.

She turned to her neighbor and tried to converse. She must make sure all saw her here tonight, so she'd not be missed too early. Effie would fib for her, say she was indisposed at tomorrow's dinner, but she had the idea Effie would not be very convincing. She turned to the older lady seated beside her. "I am so anxious to hear Geoffrey's account of Arthur's tales."

The lady seemed chiefly concerned with eating the white cheese pastries placed before them, so Ailsa soon gave up. Her mind whirled with plans. She'd spent the afternoon packing a chest with brown bread and walnuts wrangled from the kitchen on the excuse of a party of ladies in her room. She'd included a change of clothes against the wet, and two sharp knives. She'd be better prepared this time for the dangers of the road. She'd found Jamie in the stables and gone over the details with him. He'd looked unhappy. But he'd agreed to meet her well past midnight outside the gates with Nia saddled. She'd pressed her last silver in his hands to buy cheese and ale. Enough to last them to home.

"Ailsa."

Startled from her thoughts, Ailsa bumped the lady next to her with her elbow.

"Such a frown," said Hugh, leaning over her. "Whatever are you thinking on so seriously?" He smiled, but the smile did not reach his eyes.

"Hugh!" She attempted a light tone, but she was annoyed at

herself for being caught unaware. "You are excited to hear the Welsh tales, I imagine?"

He pulled her to her feet. "Come, a quieter corner will suit."

"I'm fine here," she protested.

But he tightened his hold on her elbow and guided her through the noisy crowd. He brought her to a window seat and ordered the occupants away. Seeing de Morville's fine clothes, the young man and his younger sweetheart, flushed and apologizing, left. De Morville gestured to her to be seated. His hands circled her waist possessively.

She tried to back away, but the seat was narrow. His eyes were impatient. His breath smelled of wine, harsh in her face. "You forget yourself."

His eyes narrowed, but he loosened his grip a fraction. "Everyone knows we are all but betrothed. Let us make the announcement now, tonight." He clasped her to him. His chest was hard, and his silver brooch scraped her skin, drawing blood.

"Let go," she said coldly.

"When you say yes," he said, "for you are meant to be my wife."

"Let go," she gasped, forgetting about being inconspicuous. "You are hurting me!"

"Lady!" came a clear high voice.

It was Jamie. "You must let the lady go," she heard him say, a tremor in his voice.

De Morville turned, still gripping her elbow and struck Jamie full on the face, knocking him to the ground.

"Jamie," Ailsa cried, and tried to rush to him. He was bleeding from his nose.

But de Morville clutched her elbow and turned his back on the boy.

"You must let me help him," she cried, furious. She looked around for aid. But everyone was absorbed in eating and drinking the king's feast.

De Morville yanked her away. "Leave him. He deserves to bleed."

She glared at him. "He only seeks to protect me."

"I will have that task from now on, Lady. I and no one else."

"I have not agreed to your offer. You assume too much. I will never be your wife!"

Suddenly he seemed to pull himself together. A mask dropped over his eyes. "You are right. I am at fault." He dropped her arm, and hauled Jamie to his feet. "There," he said. "True, it is his duty still. Only I wait so impatiently for your answer. You are hard on me," he said, his face charming, his voice wheedling.

She stared at him, disconcerted by the transformation.

Jamie swayed. She had no time to confront Hugh now. She brushed past him and put an arm round Jamie, leading him away. De Morville let them go, but she heard him call after her. "Tomorrow then." She shivered. I must think only of Jamie now, she told herself. And she need not think about de Morville later, for they'd be gone then, and free of him.

She took Jamie to her chamber and went to find a bowl and water in the kitchens. When she returned, she sponged his forehead and nose clean of blood, glad the other chattering women were still in the hall.

"It's nothing," protested Jamie. But he didn't seem to mind her fussing. She put honey on the bloody gash and bound the cut with clean linen. After making sure he was truly fine, she gave him leave to go. He promised to go straight to the barn to sleep right off, and to meet her by the west gate near dawn with the horse saddled and provisions ready.

"We can delay, 'tis not necessary to leave tomorrow."

"I think it is," said Jamie.

When he had gone, Ailsa paced in the tiny room, but it was far too noisy below to sleep. If only she were home already. She could never marry Hugh now, a man who could hit a child. How she'd escape she had no idea, but at home, surely an answer would come. Here, at the king's court, where she'd hoped to find justice, there was none. Only English ways and the rule of those with too much power.

She slipped downstairs and into the great hall, ignoring her normal spot at the table and standing with the servants lining the far wall, well hidden, she hoped. The storytellers had come in. She listened hungrily through the night, as they told their tales of Arthur, and his knights, and the magic that resided in the forests when they ventured out on their quests. The stories differed from the versions she knew and loved. As she listened, she wondered where Eachna might be now and what tales she told.

The weather had changed over the night hours; it would be a slow day of misty rain. Fog blew in from the sea and the damp smell clung to Ailsa's wool cloak. Most of the castle slept, after the long hours of carousing, so she slipped out unseen. She headed out the gate. The guard here often slept, she'd found, and she could escape unnoticed.

A stream ran along the west side of the castle, and she followed its banks, as it wound its way toward the woods. She walked fast, her cloak wrapped tight against the raw damp. She could smell the green scent of ferns poking up on the stream bank. Drops of water clustered on the fronds, bending them toward the ground. The air felt like a cloud, soft and thick and misty on her cheeks.

She was thinking about the Arthur tales she'd heard last night. They were well told by the two storytellers, taking on the different characters in turn, but so much had been altered, or left out entire. So much that seemed important just wasn't there. It had surprised her how angry and bereft she'd felt.

When she'd left the hall, in the hour past midnight, she'd started to tell a wandering tale of her own, just in her head and then to the three kitchen girls clustered outside the door, who she'd seen many mornings when fetching her mug of watered ale. She'd started in by accident, answering a question, as they'd found it hard to hear, but found herself embellishing and adding and correcting. She added in the parts she had known well since a small child, scenes that were part of the tales in a Gaelic telling. And she'd added in parts of her own, inspired by girls' transfixed faces, and soon quite a group of servants had clustered around her and something had happened. She'd spun off the old tales completely and invented a new story, imagining as she went, following the steps of one woman, a maid servant to the king's daughter. She'd had the maid embark on three amazing adventures, each more exciting than the last and in the end, the maid servant left the king's daughter and a life of security and ran away. She'd married and set up a home for herself, deep in the forest, away from the court, happy and independent and free.

The king's guard had come by as she wound up the story. The servants were laughing and clapping and asking for more. So she'd told them the old tale of the Queen from the West who comes over the water and again she embellished the tale, speaking of the peace the new Queen would bring and the reviving of the land, so the crops blossomed and trees grew tall and flowers carpeted the fields and no one was hungry or poor.

The head of the guards frowned when he heard the last part and ordered his men to break up the crowd. With angry shouts and kicks they'd dispersed the servants and she'd slipped away, afraid they'd recognize her and drag her to Hugh or even to the king.

But on her pallet in the last hour of night, she'd laughed silently, amazed. It was just as Eachna had said. The words were there, in her, or out there somewhere, calling to her. She just had to pull them in and weave the tale and say them right out loud.

The first birds were calling. It was time she was gone. The woods steamed and smelled of wet earth and leaves, and a spicy scent of wild garlic rose from the star like flowers under the tall elms. Her skirts, sodden where they'd trailed in the stream, wrapped around her ankles. She kicked at them impatiently. She must stop her dreaming and find Jamie. It was time, past time, to go home.

She left the meadow, turning back for a last long look, but she could see only shifting clouds and swirls of grey; even the castle was shrouded. Its high walls disappeared completely in the mists, as though it were a magical dwelling from one of the tales. As though her time there had never been. How eerie. How strange to be leaving. Strange to be going home. She thought about the story she'd told. Some part of it surely inspired by that family she and Jamie had sheltered with during the winter snows. Some part of it her own yearning to journey and be free.

What was that noise? Like the clink of metal, but certainly she was alone in this foggy field, unless it was Jamie. She hesitated, not breathing. It didn't sound like Jamie bringing her horse.

Mist blew across her face and she blinked the water from her lashes. She began to walk again but couldn't help listening. She turned, but no one was there. She shifted the pack of food and clothes from one shoulder to the other. Then she heard it again, a faint metallic clink, followed by a muttered curse. "Who is there?" she called out. Her voice sounded too loud. No one answered.

She crouched down, pulling her hood to hide her face. The fog made it hard to know where the sound had come from. She strained her ears, listening. At first, silence. Then a man's voice, too close, cursing again. Footsteps, someone wearing heavy boots, crisscrossed around her. As though he was searching. She gathered her skirts up and thrust them under her belt. Still crouched over, she moved away, or what she hoped was away. She moved slowly, hardly breathing, until she couldn't hear his boots, though she listened hard. The mists were clearing in the rising breezes and she glimpsed the castle gate.

She ran, hoping he'd not hear, hoping he was far away. She ran fast, feeling his menace behind her until she reached the walls. She stopped, her fingers on the rough granite, and waited until her breath stilled. She should go in. But who was out there in the fog? And where was Jamie?

She moved toward a stand of thick hollies by the gate. She pushed into the center of the bushy evergreens, wincing as the sharp leaves scratched her arms, and crawled forward until she could see the open gate through the branches. She could hear the clang of pots from the kitchens. She waited, cold seeping into her hands from the damp. From the kitchen came the friendly sounds of the kitchen maids clattering mugs and slicing bread.

Strong arms clamped around her shoulders from behind. Her mouth was covered by a grimy palm. She tried to scream but could not make a sound. The man holding her was huge and silent. He mounted a waiting horse, dragging her up on the saddle in front of him. She tried to throw herself against his rigid arms, but she could not shift him. His leather-clad chest smelt of burnt meat and rank old sweat.

They thundered across the meadow, riding fast, reckless, through the fog, toward the woods. She bit the hand still clamped over her mouth and the man swore and hit her with the flat of his hand. The blow struck the side of her head, and she felt the world tilting, tilting, then blackness swirling up.

PART III

CHAPTER TWENTY-THREE

ROBERT STIFLED A YAWN and looked longingly at the large window in the king's chamber. Despite the grey cold, he wished he were out there, riding his stallion away from this castle. The voices droned on. Walter was back from his most recent trip for the king, and he'd brought the suspicion that Stephen of England was revoking his offer to give Northumberland to Prince Henry. This would violate the recent truce, completed just weeks before, and David was angry. Robert watched the king pace, deep furrows drawing his brows together over his eyes, which stayed focused on the uneven floor.

Walter had insisted he come, thinking to include him, Robert guessed, shifting on his seat. Walter ever wanted to be at the center of things. He was never happier than in the middle of an argument over a legal quibble or some policy decision. While he? He should care about such things. But he'd give a lot to be out, walking, in the mist, rain, whatever. Inside, problems piled against problems. In addition to Stephen's prevarication, there was the prideful Earl of Chester, one of the many powerful border lords, to contend with. He was bitterly set against David for wresting Carlisle from Stephen and setting up court, for he regarded Carlisle as his, though he'd lost it long ago to the English.

Robert tried to focus but found himself drifting. Since coming to Scotia together, he and Walter were drawing further and further apart. Walter's dry wit and even head were welcome here, and he delighted in the endless discussions of strategy stretched out over multiple dinners or days in the council room. He was an excellent steward to the king, organized and honest. The huge household ran smoothly; supplies flowed in regularly, and the account books were neat and up to date. David relied on him more and more. Evenings, Walter often played chess with the king in his private chamber. Indeed, what with the constant travel and being closeted with the king, Robert hardly saw his old friend at all.

Decisions were being made here, important ones no doubt. But he felt like real life, or the life he wanted, was somewhere else. Now he was to be sent off yet again on the king's business, back to the rebels on the coast. It was dangerous, for they were forewarned, and would reveal nothing of note to him. And might well decide to rid themselves of a troublesome messenger and so send a message back to the king. And perhaps, Robert thought uneasily, that was even what the king hoped. Walter, he guessed, had no idea how precarious his relationship with the king had become.

Robert sighed. At least he knew Ailsa was safe. Will would see to that. He'd take her home to Caerwyn and guard her well till he arrived. He shifted on the hard seat. True, he'd not had the time to explain his thinking to her, but there was time enough for that. Time enough for words. His feelings were so new and nebulous. That he was considering a different future was an enormous leap when he'd thought, for so many years, his life was circumscribed by his vows and his past. Will had got him thinking. Arran had got him thinking. Or perhaps it was just that he was older and more aware than ever of the possibilities. At her home, at Caerwyn by the sea, there would be time, and silence, and space; he'd find the words. How he'd begun to think of a life built together, a home, children, love. Of a future, instead of a past.

"Robert." Walter, frowning, repeated his name.

The lawyers were picking up their sheaves of paper and handing pens and ink to servants, preparing to leave. He gave Walter a rueful grin. The king was in close conversation with his Constable, the elder Hugh de Morville. He was shorter than the king, stiff-backed, with dark hair threaded with grey and controlled brown eyes. Nothing like his flamboyant son.

Robert was glad that the Constable had not been here at Carlisle these past few months. It meant he could hardly have been a direct party to the attacks in the forest. The son, though. That was another matter. Perhaps now the Constable was home, he'd put an end to any plotting. Poor Peter would surely get short shrift in that affair though. Which reminded him; he must do something for the boy. He needed another chance. Relieved that the meeting was finally breaking up, he joined Walter in the hall.

Walter shook his head. "I gave you the perfect chance to approach the king," he said. "Your knowledge of …"

Robert cut him short. "It's no good. It's clear we're setting out on different paths now. Scotia will mean different lives for you and me."

Walter examined him and then sighed. "Yes," he said finally, "I suppose that's the truth. But I will miss the old days."

Robert nodded. "But the future is looking good too."

"I'm glad you see it so," said Walter, eyeing him curiously. "Yet, you have ever been one to look backward." He smiled. "Yes, I knew about your old home and lands, though you would never speak of it. I'm sorry for it. You've convinced that bride of yours I take it."

"Close enough," said Robert, thinking his friend had seen more than he'd known. "But I go to Arran one more time for the king first."

"God speed," said Walter, frowning. "Watch your back. Matters are becoming complicated in the West." He looked like he might say more, but in the end, he did not.

King David gave Robert a level stare. "If this Wimond can rally the Galwegians, along with those on Arran, Man, and Bute, then the entire mainland coast to our kingdom becomes unsafe. Even this castle would be at risk."

"Two borders at war, on the south, England and in the west, the Isles. Yes," said Robert quietly. He picked up his leather gloves and pulled them on, glancing out the window. "I go immediately."

He walked to the stables pondering the news that had arrived just this hour. Somerled,, who some already called Lord of all the Isles, had married. Without David's knowledge or permission. Worse, he'd married Ragnhilde, the daughter of Olaf, King of Man. And he was already bound by his sister's marriage to the traitor MacHeth. Troubling news indeed. If Somerled were truly David's ally, why seek these marriage alliances with David's enemies? Were the Isles on the eve of full rebellion? Robert stopped walking. What would happen, if war came to the Isles, to Ailsa and Caerwyn?

David intended to create a united Scotia, bringing peace. Or so he often said. But war was only sometimes the path to peace, and too often just the path to more violence and endless brutality. He knew this well from Normandy.

A boy jostled him from behind and blurted out a frightened apology. Robert waved him on and started walking again. Troubling thoughts, but his immediate task was clear; he needed to get information for the king, find out just how insecure David's hold on the Isles might be. He had suggested someone else might be best for this task, but the king seemed determined that he, and no one else, should go. Why that was, another troubling thought. Still, he must try to get the information, and more, see if he could persuade MacLaughlin and Fergus and any others. Peace was worth the effort and the danger. Still, the entire conversation with the king had been strange and unsettling. As though the king were testing him somehow, or suspicious.

Robert ran his hand through his hair. He must find Dugald and Torquil. They were his best hope of gaining the ear of those Arran lords who mattered. He reached the stables and called a brisk set of orders. Soon horses were saddled, supplies bagged, and ale casks slung over the pack horses' backs. He wished he could take Will with him, this whole venture made him uneasy, but he dared not. He needed to know Ailsa was safe.

There was no more time. He glanced up toward her room. There was much he needed to say. But he had to make the tide. And think, what to say and how to say it. He found Will, checking his horse's girth. "Keep her safe," he said brusquely.

"We'll meet you in Glasgow in a few weeks."

"Yes," answered Robert. He pulled off his leather glove and yanked the chased gold ring from his finger.

Will stared as he handed it over.

"Give it to her." He laid a hand on Will's shoulder, then swung into the saddle. A ship was heading around the Galloway peninsula toward Arran. It was by far the fastest way to reach the island, but he'd have to race to make the tide. He gave a last thought to Will, and to Ailsa, and then he put them out of his mind. He had a difficult task of diplomacy ahead and he must succeed, or all the coast and Isles would not be safe. War would come to peaceful Caerwyn. He'd left Normandy and England to leave turmoil and ruthlessness behind. He must not let them come here.

Ailsa's head was pounding; she seemed to be swimming through a dark sea, trying to find the light. Her shoulder hurt, quite a lot, and she was lying on cold ground. Voices, men arguing, but softly so she couldn't make out what they said. She tried to open her eyes but could only force them open a crack. And still no light. Night already? Or something wrong with her eyes? She ran her tongue over her dry lips and shivered. She tried to calm herself, and hear, but the men remained out of earshot, their voices wandering up and down and she was so tired. She slipped again into a dark sleep.

When she woke a second time, sun beat on her face and she hurt all over. She was lying on a filthy blanket. She could smell the stink of wool steaming in the sun. Her eyes could open further, one of them at least, and she could see. She blinked, red dots jumping in her vision. Still, she didn't feel so dizzy anymore. She moved, but found her hands and feet were tied, with thick ropes and unfamiliar knots.

No one seemed to be around. She guessed it to be about noon, but of what day? She felt fear rise and she pushed it down. I must figure out who these men are and what they hope to gain by taking me, she thought. Were they after ransom? It seemed unlikely, with so many wealthier ladies at court. She grimaced at the needle of pain that lanced through her head. She must be calm, use her wits, think. The swirling dark threatened again, and she swallowed hard. I must stay awake, she thought. I must know who they are and what they're after.

She lay in the sun for a long time. Midday gave way to afternoon and then evening. A cool wind blew up and she could smell the sea. Not Englishmen then; it was likely these were Islesmen or Irish, bent on heading back to their home territory, with her as their prize. Her head hurt and she was starving. Also, she needed water badly. Fools. They'd kill her before they got their silver.

She heard a dog barking, and the indistinct sound of men cursing. She narrowed her eyes to slits. Perhaps they would say something about where they were taking her. She lay still, though fleas from the blanket were driving her wild. Heavy boots crunched on the gorse and brush. Straining to pick up their voices, she concentrated. It sounded like at least three.

"You shouldna left her alone, I tell you, 'twill be your neck if she's gone."

"Gone," said another voice, scornful. "Mungo here knocked her so hard, we'll be lucky if she wakes up before we give her over."

There was a silence at this, and she listened, trembling inside, to the sounds of their arrival.

"Well," called another voice grudgingly, "at least she's still here and all." She could feel them staring down at her. She tried to appear asleep. One nudged her in the ribs with his heavy boot. It was all she could do not to open her eyes and scream at him.

"She still sleeps," he said. He sounded bleary, the worse for drink.

"Just as well," said the last, and she recognized his harsh voice. He was the one who had carried her off, the huge man who had hit her. Mungo.

"We'll get her aboard and then we're safe."

There was no more conversation. She heard them kindle a fire and her stomach rumbled at the scent of meat roasting. She had to bite her lip hard to keep from giggling, though why she should laugh was beyond understanding. They must have bagged a hare or two. Eventually, she heard them gnawing on the meat, and after another endless stretch of time, they rolled out their blankets. After a few mumbled curses there was silence, mostly, and sometimes snores and farts.

She dared to open her eyes. It was the deep grey half light of midsummer midnight. She let her eyes adjust to the dark. She must get away. Now, before they put her aboard some ship, bound who knows where. Her head pounded, but she tried to ignore it, to come up with some plan. Suddenly she remembered; she had hidden a small knife in her boot for the trip home. Perhaps it was still there?

She wriggled silently, trying to get her bound hands down to her ankles. They hadn't tied her feet so tightly, the fools. Eventually she was able to slip her hand in. It closed round the warmed metal of the handle. They'd missed it! She sawed through the coarse ropes on her ankles with the sharp blade. Her hands were harder, she dropped the knife several times on the blanket. Once one of the men shifted in his sleep. She waited, hardly breathing, till he slept and snored again.

Overhead, the stars came out. She sawed through the last of the rope and rubbed her aching hands and wrists, feeling the blood surge into them. The pain in her hands was intense, but she ignored it. Casting one look at the men, their bodies outlined in the dying fire's light, she rose to her feet, swaying with the effort. One foot in front of the other, she thought, I can do it, I must. She headed toward the woods on the edge of the clearing, thinking only that she must get away. One step, two, another. She dared to hope and moved faster. There was no sound from the men.

She reached the middle of the clearing and avoided a jumbled pile of stones. The woods were shadowy and black compared to the field, where a rising moon lighted the stones and tall grass heads and herself. She kept going, slow and careful, though she wanted to fling herself into the dark woods, find somewhere to hide. In the dark, hidden, safe, she could form some plan. She had no idea where she was, but she could figure it out. If only she could get free of them.

She hurried, though it was hard to see, the shadows under the trees drawing her in. Faster and faster, until she was nearly running. Suddenly, she fell, her foot jammed in a hole between two rocks. She grunted and bit down on the sound, as pain knifed through her twisted ankle. One of the men rolled over, mumbling, then another. Curses rang in the air as they stumbled to their feet. She managed to stand up, and took a step, but her cursed ankle gave way; sharp

pain surged through her leg, making her gasp. The men were milling about now, and she heard the pound of running feet. She dared
another step, desperate, and fell full length on the ground. Crushed
grass scraped her face as she struggled to her feet.

She threw herself towards the woods. A hand grasped her gown
and then another. She heard the rip of cloth. Then she was barreled
to the ground; gravel bit into her cheek and the smell of earth and
her own blood mingled. Her breath tore from her in sharp gasps. She
rolled over, slipping from the man's grasp, the reek of sour ale telling
her he was drunk yet. She stumbled to her feet and ran, though pain
stabbed up to her thigh as her foot hit the ground.

Her leg gave out. The ground hurtled up. The men were on her
now. One grabbed her waist and hoisted her over his shoulder, carried
her back to the fire, and dumped her on the ground.

"She's woken up," he announced to the third, who still stood by
the fire, his wiry hair disheveled from sleep. He was the big man,
the one who had carried her on his horse, who they'd called Mungo.
He eyed her, small eyes glinting like a pig in the firelight. "Aye, so
she has." He strolled over, seeming to tower in the firelight. He ran
a rough hand over her legs, down her boot, finding the knife. He
laughed and tossed it down by his pack. "Now bind her," he ordered,
turning away.

The others scurried to do his bidding and Ailsa found herself
tightly bound. Her right ankle ached terribly, and pains stabbed up
to her knee and hip. She wondered if she'd broken it. The big man
ignored her and the others and lay down. Soon he was snoring. The
two others, having tied her, eyed each other uncertainly. "One of us
best stay awake and watch her."

"She's not likely to get away now." Ailsa winced as the oaf pulled
at the tight bonds.

"Still and all," said the first, who had a whining voice. "He'll kill
us both if she gets away again."

There was a moment of silence, then the second agreed. "Aye,
and he would too. You go first."

"No, you take first watch, then I'll wake you."

"Water," said Ailsa. "I need some water, or ale."

They turned and stared at her.

"Well," said the second, "'twould do no harm." He fished a flask out of his pack and awkwardly poured some into her open mouth.

Half of it splashed out on her gown, and it tasted of old fish, but it was cool and wet. She was grateful. "Thank you." After a moment, she asked, "Where do you take me?"

But at that, the kinder one became agitated. "Can't tell you that, he'd have my head if you take my meaning," he said, with a quick glance at the sleeping Mungo.

"Be quiet, you fool," barked the other.

There was silence round the fire. Ailsa was busy with her own thoughts. She'd badly sprained her ankle, if it wasn't broken, and she'd not be able to walk away. It would be several days before she could make another attempt at best. And they meant to put her aboard a ship on the morrow. She could not place the men's accents, but English they were not. She tried not to panic, that would do her no good. She had only herself to rely on. She'd best pretend to be cowed and hope for another chance. "I need food," she said, making her voice sound piteous. The whining man grimaced but he found her a hunk of bread. She chewed on it slowly, making it last.

Night air blew across her face. She wished she were in her own bed, breathing deep, Effie sleeping, arms askew, on the next pallet. She pushed that painful thought away. I must sleep now, she thought, I must get strong. I cannot fail a second time.

The men rose early, loaded the horses, and flung Ailsa up, just like a sack of barley, she thought grimly. They rode most of the day, picking their way north. They were in the hills, still brown and waiting for spring, but coming up the coastline, for with afternoon came the scent of the sea, permeating the damp woods.

They stopped early and made camp. Ailsa was handed a chunk of dried cod to gnaw on and some runny cheese. She was ravenous, but the food made her nauseous. The kinder one, as she named him, gave her a surreptitious drink of ale. She was feeling stronger, but her ankle pained her, she was fearfully thirsty, and she couldn't help but worry endlessly. Clearly these three were working for someone; they were delivering her somewhere. It was terrible, but not unusual for a woman to be abducted and married off for her properties. Dugald had warned her many times to be on her watch. But to snatch the king's ward from the king's own castle, surely that was unheard of. She could not imagine who would hope to profit from her so. She rubbed her aching ankle, wincing as the rough bark of the oak tree she leaned on scraped her stiff back. She'd have to be patient, and keep awake, so she could make her escape. But her pounding head made her so sleepy and stupid. At least she was still on the mainland, and not on board ship yet. Perhaps they'd even changed their plans. She slept badly that night, waking often as the men changed watch or snored or fed the fire.

In the morning, they did not pack the horses; they seemed to be waiting for something. It was cold, with thickening clouds, the air swirling with moisture. They cooked some porridge on the fire, giving her a spoonful from the dirty pot when they were done. She gulped it down, though it was full of lumps.

About midmorning, Mungo pulled some linen rags, none too clean, from his sleeve. Without a word, he bound her head so she could not yell nor see. Without her sight, everything was much more terrifying. Surely if they meant to kill her, they'd have done so right off? But her dark thoughts multiplied. He hoisted her over his shoulder and carried her down a hill, toward the sea. His rank smell horrified her. She heard the others scrambling behind on the gravel, then the sound of water slapping the shore, and the creak of a boat rocking in the swells.

She tried to cry out, but she could not shriek through the tight cloth and she was silenced, as in a horrifying dream. She struggled, and the big man dropped her on the beach. Her shoulder crunched painfully into the stones. "Get this wench on board," he roared. Hands reached for her and she was hauled onto the boat. They threw her onto a pile of coiled nets; the smell of dead fish filled her nostrils. She heard them cast off; the sail cracked in the wind, the boat wrenched and then surged forward. She managed to sit up, but she could see nothing.

A man called, "We'll be there by noon tomorrow, and this keeps up." Another grunted assent.

"Unbind that woman's head," called an unfamiliar voice, but she heard Mungo roar back, "keep to yer own bloody business and I'll keep to mine."

"What, you've found a bound woman hard to handle," taunted one of the oarsman and several of his fellows laughed.

Mungo sat down near her, she knew it was him; she could smell him. He cursed under his breath, but said nothing else, nor did he loosen her bonds.

Suddenly the linen was pulled from her face. She gulped the sea air. The afternoon light glared in her eyes, though it was a dark day.

"A bad business this," said the man who'd pulled off the blindfold. He was dressed like the others, in leather boots and a short tunic, but he was clearly the leader of the galley.

Mungo scratched his hairy nose. "'Tis not for the like of us to question them," he said, "and happens he pays well too."

The captain grimaced but turned away. He called to one of his men, "Feed her and give her ale. I'll not have her die on my boat."

She was given bannocks and ale, though it was hard to choke them down with her hands bound. Still she was famished and the food unspoiled.

Night fell slowly over the water and the boat continued to head out, into the gleaming silver, leaving land farther and farther behind. They could be going anywhere, though the leader had said they'd reach their destination by midday tomorrow. That might mean the Isle of Man or anywhere on the coast of Galloway, or any of the smaller islands off the coast.

Escaping from an island would be difficult. Tears stung behind her eyes. She made herself review her chances. Jamie, he'd know she was missing when she did not meet him. If someone would believe the boy. Effie. She'd raise the alarm surely. Perhaps Robert, perhaps he'd believe. Surely Jamie would seek him out, and he would come.

He might not want her as wife, but he'd not abandon her to such a fate. Somehow she knew that was true. Calmed by this thought, she tried to get comfortable on the rough nets and shut her eyes. She must sleep; she'd need strength for what was to come. Time passed, the boat rocked on, the wind held. Finally, the listing of the ship and exhaustion helped, and she escaped into a fitful slumber.

Toward dawn she dreamed. Icy water washed over her head, and her long wool gown was drenched and heavy, weighing her down, sinking her, sinking her to the bottom of the sea. Green ribbons of seaweed clutched and clung at her legs and twined their way across her mouth and nose. Her father and her uncle floated toward her and she tried to call to them, but in the sea, all was totally silent. They floated by, eyes wide open but unseeing; she felt the water about them tremble but no sound came from their gaping mouths. Drowned, they were drowned and dead. She remembered that now. She reached for them, but they swept past on an unseen current, tumbling by her, her father's gold hair swept across her arm. Then came Niall, his muscled arm swollen and black from the blood poison, his eyes unfocused and blank. She wept then, salt tears falling in a salt sea. She felt the water like sadness filling her lungs, the cold sea engulfing her, and she screamed once, without sound or effect. And then she stopped screaming and words flowed out into the water, each in a tiny bubble of air, escaping up to the surface. Words and more words, as though they could save her.

Ailsa woke, her heart pounding. Around her all was silent but for the swish of water against the hull. The boat pushed on, and even the oarsmen slept, heads lolling on their chests. There was no moon, no stars.

No one would come for her. She was alone; she had made it that way.

CHAPTER TWENTY-FOUR

S OMETHING WAS DIFFERENT. Ailsa concentrated, trying, despite an overwhelming fatigue, to fathom what it was. They weren't moving. That was it.

She opened her eyes and saw the orange light of dawn painting the sky above the stark mast. The sail was down and rolled. She blinked, willing her head to stop throbbing.

Around her, men unloaded casks and barrels. She heard their shouts and the creak of the boat, straining against its anchor. She tried to sit up and look around, but she had to lie back, her head spinning. Before she could try again, Mungo lifted her over his shoulder. "Not so feisty now, are ye," he jeered.

She ignored him, willing herself to concentrate on any clues to her whereabouts. A small and bustling harbor, with some ten galleys pulled up on the shore. Black painted, with sails furled. Red sails. With a shock, she remembered those boats, remembered them pulling into her own bay. For her father's funeral. These were the boats of Lord Fergus. They must be on Arran. A wave of relief washed over her. Somehow just knowing where she was made her feel better. And Fergus had been her father's friend. She had only to get word to him somehow, then these dolts would be surprised.

A wagon waited nearby. Clearly, she was to be loaded along with the supplies and taken somewhere on the island. She made herself study the harbor, memorizing the curve of the shore, the crates piled in neat rows, the family of orange cats sitting on the coils of heavy rope.

They loaded her on the wagon with the chests and hitched a plow horse in front. It started off wearily enough, plodding its way west.

They were heading up into the hills at the island center. She was lying on a pile of straw, with her hands and feet still bound. She tried to wriggle into a position where she could see where they were going, but the sides of the wagon were too high. Frustrated, she slumped down on the floor of the cart. Where did Fergus have his manor, she wondered. Was it in those hills? Why had she never asked her father? Where were these men taking her, and why? Her mind spun round and round that question, for she could not puzzle out any answer that made sense.

The wagon jolted on the rough path and she feared the pile of chests would fall against her. But they held, tied with rough rope, and the horse gradually climbed to the top of the ridge, snorting. She could feel the cooler air here and smell firs, warmed by the sun. She tried to stay awake, memorizing clues, but she was exhausted.

She woke with a rough jerk of the wagon. Nothing but blue violet sky, streaked with pink clouds, could be seen. The evening far advanced already. The men were conversing. She tried to pick out what they were saying but caught frustratingly few words. "Wait," said one. And they did wait, the horse still hitched, for what seemed a very long time, and eventually a lurid pink and orange sunset darkened into the semi-twilight of a midsummer night. Her stomach was twisted in a knot of hunger. Her bound wrists were past aching, which was a relief.

Then the men, for no apparent reason, shouted to each other and the wagon lurched its way out of the pine forests and tracked through what must be a high meadow. She smelled turned earth and wet peat. After another interminable time, they passed through a gate, with only some whispered words with the guard, then rolled into a stone courtyard with a clatter of wheels.

Mungo threw a blanket over her head, smothering her in its rank smell. Gathering her up like a sack, he strode into the keep. She tried to keep track of the turns he made, but he went up and down and round, and she was confused. Finally, he kicked open a door and tossed her down. She cried out as she hit the hard floor, only thinly covered with last year's musty rushes.

He pulled off the blanket and dragged his dagger from his thick leather belt. She shrank back against the hard floor. With a horrifying grin, filled with rotting brown teeth, he slashed at her bonds, freeing her. "Good day, Lady," he called out in a sarcastic voice and the door thudded behind him.

She got to her feet, and then fell, her legs weak and her hands awakening to more pain. She managed to crawl to the door. She yanked at the rope handle, but it was barred on the outside. She called out and pounded. Her voice echoed in the small dark room. She sucked in a deep breath. Gradually, the pain lessened.

The room was small and windowless, she learned by crawling its circumference. She heard the rustlings of mice. She must be in a storage chamber somewhere in the keep. She bit her lip to keep from crying.

Imprisoned.

She must be strong. She was the lady of Caerwyn. She would think of the heroines in the old tales. They were resourceful. She would tell herself the old stories, she thought as she curled into a ball. All night, if she must. From them, she might learn. She would need their courage and cleverness and luck, just to get home.

Robert trotted down an ill-marked path through deep woods. He was on the west side of Arran and heading back to the manor of Lord Fergus. He'd already spent several days with MacLaughlin but, as expected, he'd learned little. His host had been frowning and silent, the hospitality sparse and the talk at dinner strained, but he'd come and gone without being killed so that was something.

The day was overcast, a chill wind blowing off the sea and his mood matched the weather. It had taken days just to get to Arran, what with bad weather, and finding transport for Tanet, and delays of all sorts. And once on the island, locating the men he needed had been slow.

Ahead of him rode Dugald. He'd finally caught up with him on the south end of Arran, but he'd not been able to dissuade him from another morning of hunting birds before moving north. He'd be lucky to complete the king's bidding in time to return to Glasgow to report at the dedication ceremony at the cathedral in July. Robert frowned, thinking of Ailsa. The court was becoming a dangerous place and somehow Caerwyn was involved. He was comforted that she was protected by Will, and away from the court, but the tangle of alliances was confusing and he still wasn't sure if or how she was enmeshed.

He watched Dugald's stiff back and sighed. After a long period of silent riding they reached Fergus' lands. They clattered through the gates and into the courtyard. Rain was falling. Dugald dismounted and nodded curtly in his direction before striding off toward the hall. Robert was left alone, apart from the boy who appeared to take his horse. Dugald was obviously anxious to see Fergus without him, but he shrugged. He'd find out what was going on. He went with the boy toward the stables, deciding it was more important to see that Tanet was well taken care of. "Quiet here today," he said to the boy.

The boy, blond hair stuck to his head from the rain, looked over with surprise, and mumbled, "Lord's away, sir, 'tis always quiet when he's gone."

"Away," repeated Robert. Why had Dugald brought him here at all?

"Aye, gone for some days."

Trading, or perhaps garnering information or gathering men. Robert picked up a rag and began to wipe down Tanet. Casually, he asked, "And where does Fergus trade this time of the year?"

But the boy shrugged. "Not likely the lord tells me his plans," he said with a grin.

Robert smiled back. "Not likely." Still, he thought, running a hand down Tanet's legs, he would know where Fergus ventured. It was near time for loading up the galleys for summer trading.

Robert entered the hall, after leading Tanet out to a stand of trees and tying him where he could crop the early grass, still thinking. The hall was silent, the fires unlit. Dugald stood at the far corner, looking out a large window toward the sea. "It seems Fergus is not at home," said Robert.

"Seems so." Dugald did not turn from the window.

"You knew that before we rode here today." Robert sat on an oak bench and stretched his legs out before him.

"I thought he should be back, 'tis just a routine trading trip, start of the season you know." Ignoring Robert, he continued to study the sea. "There," he said, pointing to a black spot on the horizon. "That's himself, I'll wager. He'll be joining us for dinner this night." He smiled, though the smile did not reach his eyes. "No need to fret."

Robert watched the small dot grow into a galley. They were playing him along, but to what end?

Later, Fergus welcomed him pleasantly enough in the fulsome language of hospitality, inviting him to eat beside him, but his eyes were appraising and cold. Robert found himself wishing he had Will by his side.

Through a lengthy dinner of stewed venison, he mulled over the message David had ordered him to deliver. Tell them they must fall in line or be judged enemies, outside the realm and our peace, the king had said. That had seemed unreasonably harsh even at Carlisle, seat of David's power. But here? He didn't think the ultimatum would sit well. Nor did he favor being the messenger.

What was the best way to achieve the king's purposes, and his own? Peace was what they both sought, though for different reasons. He thought about that word, letting it chime in his head. Peace. Time to till fields and harvest crops and make a life. Yet these men were suspicious of the king's version of peace, and perhaps rightly so.

Conversation was stilted, everyone ill at ease. Finally, the dinner passed. Fergus gave him a hard stare before striding out of the room. Robert took that for a sign and followed him out of the hall. In the dark corridor, cold air swirled around his knees. They climbed to a private solar above the hall. The fire was lit and the room warm, with clean rushes on the floor and colorful hangings on the walls. Already a flagon of wine and two goblets were set on a chest by two wooden stools. Fergus gestured to one and pulling off his outer tunic, stiff with colorful embroidery, he sank heavily onto the other. He downed a goblet of wine and wiped the drops from his thick beard.

"You are back," Fergus said, "and from the look on your face you've no good news to tell."

Robert nodded, trying to school his face to give no further clues. "The king sends greetings and good wishes to you, as a subject of his realm."

"Of course." Fergus poured another cup of wine.

"David seeks a new kind of kingdom, one uniting the various peoples. He wishes the Gaels and Norse of the Isles and coast to be part of this kingdom."

"What part," said Fergus. "Pulling the oars as galley slaves?" He chuckled at his own joke.

"David has a vision. He wants a nation of equals, where each group melds with the others, where all feel a loyalty to him and to the idea of a united realm. England has never been weaker in our lifetime, nor like to be. It's a God given time to meld Scotia together, to make a new nation to stand up with England as an equal."

"And what of the old ways?"

"David respects the old ways," said Robert. "He's willing to keep the culdees on, even, and abide by Gaelic customs here in the Isles, so long as he's not challenged in that which makes the regions come together as one when necessary, for defense."

Fergus stared into the fire, his blue eyes shielded from Robert's view. "I'll think on these words, which I know are more yours than the king's," he said finally.

Robert rose, realizing he was dismissed. The man had a presence like a king himself. But he paused at the door, and added, "I fear there is little time for thinking. David rides even now to gain Northumberland for Henry, but when he does, and he will, for Stephen and Matilda quarrel and so divide England between them, then he will turn west and secure these borders, if he must. At great cost to all the peoples here."

Fergus just gave him an enigmatic half smile, so he bowed and left.

He plunged down the dark corridor, and out into the courtyard. It was very late, and the night chill, with a wind off the sea. The air cleared his head of smoke, and he decided a walk in the open might be a good idea. It was certain he was too wound up to sleep.

As he crossed the courtyard, two men materialized out of the dark. Dugald, and he judged his companion to be Torquil by his build. He greeted them and Dugald mumbled a reply. Torquil jammed his face near his and said, "You don't deserve her."

Robert shoved him back. "What are you talking about?"

"I refused her, because I thought to save her grief, for who can go against the king's own writ?" He paused. "Yet, you abandon her, and take her lands. I'll not stand by for that."

Dugald put out a restraining arm. "Easy, we're under Fergus' law here, and he said no fighting."

But Torquil was past caring and thrust Dugald aside. He drew his knife.

"Have a care, I have no wish to fight you." Robert stepped back.

Dugald tried to catch his friend's arm, but he danced out of reach.

"Stay clear Dugald," he warned, "I'll fight any who tries to stop me."

Dugald glared at his friend but backed away.

Robert evaded the first wild thrust and tried to think. He must not fight here, he'd likely be thrown in Fergus' dungeons to rot, and he'd left his sword at Fergus' door. Given the excuse, Fergus would hardly pause; it was a perfect answer for the king's unwelcome messenger. Circling, he evaded Torquil's angry thrusts.

"Will you not fight," grunted Torquil. "Fight, you Norman coward!"

Robert felt a flick of pain as the blade nicked his arm. He gave a high whistle. There was the sound of charging hoofs and Tanet arrived. Rearing at Torquil, the horse thrust the man back into the night, neighing and snapping with his huge teeth.

Robert grabbed a handful of mane and leaped onto his bare back. Tanet's hoofs clattered on the rough stones of the courtyard. Suddenly, from the dark, they were challenged; guards rushed toward them, blocking the gate. Tanet darted to the left, scattering the surprised men, and gathering his legs under him, jumped the high gate. They galloped into the dark.

Robert eased the horse to a canter and then a trot and pulled to a stop in a shadowy stand of oaks. Leaping down, he led Tanet through the woods to the north bound path and set him on an easy trot away from the manor. It was past time to leave Arran and go to Glasgow, give his last report of what he'd learned to the king. The Isles and coast were a land to themselves, no longer under Norway's sway or even Orkney's and certainly not beholden to David. The Scot king had his work cut out if he hoped to meld them into one kingdom.

But it was possible, if the king could be persuaded to talk and concessions. It had to be still possible. His eyes scanned the quiet woods, seeing the burning huts and scorched fields of Normandy. Crying children. Women with dead eyes. Such horrors must not come here.

A fortnight later, noon sun beat on his bare head, making his dark hair feel like a hot cap. Robert swatted at an especially annoying fly and sighed. Glasgow Cathedral rose before him on the wide field, its stone towers solid and reassuring. The building site, busy for many months, lay quiet in the sun, the priests all busy back at the monastery preparing for tomorrow's dedication ceremony, the workers all in town readying for the celebration feast after. He slapped his gloves against his thigh. He'd hoped to find Will and Ailsa already here when he arrived. He looked down at his dusty leggings and boots. He could use some cleaning up himself. They would come soon.

He rode into the town. Wood and thatch huts clustered round a fast running stream. The monks had a more solid building of timber off to the west in the woods. The cathedral and the king's favor would turn this raw settlement into a bustling center in no time. He spotted another horse and rode toward the newcomer. "Walter," he cried, pleased to see his old friend.

Walter waved his green cap, revealing sandy hair neatly shorn. He was dressed in finery to match his cap. They decided to head to the fields with a cask of ale purchased from one of the villagers. There was little enough to do until the ceremony tomorrow and repairing to the monastery early held little appeal.

A bath could wait, thought Robert, as he settled his long form down in the welcome shade of a big oak. He could see the path leading into the village easily from here. When Ailsa arrived, he'd know. He resolved to pass the time pleasantly. "Tell me of the king's meeting in Northumberland," he said, after asking after Walter's father and brothers.

Walter frowned. "It did not go well. Stephen delayed and delayed, and finally arrived to meet us. By then David was not in a mood for compromise, you could say. The prince refused to meet with Stephen's barons, and Stephen has got no power over his own anymore. 'Tis clear the barons run the country and some have gone crazy, burning and raiding and taking all they can. Matilda masses a fleet in Normandy; no one knows if or when she'll try to cross the channel. It's all Stephen can do to pay off one baron here and another there."

"No more than we expected when we left England."

Walter looked out over the field baking in the sun, the sound of insects droning made a peaceful noise of contentment. "Yet I fear 'twill lead to problems here as well." He was silent a moment. "David is ambitious, for all he's a good and cautious king. He wants Northumberland for Henry. He'll go to any lengths to get it."

"War then," said Robert.

"Eventually," said Walter. "Not yet, not for a time. But I can't see Stephen losing his north without a fight. He's got to show his barons he can keep England intact, or he'll lose to Matilda." Walter settled his big body more comfortably. He tore off a few pieces of tall grass.

"If it's war, you go with the king," said Robert, more a statement than a question.

"Of course," said Walter. "I am his steward. And the life suits me, I'd not know what to do playing the country lord." He gestured to the fields around them.

Robert followed his hand with his eyes. "Quiet, and it suits me fine."

Walter looked with curiosity at his friend. "The warrior from Normandy?"

"I find myself changed here." He stopped, trying to put the thought into words. "Something here feels like I've come home." He shook his head. "Sometimes I think I want to make a home, make the fields grow, have a family."

Walter opened his mouth, then closed it, his blue eyes perplexed.

Robert laughed self-consciously. "Strange, is it not, after the life we led in Normandy. When last I saw David, I told him peace must come first, but now I must go further. I won't fight for him if he makes no concessions to the Isles. Or perhaps at all."

Walter drummed his fingers on his wide metal belt buckle. "Dangerous words." He frowned. "The old David might just have said fine, go to your lands and be content. The new David demands men and arms behind him. He sees opportunity. He means to take it, for Scotia, for himself. And he'll risk all for young Henry."

Robert nodded. "And I can do no less. Risk all I mean. That's life, is it not?"

Walter squinted into the sun. "You might well lose the lands." He tossed his cap on the ground. "Your life even."

"I know it." Robert frowned at the dusty road, empty in the afternoon heat. "But I must be honest with the king, tell him on what terms I would serve him, or quit his service. I can't play the middle any longer, not if war comes."

Walter pursed his lips and whistled. "Have a care. David is in a stern and strange mood these days. And he is a king, not a man." He got to his feet, avoiding Robert's eyes. "And I must not listen to such words, not any longer. I serve the king. It is dangerous, for me, and for you."

"I'm sorry Walter, that it must come to this."

"You are sure?" When Walter got no answer, he sighed and walked down the hill.

The next day, reserved for the dedication ceremony, dawned with a bright sun already glowing white in a white sky. The fields wavered green and steaming in the heat. Robert woke early, for the monks were bustling about, preparing for the big day. It was a once in a lifetime event for them, the dedication of their cathedral.

He tugged out his best tunic, pulled it on over his linen shirt and belted it, thrusting his knife in its usual holder. He stood a moment, uncomfortable in such finery, then ran a hand through his hair. His cell had only a narrow window and he could see little through it. Surely Ailsa and Will would arrive this morning. No sense to be uneasy. He stared out the window nonetheless. Then he made himself stop.

As he passed the next chamber, Walter looked up. He was rubbing his eyes, looking like he could use another few hours of sleep. "Always wide awake," he said accusingly. "And the king can't miss the message, if you wear that tunic."

Robert looked down at his tunic, embroidered at the hem in the swirling patterns of the Gaelic style. He hadn't thought about the symbolism of his clothes. He shrugged. Now that the day was here, he was excited. By noon, Ailsa and Will would be here. And he'd speak to the king today, discharging his final duties as the king's spy.

He entered the long chamber of stone, lighted on the eastern side by six narrow windows. Sunlight poured in onto the long trestle table, laid with white cloths. Big pitchers of steaming milk and bowls of fruit, cheese, and porridge were placed at intervals on the tables.

At the table's head, the king. It was a surprise to see him here so early, but just as well. No profit in delay. He bowed, and the king glanced at him, then went on talking with his advisors. The abbot hovered, vivid in his finest crimson robes, no doubt hoping for some royal attention on this important day.

Robert seated himself on the bench nearest the door, and helped himself to porridge and fruit, thinking hard. He knew what he wanted to say, but now that the moment was here, he needed to consider exactly how to say it. The news Walter had brought of the king's failure in Northumberland had to be factored in. The king needed the Isles pacified if he were to move on England, now more than ever. He'd not be in the mood to hear of the needs or wants of the Islesmen. He'd have to convince the king overtures to the Gaels were a wise move. In the long term interest of both Islesmen and French, English and Scots. He frowned into his bowl.

He had carved a wizened apple into slices when the king's advisor gestured to him. He thrust his eating knife back in his belt. The king was finishing his meal, and a bowl of early ripened pears was set in front of him. The monks must have a warm walled garden to produce such in early summer. Robert bowed and waited for the king to begin.

David took his time, examining first the pears, then looking at him long and hard, his brown eyes unreadable, though it was sure, thought Robert, trying not to fidget, that he didn't miss the designs on his tunic. He gestured to the servants to leave with an arm wave, and motioned Robert closer. "What of the Isles?" he said in a low voice. "How do they stand, with me or against?"

Robert drew in a breath. "'Tis not so simple."

"Yet it should be." The king frowned. "Explain."

"The Islesmen, and the men of the coast, for they be one and the same, they stand watchful and waiting." Robert spoke slowly, trying to choose the right words.

"For what do they watch?"

"For one who can pull the peoples together and make the sea routes safe for trading, for this is how their living is made. They watch for one who will provide protection and peace," he paused, "and be at peace with their ways."

"I am king."

"Yes," said Robert. He took a long breath. "But nonetheless, a king raised in England under Henry's shadow. And with English friends aplenty."

"Of which you are one." The king narrowed his eyes.

"I am that," said Robert. "But I am more."

David stared at him, his face impassive. His hands rested on the table, ornamented with three heavy gold rings.

Robert drew a deep breath. There was no going back now. "I mean that I am Norman in training, but Norman and Gaelic both by birth. My mother was Welsh, and my early years were spent fostered with my uncle in Wales, learning those ways." He rushed on, the words tumbling out. "For many years I told this to no man, for to be Welsh was to be a dog to the English, to the Norman French. I became the best knight I could and fought well. But always, hidden away, was this knowledge that I was not truly one of them."

There was complete silence from the king, so he charged on. "I have, by these missions to the Isles, found a part of me lost long ago, and now I realize I am the right man to be here, in the West, for I see the best of these many worlds, Gaels, Norse, French, English." He paused. "And I think you do too. I think I can help you bring the best to this region. If that is the way you truly go," he added. "If it be true you are David of Scotia, not David the Englishman."

David's councilor stepped forward, anger pulling his face into a snarl. "How dare you." He dropped back at the king's curt gesture.

David narrowed his eyes. "You are brave or a fool."

"I speak truth as I see it." He took a deep breath and spoke softly, just to the king. "I cannot support one who would crush the Gaels, stamp them underfoot, destroy their ways. One who would bring violence and war, simply because of a matter of differing customs."

There was a deep silence. The king was staring out the tall windows, his face impossible to read. Robert looked out the window too but there was nothing to be seen there, not even a raven. Long minutes passed and he felt a trickle of sweat down the small of his back. Would he lose Caerwyn, and Ailsa? Or his life? Would he be dragged away by the king's guards, plunged in a dark stone dungeon?

"Has not your friend Walter told you 'tis unwise to talk so to a king?" David picked up a pear, turned it in his long fingers, examining it for a flaw before biting into it. "Still," he said, "I need those who speak direct. Do you still wish Caerwyn and the responsibilities the lands will bring?"

"Yes," answered Robert.

"I knew of your background already, of course. We will talk more later." He waved a hand. Robert bowed and left the chamber.

Outside he paused as the hot sun hit his bare head. He felt giddy with relief, or unease. He looked out over the fields, shimmering with the unusual heat. With a king, with this king, but maybe with all kings, it was impossible to know their true thoughts.

Robert stood with a silent Walter on the wide steps to the front entrance of the newly completed cathedral. The sun beat down on the raw red rocks of the new building, bleaching them to a dulled clay. But Robert was looking out across the fields surrounding the building, his eyes narrowed against the sun. Where were Will and Ailsa? He couldn't convince himself any longer; they should have arrived by now.

"It's time to go in." Walter interrupted his thoughts.

They entered the dim coolness of the new cathedral. The walls were lit with numerous candles, but the light did not reach the vaulted ceiling, which stretched dark above him. Robert walked to the front of the chapel to his assigned spot and sank to his knees with the others already gathered. The chapel was quiet but for the whispers of the monks, still helping the abbot ready for the ceremony. David had not yet arrived, noted Robert, his eyes taking in the gathered nobles and their wives, all dressed in their colorful finest. It was a great moment indeed, for to have a cathedral, here at Glasgow, was an honor to Walter and a sign of the king's strong favor.

A fly landed on his hand and he swished it away. He shifted from one knee to the other. There was a rustle behind him, and men looked up. The king entered, severe in a purple robe of the finest wool. Stiff embroidered work of gold and blue decorated the borders. He carried the scepter of kingship in his hand. Robert felt again the ambiguity of this morning's conversation. A king's suspicion was dangerous.

The ceremony was long and even the cool chapel warmed with the heat of many bodies. The air grew close, but he'd endured much worse encased in armor in summer battles in Normandy. Finally, the bishop said the final amen, and all rose as the king and bishop left the cathedral, their long capes trailing. Walter followed close behind, as overlord of this region.

Robert let the rest of the crowd surge out of the cathedral. He walked back up the dusty road to the monastery. If Ailsa had arrived, she'd be there, recovering from the journey. He wished her there, imagined her waiting for him in the peaceful garden. But back at the monastery, all was silent and quite deserted. The evening meal would be taken in the open, out by the cathedral, and the monks and their servants were all there, preparing. Robert walked the empty hall and stared into each of the quiet rooms.

Hours later, the moon rose over the distant hills and a lonely thrush sang from the treetops. Robert sat by himself on a hill apart from the crowds, watching the king ride away. David was busy, and while Glasgow was important, now the dedication ceremony was over, he intended to return to Carlisle straightaway. Robert had bidden farewell to Walter.

"You should take care," Walter had said to him quietly as he pressed him to his chest. "For old times sake, I say this to you and I mean it." He had looked away then, and said, "We won't meet again."

Robert looked out over the boisterous feast. The brothers were scurrying back and forth, still carrying loaded platters of food, though some were starting to dismantle the large tables set up for the celebration. The nobles had departed and now the feasters were men and women from the village. Children raced and screamed. Behind them all, the cathedral loomed, its spire lit by the moon. A chapel, Robert thought, should be serene and not so grand. Still, what could he expect? David was a king, so he'd built something grandiose, something that called attention. After all, it was meant to show the English way of worship dominating. Even here on the site of St. Cuthbert, the Celtic saint, whose own church had been a small wood hut.

The moon climbed higher and still Robert sat. At first light, he'd take Tanet and head on the road to Caerwyn. He hoped he'd meet Will and Ailsa, delayed for some reason or other, and they could just turn around and ride all together back to her home. Their home, possibly. It was hard to know.

He saw one of the horse boys running toward him and rose.

"Sir," the boy called, breathless. "A man's arrived, asking for you."

Robert grinned and walked briskly after the boy. He ran up the hill toward the monastery, his eyes searching for Will's big figure. A man waited, near the stone walls encircling the monastery.

It was Peter who walked slowly towards him and bowed. "Sir. We can't find her. She is nowhere at all."

"You've lost her?" Robert felt his throat tighten. He took a deep breath. "Where is Will?"

Peter's shoulders slumped; his face creased into more misery. "We've looked all over. We thought to find her at the manor, but can't find her there. They've not seen her."

Robert frowned. "The manor? Have you lost her at Caerwyn?"

Peter looked at the ground. "Nay," he said in a low voice. "She disappeared from Carlisle. The morning you yourself left for Arran. We didn't think anything of it when she didn't appear for breakfast, but when she didn't come to dinner, we looked for her. We couldn't find her anywhere; she wasn't in her rooms, as we thought." He ran a hand over his unshaven face, avoiding Robert's eyes. "Then Will asked this Effie, her friend. She didn't want to say anything at first, but after awhile." He stopped.

Robert stared at him, eyes hard.

"After awhile she said the lady had gone."

"Where?"

"To Caerwyn. She said she was going home."

"Home, yes," said Robert, his voice impatient. "She was going home; she told me so herself. But with Will, not alone."

"Yes, but Effie . . . she seemed to think she was going home herself, or rather with the boy Jamie, you know. We talked to Jamie, of course," ground out Peter. "He was frightened, but he talked eventually. Said she was going to meet him in the early hours and go off home. He was to wait with the horse. But she was gone, and the horse too. He thought she went off without him."

Robert shook his head. She'd never hurt the lad's feelings.

"Will and I followed right after we heard that, leaving that very hour, and followed the route she'd most likely take. We thought to catch her for she had only some nag and not her mare." Peter shook his head, "We should have caught up with her in two days, perhaps three, but we didn't see her, nor hear of her at all, asking along the way. And when we reached the manor, they knew nothing, nothing at all." He passed a hand through his hair. "It's like she disappeared. We've searched between Caerwyn and Carlisle, back and forth again twice, and searched the forests all around Caerwyn and still no sign. We've sent men to Ayr and to Renfrew, but no word has come. I left off finally to come here today." His voice trailed off.

Robert noticed then how tired and dusty he looked. Peter reached under his shirt and pulled out a small pouch and handed it to Robert.

Robert took it. "What is it?"

"There is worse news yet. For that, I am full sorry." Peter stared at the ground.

Robert opened the leather pouch and pulled a folded paper from within. There was one sentence only, written in black ink in a precise hand.

You may retrieve the body of your manservant, known by the name Will, at the monastery on the road to Ayr.

Robert stared at the paper in his opened palm and slowly clenched his fingers, crushing the stiff paper into a crumpled ball.

CHAPTER TWENTY-FIVE

Arran

THE DOOR BANGED OPEN against the wall. A tall woman barged in, carrying a platter covered with a linen cloth. "Come this way. No, over here," the woman shouted to the two serving boys following her. They were undersized to be lugging such a heavy tub. "Set it there."

Ailsa watched in silent amazement from the corner of the chamber. She wasn't sure how long she'd been here, but it must be two days already. Apart from feeding her a small amount of bread, along with a flask of water, she'd been left entirely alone. Nervous, she tugged her gown down over her dirty boots and tried to smooth her tangled hair.

The boys went out. The woman made sure the door was shut behind them. Then she turned, hands on her bony hips. "Well, you're in need of a bath and no question about that. Take off those filthy clothes." She placed a linen shift on a stool near the tub, along with a bowl. "Soap for you."

Ailsa stood up, thinking the woman looked like a gigantic crow in her black linen.

"I've brought food. Eat slow or you'll be sick." The woman pulled the cloth off the platter. There were oatcakes, raisins, and a small carafe of wine.

At the sight of the food, Ailsa's stomach clenched and grumbled. She could feel tears well in her eyes. She tried to hide them, but her head still hurt where Mungo had hit her.

The woman examined her with unfriendly eyes. "The water will get cold." With that, she left, and Ailsa heard the bar over the door rammed in place. She gazed at the steaming bath water and the food, wondering why they would suddenly go to such trouble. No matter, she needed the food and the bath would be welcome. She broke off a piece of oatcake and chewed, then gulped the rest in one bite. She ate the second and drank some water and half the wine. The food cleared her mind, but she soon felt nauseous. She stared at the bath, then shrugged and peeled off her dirty gown.

She used the soap, which was gritty but lathered reasonably well, then doused her hair with water and washed that too. For a moment, she luxuriated in the warmth, pretending she was elsewhere, anywhere but here. Then she climbed out. Someone might come at any moment. The woman had left the linen that had covered the food, so she used the scrap to towel dry and wrapped her wet hair up on her head. Looking at her gown, she sighed. She couldn't put it back on, it was filthy. But she hated to wear the clothes the woman had left. She picked up a linen shift. It was delicately made and pleated, the linen extra fine.

Boots sounded outside the door. She threw the shift over her head and grabbed her gown and held it around her. The irritable woman was back, along with the two boys, who were ordered about briskly. They took the tub and gathered the old rushes and scattered new clean straw about the floor. A rough blanket was laid as a pallet on the straw and another placed near for a cover.

"There," said the woman, tucking a straggling piece of her black hair firmly back into place. She signaled to one of the lads to take Ailsa's old clothes. Reluctantly, she gave him the gown. The woman said nothing and, after a last quick look around, her face creased into hard lines, she walked out. Ailsa was left alone.

She put on the gown the woman had left, and the cloth shoes. The clothes were loose on her, but she pulled the laces tight. For the next few hours, she expected the door to swing open again every moment, but no one came. It grew chilly and then cold. She wrapped the blanket around her shoulders and tried to sleep. In the end, she dozed off and on, waking often, thinking the door was opening, but eventually the dark in the room turned to dim grey. Morning had come, and she was still alone.

Around what she thought was noon, one of the boys came in, smiled at her shyly, and set a platter of food down on the floor. "Here, Lady," he said, "new food for you." He handed her a packet, then picked the old platter up and started to walk out.

"Wait," called Ailsa, sitting up straighter. "Please, tell me, where are we? What day is it?"

The boy grimaced, his innocent blue eyes troubled. He must be only nine or ten. "I'm not to talk with you, nor answer any questions." He looked at the ground by her feet. "I'm that sorry, Lady, but she'll have my right arm if I do."

"I understand."

"You do?" he looked up, relieved.

"Aye." She smiled at him. "Do you have a name at least?"

He grinned at her. "Aye, that I do. I'm called Gowan."

The room seemed quiet when Gowan left. At least I've made a friend of sorts, she told herself, but it didn't comfort her much. She found a stone on the floor and made several marks on the wall. Perhaps she could tell something of the days by marking how often they came with her food. She forced herself to eat some of the oat-cakes and drink the ale.

There were ten days marked on the wall when the door swung open. Ailsa looked up from her spot on the floor in the corner, expecting Gowan. But it was a man dressed in brown, his face hidden by his hood. He bowed. "I want to see Lord Fergus," she said, before he had a chance to speak.

The man pushed back his hood. He was her father's age, hair greying at the temples. His round face seemed surprised. "Fergus, why?"

"He was my father's good friend and will be most disturbed to see me imprisoned so."

He seemed to consider for a moment. "Come with me then." He walked out through the open door.

Ailsa gathered her wits and followed. Relief flooded her as she walked after him out of that miserable room. She tried to marshal her thoughts as they went down the stairs. Of course, Fergus would help her. This was all some dreadful mistake.

They went down several long passages and turned into a lighted corridor. The torches threw deep shadows as they walked up a stone stairway. Finally, the man knocked at a small door and without waiting, opened it wide. "Lady," he said, a note of mockery entering his voice.

She hesitated, but what choice had she? She entered the room, which was large and lit by firelight from a huge hearth, but he did not follow. He shut the heavy door behind him.

Ailsa sucked in her breath. The room was empty. It was very warm, heated by a glowing fire. The scent of meadowsweet mingled with the smell of spiced wine, bubbling in a pot set by the fire. The room was most luxuriously furnished, piled with clean rushes, and decorated with hangings and three large pillows in jewel colors of red, green and blue. Her senses could hardly take it all in after so long in her dark storeroom. There were two windows, shuttered now, and she could see through the chinks that it was not afternoon as she'd thought, but night.

It was very quiet. Cautiously she moved to the window and tried to peer out. Was this Fergus' chamber? He would help her, unless he were a prisoner too, but that was unthinkable.

No one came. Eventually she helped herself to the wine. Her head still ached where that horrible man had hit her. She knew such injuries could take several months to heal. She sighed and sipped the wine, which was strong, and made her sleepy. She sipped more slowly, for she must be alert when Fergus came.

The fire burned low, so she stuck a log on it from the stack in the corner of the room. He must be rich indeed to have such a chamber, and heat with wood instead of peat. She frowned. Fergus had not seemed the sort of man to have a room such as this. She remembered someone gruff and hearty, who joked with her and gave her honey sweets, a big man with a wild beard and rough clothes.

There was a clunk in the corridor and the door swung open. A tall man walked in, elegantly attired in black. Ailsa gasped and the wine dropped from her hand. The metal goblet rang on the stone hearth, red wine splashing on the cushions. "Hugh!"

"You must not spill wine over expensive cloths," he said as he crossed the room to her. He bowed over her hand as though they were in the great hall at court.

Ailsa pulled her hand from his. "Where is Fergus? Why am I being held?"

"Fergus," he repeated, and helped himself to some wine. "This is not his manor, or no longer his, as you see." He took a deep gulp. "Ah, 'tis fine, is it not."

She took a step back. "Why am I here?"

He twirled the goblet in his hand. "It's good to be at rest. A long and trying journey indeed. Rough seas."

"You must tell me what is happening. I demand you tell me right now."

Hugh placed the goblet carefully on the hearth. "You are no longer in any position to make demands, obviously. You are here because I wish it. Listen well, for what I have to say concerns our future."

"Our future! We have no future together."

"You will want to hear what I have to say, so silence yourself. Otherwise, I must lock you up another fortnight."

Surely she hadn't been here that long! She stared up at him, horror slowly taking over. Hugh de Morville had abducted her. But why? She must think. If only her head didn't ache so.

"Always so vehement, a lady must not show such passion," he said, with a cold smile. "To humor you, I will answer your question. You are here because I had you brought here and here you will stay."

Her hand found the silver goblet. Swinging hard, she hit him full in the face. The shock of the blow vibrated up to her shoulder.

Surprise and then fury lit his eyes. He shoved her to the floor and stood over her. "You will regret that. You are here. Become accustomed to the idea. Indeed, soon you will beg for the privilege of doing anything I ask of you."

"That will never be," she said, shocked past all caution. She tried to get to her feet. He shoved her back down, harder. Her head hit the wood stool and sharp pain flooded her head and neck. He walked out. Ailsa struggled to her feet, needles of pain in her ear, then staggered to the window, but it was dark, with no moon. She crossed the room and banged on the door and yelled, "Let me out, anyone, help!" But there was no answer and her voice echoed in the stone chamber in a frightening way. She wiped a trickle of blood from her forehead. Finally, she walked to the fire and righted the wooden stool and sat, her arms around her knees, desperately trying to stop the swirling panic in her head.

De Morville. This was worse than she had thought. She swallowed hard and studied the hangings, the cushions, the goblet on the floor, trying to steady herself. Trying to remember her old tutor's advice for times of peril. Think. Be calm. Think.

For the moment, she seemed safe. She put her hands out, trying to warm them at the fire. They trembled in front of the orange flames. She lowered her arms. He'd not be back tonight at least. She'd have to count on that.

On the second day in the sumptuous chamber, she heard footsteps stomping up the stairs and she stood up, relieved at the thought of a human face, even if it were Hugh's. The door cracked and she tried to rush the opening, but the man who entered held her back with a strong arm. She yelled, but he said, not unkindly, "Tis no use. There's no one can hear you up here." He pulled her by the elbow, out the door and down the stairs. When she tripped, he dragged her along.

"Where are you taking me," she demanded, but he didn't bother to answer, just pulled her down a dark corridor, opened a door and pushed her in. He dragged a bundle across the floor, then left, barring the door with a resounding thump.

Ailsa sat in the dim room, smelling of mildew and rat droppings. She was in some sort of storage area once more, cramped and damp and dark. A cold wind circled above the planked floor, bare of any rushes. She crawled over and felt around until she found the bundle. Inside, she found three hunks of stale bread, a small flagon of sour beer, and a round of orange cheese, very dry and hard. She devoured part of the food, then decided she'd best hoard the rest and wrapped it in her cloak, which was cleaner than the cloth. Who knew when they'd feed her again. She huddled, trying to stay warm, thinking of the storage closet she'd hidden in months ago in the days before Lent, when she thought to evade Robert. She had vowed she was done with hiding, but now she was a prisoner in truth.

Hours later, steps sounded on the stairs beyond the door. She tensed, her fingers paused in her attempt to untangle her hair. She crept over to the door, holding her breath. She'd duck down, rush under the guard's arm and throw herself down the stairs. She clenched her fists as the door grated open and lunged. She cracked into the hard thigh of another guard, different, bigger, meaner. He kicked her back, as though she were a bothersome insect. Then he dumped a sack on the floor and left with muttered curses.

Ailsa got to her feet, her eyes filled with angry tears. She dashed them away and pushed the tangled hair out of her face. Then she stared. The sack on the floor was moving. And surely that was a groan. She yanked at the heavy rope tying the bag shut. It was hard, for whoever had been tied inside was waking up and wanted to get out. "Hold still," she said, "I'm trying to help."

She managed to loosen the heavy rope. In the dark, she could see little. She heard a sniff and then a voice said, "Lady!"

"Jamie! Not you! How?"

"They came after me," he said. His voice trembled, and he pulled the loops of rope off his wrists. "When you did not come, and once Peter and Will came looking for you, I rode toward Caerwyn alone. I was almost home when they picked me up."

"Caerwyn," said Ailsa. She sat back on her heels, silent a moment. She could practically hear the sea sliding up the beach, tumbling the pebbles.

"Will and Peter and I, we searched for you, up and down the path between Carlisle and Caerwyn. Then they had to go on to Glasgow and meet up with Sir Robert." He rubbed his knee, "Probably a big bruise there! Where are we? I know there was a boat ride."

"I think Fergus' manor, on Arran, but de Morville is here. I cannot make it out."

Jamie tried to stand up but gasped and sat down again quickly.

"You're hurt," said Ailsa. She felt his knee gently; it was hot and swollen. "I think it's sprained but not broken. Here." She turned away and ripped her shift. Fashioning a bandage, she tied the knee. "It will pain you less this way and heal the faster." She felt around with her hands, but there was nothing in the bare closet to make him more comfortable.

"No need to worry, it feels better already," he said.

"Sleep now, 'tis best you rest if you can."

He nodded and soon the soft sound of his breathing filled the chamber. Ailsa sat by him, glad of his human warmth and company, but sad he'd been captured on her account, and ashamed to need him so.

Guards appeared intermittently with brown bread and stale water, little enough for two but sufficient to keep them alive. She thought another few days had passed, but it was hard to know in such a dim place with no window.

Jamie stirred. "Sleep on," she murmured. There was little enough to do once awake. She pressed her lips together. Someone must come. Surely even now someone was looking for her. Perhaps Robert. Or perhaps Dugald; he was her kin. She couldn't just disappear. Someone would care. Someone would look. She rose and swung her arms to warm them, impatient at her weakness. She had to stay strong and ready.

She heard a shout from somewhere below, and another. Jamie stirred but didn't wake. Hoofs thudding, like several horses. Then the screech of iron gates, and a deep clang as if the gate were swung shut. If only it was Dugald, come to find her. If only it was not Hugh.

The riders, whoever they were, entered the hall and she could hear no more. She shook Jamie's shoulder gently. "Wake Jamie, someone has come."

He sat up and rubbed his eyes.

"Someone is here; perhaps Dugald!"

"Or Sir Robert?" Jamie scrambled to his feet.

Ailsa didn't answer that but went to the door and listened. "We must be ready if there's any chance to escape."

"Aye." Hope chased across his face. "I'll be ready."

A long wait later, Ailsa heard the familiar stomp of the guard coming with their food. Surely there was a second step as well. She gestured to Jamie, who swallowed hard and nodded.

The door swung open. The burly guard barged in and dumped their food on the floor. He was followed by Hugh. Ailsa felt her stomach tighten. She must not let Jamie see she was afraid. She raised her chin, staring at de Morville silently.

He motioned to the guard, who grabbed her. "No!" she shouted.

Jamie launched himself at the guard but was batted away like a small fly. She heard his dismal cry. "Do not worry, Jamie," she called to the boy, as she was flung over the guard's shoulder. They descended the spiral stairs, bumping against the rough walls in their haste. He carried her down a dark corridor, kicked open a door, and dumped her on the dusty planks. "Wait!" she called, as a confused impression of firelight and strong perfume hit her. She scrambled to her feet and banged on the door. But the guard was gone.

She turned back to survey the room. Startled, she realized she was not alone. A tiny woman was seated by the fire. "You must let me go. There's been a dreadful mistake."

The woman smiled. "My boy is back and he'll be wanting to see you. You're an odd piece, I must say. Still and all, what he wants he gets."

"You are de Morville's …"

"Nurse," finished the woman, patting her chest. "Wet nurse, so he's mine. I raised him from a tiny wailing infant." She reached out a claw like hand and pulled Ailsa toward the fire. "I raised him and he's a bad one I know, still what can one do, he's always your boy. That he is." She chuckled. The woman poured red wine in a large silver goblet. "You don't look well, drink this," she coaxed.

Ailsa pushed the goblet away, but the woman insisted. She took a sip. The wine was warmed and strong and heavily spiced. She looked over the rim of the goblet, pretending to drink more. This chamber had a window. She set the goblet down and went over and looked out into a cloudy afternoon, the air humid and threatening rain. Servants were brushing horses in the courtyard and two kitchen maids went by, lugging a big pot of stew. Everything so normal that tears welled in her eyes.

The old woman muttered as she bustled around the room, straightening the two stools and the hanging on the wall. She brought the wine again.

Ailsa shook her head, but the woman just stood, with her arm outstretched, so she took the goblet and drained it. Perhaps it would strengthen her. She feared Hugh would come all too soon. The woman gathered her cloak and slipped out the door. She spoke with the guard, and they laughed, as if at some joke. Then the wooden bar clunked into place, locking her in.

Ailsa paced, examining the room and the window, too high up and too narrow for escape. The room was overly warm. She was worried about Jamie. She had to get him out of here. It was her fault, all of it. She put her hands to her cheeks, flushed from the hot wine. What might Hugh be doing to him, even now. She took a deep breath and let it out slowly. Such dire thoughts would not help. She sat on the floor, her chin in her hands, and stared at the fire, which wavered and flamed. She must rouse herself, think, come up with a plan.

Yet the room seemed to be spinning slowly around her. She closed her eyes, shutting out the chamber, and thought herself away, away, to the fresh scent of home. Her head felt strange, heavy and twirling, and golden light shattered at the edges of the room. She needed to do something, but it was hard to think what, and she was so very tired. She lay down on the floor, close to the flames like a cat, and stared into the glowing coals.

Ailsa woke shivering some long time later. The floor was freezing and the chamber dark and the fire gone out long ago. "Jamie," she called uncertainly. Then she remembered the strange small woman and the glimpse of Hugh. She managed to get to her feet, but she was panting and breathing hard. Foolish, they'd drugged her with the wine.

She dragged herself to the window. It seemed that hours had passed. It was midnight or beyond and nothing to be seen. How long had she slept? Had another whole day passed? She hugged her knees by the dead fire, trying to erase the strange and awful dreams from her mind.

A long time later, the door creaked open and Hugh walked in, his face unreadable in the dim light. "Come, come, haven't you a better welcome for me? I've ridden hard to return to you so quickly."

Ailsa scrambled to her feet, confused by his affable manner. "Why are you holding me here? Where is Jamie? You must bring him to me immediately."

"All in good time." He reached out a gloved hand. "Won't you sit by me? I have much to tell you."

She hesitated, but she needed more information. Gingerly, she sat on the edge of the stool. Out the window, the sky was beginning to grow light.

"The king and the prince ride once again to treat with the English. The king hopes to avert war, but he means to win Northumberland, whatever the cost."

Ailsa nodded cautiously. This news did not seem particularly important right now.

"The rebel Wimond plans further risings here in the West. The king means to squelch any rebellion, but even now rides the wrong direction. While the cat is away…" He paused. "The Islesmen sway this way and that, one day for the king, one day for Wimond. And this Wimond claims royal blood too. Did you know?"

"I have heard it said," said Ailsa, wondering if he meant to trap her into treason. If only her head weren't so heavy and dull.

"Yet I see you are thinking and what has all this to do with me?" De Morville stood and stretched. His clothes were black, as always, and of a fine wool cloth with an edging of gold to the tunic. "Oh, but it does affect you." He placed a finger under her chin and moved her gaze to meet his. "It does affect you, for I must decide for the king or for Wimond."

Ailsa pulled back. "You would betray the king," she said, "for this fake bishop from Man?"

"You must admit this Wimond, fake though he may be, has his points. The king suppresses trade here in the Isles, costing me much coin. And many say David himself stole the throne. And then, there is Somerled, there is always this Somerled, in the background. One wonders which way he will go in the end. One wishes to be on his right side when all is done."

"But you are son of the king's own trusted Constable. What Somerled does should not matter to you, except that you inform the king," said Ailsa slowly. The de Morvilles were no old family from the Isles, they were English, and owed their lands and manors and wealth all to the king. None of this made sense. "In any case, what you decide has naught to do with me," she said, moving toward the door. She wondered that he had told her this much. And now that he had. She pulled at the door latch, which did not budge.

De Morville laughed right behind her. He wrapped a tight arm around her waist and pulled her toward him slowly.

"Does your father know what you do?"

Hugh frowned. "I do what I do for the de Morvilles. My father is old. His day is past, and he doesn't know it yet. The world is more complicated than he imagines."

"Or perhaps it is you who does not understand loyalty," said Ailsa.

He yanked her to his chest. His brooch bit into her skin. "Don't you want to know why?" he whispered.

"Nothing you do is of interest to me."

He laughed. "You must try harder to please me. For all of this matters to you now."

He must be mad! How would she get away? As she thought this, he suddenly loosened his grip. He brushed off his clothes and picked up his cloak, a new one, lined with sky blue silk.

"What do you want of me?" Her voice was shaking and to stop

it, she pressed her lips together. "You must let me go, and Jamie too, immediately."

He moved to the door. "Fix yourself. I wish a beautiful bride this afternoon and it is dawn already."

Ailsa choked out, "I'd not marry you. I'd never marry you."

"I think you will." Hugh's voice was calm. A knock interrupted them. "Come."

Three guards entered first, and then a fourth dragging Jamie. He staggered and fell to his knees at her feet.

"What have you done," she cried. Her fingers ran over the dark bruises on his face, the finger marks on his neck. She gently lifted his head, "Jamie!" His eyelids fluttered, but he did not speak. "You beast," she cried to de Morville, "what have you done to this child?"

He swung his cloak over his shoulder and crossed to the door. "You will marry me this very afternoon."

"Never."

"You will, or the boy dies."

There was silence, the air in the room suddenly thick, like deep water moving in a purposeful current. It seemed hard to hear properly or breathe. Ailsa could feel Jamie's pulse jittering under her palm. They had beaten him. In truth, it would not take much more to kill him. "You would not." She drew the boy to her.

Hugh shrugged. "It is entirely your choice."

"Not today," she murmured, desperate, "not this afternoon, I need time, I must have time, to prepare." Any delay, she thought.

He looked at her, eyes narrowed. But after a moment, he nodded. "When?"

"In three days," she said quickly. "I'll marry you in three days. But only if the boy lives."

"Three days then."

"I must have hot water and bandages and herbs for him," she said.

De Morville ignored this and swept out.

"Jamie, Jamie," she murmured. She carefully felt his bones and found none actually broken, though he had some terrible bruises on his arms and one on his belly that stretched up over his ribs.

A servant appeared with a bowl of warm water, and some healing herbs, though she would not stay to answer Ailsa's questions. At least she had the herbs. She crumbled them and sprinkled them in the water, and bathed his face, sponging blood off the worst off his bruises. After a time, he opened his eyes.

"Lady," he whispered.

"Aye, don't try to speak," she said, "they're gone for now." She tried to smile in a comforting way. He nodded and sank into a restless sleep again. She covered him with a linen hanging, which she dragged from the bed, then sank back on her heels to let him sleep.

Three days. She'd bought them some time. Though why Hugh had agreed made her wary. They must escape well before the third day. She looked down at Jamie. They'd not be leaving tonight, it was sure. In the morning though, surely by morning. He was young and strong. She looked down at his face, cheeks still smooth as a child, his forehead gashed and one eye near shut and purpled. In the morning, for certain.

CHAPTER TWENTY-SIX

Irvine

ROBERT STARED INTO THE DARK TREES outside the firelight, thinking of everything and nothing. He'd ridden hard all morning and half the afternoon, heading away from Glasgow and toward the monastery. He'd found Will there, Will's body that is. Until that moment he'd been sure in one part of his head that it was all a mistake, that Peter was confused, that Will had outwitted his attacker somehow. It had happened before, so many escapes, in Normandy, and even here.

Will's body, cleaned up by the monks so the dagger slashes in his chest gaped open but bloodless, seemed to set his own head loose from his body. Where his thought and feeling should be was only air, a kind of wind, with a restless noise that didn't let him sleep or even rest.

He was headed to Caerwyn. He had placed Will's body over a second horse he'd borrowed from the monks and roped him on so he wouldn't slide off. He would bury Will at Caerwyn, alongside Nevin. After that, who knew. The wind in his head made thought impossible. Peter kept the fire built high, to keep the wolves off, and tried to give him food. He shoved him out the way and resumed pacing.

The woods were dank and silent. That Will was actually dead seemed impossible. That it was his fault was sure. He'd sent him to keep Ailsa safe, knowing there were risks. There were always risks. But Will was clever and wily. He'd made it through countless tough times, and saved him too. Why should it all end now? He should have taken Ailsa to Caerwyn himself. Even though the king had ordered him to Arran, he should have seen Ailsa home safe, and if he had, he'd know exactly where she was right now, and Will would still be alive. It seemed another world or another lifetime when the needs of a king were important or even relevant. A king could have you imprisoned or killed, that was true. But wasn't this worse? He stopped, his hands on his temples, pressing his forehead which felt like it would burst.

He picked up an iron pot and walked to the stream flowing by the campsite, filled it with the freezing water and set it on the fire. He imagined he heard Will coming out from the forest, chuckling at some joke. He slumped on his blanket and stared into the flames.

A twig cracked. "Just me, Sir." Peter materialized out of the woods, his hair curling in the misty air.

A week had passed, a long strange week. They'd ridden to Caerwyn and buried Will. On the hill beside Nevin. Never in all his imaginings of the future, his dreams of revenge, his new thoughts of a home of his own, never had he once thought of losing his friend. His best friend, though his servant. His only true friend, if he were honest. Even Walter was already gone with the king and taken up with his ambitions and he knew, as Walter had said, it was best they did not meet again.

Peter cleared his throat.

Robert ignored him. They were camped in the forest east of Caerwyn. Once Will was buried, he'd been unable to settle, unable even to sleep. Out here, in the woods, in the open, he could breathe at least.

Peter interrupted again. "I've been thinking, strange how the de Morvilles been shadowing you ever since you came to these lands."

Robert sighed. "I've been going over that in my mind. But I can't think it's connected. What would they gain by killing Will or taking Ailsa? She's not wealthy and they could get no large ransom. It all makes no sense." He rubbed his aching eyes.

"Unless," said Peter and stopped.

Robert turned away. Unless. Was Ailsa in danger, or was she casually laughing with Hugh de Morville at how easily she'd tricked him? And who had killed Will? Whoever it was, he would find him, and kill him. He owed that much to Will. He'd failed his friend, who had never failed him. Unable to sit, he took a bag of oats from his saddle bag and dumped some in the simmering water over the fire. He carried the rest down to Tanet. The big horse stuck his nose in the bag and snorted. Robert leaned his forehead against the grey's neck.

He returned to the fire and Peter took the pot off the flames and set it to cool on a flat rock. They shared a spoon between them, scooping up the hot oats. Robert felt them burn his tongue and throat. He thought of the many times he'd shared a meal with Will. It was not Peter's fault, but he had no patience for him. "We must go to Irvine, to de Morville's keep," he said. "'Tis past time to confront them."

"Right into their castle?" Peter tugged at his ear.

Robert squinted at the sun, barely visible behind the cloud cover. "We can be there by noon. You can come along, or not." He kicked earth over the fire.

Peter nodded, looking worried.

Robert approached the de Morville lands later than he had hoped. Peter's horse had pulled up lame and he'd sent him to the nearest village to rest the horse and told him to return to Caerwyn after. He preferred to be alone anyway. He didn't need to be responsible for another death and entering Irvine was a crazed venture.

"That's her there, Irvine," he imagined Will saying. "Quite the castle." Robert squeezed his eyes shut and opened them again. He had to stop doing that, imagining Will here, riding alongside him, talking, always talking, or worse, laughing as he'd always done.

He stared at the castle above the rock cliff, eyes narrowed. The sea was gilded with late afternoon sun, and a stiff wind blew off the water. It carried the smell of salt, mixed with a disturbing earthy scent of too much green and rotting leaves. Tanet nickered and he quieted him with a touch to his neck. The de Morville's main castle was in the east, in the fertile lowlands, but this place was well built and looked newly fortified. The stockade fence showed raw patches of new cut wood.

Even as he watched, the gate swung open and several riders passed out, trotting up the road. Robert slid off Tanet and led him further into the woods, then crept closer to watch. Soon, he could hear the jingle of harness and snatches of men's voices. There were three, two riding abreast and one following, clearly a servant, riding a donkey and leading another donkey piled with baggage. He'd wait until the party entered the forest, out of sight of the castle guards.

"'Tis late indeed for such a ride, but the master's not one to think on anyone else's comfort, is he," one was saying.

"Must be important," said the other, "and he pays well. I'm not averse to an occasional night ride."

The fickle wind shifted, and the man's reply was lost. Robert strained, but he couldn't catch any more. He peered through the thick leaves. Only when he heard their voices coming up the path clearly, mixing with the creak of leather and the plod of hoofs on the damp ground, did he step out into their path.

He sprang for the first. Surprised, the man tumbled off his horse onto the moss, silently, groaned once, then lay in a crumpled heap. The second rider swung about and galloped away, back toward the castle. The servant gaped, and tried to turn the donkey about, shouting for help.

Robert grabbed the unresisting servant and wrapped a cloth round his mouth and tied it tight, to silence him. He shoved his hand in the sleeves of the first rider. There could be a parchment of some sort. If not, the message was verbal, and he'd have to wait till he awakened to get it out of him. That would take precious time. He searched. Nothing. Then, in the man's left boot, he found it, a leather pouch sewn tight. He held it up. The man was groaning; it was time to be away.

Robert turned to the servant. "Be quiet and ye'll not be harmed." He yanked the cloth from the man's mouth. "Where were ye headed?"

"I know not, sir," stammered the man, his round eyes wide.

Robert sighed. It was probably true. "Is your master in the castle?"

"Nay." The man swallowed, his Adam's apple bobbing in his thin neck. "He's with the king. And young master be away too." The fallen rider stirred again and sat up, swaying.

Time to be gone. Robert sprinted for Tanet, stuffing the pouch into his tunic as he ran. He galloped away, leaving the path soon after to follow a stream. This might confuse the pursuit that would certainly come. After a long stretch of fast riding, Robert pulled Tanet to a halt. "I doubt they'll follow us this far," he said to the horse. All the light had gone, here under the trees. They were deep in the forest and far off the path. He rubbed the tired horse down and loosed him to find grass, then sat on a damp rock, his cloak wrapped around his shoulders. He pulled the pouch from his tunic and fingered the leather. The message would have to wait until morning. He dared not light a flame and the darkness made reading impossible.

Morning dawned grey and chill with light slow to enter under the spruce branches. Robert carefully slit the pouch open and drew out a stiff square of parchment. He examined the elaborate script, noted the king's seal, and holding it up to what light there was, he read. And read once more. It was not a long document, though it was signed by a long list of landowning men. He pulled his own leather pouch out and unwrapped the precious parchment he'd carried inside for months and held it up. They were identical as to the seals, and the elaborate initial D at the bottom, both parchments signed David, King of all Scotia.

Robert placed both parchments back into his leather pouch, wrapped them well against any damp, and hid them in his pack. He began to pace between the trees, avoiding the twisting roots. Tanet lifted his head to watch. He was thinking, and what he thought was that it was impossible. Except it was not. Kings could not be trusted. He knew that and he had known it all along. His hope had made him vulnerable.

One parchment said Lady Ailsa, the king's ward, would marry Sir Robert, newly from Shropshire. She and the manor and lands of Caerwyn would be given to Sir Robert by will of the king.

The other, which should be an identical copy, was not. Robert stopped short. Had Will discovered this? Was that why he was killed? Robert groaned. If only he'd been less trusting, less dutiful. His friend would still be alive.

The other parchment, dated the same day as the first, said Lady Ailsa, the king's ward, and the entire estate of Caerwyn, were given over to Hugh de Morville, for his many services to the king, and in recognition of the love the king held for his father, Scotia's Constable.

David had never intended to give him the land. He'd never been grateful for his life saved. He'd just seen an opportunity to get information from dangerous lands. He'd used him. Set him up in the dangerous role of spy. Intending all along to deceive him, or perhaps just to get information and then get him killed.

Robert blinked hard. He rubbed his eyes and face. He dumped some water on his hands and then, wiping his fingers dry on his tunic, he pulled out the pouch again. He laid the two parchments on his knees, trying to see something in the Latin lettering that he had missed, something that would lead him to Ailsa. He'd been too late in understanding to save Will, his friend. Now Will was dead. But Ailsa was still alive. At least he hoped so. And if alive, she was in danger. They needed Caerwyn, for some purpose, and for that they needed her. He hoped they needed her. He must find her. He must not fail again. For too long he'd been suspicious, but of the wrong person. He'd suspected her, but all along it had been the de Morville's and behind them, the king.

He stared at the dark letters for a long time, trying to see, to find some clue. Then he thrust them back in his pouch. He rode Tanet back through the forest, straight back toward the de Morville castle. When he reached an outcrop with a view of the fields and castle below, he peered down. Something was brewing. Men were pulling in cows and sheep rather than putting them out to graze and others were lugging barrels of water or ale. "They fear a siege," muttered Robert aloud. Who'd be interested in controlling this region, and willing to risk the king's ire to do so? Yet perhaps, and more likely, he realized, it was the opposite. Perhaps the de Morvilles played a dangerous game and prepared themselves for the results?

In the distance, beyond the forest, he could see the cleared fields and solid walls of a monastery. "Let's pay a visit to the brothers," said Robert. "They will know who threatens their wealth, be sure of it. And I mean to find out this day too." Tanet flicked his ears at Robert and tossed his head.

When he rode into the dusty courtyard of the brothers of Ainsley monastery, the sun had burned through the fog and it was hot. A short cleric, his tunic overlong and dragging on the dusty rocks, wandered out to greet him.

"Good day, father," said Robert.

The monk surveyed him with cold eyes, pale blue under wispy brows. "Good day to you," he finally responded.

Robert pretended not to note the lack of friendliness in the greeting and swung off his horse, clapping the brother on the back. "I'm fair parched from our long journey, I've been traveling all day long and nary a drop of water anywhere. Is this country hereabouts always so dry?" He rattled on, impervious to the monk's frown. "Aye, I'm ready for a good meal and a quiet night indeed. I'm a merchant, coming to the market on Saturday. I usually go to Renfrew but my friend said why not try something new, could be coin to be made and I'm always game for that, so I said yes." He tied Tanet to a hitching post, as there seemed to be no stable boy about. "Not that making money is the only thing, you understand. I know the Lord said 'tis hard for a rich man to enter the kingdom of heaven, but even so, a man has to survive, hasn't he. Especially if he has daughters at home." He winked at the monk.

The monk frowned back at him. "That be a fine horse for a merchant's needs."

"True, but a man has to have some vices." He gestured toward the monastery. "Show me around. I've not seen this center before. It seems to be stoutly built."

The monk sighed, but handed him off to a youth, dressed in the robes of a novice. The skinny boy showed Robert the chapel, kitchens, and monk's quarters, rushing them through with nervous haste and never a smile. Robert tried to question him about the preparations at nearby Irvine, but the young man only managed to stammer out that he knew nothing of a threat. Robert didn't believe him, but there was little use to question him further. He told the boy he'd be staying the night. He was shown a small cell with a single lumpy pallet. An hour later, the boy returned and plunked a bowl of milk and a loaf on the floor and rushed out. Robert ate the food, then stretched out on the cold floor rather than the pallet, which seemed to be leaping with fleas.

He woke just as the monks were hurrying to matins. Quiet whispers and the creak of leather shoes on the stone walkways were the only sounds. He checked that his dagger still sat on his belt and wished he had his sword. Peering out the door, into the dark corridor, it appeared empty and he decided the monks should all be in the chapel by now.

He edged out of the room. A single torch lighted the hallway and he walked carefully, anxious to make no noise that would alert any of the brothers. He reached the hall, where the lingering odors of smoke and grease met his nostrils. He slipped out into the courtyard.

Fresh cool air hit his face. He tightened his hand on his dagger and crossed to the stable. He whistled once softly and Tanet nickered in response. He found the horse in a dark stall at the end of the barn, and tied him outside, at the back of the stables, where the shadows were the darkest and might hide the horse's grey coat. Then he crossed to stand just outside the chapel.

Inside, the monks were still chanting. Their sleepy voices wandered up and down, intoning the Latin phrases. Following the words in his head, he decided they were about halfway through the service. Good, there was time.

He made his way to the one building in the courtyard they'd not entered on the tour of the monastery earlier. On the far side was a window, shuttered with wood, but through the chinks he could see the gleam of light. Someone was inside, yet all the brothers should be at their prayers. He circled the building. There was an oak door, tied shut with thick cord. No other entrance.

Robert risked a peek through the window to the inside. The

dark shape of a bound man lay on the floor. He was unconscious, or perhaps asleep. Or dead. Darker stains of dried blood marred his clothes. But no, the man was alive; a hand moved.

Robert heard a creak and he moved round the side of the building. The night breeze blew the scent of mint to his nose. The big door swung open and a monk dressed in dark robes came out. He retied the door shut. Then he looked about fearfully and waited. Eventually he appeared reassured for he glanced up at the sky, where the moon was weaving in and out of fast-moving clouds, then started cautiously across the courtyard, heading for the chapel. I must seize him now, Robert realized, or he'll fade in with the others and I'll not be able to tell them apart.

He rushed forward and wrapped an arm over the monk's face, silencing him, save for a deep grunt of surprise. The man twisted in his arms, his back corded with surprisingly strong muscles for a monk, but he could not get away. Robert wound a gag of cloth into the man's mouth, then picked him up, and threw him over his shoulder. He led Tanet quietly out the gate. Then he mounted, with the man slung in front of him, and gave Tanet his head. They galloped across a wide meadow and entered the deep forest, with its smells of water and ferns and moss.

When Robert felt reassured there was no pursuit, he drew rein. They were deep in a stand of evergreen, and the scent of pine filled the early morning air. Water dripped from the branches onto his head as he listened for any sound of pursuit.

"Do you think it was wise, taking a monk?" Robert could hear Will say. He felt a stab in his gut, but it made him almost laugh as well. He pulled off the gag.

The monk rounded on him in a righteous fury. "You'll burn in hell for this, you God forsaken bastard."

Robert grinned. This man was no monk. "Enough," he said suddenly, making his voice cold and commanding.

The man stopped, his eyes full of rage.

"You will tell me what you're doing, masquerading as a priest."

"I'll tell you nothing at all," said the man.

"I think you will," said Robert, keeping his voice calm and reasonable.

The man's pale eyes narrowed.

"Who lies injured and bound in that outbuilding?"

"I'll say naught to you, you bastard."

"Who do they hold in the building, and why," said Robert, his voice growing even colder.

"I'll tell you nothing," boasted the man, so angry his voice shook. His cowl slipped off revealing thin, greying hair.

Robert stared at him. "I know you."

The man's eyes widened. "You do not."

"You are fitz John's man," said Robert. He jerked a length of rope from his saddle bag.

"You'd not dare," stammered the man. "Fitz John would skin you alive for it."

"Would he?" said Robert, "and why should the great lord care so much for your worthless hide?"

"You can't do this," the false monk said, his voice rising. He looked around, as though help would come riding out from the trees.

"I will, unless you tell me all." Robert stared into the man's eyes, feeling all the old anger and need for revenge, a hard core seemed to settle in his chest. He wound the rope around one fist and then the other. "Have a care Robb," he seemed to hear Will say. "You don't want to do this."

I do, actually, thought Robert. His anger at fitz John and despair over Will seemed to gather in a dark place in his chest. He turned his back on the fake monk and walked ten paces away, breathing hard. His head felt strange, as though a belt tightened around his forehead. Will, decent laughing Will, who always told him the truth. Fitz John who stole his father's land and his own future. He turned to the fake monk.

Something in Robert's face decided him. The monk gaped, then stuttered, "All right, all right, what do you want to know?"

"Why are you here, in Scotia?"

"I do what my master tells me. Do you think I want to be here in this forsaken heathen country? I'd go home in an instant."

Robert stared at him, considering. "What else can you tell me?"

"Nothing. I know nothing. I was told by fitz John to do the bidding of Hugh de Morville."

"Where is your home?"

"Gwynnedd, in Wales. "'Tis all in turmoil there. With no strong king in England, there be risings all over the land. Since fitz Gilbert died . . ."

"What?" Robert grabbed the man's shirt. "What happened to fitz Gilbert?"

"The Welsh, they killed him."

"Richard fitz Gilbert is a powerful man. How would they kill him?"

The monk shrugged. "He was over proud, too sure he'd never be taken. He was traveling through a mountain pass, near Abergavenny, traveling openly with no caution."

Robert stared into the dark woods. Richard fitz Gilbert of Clare, Lord of Ceredigion. Dead. He felt sick. He had wanted, for so many years, to kill the man himself. "Why would fitz John send you here, why not keep you near him, for protection?"

The man sneered. "I angered him. He said I'd learn caution if I spent some time in the North." He spat into the woods.

That sounded like fitz John. "Who's the man in the cell?"

"Some Islesman."

"What Islesman?" said Robert. "I grow impatient with you."

"His name is Dugald," sniveled the man.

Robert grabbed the fake monk by his neck.

"Where is the lady?"

"What lady?"

"Where?"

"I don't know what you mean."

Robert wound the rope around the man's neck.

He spit out, "Arran, the lady is on Arran."

"Where on Arran? Tell me," he said, shaking the monk. Would fitz John take everything he valued in this world?

The man stammered out, "Fergus' manor."

"Why?" said Robert.

"I don't know, I tell you. There's some pact with the de Morvilles and fitz John. 'Tis all I know, truly. Don't kill me, don't."

Robert pulled out his dagger. The man, quavering at his feet, wailed even more loudly. Robert hesitated a long moment, then sliced through his ropes. "You live because you've given me the information I seek but let me never see your face again."

He threw himself up on Tanet. That dog of a man, de Morville. And clever Fergus. Playing two sides at once. And behind it all, fitz John. Always fitz John, his nemesis. No revenge could be more than he deserved.

But that must wait. All that must wait. Now he must find a boat, he must get to Arran, before, once again, it was too late. Through the whirl of his thoughts, he remembered. He must get Dugald. "God's blood!" he shouted and Tanet leaped into a gallop. But it was true, he must. And then, a boat.

"We must find Torquil first," insisted Dugald.

Robert clenched his teeth. "There is no time." He struggled to keep his voice calm. Now that they'd landed on Arran, he was in a furious hurry to reach Ailsa. He had sprung Dugald from the outbuilding with no trouble. And the voyage from the mainland had been quick, for they'd found a boat pulled up onto the sands, launched her before they were seen, and then they'd been lucky with the wind.

"Torquil knows Fergus' keep well, he was near raised there. He'll know where she's being held, and he's another man and God knows we need another arm." Dugald's voice was curt and he rubbed his head as he spoke, where a large lump showed, no doubt painful.

Robert frowned. Dugald had a point.

"The lass's feisty," continued Dugald. "They will not dare harm her. She's under the king's own protection after all." Dugald fingered the lump. "I can't think why de Morville's taken her anyway. It makes no sense. She's always in trouble, that one."

"That bothers me as well," admitted Robert, slapping a glove against his leg. And he hadn't even told Dugald of the shadowy connection to fitz John. "You were tied up at that monastery for two days, but no one mentioned ransoming to you." Dugald had still not told him a convincing story of why he was tied up at the monastery at all.

"And if they're not after ransom, then they must be after marrying her. But Caerwyn is a poor holding compared to Irvine. What need has a de Morville of her lands?" Dugald stretched his long arms. "And Fergus involved? Hardly seems likely." He was quiet a moment. "She may be married already." He cast a quick look at Robert.

Robert said nothing. That thought had come to him already and he had thrust it away. He rumpled his hair, exasperated at the round of his worries. He was missing some piece of this puzzle. Still, Dugald was unfortunately right. They needed Torquil. "Where will we find him?"

Dugald pointed north. They headed off on foot, for they'd left the horses with the boat. Robert tried to control himself as they hiked. He'd find Ailsa by tonight. Get her away. And then he'd figure out what he wanted to say to her. He ducked as a tree branch slapped toward his face. The ground was spongy underfoot and morning mist wafted between the green branches. He picked up the pace, crowding Dugald, then striding ahead.

After half the morning, they arrived at a small glen. Water flowed down a tumble of rocks, splashing into deep pools. It was a beautiful spot, but Robert couldn't appreciate the green water. "Are we near?" he demanded. "Where is he?"

"Fishing," said Dugald. They walked upstream and spotted Torquil, hip deep in the water, throwing a line with a hook tied with bits of feather. He had two silver fish in a basket already.

He greeted them with a scowl. "You're scaring the salmon."

"We need your help," said Dugald.

Torquil took a look at them and pulled in his line. He waded to the shore, water dripping down his legs.

"It's Ailsa again," said Dugald. "Someone has taken her. We've traced her here."

"Abducted Ailsa!" said Torquil, raising his eyebrows. "For ransom?"

"We know not, but we think we know who. The de Morville clan. And Robert here suspects Fergus is in with them."

"Fergus? Nay, why would he mix up in such a deed?"

"I know not, but she's on Arran and I warrant she couldn't be here without his knowing it, not for long."

Torquil reflected, and said reluctantly, "It's true that." He turned to Robert. "I suppose you have a plan?"

"Not yet," answered Dugald. "But let's eat those fish there and start thinking."

Robert grimaced at the further delay. He paced up and down as the fish sputtered and smoked over a small fire. He gulped his portion and washed it down with water from the stream. "We must go," he urged.

Dugald stretched his legs out toward the fire. "We can move closer, for sure. But we canna enter Fergus' manor 'till nightfall. Though I don't know how we'll enter even then."

"We'll think on it as we walk," insisted Robert. The two others glanced at each other, then agreed.

They headed down a winding path that ran along the high ridge, in the general direction of Fergus' manor, Robert thinking of plan after plan, discarding them as they went. He barely felt the rough branches slap his legs, or brambles tear at his arms. There had to be a way in. They were only three, so entering boldly through the gates was impossible, but by subterfuge, there must be a way.

Toward sundown, the three men lay flat on their stomachs on a ridge, looking down over a deep valley and long meadows, grey now in the summer twilight. Fergus' manor lay on the far side, by the sea. They could see guards patrolling the earth ramparts and moving about the iron gates, tiny ants from here.

Robert turned to the others. "There seems a fair amount of activity. Is that normal?"

"No," frowned Torquil. "Few dare to trouble Fergus here, and all must come by sea and can be seen far ahead of their landing." Even as they watched, a messenger arrived, spurring his horse through the gates.

"He had de Morville's colors on, did he not?" whispered Dugald, for de Morville followed the new fashions and had his tunics and banners all done up in black and brilliant gold.

"Yes," said Robert.

Dugald grunted. "I still don't understand."

"I fear it has to do with the rebel Wimond," said Robert, but he had to tell them something more of his suspicions. "With the king off in England. He leaves this coast open to rebellion." He paused, assessing the two men. "Why they want Ailsa, what use she is to them, why they want Caerwyn, I haven't puzzled that out."

"How will we get in?" said Torquil, after a silence. "I had no thought to find the manor so well guarded."

"I have a plan." Robert shifted his weight on the damp ground. "It will be dangerous. There is no call for either of you to join in if you don't wish."

Dugald was irate. "How say you, she's my cousin! What is your interest?"

"You forget," said Robert, "she is to be my bride."

"Ailsa may not wish you as her husband," Dugald said, "remember that well. But she needs to be rescued first. With that I agree." He fingered his dagger and added, "Ailsa might be difficult, but she is my kin."

"Just listen," Robert said. "Here is the plan."

CHAPTER TWENTY-SEVEN

AILSA STROKED JAMIE'S HAIR as he slept. Tension drummed through her but she made herself sit very still. Jamie was feverish, the effects of the beating. With a swallow, she forced down the lump of her fear. He would be all right. She must believe that. And she still had two more days until she had to marry de Morville. She'd not be here then, she vowed. But Jamie had to heal first and the more he slept the better.

Her legs cramped but she didn't move. She tried to still her mind, shrinking away from the danger of Jamie's fever, thinking through her plan of escape. It wasn't much of a plan. But she had a hope it could work. She thought the plan through again, detail after detail. The good thing was that whether she got away or not, Jamie would.

By late afternoon, Jamie seemed better. He woke and spoke to her; his voice was weak, but he wasn't delirious. He gulped some water and ate the stale bread. She gave him all of it, telling him there was plenty more for her. By evening, he could sit up, though his face was white where not purpled with bruises.

"There seems an uncommon commotion," he observed.

"Aye," said Ailsa, peering out the tiny window, "riders going to and fro and more guards about." She judged him strong enough to speak. "I have a plan."

"Good," he said, as though he'd known all along she would.

"You must listen carefully," she said, "and do all I say."

"Of course, Lady," he said, looking shocked.

She smiled again, truly cheered this time. "You are a good man, Jamie. I'll not forget your service." She left the window and sat beside him. "When they come with our evening meal, you must lie here looking fevered and very ill. I will make a fuss, saying you are dying and must have aid." She paused. "I think they will want to calm me and will eventually agree. I will say you must have a doctor, and they will take you to a healer."

Jamie frowned, and looked like he would protest.

She placed a finger on her lips. "Shush. You must do exactly as I say. You will go, pretending to be quite ill. As you will look so incapable, they'll not bother to guard you overmuch. I think, after all, you have served your purpose for them," she said, a bitter note in her voice.

Jamie looked puzzled.

"Never mind. You must have your wits about you and when you can, you must make your escape. Maybe at night when they leave you to sleep. Take one of the fast ponies if you can, from the meadow you mentioned, the one you passed to the south coming in. You can ride with no saddle or bridle?

"Of course," said Jamie. "But where do I go?"

"You must ride fast as you can to the village on the south side of the island. There lives an old man, good friend to my father; his name is Craig. Tell him it is urgent, you must get word to Sir Robert, at Caerwyn. They must tell Sir Robert . . ." She stopped. "Tell him I am held against my will and seek his aid."

"I do not like to leave you here."

"But you must," she said urgently. "You must, Jamie. It is my best hope."

Jamie stared at her somberly. "Aye," he said finally. "And Sir Robert will come. You need not fear."

Whatever else was between them, she hoped Robert would not fail her in this. Though likely it would be too late. "How do you feel?" She placed a hand on Jamie's cheek, and smiled to find it no longer hot. "Can you stand?"

"Aye." He demonstrated, wincing only a little.

"Good. Then let us try for tonight when they bring the food."

"Are you sure?" He frowned at her, then grimaced at the pain in his jaw.

"I think they'll be tricked by this. Can you do it?"

"Aye," he assured her. "I often act in the plays at Eastertide. I am very good." He laughed. "You will see."

The rattle at the door startled them both. Jamie dropped to the floor and groaned. She bent over him, pinching his cheeks to make them red and straightened as the guards entered the room.

"You have finally come," she said, making her voice trembling and weak.

The bigger guard frowned.

"My servant, he is so ill. You must fetch a physician quickly."

"A physician," laughed the other guard. "For a servant boy. I think not."

"You must," she said, straightening up to her full height, "or at least bring a healer, he is just a boy. He is ill."

Jamie emitted a convincing groan. Ailsa dropped beside him, on her knees. "Please," she entreated, willing tears to fill her eyes.

"Perhaps…" The younger guard was weakening. Ailsa turned to him. "Kind sir, please, he is dear to me, a boy from my home, and so good with the horses." This caught the older man's attention.

"He's valuable, eh?"

"Very, he has the golden touch with the horses." She turned to Jamie, hiding her face from the men. But she could feel them thinking.

The kinder guard frowned. "If the boy's so useful, the master'll not thank us for letting him die."

"He don't look like dying yet." The older guard snarled.

But Ailsa read confusion on his face. "Lord de Morville would have a healer for him," she said. "Ask him."

"De Morville's not here."

That was welcome news. She strained to keep the relief from her face. Clasping her hands, she said, "Where is he?"

"That's no business of yours," said the guard.

Jamie groaned again, a hand on his stomach.

The young guard said, "We could take him to Nell."

"This Nell," said Ailsa, turning to them swiftly, "is she a healer? Have her brought here to help him."

"Have her brought here," laughed the older man. "Nell goes only where she wishes." He cursed, then turned to the younger guard. "Take him if you want. I'll have no dealings with that witch." He strode out. "And be quick about it."

Ailsa caught her breath, trying to keep the elation from her face.

A step echoed from the hall. She kept her eyes on Jamie.

"What is this?" The voice was icy and familiar.

Ailsa lifted her eyes to Hugh, feeling the blood fade from her face.

The young guard stammered. "Lord, we thought you were still away. The boy is ill; she wants a healer."

"Does she," said de Morville, his eyes sweeping to Ailsa. "Leave us. But take the boy."

"I thank you," said Ailsa, lowering her eyes. "He is so ill."

De Morville turned back to the guards. "Take him to the hall and tie him by my chair. I shall keep him by me until the ceremony."

"He must see a healer straightaway. He is ill." Ailsa stood up, wringing her hands. But the guards left the room, carrying a limp Jamie, still playing his part. They avoided her eyes. If only she'd had one more hour.

"He will have a healer, and his freedom, if you but follow through on your agreement."

"I will," she agreed quickly, "but he needs a healer now."

"Well, that suits my new plan as well." He tossed a packet to her, a large packet with something soft inside. "Open it."

Obediently, she opened the linen package and pulled out a gown, brilliant red, with golden braid as trim. She'd never seen such expensive material, though she did not favor the bold color. She looked at him, the cloth in her hands, dread pooling in her stomach.

"Your wedding gown." De Morville drew off his gloves. "Two days more is too long to wait, there are important matters that need tending. We marry tonight. Be ready."

"But you agreed to three days. Only one has passed."

"It has become inconvenient to humor you."

"And what of Jamie?"

"The boy will be freed. I'll send him on his way after the ceremony." He stopped, leaving an ominous silence. "All is now in your hands."

"You cannot force me. I must consent at the chapel door and I will not."

Hugh ignored that and signaled the guard, who opened the door. When he left and the bar clunked down into place, Ailsa stood for a long time and stared at the floor, the garish gown slipping out of her hands to pool at her feet. Hugh was right. He had her trapped. For no matter what, Jamie must not pay.

Robert knelt in a mass of pine boughs, looking down over Fergus' manor. The sky was still lit by the summer sun and twilight would not come for hours yet this month of the year. Eventually, the manor would sleep. He must not let impatience ruin his plan.

He watched the guards at the gatehouse. He thought they would change shifts just before full dark, or what passed for full dark in summer. He hoped to find Ailsa and get away just before the old shift changed to the new. They'd be tired then, distracted, ready for a meal and their pallets.

He glanced over the meadow to the north. He could just make out the stand of firs where Dugald and Torquil crouched. He hoped they'd stay awake until they were needed. He ran a hand through his hair. He had thought over the plan, seeking any flaw. It would take luck, that was sure. But it could work.

His eyes swept the manor for the hundredth time. There should be some clue, some hint to tell him where they held her. The interior of the hall was brightly lighted, and torches flamed along the walls at regular intervals. It was an impressive building, clearly built in stages over the years. The center tower was tall and flat topped, with rambling buildings threading out to the west and east. They could search through the night and never find her in the endless storerooms. At best, he thought, they'd have till dawn, then they'd surely be discovered as servants and guards rose from their sleep.

And if de Morville had her with him in the hall, that was worse. What were all the torches for? Were they holding a feast tonight of all nights? That would be more than inconvenient. Although perhaps they'd be less aware, he thought, searching for reason to hope, perhaps drowned in drink. Still, it would be the longer before the castle darkened. He settled back with a sigh.

After a time of silence, broken only by leaves rustling in the oak above him, he caught a flicker, a faint spot of gold, in one of the rooms far from the hall. A candle had been lit. It was possible it was a servant, gathering up some forgotten item of clothing. But it could be where they held Ailsa. He memorized its location; he'd look there first.

Finally, though people still bustled in the courtyard, he judged it sufficiently dark. There would be three, perhaps four hours of semidarkness and then light once more. He needed to find her and be back on the boat by then.

He whistled once, twice, and listened. An answering call from Dugald came on the wind. He slipped from his hiding place, keeping to the shadows of a line of oaks, and made his way to the road. Then, he walked, stooped over to disguise his height. The plan made him a merchant, from Ayr, seeking to set up a trade agreement with Lord Fergus.

At the gate, he passed through with surprising ease, telling a tale of a lame horse to explain his late arrival. The guard was distracted, as he'd hoped, and let him in without much inquiry.

He kept watch for Torquil and Dugald, and saw them enter the gate behind him with a stir, gathering the attention of the servants still cleaning up from the evening meal. Their task was to distract Fergus long enough for him to get Ailsa away. Would Dugald and Torquil play their parts? Or would they betray him for something Fergus might offer? It was no secret Dugald preferred Torquil as Ailsa's future husband and lord of Caerwyn. Robert shook his head. It was not the time to worry. Now, finally, was for action.

When a servant passed by, he begged a skin of wine. Turning to the wall, he sprinkled it liberally on his clothes, then pulled his shirt out around the neck of his tunic, seeking the look of a disheveled and tipsy merchant. He moved down a corridor, heading in the direction of the light he'd seen, found a quiet corner, pulled his hat down over his face and pretended to sleep.

The corridor seemed little used. For a long while no one passed but a yellow tabby cat, who ignored him. He got to his feet. He calculated Ailsa's room, if it were the place where he'd seen that gleam of light, should be upstairs toward the end of the corridor. There must be stairs. If not, he'd have to go through the hall and that would be complicated.

Spurred feet clinked on the rough stones and he sank to the floor, pressing against the wall, feigning sleep again.

"What's this?" said a deep voice. "You canna lie here." He felt a kick to his foot. The bright light of a torch shone alarmingly close to his eyes.

"What?" Robert stirred, trying to look convincingly drunk.

"He's sleeping it off," said another voice. "Come, we've more important matters to attend to."

"He canna stay here," insisted the first voice.

"Nay, it will not matter."

They marched off and Robert got to his feet. He reached the end of the corridor. There were no stairs, only a window. He climbed out to the courtyard and immediately stumbled on a block of granite. He felt with his hands, searching for an outside stairway. Then his hands closed on a block of granite, and as he felt higher, another. He climbed the steep blocks, moving up a narrow path along a stone and packed earth wall. He reached the top and looked around in the dim light. Yes, there was a door. He ran his fingers over the rough wood. Rust flaked off on his fingers when he touched the handle. Not used often then. Did it lead where he wanted? Or was this a dead end, a waste of precious time?

He took his knife and pried at the corroded metal. Rust fell off in chunks but he got it off. Carefully he pulled the door, trying to make little sound in the still air. Music still floated from the hall. He tugged again at the stuck door. The hinges screeched. He froze, but no one came.

Inside, it was even darker and the air stuffy. Cobwebs draped over his face. He'd have to risk a light, just to see where he was going. He lit a taper and looked around. He was in another long corridor, apparently unused for some time, for it was littered with debris and mice ran before him, squeaking.

Then he heard voices and the tramp of booted feet. He doused the light and drew up against the wall. The voices stopped, still far down the hall. A door opened and banged shut. He crept closer, hoping to hear something that would tell him if Ailsa were indeed held here.

The door banged open again. He flattened against the wall. There was the clank of a soldier's sword against the stone wall and the thud of heavy boots. "Ready yourself, we come for you soon."

And then unmistakably, Ailsa's voice. "I must see the boy."

They did not reply, and she said no more.

Robert crept closer. Down the corridor, a door opened wide, spilling light into the dark corners. He retreated, cursing under his breath. Two manservants, grunting, came down the corridor, carrying a great cask of ale.

"Wine and ale all the time," grunted one, "foolishness." They stopped in front of the door and waited as the guard fumbled with the bar, and finally swung the door to the chamber open wide.

"Quiet!" cautioned the other servant. "Or the lord'll have your hide." The first man laughed.

Robert leaped from his hiding place. He knocked one man to his knees and pushed him to the floor. The other dropped the cask, yelling as the heavy barrel crashed against his knee and ale leaked out, splashing. Robert shoved him. The man hit the wall, groaned and slumped to the floor.

The guard, recovered from his surprise, had pulled his knife. Robert slashed the air in front of him with his own dagger. "Drop your weapon," he said, and the man dropped the knife with a clang onto the stone floor and ran out the door.

Ailsa was standing still like a tree with no wind to liven its leaves, staring at him.

"Come," he called, holding out his hand, "come!"

"I," she stammered and did not move.

He frowned. There was no time. "Come now, you're free," he said gently. The servant on the floor stirred, but it was the guard who had run that was the danger.

"I cannot," she said, her voice flat.

He registered the words but could hardly believe them. "Why not?"

"I marry Hugh de Morville this night," she said. So softly he could hardly hear. He shook his head.

"No." He grabbed her hand. "You are free now, you need not. Dugald is outside. We must go, now."

A wrinkled old lady entered the room. She immediately set up a loud wail. "Help, we are betrayed, help!" Behind her, came the pounding of men's boots running up the stairs.

"Ailsa!" He grasped her shoulders. "There is no more time."

Her eyes avoided his. "Then go now, go quickly."

He felt his arms turn to ice and drop by his side. She refused to meet his eyes. "I see I have been mistaken."

She looked up then, but said nothing. He turned on his heel, brushing past the tiresome old woman, who tried to grab at him. Out the door, he hesitated, but there was no sound from her and already the thud and clank of armed men was far too near.

He raced back the way he'd come, a confusion of voices and the clang of weapons hitting the walls close behind him. He reached the door and leaped down the flight of stairs. Outside, he ran, the guards pounding behind him, shouting. He raced to the stables and slipped in the propped open door. It was quiet; he tried to stifle his heavy breathing. Everyone was in the hall, drinking, as at a feast. A wedding feast, he realized.

He grabbed a horse and swung on, using a rope as reins. The horse skittered under him, but he turned the beast and dug his heels into its sides. The horse leaped forward and they galloped out the door and toward the gate. Dugald and Torquil would be fine; they would see what had happened. No need to explain. The horse was tall and sturdy; he set him toward the massive gate and they sailed over. He tried not to feel the gash she'd opened in him. She chose de Morville. So be it.

CHAPTER TWENTY-EIGHT

Hugh stepped out from behind the bed curtains. "Well done," he said.

Ailsa ignored him as the old woman adjusted her skirts. Her mind raced back and forth, seeing Robert's face, alight with entreaty and then rigid with anger, as she told him to go. She tried to swallow the lump in her throat and failed. He would have tried to save her and Jamie both, and with Jamie tied to a chair in the great hall and helpless, and Hugh hiding behind the bed hangings, sword drawn, Robert and Jamie both would have been killed.

She shut her eyes, but she could not shut out his face. His eyes had told her something new. Then they had slammed her out.

Her stomach wrenched with a sharp pain. She wished she could faint, but of course she did not. Hugh left, laughing and talking with one of the guards. The old woman fussed around her, twitching the cloth of the strident gown this way and that. But it didn't matter. Nothing mattered any more. No, she thought, that wasn't true. There was still Jamie. She must play her part, for Jamie must not be harmed.

De Morville's nurse stood back and admired her handiwork.

Ailsa regarded the disgusting old woman with dislike.

"No need to look like that." The old woman laughed. "You'll be getting your comeuppance tonight, I'll wager. Too proud you are by half. But no better than the rest of us, you are."

The door creaked open, and three guards spilled into the room, along with the smells of sweat and wet wool and iron. "She ready? Our orders is to bring her down."

"'Tis early yet," protested the nurse, her wrinkled hands holding up the bright cloth as she fussed. "We've not finished."

"Finish then, and fast. He grows impatient."

The old woman placed a gauzy headdress of silver mesh on Ailsa's head. "There," she said, stepping back to admire her work.

"Are you ready?" asked one of the guards. Ailsa realized, after a moment, that he was talking to her. It was the young fellow with the kind green eyes.

"Aye," she said. Her voice seemed to come from so far away. A roaring filled her ears. Like the sound of the sea, yes, the sea. Concentrate, she scolded herself. You must hold together until he lets Jamie go.

She walked down the corridor, the red skirts sweeping behind. They reached the hall and one of the guards grabbed a cloak for her. The air felt good on her hot cheeks. It seemed long since she'd been outside. She smelled green leaves, wet stone, and salt. They guided her across the courtyard, toward the chapel step.

Hugh waited at the door. She stopped. "Tell him," she said to the guard, "that he must let Jamie go now." She heard her voice as in the distance, clear and imperious.

The guard frowned, but after studying her face, he went to de Morville and whispered her request in his ear.

Hugh called out. "Do you doubt my word?"

"I will not marry you until he goes free. You must set him on a horse, and I must see him go out of sight. And none of yours to follow him."

Something in her face decided him. He called a guard who disappeared into the hall and emerged with a tousled looking Jamie. Ailsa rushed to him and pulled him to her in a hug. "Ah Jamie, truly sorry I am for the pain I've caused you," she whispered.

He drew away, his face red and shocked. "Oh no, Lady," he said, "'tis none of it your fault."

"You must go now."

Jamie scowled. "I won't leave you here."

"You must, you have a task to do," she whispered. "Remember, I count on you."

He hesitated, but then he nodded and she took a deep relieved breath. "A horse." She turned back to the men, her voice commanding. De Morville grimaced but nodded to his guard and a black pony was led out of the barn.

Jamie mounted.

Ailsa touched his leg. "I thank you." She stepped back.

Jamie looked at her one more moment, indecision on his face, then setting his chin he dug in his heels. He tore out the gate at a gallop.

Ailsa watched him go with immense floating relief. At least she'd succeeded in this one thing. It was all her fault he'd been in danger, but now he was free. She doubted he would go to Craig. He'd probably attempt the journey straight back to Caerwyn. The ride would be long, but Jamie had proved clever and brave and resourceful. He'd deliver her message to Robert. It would be too late to save her from this marriage, but Robert would understand then, at least. He'd know she had to do what she did.

Hugh interrupted her thoughts, bringing her back to the farce of a wedding she must perform. "We have guests to entertain, but first, the wedding," he said.

She felt her heart racing. But Jamie must stay free, and Hugh had only to say one word and a troop of his guards would be off after the boy. She took a deep breath and walked to the chapel door and turned to face him. Her face felt rigid as a stone mask.

The priest stood by the door, a pudgy man with ears that stuck out from his head. He did not look her in the eye. Only the guards and the loathsome nurse stood by as witnesses. Fergus was not here. Did he even know? This was his manor. He'd been her father's firm friend. Loyalties were coming unraveled. Everything was changing. She concentrated on breathing. Hugh began to speak, and she heard the words despite the thrumming in her ears.

"I, Hugh de Morville, grant these lands to the Lady Ailsa of Caerwyn in exchange for her hand in holy marriage." He named the lands he gave to her. The list was long, but the lands he named were small and inconsequential holdings. He was not being generous, though it hardly mattered. Why did he want her? She thought over what he'd said, about Wimond, and what he'd not said. About Somerled and the king and which way to go, if it came to it. Though it mattered not at all now, the why of it. She realized he was handing her a sack of coins. She took the symbol of his wealth, though her hands felt stiff and cold.

Then, too soon, it was time for the vows.

"I, Hugh de Morville, of Lauderdale and Irvine, take Ailsa, Lady of Caerwyn, to wife, to have and to hold, from this day forward, till death doth us part, as holy church doth ordain."

She felt her limbs turning to ice, but she held her head high and said her vows clearly. She felt him kiss her cheek, so far away she could hardly feel his cold lips, and then the wedding was done.

He turned her around like a doll, facing the small band of servants assembled around the chapel. They cheered dutifully. She belonged to this man now. She heard the contrived shouts of the servants, a distant useless clamor.

They led her into the hall, and she stopped, the long gown suddenly so heavy, weighing her down. She thought they'd eat now, but Hugh urged her on, up the stairs to a private chamber. Surely, he did not mean to take her now. How would she bear it? She bit her lip. She must, for Jamie's sake.

The door to the solar was open. He pushed her inside.

"Chat with our special guests. I have business to attend to." He shut the door and she heard the bar clunk down on the other side. Why lock her in now, she thought wearily, and turned.

And stared into two familiar faces. Torquil and Dugald, disheveled and bruised, stared back at her, surprise writ clearly on their weary faces.

Robert slid off the borrowed horse. Time to give him a rest. He had ridden half the night and then onward into the grey dawn. He was too keyed up to rest himself and paced back and forth under the pines as the horse nosed about for grass. He cursed out loud as he stomped back and forth. Once or twice the horse looked up, with seeming curiosity, as he kicked at the grass and stared into space.

I can't come with you! Who could believe it! He had chased all over the Isles looking for her. She was in danger; he'd felt it. He had been sure. But all the time she was planning to marry Hugh de Morville.

Robert kicked at a rock embedded in the path. It was firmly wedged in the ground and he swore again as pain ricocheted through his knee. The small meadow was annoyingly peaceful in the sun; bees in the tall clover were the only sound apart from the occasional snort of the horse and a clunk of a hoof against stone.

He considered waiting for Dugald and Torquil, but they were most likely sleeping off the wedding feast even now, pleased at tricking him. He recalled the glances they'd exchanged. So, he would cross back to the mainland, and then what? Head to the king, who could be far south by this time, engrossed in England's affairs? He'd be little pleased at the news of the Islesmen's wavering loyalty. And Ailsa's marriage? That would not please the king either, or would it? Her marriage to Hugh had been the king's plan all along. He slumped down to the ground and then lay down flat, shielding his eyes from the sun. Why return to the king at all? He owed the king nothing anymore. Certainly not loyalty.

It was all too confusing and his mind kept wandering. Why did Will have to die? The king had betrayed him and Will had paid for it. He had to go to Caerwyn and stand by the grave once more. That much was certain. He'd known, all along, Ailsa might be part of some plot against him, but even so, he'd never quite believed it. In the end, he'd been wrong, and so Will was dead, and his own future utterly uncertain.

A few hours later, he launched the boat himself, with some difficulty, and pointed her back to the mainland. After a choppy crossing, he walked into Ayr, and dug some of his last silver out of his pouch to buy a horse. He ate a greasy meal at the local tavern, some sort of stew, light on the meat. He downed a mug of sour ale to cut the taste. Then he got on the horse and headed toward Caerwyn. As he rode, he tried to think about his future. He could travel back to Carlisle. Maybe fight for the king in Northumberland. Fighting was something he knew how to do. But the thought of seeing David again put a bad taste in his mouth. He could return to Normandy. They were always fighting there. But he was tired of fighting. He put off trying to think ahead and let his mind drift. He thought of Ailsa, and he wondered about Caerwyn, and how it fit in with Fitz John and de Morville, but it was all a puzzle and his head ached.

By afternoon he approached the Roman Road. The horse, lazy all afternoon, raised his head and pricked his ears at a new sound. Robert pulled his dagger and jumped down, grabbing the reins. He hid behind some brush. Horses, three or maybe four. Pounding along. In a hurry. He faded back into the brush hoping the strange horse would keep quiet. He watched the riders race by until their thudding hoofs faded.

He was about to lead the horse back onto the road when he heard another horse, one by the sound of it, pushing hard. Horse and rider swept into the clearing and the rider pulled up. The horse snorted and reared, the rider clinging to his bare back. It was only a boy. He was looking around, cautious, as though he expected to find enemies. Then he jumped down.

Robert squinted into the sun. There was something about the way the boy stood. "Jamie?"

The boy grabbed the horse's reins.

"Jamie, wait!"

Registering that he'd heard his name, Jamie turned, his eyes searching the shadows under the trees. "Sir Robert, is it really you?"

He was breathing hard, his face flushed. And bruised too, by the look of it. What had happened to the boy?

Jamie fell down on his knees before him. "You must save my lady."

Impatience and anger filled his throat, but he took a deep breath. The boy was close to tears. "Your lady does not need my help," he said gently.

The boy broke down, sobbing, "It is all my fault."

"None of this be your fault, boy. How do you come to be here?"

"She did it for me."

Robert frowned. This was making little sense.

Jamie wiped his cheeks with a dirty palm. "Stayed with that beast because of me."

"What are you saying?" But Jamie just shook his head, then hid his face in his hands. Robert offered him water from the flask he carried, then sat beside the boy. He hoped the armed riders would not return too soon. "Explain."

"She gave me a message for you."

Robert felt his breath catch. "Tell me," he said, "from the beginning."

Jamie hiccuped. "They captured me as I rode back to Caerwyn. And took me where they held her, on a boat, full of the stink of dead fish it was."

"Who?"

"De Morville. His men that is. They had her in a dark and dirty storage room. With damp straw on the floor. They beat me good. I tried to help her. We tried to escape; 'twas my lady's plan and a good one too. But they saw through us. I tried to stop them, but I couldn't." He hung his head. His brown curls were plastered to his head with sweat.

"You've not reached your full growth boy, you can't expect to stop armed men."

"I failed."

"You have found me. Where did they take her?"

Jamie swallowed.

"I didn't catch it all. I just heard my lady say, if you set him free, I will do it."

Robert batted a bee away. "And then."

"Then," the boy faltered. "They had me tied to a chair, and they dragged me out. My lady ran to me. She said I must go free. De Morville had me set on a pony, a proper nag, not this one here, this one I snatched from his fields."

Robert felt his lips twist in a half smile.

"My lady ordered me off. I did not want to leave her." Jamie screwed up his face. "Find Sir Robert, tell him I seek his understanding for what is done." Jamie wiped his nose with his tunic. "She could say no more. De Morville was there, watching, listening. She bid me hasten away." He stopped. "Did I do right, to leave her?"

"You did right." Robert heard his voice, as though far away, reassuring the boy. He had failed her. He'd been ever suspicious and skeptical, never daring to trust. "When did you leave her?"

"It took me the rest of the morning to reach the bay, and it was afternoon before I could sneak onto a boat," said Jamie. "After we landed, I stole this horse. I needed to reach you quickly. That's why they were chasing me."

She could have been away with him, had he not been so blind and stupid. "You've done a good day's work here, Jamie. You have call to be proud."

The boy's face shone. "You'll save my lady?"

"Yes," said Robert, though how was the devil's own question. The boy nodded, apparently satisfied. "Now, climb on that horse you've helped yourself to and take him to Caerwyn, stable him well and get yourself tended to. You've done your part. Can you make it?"

"Oh aye," said Jamie, looking renewed. "Or I could come along and help you."

"No. Time for you to head to Caerwyn. And take care. Those riders ahead of you, they'll circle back."

"Aye," said Jamie. "But I know a wee path just north of here. I can reach it by dark, then I'll be just fine."

Jamie rode off, looking relieved he'd done his part.

Robert stood in the quiet meadow, not hearing the bees in the clover or the swallows calling as they swooped among the birches.

Robert waited until dusk covered his actions, though it was difficult to sit still, and dusk came so late this time of the year. He had returned to the coast in the afternoon, but finding a boat required darkness. When he judged the time right, he ran across the meadow and his nose caught the scent of salt and bait fish. A breeze, light but steady, blew off the land. That was good. There were three boats pulled up on the beach. One looked like it would leak like a sieve. He crept closer. One had no sail, so that made the decision easy.

The third was heavy, but he thought he could drag her in on the rollers. He dropped his weapons aboard and pulled her along, her old beams creaking. It would wake the dead themselves. But no one happened along. With a last mighty tug, he got her into the water.

She was leaking, but she'd swell, he hoped. He found a pot aboard he could use to bail her meantime. He grabbed the oars and prodded her out beyond the swells, then raised the sail. Just as the wind caught, he heard shouts from the beach. He could make out men, shouting and dancing on the shore. He waved to them and turned away. Later, he'd return the boat and pay them well. But for now, on to Arran as fast as the wind could take him.

A fog bank crept closer and brooded over the waves in swathes of white. He sailed on, the fog thick and his cheeks and eyelashes were soon beaded with moisture. After some hours of sailing, watching the wave and tide direction, he had some luck. The fog lifted and he prodded the boat into the small cove on the eastern side of the island that he and Will had used before.

Just thinking about Will was a stab in his stomach. He took a few deep breaths and the pain eased, then he rowed the boat until he heard the grinding of wood on rock. He yanked at the sail, letting the heavy linen pile on the deck and leaped ashore, pulling the boat off the rock as the next wave lifted her, guiding her onto the pebbled beach. He pulled her up as far as he could. The tide would be rising. He'd have to tie her well and hope for the best. He'd be needing the boat before long. If he was successful. Though there could be no question of that. He must find Ailsa and get her away from de Morville.

He started walking, thankful no one seemed to be around this late, or rather this early in the last hour before dawn. A tree limb snapped against his cheek. Robert cursed under his breath and listened. But the soft crackling of branches swaying in the wind was all he heard. He moved down the narrow path threading though the trees. He worried he'd miss the path and stray into a bog or a blow down that would slow him. He ducked under a low branch and then stopped. Yes, there it was again. Voices. His nose caught a whiff of smoke. Men ahead, camped in the woods. Whose men was the question.

He slipped out of the evergreens and made his way toward the smoke, staying away from the path, feeling his way from trunk to trunk. Voices again. And laughter. Good, they were relaxed and suspected nothing. Where were their guards? He was getting very close. He could smell the meat they cooked over their fire now and distinguish their words. He crouched in a clump of hemlocks, slipping through the thick branches until he reached the top of a rise. He peered down. In a clearing, a cluster of men stood before a fire. Another small group sat off to the side, eating.

His eyes scanned their colorful cloaks. Their clothes were much too fine for farmers or even the local smugglers. One, in the center by the fire, caught his gaze. He was tall, dressed in the dark outfit of a churchman, but somehow his dress caught the eye more than the bright colors of the men surrounding him, hanging on his words. Robert held his breath, trying to hear what he said. The breeze cooperated, and a string of words floated clearly to him. He frowned. What manner of speech was this? Then he realized; the man was declaiming in Latin.

The tall man stopped speaking and laughed at the puzzled faces around him. Bending toward the fire he picked up a burning stick and swung it in the air. "In other words," he said, still laughing, "we have accomplished our purpose here. Drink deep for this night is our last as servants to a false king. Eat your fill, for tomorrow, we head to Galloway." A few of the men cheered, fists raised in the air. "Aye, first Galloway, and then, all Scotia!" Cheers rocked the quiet woods and the birds grew silent at this invader in their midst.

Crouched in the trees, a branch sticking into his ribs, Robert examined the man, noting his height and his thick brown hair and heavy brows, his long nose and eloquent hands. The men hummed around the tall figure, and the clamor of their excited voices filtered between the trees. A cask of ale was opened and passed about. The tall man said no more, but walked to a boulder near the trees, where he sat, alone.

Robert examined the man's profile, wishing he could see him

straight on. Seeming to feel the scrutiny, the man turned his head and stared into the woods. Robert froze and shifted his gaze.

The man got to his feet again and when he spoke all the others turned to him, faces alight. "Be calm. I come to free you, if truth be told, from the tyranny of English rule and foreign ways. Aye," he continued, "I come in peace, as a man of God, and bring a message of hope for these Isles. 'Tis nearing the time for all true men who love these Isles to rise together, for the benefit of all, to throw off these foreign invaders, these Englishmen." His voice rose and fell, scornful. "And our good friend from the North, he will come too. I have his word."

The men exclaimed and Robert heard several of them call out the name Somerled. He leaned closer, hardly breathing.

"I tell you Fergus has not yet fully appreciated the benefits and truth of our mission. But he will. And many others have already joined our cause."

For certain it was the rebel bishop himself, Wimond. Here, on Arran! If the king knew, he would be outraged. The man's own words branded him traitor. Though many would follow him, thought Robert, staring at the cluster of men surrounding the bishop, landowners by their dress, powerful men, clearly in awe.

Wimond was speaking again, perhaps to still their doubts, weaving a story of English betrayal and tragedy, urging the men to fight for their way of life. And there was truth to the man's words. Though he mistrusted the too elegant phrasing and frequent calls on God. And then there was the matter of the man's method and aim. War, in short. Robert looked at the peaceful sky up over him, the small brown wrens hopping from branch to branch above his head. Bringing violence and devastation to this Isle was not the way to keep English ways out. There had to be a way to meld Gaels and Norse, Irish and Scots, French and English. To fuse all into the new Scotia King David was always talking about. If he'd truly meant it.

Robert swallowed, seeing in his mind the desolate war fields in Normandy, a child wandering alone, crying. Corpses lying maimed and bent in the mud. He must get this information to the king right away, that trouble, serious trouble brewed in the Isles. No matter the danger to himself. He must summon eloquence of his own. Somehow, he must make the king see the value and beauty of the ways here. See that there was something of worth to bring into the new Scotia. Else war and all its devastation would come here, to Arran and to Ailsa's home, that was certain.

CHAPTER TWENTY-NINE

AILSA STARED, THEN SHUT HER OPEN MOUTH with a sharp click of teeth. "Dugald, what are you doing here?" Suspicion flooded her mind and she backed away. "You haven't been a part of this?"

Dugald stared at the floor, saying nothing, his face flushed a furious red.

"What have you done?"

"I didn't know he truly would harm you," said Dugald, raising his eyes to hers. "I might not have seen eye to eye with you cousin, but you must believe I'd never of harmed you."

She stared at him, trying to understand what he was saying.

"When Robert said he was coming to fetch you, well, I just thought..."

"You thought what?"

Dugald lifted his head and glared. "I thought you'd be better off with one of our own kind. Like Torquil here, you always had a liking for him."

Ailsa looked at Torquil. He was examining the floor, his face red and miserable as Dugald's.

Ailsa closed her eyes for a long moment. When she opened them, the two men were still there. They were battered, she realized, and Torquil's arm was bent at an odd and painful angle. "I recall as how he wasn't entirely interested in me, once he heard he'd have to fight for me. And maybe with the king himself." She addressed Dugald, but both men stared, as if absorbed, at the planks of the floor. "What did you do, Dugald, exactly?"

"Well, just that I mentioned to Fergus, some time past, you'd be better off with one of our own. Not much else…"

"I want to know exactly."

He blurted out, "We came with Robert on a boat here to Arran and gathered up Torquil, after Robert got me from the monastery."

"What monastery?"

"Near Ayr." Dugald frowned at her interruption. "I fell afoul of that bishop there and he gave me a crack on the head." Robert just assumed it was about this de Morville plan, so I didn't tell him otherwise. I mean, how it was more a difference of opinion about some merchandise."

"You mean, he saved your skin, and this is how you repaid him."

"Well, aye," stammered Dugald, looking uncomfortable.

Ailsa frowned at him, though he didn't seem to notice.

"We came to Fergus' manor and we were supposed to feel out the lords and distract attention from him. Spirit you out and head back to Caerwyn that very night." He stopped. "Only it didn't quite work that way. You see Fergus got talking, and we all got drinking, and then it seemed this de Morville had some point, talking about easing the trading and all."

"And you left Robert on his own. Obviously, de Morville threw you in here to sober up and hasn't let you out yet." Ailsa cut in, her voice weary. The fools, Robert had found his way in somehow and found her despite them, and then she'd turned on him too. That must be what he thought. And now none of that mattered, as she was de Morville's wife. She walked to the window and traced the rough stone with her finger. "And Meriel? Did she know too?"

"No, no." Dugald scratched his head and winced. "She wouldn't have liked it, I suppose."

Ailsa blinked back tears. She missed Meriel, and her old life, and Jamie, and Robert, and Nia her mare and Caerwyn and all of it, all of it was gone now and no longer her life.

Dugald raised his voice. "What do we do now?"

"Now?" she said, still staring out the window, no longer surprised that she seemed to be the leader, "there's nothing to do now, but only wait."

"But," protested Torquil, "we can get you out of here, somehow. We'll find Robert and explain."

"For all that, it is far too late."

Bells rang for evening prayers. Ailsa watched the shadows outside in the courtyard lengthen into night. An orange moon began her rise. Torquil and Dugald sat by the fire, playing a game of droughts. She watched them as from a distance. It was hard to stay angry. They lived by a set of traditional rules, but she could see that all the old rules and ways were no longer enough. Everything was changing, and Norman and English and Gaels and Norse, they would all have to learn to get on or there would be troubles and violence. Once she thought Caerwyn was a world apart, and could stay unaltered, but now she knew better. Change had begun when she was but a child and come on even faster once her father had drowned. And when David became king and brought the English, nothing could stay as it was.

The tramp of feet in the hall made her freeze. The door burst open and two guards marched in. "Lady," said the first politely, and gestured to the door.

Ailsa said nothing. Her heart was in her throat; she felt she would choke.

Torquil said, "You can't take her."

Dugald clambered to his feet, awkward in his pain, and lurched toward the guard, fist raised. "No, Dugald!" she called, too late.

The guard struck him across the face, and he crumpled to the floor. The second guard crowded into the room and kicked him.

"Dugald!" Ailsa called as the guards hauled her away. "Poor Meriel," she thought, as they rushed her down the dark stairs, knocking her against the rough timbers. The guards yanked her along and thrust her into a chamber, slamming the door. "Let me out!" She'd married him; he had no right to treat her this way. She rushed to the one window and saw it narrowed as it went through the thick stone walls. It was nearly a man's length deep and let in only a sliver of light. Outside all was quiet and despite the moon, she could see nothing.

Within the chamber, embroideries decorated all four walls. The most obvious feature of the chamber, she avoided. But the giant bed, with its black hangings, dominated the room. She walked to the fire and sat down on a stool. She had made a bargain. Jamie's life for this. She covered her face with her hands and squeezed her eyes shut.

Hours passed, and no one came. Eventually, she dozed, and woke suddenly, dazed from a dark dream, and saw the fire burned down to coals. She heard a loud thud. She got to her feet, stumbling over the stool. Another dull thud, a sort of boom, and shouts. A crash, perhaps of timber splintering, or a huge trestle table falling to the stone-flagged ground. Then the clang and clunk of swords on shields. She gripped the slippery cloth of her awful red gown, twisting the material in tense fingers.

Boots pounded in the hallway and men shouted. She ran to the door, but they raced past her chamber. She pressed her ear against the door, banged, and called, "Let me out!" Outside, she could hear horses neighing and the clash of metal, of weapons. She had no idea what was happening, but there must be some way to take advantage of this chaos. She must get out. She was safer with any attackers than with de Morville, no matter who they be. She banged on the door again, until her hands bruised, but no one came.

She grabbed the iron shovel by the fire and yanking at the cloth with her free hand, she ripped off a strip of the red cloth of her gown. She threw it on the coals and the cloth flamed up, catching strength from the draft from the window. She jerked the bed hangings down and tossed them on the fire. It sizzled and smoked and then burst into flames. For a moment, she watched as the flames bit into the cloth and flared up and up. Then she ran to the door and yelled, "Fire, fire!"

Still no one answered and the fire was dying down, so she grabbed feather pillows from the bed and thrust them on the flames. The orange flames danced and flared and she piled on the stool and then yanked down the wall hangings and threw those on too. The fire roared up suddenly, forcing her to the window. It was fearfully hot now and smoke poured out the window but much hung in the air, making her cough.

She shouted from the window and tossed out the goblets and the fire iron and whatever else she could find. Her throat felt raw and the air was hot and full of ash.

"What in the devil's name," she heard from the corridor and the door swung open. Coughing, sucking in cold air, she ducked under the manservant's arm, and raced down the spiral stairs, stumbling toward the bottom and falling on her side. She picked herself up, groaning, eyes streaming, and ran.

Armed men and servants alike were rushing around the courtyard. She ran to the hall and found it deserted. Much smoke and eager flames leapt from the rushes and as she watched, flames caught the cloth on the trestle table in the center of the room. The fire burst into tall spires, and smoke rose in spirals. Sparks exploded and lit the roof thatch and soon even the giant timbers were creaking and smoking.

She stared, astounded that the fire had roared so quickly out of control. Coughing, she made her way through the smoking hall to the room where Dugald and Torquil were imprisoned. She struggled with the bar. The door creaked as it swung open and smoke poured out. So much smoke. "Dugald," she called. There was no answer. Her eyes watered and burned. She bent low and held her breath and entered, her arms outstretched, feeling along the floor, searching for her cousin and his friend. Lungs bursting, she took a deep breath and coughed and coughed.

They were not here. Gone. Smoke swirled around her head and in her lungs. She felt her way back to the door and the rush of cold wind up the stairs and gulped precious air. A beam fell, in a room above, with a crash, and sparks scattered down the stairway like falling stars.

Ailsa ran down the stairs and out into the grey dawn, into the clamor of men shouting and servants running with buckets, and horses neighing. She ran to the stable and opened the doors wide and loosed all the frightened horses, ropes burning her palms. Leaping on the last, a white mare, she galloped off into the night.

Robert stared in horror at the burning manor. Men were fleeing down the road, driving cattle and panicked sheep before them. The bellows of the frightened cows mingled with men's shouts and the clang and clash of metal. Who was attacking Fergus? And where in this inferno was Ailsa? Orange flames leaped into the black sky. Acrid smoke filled the air. He choked on it, and ran forward, coughing and shoving through the crowd and lines of loaded carts, pushing men out of his way.

He reached the courtyard. Servants were emptying the storerooms. Shielding their heads from falling sparks with soaked rags, they lugged casks and rolled barrels and balanced piles of cheeses and flat breads. Robert ran toward the keep, hoping to find someone, anyone, who would know of Ailsa. Avoiding overturned benches and hurrying lads carrying sacks of flour, he entered the kitchen. In a corner, he spied a big man, covered in soot and flour, but recognizable for all that. "Fergus!"

Fergus glanced at him and frowned. "I have no time for you now, as you can well see."

Robert leaped over the table and grabbed Fergus by the shoulders. The big man flung him off. Robert scrambled to his feet. "Where is the woman?"

"You're mad. Get out of here, I've work to do."

Ignoring the kitchen girls, who clustered in a frightened circle, Robert drew his knife and stuck the point to Fergus' throat.

Fergus hesitated and swallowed, but then he pointed to the stairs at the corner of the hall and made to turn away.

"Not so fast," said Robert. "You've violated the king's peace. I would know why."

"Hardly time to talk of such things now." Fergus shouted to the kitchen girls, and they resumed their carting of grain sacks, bags of apples, and other foodstuffs. "The whole village needs this food, even you can see that."

"Why join with de Morville's plotting? Is he in league with Wimond? Does he seek to overthrow the king?"

"Who can say?" responded Fergus, with a shrug of his giant

shoulders. "I have one duty only, to my lands, here and in Galloway. These are MacLaughlin's men. He's thrown in with the English I'd say, or just out for gain more likely."

A crash sounded from the kitchens, and Fergus, ignoring Robert's attempt to restrain him, bounded through the open doorway and disappeared into the swirling smoke.

Robert grabbed one of the servants rushing by. "Where is the woman held?"

"I don't know," shouted the frightened man.

Robert loosed his grip and the man ducked away. The clash of weapons had stalled, as everyone turned to putting out the flames and carting off supplies, but smoke was swirling thicker. He turned to the stairs. He heard another crash from the kitchen, and realized the shelves were toppling, tipping piles of crockery onto the stone floors. He ran up the stairs.

The first room was empty; smoke swirled in the door behind him and out the open window. He lunged back across the hall. He forced the second door open. Empty. He stared a moment then raced back down the stairs.

In the courtyard, he avoided a wagon piled with hens and ran into a tall man. "Torquil!" His eyes were ringed with black soot and he supported a sagging Dugald.

"Where is she?"

"They took her. We don't know where." Dugald could barely stand. His forehead was bleeding, and he had a swollen jaw.

Torquil said, "It's de Morville has her, and Fergus, and that crazed Wimond as well. They're all in this somehow. Tied together."

Robert took Dugald's arm. "You're weak as a cat."

Hot winds laden with ash blew against their clothes and ruffled their hair. Robert grabbed one of the donkeys being led by, waving off the startled boy. "Set him on here and make your way to the bay above the main town, I've a boat there," he said to Torquil.

Torquil nodded, too weary to argue. Robert watched them tangling with the frightened donkey for a moment, then dismissed them from his mind.

He entered the keep again, shoving his way through the crowded corridors, packed with farmers looting food, chests, and heaps of clothes. It was clear the main beams had caught now, it wouldn't be long before the whole place torched up. It was chaos away from the kitchens, without Fergus to keep order. A small child stood by the window, wailing. Robert hoisted him over his shoulder and ran outside into the courtyard again. Finding an anxious group of women clustered by the stables, he thrust the child into one woman's arms and turned back without a word.

A hand plucked at his sleeve. "What?" he demanded.

"Sorry sir."

He looked down at a young face.

"Aye," he said, more gently.

"Do you seek the lady?"

Robert turned eagerly. "Where is she?"

The lad bit his lip. "Jamie. He was my friend you see, at Carlisle. I didna like to see him treated this way. But there was nothing I could do."

"But what of the lady?"

"They seized her and carried her to up the stairs." The boy gestured. "She was struggling and yelling and so I chanced to see. The lord cuffed me and said keep my mouth shut and I would. Only Jamie is my friend." The boy pointed to the far end of the keep. Robert moved forward blindly.

"Sir!"

He brushed the boy away. He needed to get there, but how? The middle chambers were already alight.

"She isna there now." The boy's words penetrated the panic in his head. "She got away. On a fast horse. I saw her, and I told no one."

Before he could question him further, the boy scurried away. "Wait," he called, but the boy was gone in the smoke and commotion.

He ran to the stables, but all the horses were gone. In the fields, past the road, he found a huddled group, a mare and two ponies. He grabbed the mare and vaulted on. Where would she have gone?

Ailsa pulled up the white horse and slid off. She rested her head against the horse's neck and tried to slow her breathing. She had escaped, but she was still trapped on this island and in this marriage. De Morville might find her at any moment. She clutched the horse's mane in her fists and tried to think.

She would ride east, she decided, once the light permitted, and search until she found a harbor with boats. Persuade someone to hide her on their boat. She had no silver. No matter, persuade them somehow she would, and cross to the mainland. Go to Caerwyn.

But Caerwyn belonged now to Robert, or maybe to de Morville. It didn't matter. If she tried to return, the king might send men to take her, and de Morville would certainly look for her there. She no longer had a home.

She sat down on a cold rock, rough granite and damp moss under her fingers. She felt the burn of tears and wanted to let them flow but if she started she didn't think she could stop. Think! Where else could she go? Somehow she and Caerwyn were of use to de Morville and he'd entrapped her. But she had made it possible. She had been too naive, too sure she could persuade a king to see justice her way. Too ignorant about how a king's power worked. And then with her story telling, she had angered the king, feeding the myths of an independent west. She hoped Dugald and Torquil were safe. Though she was angry with them still.

She began to walk, leading the horse, trying to escape the round of her thoughts. She'd escaped de Morville but she was still caught, already de Morville's wife. She no longer had a home. She had only the shift she wore and this white mare she'd stolen.

She was in a dark part of the forest, soft dripping evergreens stroked her arms as she passed. Feathery and scented. Above her, sky stretched a pale pink, still lit by a morning star and a fine crescent of moon. She stopped walking and stared up at the sky, until the horse nudged her and nickered. It was crazy, but suddenly at that moment she felt so relieved, so strangely happy, so hopeful. She threw her arms around the startled horse's neck and breathed in her warm smell.

Hugh de Morville was disloyal and cruel, a man of no honor. He'd stolen her and forced her into marrying him, but no matter what he said, he and his English priest had no hold on her. She had only to get away. She had done it already, almost. She had only to keep on, go further and further, escape well beyond his reach.

And if she could? What might her new life be? Robert's face rose into her mind and her breath caught. Even if he would never be hers, at least she could try to find him and explain, and at least she'd not stay to be trapped and imprisoned as de Morville's wife.

She heard loud voices coming over the rise. She got to her feet and looked around, unsure which way to go. Men's voices, shouting, and the deep baying of dogs. The horse tossed her head and reared, spooked by the sounds. Ailsa was knocked to the ground and the mare disappeared with a rush into the trees.

Ailsa scrambled to her feet and ran. Ducked under trees and dove through brush, shielding her eyes as best she could, brambles scratching at her cheeks and arms and back. She entered a clearing and darted across.

She tripped on a rounded stone and landed hard on her chest. Before she could get her breath back, strong arms flipped her and pinned her against the ground. The damp cold grass drenched her back, and the large dogs circled, barking and growling, teeth bared. The man holding her shouted and the dogs backed away a few feet, their yellow eyes on her throat. The man hauled her to her feet and dragged her along, then dumped her at the feet of three men. One, Ailsa saw through a swelling eye, was Hugh.

"You forget," he said quietly. "We have made a bargain, you and I. The boy is safe, as you wished. Now is the time for you to fulfill your part."

"Never," said Ailsa.

"Bind her arms. Then get back to the port." The men wound and knotted thick cord about her wrists and left. Hugh grabbed her cloak and pulled her close to him. He spoke softly. "Never is a strong word but I think, before this day be well started, you will rue defying me. And look, dawn is already breaking."

Ailsa looked at the sky over the dark oaks and indeed it was a streaked and queasy grey. Angry orange streaks lit the hills. "You forced me. The marriage is not binding. I will never belong to you."

Hugh placed a hand at her throat. "My men have long arms. It is an easy matter to pick up the boy again. Or that cousin of yours. Or his little wife even."

"You couldn't, you wouldn't dare."

"Who can stop me?" he said. "My father has the king's ear. I will do that and more, you can believe me. And after that tale telling of yours, all that nonsense of a true Queen coming over the water from the West, the king will never trust you."

"Fergus then, he was my father's friend. In honor, he will help me."

Hugh laughed. "After you fired his keep? Men will do much for money. Besides, your Fergus was already working for me." He pushed her forward until they entered the woods again and came upon a small house hidden in the trees. He opened the door and tugged her inside. He forced her to climb a rope ladder to an upper chamber, small and dark. "I will return, wife." He pulled the ladder away and went out, slamming the door shut.

Ailsa ran to the one window. Below, two people murmured, their voices carrying in the still air. Gowned in black silk, unmistakable gold hair gleaming loose against the dark cloth, Alice stood facing de Morville, her two white hands on his chest.

Ailsa listened to the rise and fall of their voices, trying to make sense of them. Hugh bent toward the woman, and she heard Alice's melodious laugh. "Not long now," she caught, the words carried up to her on a breeze. "Tonight, it must be tonight…"

He was her lover. How obvious. She had been so naïve. She tried to strain her ears, to hear more. The wind shifted and their voices came her way.

Alice said, "She will seem ill and will not wake."

"And the king?"

"Fergus will protect you from the king, even if your father will not. He has a pact with Somerled, does he not? This king's days are numbered. And the Prince is so ill, he has not long to live surely. Soon we'll be rid of all of them."

"The king might be displeased? This Robert did save the king's life."

"Robert is a problem for the king and a king will always be happy if a problem is removed." Alice smiled and kissed Hugh. "You deal with him and I will meet you at Carlisle."

They moved down the path and Ailsa heard the distant jingle of their horses' bridles and hoofbeats as they cantered away.

She gripped the window sill. She must find Robert. Immediately. He was in great danger. She must warn him. There was no one else.

She leaned out the window. It was far to the ground, too far, but a branch from an old apple tree leaned toward the house. Too far to jump. She walked around the bed chamber, running her hands along the rough walls. There was little but the bed. And its linens. She grabbed a sheet and using her teeth, made a hole. She ripped the cloth into strips, knotting them together to make a long rope. It was slow work.

Finally, she leaned out the window and threw her makeshift rope over the leaning branch and reached out as far as she could. She just managed to catch the end when the wind swayed it in her direction. She tied the other end to the bed frame, using the knots she'd learned when fixing her father's nets. She tested it, yanking, but she would just have to trust it would hold. She climbed up onto the wide sill and looked out, her stomach clenching.

She wrapped the linen three times around her palms and took a long breath and then she jumped. She missed the branch she aimed for, but grasped at the next, banging her shoulder and her wrist as she slammed against the house wall. She swung in the air, clutching at the end of the rope of linen, as it yanked her elbows and shoulders until they burned.

The rope held, but it was too short.

She looked down and then up, quickly. It was far, too far. But there was no help for it. She took a deep breath, unwound one wrist, then the other, and let go. She hurtled down and landed hard, and lay for a moment, winded and sick.

Then she gasped and rolled over, breath coming again, uneven and painful. She stumbled to her feet, clutching her injured arm, and ran.

CHAPTER THIRTY

WHEN AILSA WOKE, she was warm, enveloped in a soft blanket smelling of lavender, and she seemed to be in her room, her own room at home at Caerwyn, though how could that be. Late afternoon sun slanted in her window and the familiar scent of the sea floated in on the fitful breeze. She struggled up, shaking her head to free her from this too pleasant dream.

"Oh miss, you're awake!"

"Osla?" She looked around the room. "Am I really home in my own bed?"

"We're that happy to have you back miss, just like old times. Cook is making your favorite soup of onions and cheese and ..."

"How did I get here?" interrupted Ailsa. Then she remembered and tried to climb out of bed. Her shoulder and arm stabbed with needles of pain. She stared at her wrist, wrapped in linen. "Robert, where is he?"

"Sir Robert is gone."

"Gone? Gone where? When?"

"There there, you must stay calm," Osla said. "You've had a shock and you're injured. You must rest." She tried to put the blanket around Ailsa's shoulder.

Ailsa twisted away. "Who brought me here?"

"You came with Sir Robert, in the dead of night, both of you bleeding and limping. We brought you up here right off. You've been sleeping that deep you never stirred for an entire day and a night. Sir Robert, he told Jamie to saddle up that big stallion of his and..."

"Jamie is here?"

"Aye, miss. Of course."

"That's good." Ailsa smiled. It was good, it was wonderful news. She slid down from the high bed, ignoring the ache in her shoulder and wrist, and something wrong with her knee. She limped to the window and stared out over an empty field, the earth brown despite the season. "Why hasn't the east field been planted?"

Osla ignored that and chattered on. "Torquil and Dugald are in the stables, and Lady Meriel will be here by dinnertime, for your cousin has sent for her, 'tis a grand homecoming indeed."

"Did he leave a message, Osla?" Ailsa pressed her lips together, embarrassed at having to ask.

"Sir Robert? Not as I know of." Osla was pulling gowns from her chest. "You must wear something fine."

"Aye," agreed Ailsa absently. Sudden tears dimmed her view of the sea below.

She remembered. Stumbling barefoot through the forest, thorns stabbing her feet and rocks scraping her shins, thinking to make her way to the harbor, desperate to search out Robert's boat and find him in time. Finding the path. Fearing running into Hugh or Alice. Fearing they would find Robert first. Then shouts and the thud of hoofs. She'd crouched in the brush. Robert on a stolen horse, unmistakable to her, and in the distance the ominous sound of hoofs and de Morville's men. Without thinking, she'd rushed straight into the path; she must have seemed a ghost of sorts, rising up from the ground like the mist come to life. Certainly the horse had reared and someone screamed and Robert had cursed and then shouted her name twice and laughed. He'd pulled her up on his horse. And so they'd escaped.

The sun felt hot as July, though it was late in September. Ailsa brushed her hair back from her face, feeling the dirt on her hand grind onto her cheek. She was winding her way toward the woods, where she'd left a basket of mushrooms, gathered that morning, in the shade of some beeches. Her legs ached and the sun burned the back of her neck. She stopped a moment and took a long breath. It looked so far to the edge of the woods. It had taken a long time to recover from her ordeal with de Morville, that was all. Soon, she would be herself again.

She reached the cool greenness of the woods and entered, feeling the trees surround her with their welcoming arms. She located the mushrooms and turned back. She had to get them to Cook before dinner time. But when she reached the edge of the trees, she stood a moment longer in the shade and looked out across the baking field. A half dozen workers were raking hay; soon it would all be carefully stored away against the winter. She hoped there would be sufficient. Two more fields had been abandoned in her absence, and more families, too many more, had packed their goods and fled. Only a score of houses were still occupied and she knew many grumbled at the extra labor and worried about the precarious winter ahead. And in the next month there was so much more to be done, gathering in barley and oats, drying and preserving beans, peas, and apples, picking and preserving the last berries. And then it would be slaughtering time. With so few hands to do the work. It made it harder for everyone, each family that left. Yet she found she couldn't blame them.

She headed back across the field. Her eye registered someone approaching from the manor. As always in these last few weeks her heart leapt. She quickened her pace, no longer feeling the heat, though the glare struck her eyes. The visitor was tall certainly and dressed in dark clothes and strode along with something like Robert's firm assurance. She wanted to believe it was him, but even as she hoped, she knew it was not. The man waved, so she walked toward him, pushing down the thoughts that troubled her nights. Where was Robert? Why had he left without a word?

But what was the good of wishing he were here? The truth was bitter. De Morville might be a traitor. He was certainly a disgraceful excuse for a man. But he was still her husband and his father still had the king's ear. Robert was wise, no doubt; there was little profit in talking of what they would not have. The man waved again, and she recognized Torquil.

"You shouldn't be doing so much," he said and took the heavy basket of mushrooms from her. "Are you fully recovered?"

"That's a very fine hat."

He adjusted the bright blue cap on his head, with a self-conscious grin. "The latest style. I had it made in Renfrew." He touched the hat again. "Shall we walk? I have something to tell you." He kicked at a tuft of grass, avoiding her gaze. "I hope you will congratulate me, I'm to be married."

She felt a prick of something, envy perhaps. "That's wonderful news." She tried to sound sincerely glad. "Who is the lady?"

"She comes from Ayr. Her father helped us with the horses when we were after finding you." He glanced at her, half-apologetic.

"I hope you will be very happy in your marriage and blessed with beautiful sons and daughters," she said.

His face cleared. "You are sure?"

"Dugald and Meriel should be back from Renfrew by dinner time as well. We'll celebrate your good fortune," she said firmly.

A fortnight later, Ailsa stared out the window of her bedroom as the last afternoon sun glinted on the sea. She twirled the ring around her finger. It was heavy; the twining pattern of stylized leaves chased in the gold sparkled in the sun. It was on her finger when she had awakened, that first day back here at Caerwyn.

She smoothed down the linen of her gown, dyed a rich blue-green, and flipped her hair, dressed in long braids, onto her back. She'd stuck some of the first red and gold leaves in her braids. After her long absence, home seemed to surround her with warmth and comfort and beauty. She admired the timbered beams, the long windows overlooking the sea, the rich fields stretching toward cool forests. She admired it all, but she had gone away and come back, as those stolen by the faeries, the same on the surface, but far different underneath. This was her home, and yet now, somehow, it was not.

She went down the stairs and paused at the threshold to the hall, filled with family, servants, and minstrels setting up their instruments. She entered, greeting all as she passed, playing her role of lady of the manor. She motioned to the servants that the harvest feast should begin and turned to her guests, trying to forget all in her role of hostess. It was as though everyone at Caerwyn existed in a play and continued to say their lines, and somehow only she knew that all this was over, and what was left only a farce.

Late that evening, Ailsa wandered through the hall, saying a last word to her guests. She stopped by a crowded table, where the conversation seemed lively despite the hour. She slipped onto the bench beside Desmond, who had a small manor and lands inland toward the hills. Desmond and the other men raised their cups to acknowledge her, then went back to their conversation.

"But how can ye think it will no matter?" said Malcolm, a tall man seated opposite. He was dressed in thick green wool, his grey beard neatly combed.

Desmond shrugged. "What the de Morvilles do is no business of mine, nor yours. 'Tis Normans they are, and their ways strange to us."

Ailsa felt a shaft of cold in her back at the name. A chorus of agreement sounded around the table.

Malcolm frowned. "Ye think it will not matter to you, as you hail from Bute, and 'tis far away. But what the de Morvilles do will affect us all, I tell ye."

"What have they done now?" she asked in a quiet voice.

All eyes swiveled to her, and the men shifted uneasily on the benches. "'Tis what they plan to do…" said one.

"You do not know that for fact," snapped Desmond.

"We know there are preparations at Irvine, as though for war or siege," said Malcolm calmly. "And we know too that David is far from here, meeting with Stephen in England. 'Tis an odd time indeed for the king's ally to stockpile weapons and food."

"He could be preparing to defend the Isles," said a third man, his tunic stretched tight over his giant chest. "Ye cannot be sure. And besides, what Normans do among themselves, it matters not to us."

Desmond stood. "I cannot be sure what they are doing at Irvine," he agreed, "but you are wrong. What these English and French do will affect us all. The times have moved on and we must too."

The others muttered, but Desmond had no more to say. He bowed to her, apology written on his face, and left. The rest of the men made an effort to cover the glum mood with jokes and laughter as they bid her good night.

Ailsa passed through the hall, stopping here and there to ensure that all were comfortable, that there were sufficient blankets for those who would sleep the night. Finally, she reached the door. She stood a moment, shivering in the cold air of the corridor. The de Morvilles. Preparing for war or siege at Irvine. So close to Caerwyn. What would her good neighbors think if they knew she was married to the man?

She forced herself up the stairs to her chamber. If the de Morvilles were indeed contemplating open rebellion against the king, then what of Hugh? Would he come to claim her and Caerwyn now? And if he did not, would the king's men come to imprison her, now that her husband was a known and open traitor?

She had already doubled the guard around Caerwyn, taking even more men away from the fields, and rebuilt the timber fences that had once encircled and protected her home, but this was worse, much worse, and besides, she could not hide away here forever. Time had been standing still, but now it would begin to move again. She feared she would never again be safe, from Hugh or from the King.

"'Tis clear as day, Lady," Mirren the steward said, "though I'd not have foreseen it, but he has scrambled off for good. Perhaps he's gone over to your neighbor's manor." He paused. "Or perhaps he's headed for de Morville territory, what with all the rumors."

Ailsa frowned, winding her long braid in circles round her fingers. "Surely he would not," she said, "not Bowie from our own lands. He's been in the stables since I was a child. He would not betray me so."

"Some men will do much for money," answered Mirren. "He's been gambling and losing for a time. There's word the de Morvilles have sent a man or two nosing about. And there's little enough food in our stocks. He'll not be the only one thinking of leaving, one way or another."

"What do you suggest?" She kept her voice even, but Mirren glanced up at her, sympathy in his eyes.

"Bowie was a good one with horses, though not with men, and

we must replace him." Mirren said. "You have some fine horses; they must be cared for proper, not haphazard like. It's not everyone has the knack."

Ailsa stared into the fire, half seeing flames and half seeing Robert's stallion winding through the woods, grey in the misty light. She shook her head impatiently.

"I know you be in a hurry," said Mirren, "but I'd caution to look into any new man well for we'd not want more trouble here."

"Aye." She was quiet, for rumor had filtered to the manor but two days ago that Hugh de Morville had been seen near Renfrew. She made herself take long deep breaths. If she could not feel safe here at Caerwyn, surrounded by those who loved her, where could safety lie? Still, who would have thought Bowie could betray her for coin?

"We will sell the horses," she said decisively. "It is time. And I have been thinking of Jamie, and what to do with him."

"Sell all the horses? What about your mare?"

"You know Jamie has the way with horses, and when on Arran with me he proved himself true beyond any doubt. I have asked our neighbor Thomas to take him on as his head groom and he has agreed. And I will give Nia to Jamie as his own."

Mirren looked unconvinced. "It's a heavy responsibility."

"In Carlisle at the king's stables, Sir Robert trained him. He knows exactly what to do. Robert was well pleased."

The old man's face cleared. "Well now, that does seem a good answer then."

"I've been thinking I must find a way to reward him for his service to me," said Ailsa, "but not sure what to do not to offend his pride."

"This will suit." The old man rose to his feet.

She grabbed an oiled linen cloak from the hook by the door. "We can tell Jamie together." They walked out into the cold courtyard. An autumn rain was pelting down, drumming on the slates. Ailsa ran ahead.

Jamie materialized out of the warm gloom of the barn, his usual grin wide when he saw her.

She threw back the wet hood and stamped the water from her boots. "You know Bowie is gone."

"I do." His face darkened. "I am sorry for it."

"'Tis not your doing. But it's got me thinking. We must be selling off the horses here. There is not enough hay for the winter." She paused. "I'd like you to go to Thomas, be his head of stables."

"'Till someone new is hired?"

"No, you to be head," she repeated. "He has already agreed and glad indeed to have you. And Nia will be yours. You'll care for her well, I know." She blinked. It would be hard to give up her mare.

His eyes glowed, vividly blue in the dark room. She heard the soft rustle of the horses behind him. "It would be my fondest dream," he said solemnly.

"Good then," she said firmly. "It is settled. You and Mirren will take the horses to the market on Tuesday, and once they are gone, you will go to Thomas and take over immediately."

"Aye, Lady," he agreed, his mouth stretched in a wide smile.

Mirren winked at him, and they all laughed. It was comfortable together in the dim light of the barn, with the soft rustling of the horses munching their hay. But later, staring out her window, tears tracked down her face. Change, however necessary, was hard. A week later, she waved Jamie farewell, as he rode Nia away, his bag with all his belongings tied on behind.

Two mornings after Jamie left, five of the village men came to her hall first hour in the morning. They stared at the ground and shuffled their feet and she knew what they would say before they said it. She got to her feet. This day had been coming for years, and now it was here.

"We're for leaving, Lady. It's sorry we are, but the chance is here and we must grab it now. Renfrew is growing into a town and there's plenty of work there. And coin. Plenty of food and company for the women."

She didn't say what of your long years on this land, or your loyalty to my father, or your ties to me or to Caerwyn. In the Isles, men had always been free to make their own way. It was just the new English idea to tie them to the land, whether there was food enough for all or not. She would not see them or their children starve. "I will not seek to keep you here, if your minds are made up. I only wish I had more to give you. Come tomorrow morning and there will be a cart load of supplies to be divided among you, your share for the work you've put in this season." The men nodded, their faces tense, but relieved. "And I wish you and your families well in your new lives."

Ailsa instructed the kitchen girl to load three hams, six wheels of cheese, eight loaves of bread, and two ale casks into the good cart. She added blankets, and she gave each family a table or a bench and linen cloth along with the rest. Next day, when the cart was heaped and covered with an oiled cloth, she had them put the two donkeys to pull it. When the men and women and the excited and fractious children were all gone, the courtyard felt silent and deserted.

Later that difficult week, the small brother of Osla appeared at the gate, a little lad named Arthur, looking confused. Ailsa called him over and he approached, a heavy packet in his hands. He handed it to her. She smiled at the boy, who grinned back, pleased to have finished his task. He bounded away. Ailsa stared after him. Osla had refused to go with the others, but it was just a matter of time. She had a sweetheart, and he was for going.

She stared down at the letter, sealed in an oiled packet. Her name, Ailsa, Lady of Caerwyn, was printed in broad capitals across the front. Lady of Caerwyn. No longer, in truth.

She pried open the seal, then drew out a single sheet of parchment. She held it in her hands, a breeze fluttering her hair to tickle her nose. Could the note be from Robert after all this time? She looked down at the missive in her hand and saw the closing signature. She blinked and forced herself to read.

Greetings to my dear friend Ailsa,

I trust this letter finds you in good health and spirits. It seems long indeed since our days together at Carlisle and though I still hope to come and visit you some time in the future, I have news that will not wait. Davy and I have married, quietly, in the chapel at his parent's home at Liddesdale, and now I find myself awaiting the birth of our first child. My mother is with me so I am not too frightened, though in truth my health has not been the best. My Davy however has been the best of husbands. He is gone much, with duties for the king in his quest for Northumberland. I confess to being lonely and wishing you were with me. But I write urgently not to tell you my troubles, but to tell you that I have heard much from the court that concerns me. I believe you are in some danger. I dare not say more in a letter, but implore you. Do not trust. Do not tarry. Flee.

With much love, and hoping to meet with you some finer day,

Your friend Effie.

Ailsa replaced the parchment in the oiled paper and put the packet down on the bench beside her. She sat for a long time, staring into the blue sky, streaked with high white clouds, flying on by.

/ # CHAPTER THIRTY-ONE

Carlisle

ROBERT FELT TOO RESTLESS TO SLEEP. He wished Will were
here with him, lurking in the forest along the River Eden, near
Carlisle. He'd been thinking for some time he must go to the king's
Constable, tell him what news he had of his son. Give him a chance
to deal with it, or head it off, before open treason and war erupted.
The king was still away down south and he had a feeling the Constable
cared more for Scotia's peace than the king, caught up as he was in
England's quarrels. Besides, he didn't feel he owed the king anything.
And at one time, the Constable had been kind to him.

He could almost feel Will's frown in the dark. Unlikely to be
pleasant, he imagined Will saying, and the Constable is a powerful
man. He will not want to hear this, bad news about his troublesome
son. Maybe knows it all already and has turned his eyes away. True
enough. It was certainly dangerous and could be foolhardy. Caerwyn
had proved to be a most dubious gift. In truth, he should not be
anywhere near Carlisle. Still, somehow, he felt he owed it to the
father. What he owed to his own father's memory was still unclear.
He rubbed his eyes and got to his feet.

Near the castle he found a serving boy sent out to gather firewood
and only half awake. He gave him a coin and the boy's face lit up.
He led Robert through a back door into the warren of storerooms
behind the kitchen and raced off with a message. Robert waited in
a small room, barely larger than a closet and smelling of sour milk

and cheese. He sat on a crate in a dark corner, hoping he wouldn't have cause to regret this.

The door opened, without a knock. The Constable walked in, his full cloak billowing in the wind. "God's blood, 'tis cold in here."

Robert stepped forward. "I thank you for coming."

The Constable examined him and gave no greeting. "What urgent news could you have for me?" His voice was impatient.

"News of your son and of the fate of the king's peace," said Robert quietly.

The Constable considered him, no emotions visible on his face. "And why bring me news, I who have disowned him?"

"A father is always a father."

A flicker of the Constable's eyelids was the only response. "Your news then."

Robert gestured to the stool and the Constable sank down on it. He told him Hugh had abducted Ailsa and she'd escaped only by firing Fergus' manor.

The Constable's fingers were still on his lap. "This I have heard already." He met Robert's gaze. His eyes were dark, like his son's, and harder to read. "The woman is free now, and I know already Fergus plays a tricky double game, so I assume you have more to tell me. What of this Somerled of the Isles. Does he, like Wimond, preach rebellion against the king?"

He sounded so casual, thought Robert, as though he spoke of a feast at a neighbor's manor, and not of treachery. "'Tis whispered by some that Somerled has ambitions," he said carefully.

The Constable gestured impatiently.

Robert ran a hand through his hair. "I do not think he's behind this rebellion."

"Why?"

"I think your son is counting on it—that David will think it's Somerled. Your son means to provoke war."

The Constable's mouth twisted, and he turned his eyes away.

Robert shifted his weight. It was no comfortable business, telling a father his son was a traitor, disowned or not. "The grievances are there, as you know, for any man to rouse up," he said.

"So you indicated to the king." De Morville tapped his long fingers on his thigh. "I have worked long to aid the king in bringing the best of English and French ways to Scotia. Coin, lands, and power are the reward for my hard work, but there are many who are envious."

"No doubt," agreed Robert. "But I talk not of rumor. I saw and heard your son myself."

The Constable got up and walked to the door.

"Violence and war in the West will help no one."

The Constable took a long breath. "My son has made mistakes, but as you say, he is my son. I thank you for this information." He opened the door. "And in return I will tell you this. Troublesome times are coming. You know far too much. You should quit this place and come not to Carlisle again. The king has already decided your fate." He looked away, down the dark corridor. "And do not tarry."

Ailsa sat at her table, dressed in her second finest gown. She knew she looked the part of the manor lady and she was trying to play her role well, with all the household gathered for an early December feast.

Dugald and Meriel were seated near her, but at her side was a man Dugald had brought from Galloway. Her cousin was ever scheming to see her married and safe. She knew he tried because he loved her, and he seemed so sure she should agree to this man's protection. He was rich, he would be able to bring mercenaries and protect Caerwyn, and most importantly, he had laughed about the marriage to Hugh and said it was hardly binding and mattered not. Dugald was urging her every day and Meriel as well, in her quiet way. Her cousin needed to go voyaging come spring and he couldn't leave unless Caerwyn was protected. Unless she was protected. For what if Hugh did decide to come after her? He was likely to, she knew that. She gulped more of the wine. If only the old curse the villagers whispered of were true, that any she married would die horribly and soon; Hugh would be stricken and she would be free.

One of the serving boys appeared at her side. Her messenger was back. She excused herself, and hurried to the kitchen, not stopping to grab a cloak, though a bitter sleet was falling outside. The messenger was warming by the fire, ice melting off the ends of his hair. "What have you learned?" she asked eagerly. She'd sent a message, a last effort to find where Robert had gone, before it was too late.

"The king was not in Renfrew," the messenger said, "but I heard much of the court nonetheless, for many merchants trade between Glasgow and Carlisle, what with the cathedral building and the king's interest."

"Is the king expected?"

"Nay. The king and all the court stayed south for the winter. 'Tis not known where Sir Robert went, though all said he was not with the king."

Ailsa thanked him, then asked the cook to prepare him a hot meal. He gave her a gap-toothed smile. "One thing more, Lady."

"Aye?"

"The rebels under this Wimond be raising a fuss in Galloway and Lord Fergus might be helping them out."

That was true certainly. "What else do they say?"

"Could be Somerled himself is leading them. He might be breaking from the king and all folks around her will have to take sides."

Ailsa frowned.

The man took a step toward the door. "And 'tis said of the de Morvilles at Irvine, that the son of the house be with the rebels."

Ailsa backed out of the kitchen. The wind clutched at her and she pulled the hood over her head. She hesitated, knowing she should return to the hall, but instead she headed down the winding path to the beach, ever her solace, though lately she'd avoided venturing forth alone. But on this storm driven night everyone would be safe inside, including Hugh's men.

She followed the narrow twisting path, taking care for the stones were glazed with ice and the wind so strong it caught her skirts and billowed them until she caught them up in her belt. Gravel and ice crunched beneath her boots.

At the beach, the sand stretched white and eerie in the darkness.

So Hugh had finally chosen sides. And if Hugh had joined this rebellion, she and Caerwyn must figure in his schemes. She realized she was holding her breath and let it out in a long, ragged sigh. He would come after her. And the king too would send men after her. Caerwyn was somehow a strategic prize in all these twisting alliances and she was now the wife of a traitor. More than reason enough to seize her land and toss her in a nunnery, or an iron cage. And that story incident. A Queen sailing in from the Western Sea. The king would recall and be angered all over again. He'd think she joined her voice with Hugh in rebellion, or even that she'd talked him into it herself.

She shook her head. Yet still she found herself glad she had told that story. It meant something different, something private and important to her, apart from all the quarrels of these ambitious and ever troublesome men.

A gust of wind tossed her hair. She looked around uneasily. But she was alone on the dark beach. Spray from the waves spattered her cloak. The water was black. Long swells rushed up the beach and tumbled the smoothed stones in a constant clacking that blended with the howls of the wind.

It was the turning time of the year, and time to face reality. Caerwyn's people were nearly all of them gone; the estate was finished. The king and Hugh between them would end it and they would come to deal with her. Both would be angry she'd simply let the workers go. Hugh would turn Caerwyn into a landing place for rebellion; the king would make it a staging place for dominating the Isles. Whoever won out, she would be no longer needed for their schemes. She would be an inconvenience and a danger. How easy it would be for her to have an accident or simply disappear. She swallowed, suddenly flooded with the fear she had kept back for days.

And it seemed that despite all she'd imagined she'd felt and heard, Robert was not coming back.

She threw a handful of pebbles into the waves, her hands clumsy with cold. The ring on her finger clanked against the stones. She twisted the gold ring round and round, and abruptly yanked it off. The water crawled before her, inky and glittering. She should cast it in. She held the ring for a long moment in her hand, heavy and warm. Then she sighed and placed it back on her finger.

She would not marry the man up in her hall, nor go with him to Galloway. But she couldn't stay here any longer either. Effie was right; she must flee. She would pension off Mirren and Osla and the few servants left, send them on to Renfrew and safety with the other families, and then she would go. Reality had come and must be faced. She must step away from her past and into her future. What that might be, she couldn't imagine.

She trudged back up the hill, sliding on the ice and scraping her knee. She'd have to leave a note for Dugald and Meriel to find after she was gone, for they'd never let her go if she told them. Her going must be in secret; no one must know where she went. For their safety as well as hers.

She stopped mid hill and stared out over the black sea, sleet pelting her and her cloak snapping. She didn't know where she would go. But she would go. And it must be soon.

CHAPTER THIRTY-TWO

WHEN SHE REACHED THE TOP OF THE CLIMB, Ailsa lingered staring out over the dark water until her knees stiffened and ached with the cold, the fierce wind twisting her cloak around her ankles, so she narrowly avoided tripping. The roar of the wind filled her ears. Then she heard something else, a clatter or clink, like a rock rolling on the icy path. "Who's there?" she called out.

No one answered, of course. Just the dark and her darker thoughts. There was her manor, lit up by candles and torches; music came to her in spurts on the wind. Her home, but not for much longer.

Below her, a rock rattled down and clunked as it hit the stones on the beach. Followed by a muffled curse. Ailsa grabbed her skirts up and ran toward the gate. Her legs felt stiff with cold and fright, her skirts bunched and hampered her, and she clutched them higher and stumbled over a rock.

Boots scrambled on the gravel behind her.

She ran toward the light.

"Kyle," she yelled. "Kyle, open the gate!"

A man's arm wrapped around her waist and yanked her away from the gate. His cloak reeked of sour ale and old sweat.

"No!" She jabbed her elbow into the solid belly and heard a grunt. But the arm tightened around her, crushing her. He whirled her away from the wall and towards the shadows. She could hear Kyle calling now, and the screech of the gate. She tried to yell, but a hand smothered her mouth. She bit down on the man's fingers and he yanked his hand back and yelled. She shoved him away. "Kyle, here!"

The man clutched at her shoulders, swung her around, and slammed her to the ground.

"Mistress, where are…" Kyle's voice was cut off by a choked scream.

Now she heard the thud of horses; men poured into the square of orange light at the opened gate. A trap. Men, in black, mounted on dark horses, crowded through the opened gate and milled about in her courtyard. Caerwyn was open to the outsiders. She struggled to get away but couldn't budge her assailant's hard arms. He dragged her through the gate and into the mass of men and stamping horses. The silver of mail and masked faces and spear tips gleamed. Shouts echoed from inside the hall. Caerwyn's men were alerted, but they were too few, and no match for these armed men, and soused besides from an evening of drinking. She felt sick. Dugald was in there, and dear Meriel, finally once again with child.

A strange whirring sound filled her ears. Like angry bees in hot summer. Around her she heard a thudding. The grip on her arms loosened and she almost slipped away, but the man remembered her and yanked her with him toward the stable. Men were falling now, tumbling from their horses, and screams ricocheted from the timber walls. Arrows, pale feathers picked out in the light, stuck from legs and necks and men were shouting, wheeling their horses. "Devil take the bastards," cursed the man holding her, but he didn't let her go, just shoved her further, past the stable, into the darkness along the walls.

A man rode into the square of light. His horse was a grey, shining under the torches like the moon on seawater. "Robert!" she called, "Robb!"

The man holding her circled her neck with his thick fingers and whispered into her ear. "I will twist your head from your neck if you utter another word." The sharp stink of sweat filled her nostrils and her chest seized up so she couldn't breathe.

The horseman rode directly toward them, dropped his reins and raised his longbow. The man holding her cursed and laughed and pulled her tighter to him.

She heard a hissing sound and a thud. The arms around her chest seized tighter and then slackened. The man fell, dragging her down with him, an arrow sticking from the center of his forehead, blood leaking down his face and neck.

"Ailsa!" Arms reached for her, crushed around her, pulling her tight. She shut her eyes. She couldn't seem to catch her breath. Robert smelled of horses and exertion and cold night. The harsh wool of his cloak scraped against her skin and then he was cupping her face, warm hands on her cold cheeks. "Are you harmed, has he hurt you?"

"Nay," she managed to stumble out and then he was kissing her. She pushed him away. "Where have you been these long months, with no word to me!"

He held her hand up and found the heavy ring. "You have my word here, my pledge. Did you not know it?"

She stared at the ring. "You've been gone long. I did not dare hope." She could feel hot tears welling and turned away. "And perhaps you were injured or hurt."

Her men were crowding, wide-eyed, at the gate, weapons in hand. The intruders were gone, vanished into the night. "Kyle?" she asked.

"He took a sword thrust, but he'll make it," said one. "He's in the hall already. Lady Meriel is tending to him." The big gate creaked shut and she heard Robert organizing men to guard the walls.

Inside, she checked on Kyle and saw he was indeed pale, but already bandaged by Meriel.

"Where have you been, Ailsa," she whispered. "I've been so worried, and Dugald's friend is wondering." She stopped, her mouth open as Robert entered the hall.

Robert bent over Kyle, nodded to Meriel, and took Ailsa's arm. "Come sit by the fire. You are quite pale." He called for wine and waited until she drank a goblet down. "I have something important to show you."

He pulled a pouch from his sleeve and drew out another smaller pouch of soft leather. Inside were two squares of parchment. He handed them to her.

Ailsa swallowed. The words danced before her, in Latin, a large

D at the bottom center of each parchment. She looked up at him. "From the king?"

"Read."

She read one and then the other, slowly and carefully, then once again, to be sure. "What does it mean?"

"You can read as well as I."

"The king always intended to rob you?"

Robert shrugged. "Who can read the mind of a king? He does as he likes and answers to no one. Certainly not to a landless Welsh-born knight." He put a finger under her chin and tipped it up. "He always meant to take Caerwyn from you, in any case. However he could. They will use it as a landing site, to fight the rebels here on the coast, or to mount a rebellion of their own."

Dugald came up and Ailsa handed the two charters to him. He had Meriel read them aloud and shook his head. "A bad business."

Robert turned back to Ailsa, ignoring Dugald and the crowd of guests in the hall. "We can make a new beginning," he said quietly, "if we so choose, you and I."

She frowned and stared at her hands. "Hugh made me his wife."

"Do you believe that?"

"No."

"Nor do I."

Ailsa woke first. Robert lay warm at her side, asleep, the moss coverlet twisted round him. Her other side was uncovered and cold. She slid from the bed and reached up to the window. She moved the shutter aside. A blue-grey dawn sky gleamed into the chamber and the sharp scent of the winter sea drifted in on the cold air. She climbed back under the covers and stared at the clouds. She thought of lying here with Niall in the warmth of that one summer and there was the familiar stab of sorrow and loss.

Robert's eyes opened and he touched her cheek. "'Tis good to wake here with you." He hesitated. "Are you well? It can be difficult and confusing to leave the past behind."

She thought for a moment, images tumbling over in her mind.

"I am well. It is good to have a past, but also good to think on the future." She touched his shoulder. "I am glad to have found a future."

He pulled her into the crook of his arm and they watched the clouds together. After a time, Ailsa pulled away and looked into his eyes. "I know already what you don't wish to say. That we cannot stay here. The days of Caerwyn as my home are gone."

He pulled her close and whispered into her hair. "Let us speak of all that later. We will live in the dream for a while longer."

Later that day, after Robert saw to the horses and set his men to repairing the damaged gate, they walked together up the stairs to the walls and looked out over the estate. "I have something to tell you that cannot wait," said Ailsa. "Caerwyn's families have all been leaving. I have tried to hold the estate together but in the end I've failed. Perhaps they got wind of troubles to come, or perhaps it was just time for new havens. I have let them go with my blessing. And given them food and other things from the estate, tools and furniture."

Robert surprised her. "Good. Men should be free to go where they will and raise families where they wish."

"We think alike on this then. I am glad."

There was much to do in the next few days, for they were leaving too and soon. Either de Morville or the king's men would come, that was certain. The only question was when. Though it was winter and travel would be hard, they decided to go now and not wait. So the remaining servants and Robert's guards were told; supplies were divided and parceled out. Kyle recovered enough to go to Thomas, along with Mirren and Osla. They would be safe there and content. All the farewells were difficult, but Ailsa found she was glad she could see them well settled and she had news of Jamie, who was doing a wonderful job with the horses. In the end, Thomas had proved a faithful and steady friend.

Dugald and Meriel had to be told and convinced and argued with over and over.

"You must come to Arran. I'll give you land and help build you a house," said her cousin.

"No."

"Where do you think to go?"

Ailsa shook her head. "I do not know. Only that it must be somewhere far, out of the king's reach. And better for you not to know."

"Out of his peace you mean," said Dugald irritably.

Ailsa shrugged. "His peace is mostly illusion, is it not? I will go somewhere where I can be free. Where we can have a life, and perhaps, in time, children, a home. We can have a future." She stared at Dugald, who stared at the ground. "Don't you wish that for me?"

"You know I do. I'm thinking if I'd taken you voyaging, all that long ago, maybe none of this would have happened."

"Perhaps. But this land was coveted, by those with power. Our grandfather chose too well. It would have happened, now or a few years on, it doesn't matter when. I think I have always known that I had to go away." She frowned. "I never saw my future here, you know that."

Meriel approached and put a hand over hers. "But will Hugh come here looking?"

"He will, unfortunately. Which is why you and Dugald must be gone as well, tomorrow or by week's end at the latest. On Arran, among friends, on your own lands, you'll be safe."

"You can't mean to just give up Caerwyn." Dugald looked appalled.

"I do mean to," said Ailsa. "I have given it up in my mind, long since. And you must let it go as well."

Dugald looked to Robert, who shook his head and said, "I've clung to the past too long in my life. I won't make that mistake again."

"Come." Robert patted her hip as they lay twined together in her narrow bed. "I have something to show you."

The last night's rain had melted away in a warm wind, and though she knew there was still much winter to come the sun held a warmth this morning that promised spring. They reached the beach and walked along it, water slapping the shore and the smells of sea creatures carrying on the soft winds.

"Where do we go?" queried Ailsa, though hardly caring. She felt the happiness of holding his warm hand as they walked down the sands.

"To our boat of course," he answered, as they rounded the bend. Drawn up on the sands was a galley, some twenty feet long, with a mast of oak and planked sides painted a gleaming green.

Ailsa stopped, struck silent.

"I had two men building her the whole time I was gone." They drew nearer and she smelled raw wood and paint.

Robert examined the wood planks and mast and lines, while she exclaimed over the smoothness of the paint and the careful sanding of the seats. Finally, he turned to her, "Will you like to voyage on her?" His voice held a touch of anxiety.

"I will love her," said Ailsa. "And our journeys together."

In the end, they had word. From his old friend Walter, with just the message "Go now." Robert blinked once, twice, as he studied the note and tossed it on the fire. "We both have faithful friends, it would seem," he said. "The time has come."

They sailed that very afternoon, after a tearful good bye with Meriel, round with her child. Dugald was out hunting and they could not wait.

Robert took only one extra hour, to sit by Will's grave. When he left, he knew he'd been forgiven for not seeking out and killing Will's assailant. Will had always said leave the past where it belongs, in the past. He stood up, a failure at revenge, and he felt closer to Will and to his own father than ever before, which was strange.

They pushed the boat out into the surf and climbed aboard and Ailsa studied her home and then turned her face away. They were alone, with no extra men to row if the wind gave out. There was no one they could endanger. But the wind held steady and the boat rode easily over the long swells and the sun even appeared through the clouds toward mid afternoon, a pale disk that promised spring though the bite was sharp on their cheeks.

Next morning, after a long dark night, they adjusted the sail and headed north. The sky glared red and orange, and over the day the wind built and grey clouds piled thick and dark and full dusk came down hours early. The boat flew with the sail bellied out and the waves grew, topped with white spray. Purple swathes of cloud lay on the hills. They watched the rain reach from the clouds to the hills and soon the rain fell on them, first a few drops and then drumming down. The water was pitted with the heavy drops; the waves swelled and climbed, and their boat rose and fell and rose again. They were cold and drenched and shivering despite their leather cloaks and hoods. The rain turned the sky and water the same dark grey, impossible to see where they were going.

They threaded through the islands they knew, heading north always, trying to keep to the lee, but the further they ventured, they didn't know the land and they were fearful of reefs and rocks in these unknown to them seas. Ailsa worried endlessly as they sailed. Would they be chased? Would those she loved be safe? Hugh was persistent. His pride would be hurt. A king's reach was far.

The waves built as night fell until the storm and the dark forced them to pull into what seemed a deserted cove. White surf roared up a sand and pebble beach. Ailsa listened to the crash and pull of the waves and thought perhaps Hugh would think them overturned by the storm and drowned. But then she thought he would send men after them, to be sure.

The storm settled right over the cove and the waves crashed on a granite cliff they couldn't see in the dense fog. Rain poured through the night. They huddled in a dripping crevice under the granite. Sleep wouldn't come and she found herself remembering and repeating Eachna's lessons as rain sliced through the night.

Night passed and grey light came to the sky. The storm passed over and moved out to sea. The swells remained but the rain was gone and a pale sky stretched blue overhead. Seabirds squawked and dove for fish and a vee of migrating ducks flew by.

They sailed on, ever northward, and came at last to the far tip of the Isle of Jura. Their clothes were wet and tattered and their food nearly gone. But the water ahead gleamed smooth like a black mirror in the winter twilight.

They sailed on and a moon rose and where the fog parted, in the silver light glimmering, they could just see the swirl and upheaval of the great whirlpool ahead.

Ailsa thought of all the stories she'd heard of the famed waters of Coire Bhreacain, tales in which the waves mounted and whirled, malevolent, ferocious, and hungry, stirred by the fierce goddess of winter snow and sleet and ice. The boom and roar filled their ears.

They rested for an hour, or maybe two, drifting in a sheltered cove, watching the waves circle, waiting for the right moment, gathering their courage. Then they cast off and climbed and raced and swirled. The wind blasted their faces and spray soaked their faces and poured down their necks. Ailsa clung to the mast with both arms and in the sudden calmness of the center, Robert tossed three oak oars and their bag of provisions into the water, hoping the chasers would think them smashed and sunk and cease their search.

In the end, they made it across. They sailed into the far reaches beyond. Into the white light of a winter midnight. They saw the grey and silver porpoises dancing over a black sea. They headed north, always north. A round moon lighting a path. Not worrying about where they would finally land. And as they sailed, they had time finally, and told each other all their stories. They remade their pasts and imagined new and wondrous futures.

ACKNOWLEDGMENTS

Sincere gratitude to all the scholars whose works helped inform me about 12th century Scotia. I have stayed generally true to the facts as I understood them, but this is a work of fiction and I've altered a few locations and time frames and ignored certain issues like language difficulties to suit the story. King David, his steward Walter fitz Alain, the de Morville family, and many others were real people, but Ailsa and Robert are inventions. Arran and Carlisle existed and exist, but Caerwyn is an imaginary place. A list of books I consulted can be found on my website for those interested in the challenges and complicated cultural interactions of this period.

This book, oddly enough, is both my first and latest novel. Some pieces remain from the very first novel I wrote, which resides now in a green box in the closet by my study. Ailsa only emerged in this latest version, when her quest took over the story. Along this bumpy way, so many kind and thoughtful writing teachers have contributed to this work, in person and through their own books on writing craft. Also so many observant and generous fellow writers have helped me along. Thank you to all my fellow travelers on this storytelling quest; I am grateful to be one of you.

I was fortunate to first travel to Scotland on a trip encouraged by my husband's father, PopPop. On this family trip, along with my husband and our son, then seven, we spent many happy hours exploring ruined castles and hiking through incredible forests and along the sea in the amazing Midsummer evening light. The ocean and islands were haunting and I knew I'd write a story centered on this place of sea anemones and ancient oaks and curious songbirds.

I visited western Scotland again with my husband recently. We took many long walks in fleeting sun but more often in soft drizzle and wind. Fog moving in and out. Light on the sea and fields. Without these trips I couldn't have written a word, so thank you to all who welcomed us and to my family for accompanying me and making the time joyous.

To all my extended family, a huge thank you for your support and encouragement and kind words. Special thanks to Mark for all the maps. And to Liz for the photo shoot. To Morgan and Hannah, thank you for the months together, when there was less time to write but more wonderful time to be a family together. For dear Simon, who sharpened so many pencils for me and always checked to see if I'd used them yet; thank you for keeping me company in my study. And to Bruce always, for everything with and beyond words.

ABOUT THE AUTHOR

Arlene MacLeod grew up in New England and upstate New York. She earned her undergraduate degree from Bowdoin College, where she studied government and history, and she holds a Ph.D from Yale University in Political Science. She taught comparative politics and political theory at Bates College, where her courses combined her interests in literature, power, and imagination. She lives with her husband near the coast in Maine, where she enjoys long walks, swimming in the ocean, and painting. She has always loved to read, especially books that transport the reader to a different time and place. She is the author of *A Necessary Garden*, and with her son Morgan MacLeod, of *Ruins*, a collection of short stories and photo essays.

www.arlenemacleod.com

www.ingramcontent.com/pod-product-compliance
Lightning Source LLC
Chambersburg PA
CBHW032113110726
47902CB00003B/569